# The Cornish Cream Tea Christmas

Cressy was born in South-East London surrounded by books and with a cat named after Lawrence of Arabia. She studied English at the University of East Anglia and now lives in Norwich with her husband David. When she isn't writing, Cressy spends her spare time reading, returning to London or exploring the beautiful Norfolk coastline.

If you'd like to find out more about Cressy, visit her on her social media channels. She'd love to hear from you!

 /CressidaMcLaughlinAuthor
@CressMcLaughlin
@cressmclaughlin

Also by Cressida McLaughlin

Primrose Terrace series
*Wellies & Westies*
*Sunshine & Spaniels*
*Raincoats & Retrievers*
*Tinsel & Terriers*
*A Christmas Tail* – The Complete Primrose Terrace Story

The Once in a Blue Moon Guesthouse series
*Open For Business*
*Fully Booked*
*Do Not Disturb*
*Wish You Were Here*

The Canal Boat Café series
*All Aboard*
*Casting Off*
*Cabin Fever*
*Land Ahoy!*

The Canal Boat Café Christmas
*The Canal Boat Café Christmas – Port Out*
*The Canal Boat Café Christmas – Starboard Home*

The House of Birds and Butterflies series
*The Dawn Chorus*
*The Lovebirds*
*Twilight Song*
*Birds of a Feather*

# The Cornish Cream Tea Christmas

### Cressida McLaughlin

HarperCollins*Publishers*

HarperCollins*Publishers* Ltd
The News Building
1 London Bridge Street
London SE1 9GF

www.harpercollins.co.uk

This paperback original 2020
2

First published in Great Britain as four separate ebooks
in 2020 by HarperCollins*Publishers*

Copyright © Cressida McLaughlin 2020

Cressida McLaughlin asserts the moral right to
be identified as the author of this work

A catalogue record for this book
is available from the British Library

ISBN 978-0-00-840871-8

Typeset in Birka by Palimpsest Book Production Ltd, Falkirk, Stirlingshire

Printed and bound in Great Britain by CPI Group (UK) Ltd, Croydon CR0 4YY

MIX
Paper from
responsible sources
FSC
www.fsc.org
FSC™ C007454

This book is produced from independently certified FSC™ paper
to ensure responsible forest management.

For more information visit: www.harpercollins.co.uk/green

For Kate, Tim, Clara and Pete

# Part One

## Rudolph the Red Velvet Cupcake

# Chapter One

Hannah Swan sat in her allocated window seat and felt a faint pang of disappointment. On the walk from her flat to Waverley station, despite the early hour, Edinburgh had been so full of twinkling Christmas lights – strung up in the trees of Princes Street Gardens, and as part of sumptuous festive window displays – that the faded fabric of her seat and plain Formica table were a letdown. The only burst of colour came from a poster advertising mini-breaks in the Scottish Highlands, and the lush greens and endless blue sky were entirely wrong for this time of year. Hannah loved Christmas, and her train was sadly lacking in adornment.

It was the fourth of December, a Friday, and she was on her way to the other end of the country; to a Cornish village called Porthgolow, to spend a week assessing the green credentials of a spa hotel. She gave a brief shake of her head as a man settled into the seat opposite and held a newspaper open in front of his face. All her carefully orchestrated plans:

the friends' Christmas that she always held on the twenty-third; present-buying and -wrapping; decorating her tiny flat and helping her mum put up her tree. She would somehow have to fit them all in when she got back.

She had only been working as an eco-consultant for Green Futures for six months, and this was her very first client. Gerald, her boss, had initially been reluctant to send Hannah on her own, but when her colleague, Brad – who unsurprisingly had a myriad of reasons why he couldn't take such a long trip a few weeks before Christmas – had suggested Hannah could work with one of the freelancers based in Cornwall, Gerald had agreed. It was the best of both worlds: a member of his core team to show the hotel owner, Daniel Harper, how committed they were to his case, and an experienced freelancer who had local knowledge.

Sitting in the cool meeting room with a view of Edinburgh Castle beyond the rain-splattered glass, Hannah had been overjoyed. It wasn't until she was on her way to meet her friend that evening that reality had set in.

'Why did you accept it?' Saskia had asked once they were settled in the pub, festive foil decorations looped across the ceiling. 'Why go now, just before Christmas, instead of taking the next case he offered you in the New Year?'

'I have to show willing,' Hannah had replied. 'I have to prove myself.'

'Do you think Gerald had that in the forefront of his mind when he let you accept a case that nobody with any sense would take?' Saskia's dark eyes had flashed. 'It's bloody freezing, it's nearly Christmas and it's hundreds of miles away. Not to mention your company policy means you can't hop on a plane and be there in a couple of hours.'

Hannah had squirmed in her seat. 'Gerald's not a game

player. He's keen for me to get out there. Also, Sask, how can we tell people how to look after the planet if we're flying everywhere? Trains are the best option.'

'But what about your plans?' Saskia had pressed. 'The friends' Christmas? Strategy is your middle name, and I can't imagine how you're going to fit everything in once you're back. You know I'll help as much as I can, I just don't want you getting stressed.'

'I'll *re*-strategize then,' Hannah had said, hoping Saskia couldn't see that she was slightly hurt to be given no credit for spontaneity. It was true that she liked to be prepared, but she wasn't a total stick-in-the-mud. 'Besides,' she'd continued, 'I'm not solely responsible for the Crystal Waters project, so I won't get stressed.'

'Ah yes, your babysitter,' Saskia had grinned. 'Gerald's covered his bases.'

'Exactly.' Hannah had nodded, determined. 'My *freelancer*.' She didn't like to think of someone babysitting her – that person being somebody called Noah Rosewall, apparently one of Gerald's trusted contacts, who lived an hour away from Porthgolow.

It was a strange situation where Hannah, as a Green Futures employee, would be leading on the case, but Noah would have more experience. Hannah hoped they would work well together, despite the unusual set-up and the fact they'd never met before, and that she could prove to Gerald she deserved her place on his team.

The train juddered awake and Hannah held on to her coffee and her almond croissant. It had been too early to have breakfast at home, and she needed fortification for the long journey. What she hadn't told Saskia was that, as well as wanting to get her first project under her belt, she had felt the pull of Cornwall like a familiar song tugging at her heartstrings.

Her mum had taken her and her brother there on holiday when they were little; they had stayed in Newquay and made the most of the surrounding beaches. Hannah remembered the way it was almost surreally beautiful when the sun was shining, the colours pure and bold. Those holidays had ended when they'd moved to Scotland, but the snippets of memory Hannah had retained were magical. Cornwall in December would be very different from midsummer, and she would be there for work, but the thought of seeing the sea and the rugged coastline still gave her a thrill.

Tucking a strand of long blonde hair behind her ear, she took out her iPad and opened Safari, Porthgolow appearing as a search option after she'd typed the first two letters. She'd already done this several times, but nothing about the village's internet presence had so far jogged her memory, and when she'd spoken to her mum on the phone – she hadn't had time to visit her before the trip itself – her mother had been vague.

'Of course we didn't just stay in Newquay when we went, love, but that's what a holiday's for – travelling around, visiting new places. What's the name of this village again?'

'Porthgolow,' Hannah had said, and then repeated it, trying out a slightly different pronunciation.

There was a pause, as if her mum was considering it, and then, 'Nope. Doesn't ring any bells. Maybe we passed through it, but all those Cornish place names are so similar . . . It was twenty years ago, love.'

They hadn't lived in Edinburgh when Hannah was little; she'd been born in Oxford, and they'd moved to Scotland when she was nine, her mum wanting a fresh start after divorcing Hannah's dad. After that, the Cornwall holidays had stopped. It was a long enough journey at the best of times, as she was about to experience for herself, let alone with two young children.

From her online search, Hannah had already discovered one point of interest in the village she was visiting: the Cornish Cream Tea Bus. It was a vintage Routemaster that had been turned into a café and was based on Porthgolow beach. It gave tours around local beauty spots, was the focal point of a Saturday food market and had even, earlier in the year, been part of the catering team for a lavish BBC costume drama filming in the area.

Hannah went to the website now, and once again pored over photographs of the bus standing on the beach, its red paintwork contrasting with the pale sand and dizzyingly blue water. There were pictures of scones, crumbling under healthy dollops of jam and cream, steaming cups of tea, sausage rolls and mini quiches, Danishes and doughnuts, slices of lemon cake. Hannah's mouth started to water and, as she went on to read about the variety of culinary delights on offer at the food markets, she was almost drooling. Would they be holding them in December? Would the bus even be open?

Hannah felt a pang of longing for her sous chef job at the Whisky Cellar, an upmarket restaurant in Edinburgh's old town. It had kept her in rent money throughout her university course, but it hadn't just been a way of staying afloat. She had loved the simple pleasure of creating original, mouth-watering food, though she hadn't admitted to anyone quite how much she missed it. She decided, as she eyed her almond croissant with disappointment – it didn't look anywhere near as good as the photos she'd just been looking at – that while she was in Porthgolow, she would fit in at least one visit to the Cornish Cream Tea Bus. She wondered if Noah could suggest other local eateries for her to try.

The train picked up speed and left Edinburgh behind, and Hannah turned to her notes. It was just after seven, and she had at least ten hours of travelling ahead of her. The first train took her all the way to Newton Abbot in Devon, so she was pleased she'd got a table and a window seat.

The Crystal Waters Spa Hotel had been established in 2016, taking the place of the old Clifftop Hotel which had, according to the owner, Daniel Harper, been rundown and unsafe when he'd bought the site. Mr Harper had built his new retreat to a high standard, securing it into the cliff in a way that must have been eye-wateringly expensive to achieve.

From everything she'd seen and read, Hannah thought that this would be a straightforward job. Ecological concerns were already on everyone's radar when the hotel was built, and it looked as if Crystal Waters was ahead of the game. But there was always room for improvement, and that's what she and Noah would be able to advise on. Excitement danced through her at the thought of it: walking through the rooms and grounds, assessing the building's suitability for solar panels or an energy-efficient air-conditioning system, discussing water reclamation, eco-friendly toiletries and reduced packaging. Even the smallest changes would make a difference.

Done with her notes, she looked at her messages. The first contact she'd had with Noah was an email exchange once Gerald had confirmed the visit and put them in touch. He'd offered to pick her up from Newquay station, which she'd readily accepted. Her train was due to get in just after five that evening.

*Hi, it's Noah. So you have my number if you need to get in touch.*

*Hi Noah, thanks so much for this! Really looking forward to working with you. Hannah.*

*You too.*

So far, so straightforward.

Hannah read and dozed, and returned to the buffet car once her croissant – great flavour, a little on the soggy side – had disappeared. The weather changed as frequently as the view beyond the glass; bright rays peeping out between clouds, rain battering the windows moments later, the dense greys and brick reds of towns and cities replaced by dun-coloured December fields and the charcoal lines of leafless trees. The man with the broadsheet seemed disinclined to make small talk, leaning his head against the seat and closing his eyes once he'd finished with his newspaper.

As morning slipped into afternoon, Hannah noticed the increasing frequency of the announcements, her skin prickling when one started with: *We regret to inform you that . . .* There was a signalling problem ahead of them, and the updates were soon accompanied by stops and starts, the hitherto-moving backdrop now pausing on views of fields and cows, rows of neat back gardens with colourful children's slides and washing lines.

The man opposite Hannah woke up and blinked, his gaze settling on her. He was attractive, in a 'distinguished older man' sort of way, dressed in a navy and white checked shirt, his dark hair greying at the temples.

'We must be nearly at Newton Abbot by now,' he said.

'I'm afraid there have been some signalling problems,' Hannah replied, 'so we're forty-five minutes behind. They're keeping us up to date with announcements, though,' she

9

added brightly, trying to find something positive amongst the gloom.

He swore under his breath but gave her a tight smile. 'Isn't this bloody typical? I'm going for a coffee. Want anything?' He gestured at her empty water bottle and sandwich packet. Hannah was about to decline, then realized she was cold and that, also, she wanted a reason to keep their conversation going. 'A tea would be lovely, if you're sure?' She opened her handbag to get her purse, but when she looked up he was already striding through the carriage.

She messaged Noah.

*Hi. We're running 45 mins late. Signalling problems! :( I'll miss my connection but there should be another train. :) I'll let you know. Hannah.*

His reply came half an hour later, once her table companion had returned with tea and chocolate biscuits and refused to let her pay for them.

*Keep me updated.*

Noah, it seemed, was a man of few words.

Her table companion, however, was not. Mark was a business consultant on his way to visit his elderly mother in Devon. Hannah enjoyed his company, glad that he'd eventually chosen conversation over silence. Saskia had often said Hannah's main superpower was friendliness, and Hannah would be the first to admit that she wasn't self-conscious when it came to getting to know people.

Mark told her about the village he'd grown up in and where his mother still lived, how he'd go to the pub and pick up conversations with people he hadn't seen for years as if the intervening time had never happened. She told him about the reason for her journey, and about planning her friends' Christmas. She explained that she always chose a non-traditional menu so nobody overdosed on turkey, and how it was always the maddest – but the best – part of her festive season.

As they talked, an image of Seth popped into her head. Dark hair and even darker eyes, a smile that could be insolent and heart-meltingly attractive all at once. Seth was one of her group of friends, and the object of her secret desire for many years. He had also broken up with his girlfriend, Laura, in the summer.

Hannah hadn't spent *too much* extra time planning this year's meal – she had been going to research ways to make her Dauphinoise potatoes especially rich and extra crispy on the top anyway – but she couldn't deny that Seth's recently single status had been on her mind.

By the time the train pulled into Newton Abbot it was an hour and twenty minutes late, but Hannah had barely thought about it.

'Need help with your case?' Mark asked as they stepped onto the platform. He had lifted it down the train steps without asking, and was now hovering, waiting to see if he could be useful. The wind was icy, the sun low in the sky, the night edging closer.

'I'm fine, thank you though. You should go and find a taxi. Your mum will be wondering where you are.'

'She'll be asleep in front of the telly,' he replied with a good-natured eye-roll. 'Good to meet you, Hannah. Good luck with the hotel and, when you get to it, have a great Christmas.'

'You too!' Hannah watched him stride off, burying his chin in the collar of his coat.

She searched screens for the next train and platform to Newquay, accepting the help of a staff member who was

11

directing the late passengers to their onward journeys. She followed the stream of people, waited ten minutes for the smaller train, then texted Noah her updated arrival time.

It was close to seven when the train finally pulled into Newquay, and despite her tiredness after hours of travelling, her stomach was a ball of nervous anticipation. She was in Cornwall. She would be able to taste salt on the breeze and hear the crash of waves against the sand.

She smiled at the guard as she went through the turnstiles, cheered by the band of silver tinsel round his hat, and stepped outside. The darkness was complete, the soft glow from the station's outside lamps reached barely beyond the taxi rank, and the crisp night had no hint of warmth. Hannah wrapped her scarf tightly around her neck. It was made up of rainbow stripes of the softest wool, a long-ago present from her dad. It was only just holding together but she refused to give up on it. She peered into the car park and pulled out her phone.

She had no idea what Noah looked like or what car he had. He was thirty, two years older than her, but there hadn't been a photograph accompanying the Pen Picture Gerald had sent across to her once his involvement had been confirmed. She was about to call him when a loud *beeeeep* made her jump. She spotted a gleaming black Land Rover, its headlights shining like twin suns, obscuring the driver. Could that be Noah, expert eco-consultant, driving a huge, gas guzzling car? She turned away, perusing her surroundings for someone more likely.

The car horn sounded again and Hannah's head whipped round. Whoever it was seemed desperate to get her attention, but she remained wary. She didn't relish the thought of being kidnapped and thrown in a dank cave, or her lifeless body being dumped on a beach at first light, the waves creeping up to her blue toes.

She shook her head: she should have asked Noah what car he drove.

Finding his number in her phone, she hit call just as a man leaned his head out of the Land Rover's window.

'Hannah Swan?' His voice was low, with an edge of irritation.

'Noah!' She beamed, cancelled the call and wheeled her suitcase over to join him.

He got out of the car and came round to meet her. He was taller than her, dark hair tamed away from his face with a shiny coating of styling product, his eyes meeting hers behind black-framed glasses. His jaw was square and, even this late in the day, impeccably clean shaven. He was wearing a formal shirt the colour of forget-me-nots and black trousers, no jacket, despite it being Friday evening and utterly freezing. He held his hand out, and she felt the strength in his confident but not overpowering shake. His gaze didn't leave her face, and Hannah felt suddenly flustered.

'I'm sorry I didn't come over immediately,' she said. 'I wasn't sure –' *if you were going to abduct and kill me* – 'if it was you.'

'Because of the car,' he said, raising an eyebrow.

Hannah nodded as he took her case and lifted it into the boot. When he closed it, he pointed to a shiny silver decal just above the bumper. 'It's a hybrid. You have to have weight behind your wheels on these roads, especially in winter, so I had to compromise.'

'It's a very . . . smart compromise.' Hannah knew from work how much hybrid vehicles cost, and this one was not cheap.

Noah gave her a tight smile. 'Some people might say it's an indulgence.'

'*I* wasn't saying that,' she replied. 'I'm so sorry I'm late, and I didn't mean to—'

Noah held up a hand, stopping her. 'Let's get in, shall we? It's bracing out here.' Without waiting for her reply, he climbed into the driver's seat, and Hannah headed round to the passenger side. Once inside, she immediately regretted commenting on the car. It was glorious, the plush seat cushioning her weary body, the interior warm and softly lit. She risked a glance at Noah and saw that, beneath the wax, his hair was desperate to curl. It sat up in little peaks – like lizard crests, she thought, and hid a smile.

He drove out of the car park and onto the dark road. 'You must be tired after your journey,' he said into the quiet, the car's engine no more than a gentle hum.

'It was annoying that we got held up,' she said, 'but all I had to do was sit there and wait for the train to reach Newquay. You're the one who's been put out, not knowing when I'd finally appear.'

'It's not a problem,' he said. His voice was low and measured, but she'd detected the faintest hint of a Cornish accent, some of the vowels lengthened slightly, words not ending as sharply as they might.

'It's kind of you to come and get me at all.'

'You wouldn't have had much luck with public transport from Newquay to Porthgolow on a Friday night in December.'

Hannah waited for the accompanying laugh or smile, but none came. His arms seemed constrained by his blue shirt, the muscle definition obvious once you started to look. He seemed tightly held together, every action careful, giving nothing away: not curls or emotions or warmth. Hannah

14

hoped it was simply that this was their first meeting, or that he was tired and desperate to drop her off and get back to whoever was waiting for him at home.

'Do you know Porthgolow well?' she asked.

'I know most of Cornwall well,' he replied, 'so I know Porthgolow. But I haven't been in the hotel, or met the owner.'

'Have you been on the bus?'

'The bus?' She could hear the frown in his voice. 'I tend to use this, seeing as I paid so much for it.' He patted the steering wheel.

She couldn't detect any sarcasm in his voice, so she had no idea if it was a joke or if he was annoyed by her earlier comment. She felt cowed, as if she'd done nothing but irritate him since the moment they'd met.

'I meant the Cornish Cream Tea Bus,' she said quietly. 'It's in Porthgolow, and from what I've read it's really popular, a tourist destination all on its own. The cakes look delicious.'

'Oh. That. No, I've not been on that.' Hannah watched a muscle move in his jaw, waited for him to say something else and then, when he didn't, turned to look out of the side window, where there was nothing to see except darkness. Her confidence wavered. If Noah was going to be like this the entire week, then her supposed superpower of being able to make friends with everyone was going to be sorely tested.

# Chapter Two

Hannah didn't have the joys of the Cornish landscape to distract her as they drove up the coast from Newquay, and Noah remained quiet in the driver's seat. Either he was concentrating on the dark road, or he didn't want to get to know her. Or maybe, she thought, shifting in her seat, she was giving off antisocial vibes by looking out of her window.

'Not long now,' he said, surprising her. 'Don't fall asleep on me before we get there.'

Hannah laughed, then cleared her throat. 'I can't seem to slow my brain down. I feel as if I'm still moving, the world shooting past the train window at a hundred miles an hour.'

'You are still moving, though,' he said softly.

'Oh.' Heat blossomed in her cheeks. 'Yes, of course.' God. She wasn't sure it was possible for things to get more awkward. She burrowed in her bag for her phone, and tapped out messages to Saskia and her mum, letting them know she'd arrived. She didn't tell Gerald – she would settle for emailing him once they'd made progress at the hotel. When she looked up they were turning into another car park, a metal sign on the wall announcing that this was the Crystal Waters Spa Hotel.

Hannah gasped. She had seen photos of it online, but they hadn't done justice to the beacon of glass and elegantly lit, honey-coloured brickwork that appeared like a mirage out of the dark. There were lollipop bay trees either side of the doors, everything about it screaming quiet opulence. She thought of the bed she would sink into not too far in the future, and sighed dreamily.

'It looks impressive,' Noah murmured, as he turned the car expertly into a space. Hannah could hear the sea, the gentle shushing of calm waves hitting sand. Anticipation ran down her spine and, relieved and tired and eager to get to her room and take her shoes off, she turned to Noah, awkwardness forgotten.

'Thank you for dropping me off. When do you want to start work? Tomorrow? I'm here for a week, so if you're keen to get going then I don't mind working the weekend.'

'I thought we could have a quick meeting now. Have you eaten?'

'Now?' Hannah balked. 'I was going to see if I could grab a snack.'

'Great. Let's get you checked in, you can take your things to your room and we can get a bite to eat.' He pushed open the door and went round to the boot. Hannah sat for a moment before getting out, wondering if her confusion had been obvious. She had been expecting Noah to dump her and go, not prolong their torturous time together.

He led the way through the doors, wheeling Hannah's suitcase, and she followed, entranced by the beautiful foyer. Everything was surrounded by glass, glossy and shimmering, a golden pattern in the stone floor catching her eye. The tones and textures were natural: greys, greens and muted blues. It was organic and luxurious and wholesome all at once, and every inch exuded class.

She stood next to Noah while another guest checked in.

The woman ahead of them was wearing a knee-length red corduroy coat and purple Doc Martens. She had reddish-brown hair in a frizzy cloud around her face, her pale skin contrasting against the bright blue frames of her glasses.

'I have my reservation number here somewhere,' she said, burying her arm in a large canvas bag.

'Your surname will be fine,' replied the neat woman behind the desk. 'We'll be able to look you up on the system with that.'

'I just feel so stupid,' the woman continued. 'I packed so carefully this morning. Maybe I've left it in the car?' A couple of pens spilled out of her bag and onto the floor. 'I could have a quick look in the glove compartment.' She gave an exasperated sigh and a small bag fell out of the larger one, a lipstick and powder compact scattering across the polished stone.

Hannah bent down and retrieved them, the woman giving her a grateful smile when she handed them back. She had hazel eyes and long lashes, her lips coral – presumably from the lipstick Hannah had just returned – but her brows were lowered, as if she was permanently puzzled.

'Thank you,' she said. 'I mean *honestly*. You would think I could manage this one thing.'

The receptionist smiled. 'It's fine, Ms . . .'

'Benson. Audrey Benson. I am sorry about this, it's just I'm *sure* I had the email printed out.'

'It's not a problem,' the receptionist assured her again smoothly. 'I've got you here. Let me print off your form, I'll just need a signature and a date, plus your car registration number, and you'll have your room key in no time at all.'

Hannah smiled, enjoying the good-natured chaos, and glanced at Noah. He was so still and sombre, it was as if he couldn't see what was happening in front of him. His eyes, she saw, were a bright, clear blue. She hadn't noticed under the station lamps or in the car. Hannah gazed at him a moment longer and then, when it was her turn, strode forward to check in.

'Hannah Swan?' the receptionist repeated when she'd given her name.

'That's right, from Green Futures. And this is Noah Rosewall. I think we're expected, though it's only me staying here.'

'I live in Mousehole,' Noah added, joining Hannah at the desk.

'Of course.' The woman, whose name tag read Chloe, gave them a warm smile. 'If you could hold on just one moment?'

She went through a door behind her and returned with a tall, wide-shouldered man who, Hannah couldn't help noticing, was very handsome. He met her gaze easily, and she felt the full force of his charisma. He strode forward, coming round the desk to meet them. He shook her hand first, then Noah's.

'I'm Daniel Harper. Did you have a good journey?' He glanced between them. 'I have to say I was expecting you slightly earlier.'

'Train delays,' Hannah said. 'There's plenty of time for

problems to crop up when you're coming from Edinburgh.'

Daniel winced sympathetically. 'It's a long journey, but it gives me confidence that I'm worth it – or at least my hotel is, if you're prepared to travel all this way. And you, Noah? You're local to the area?'

'Mousehole,' Noah said again. 'It's still an hour's journey, but that's Cornwall for you.' She thought he sounded indulgent rather than angry, as if he was proud to live in a place where the roads resembled farm tracks and short trips took half the morning.

'It is indeed,' Daniel said. He was smiling, giving them his full attention. The perfect host. 'Hannah, I've given you one of the sea-view rooms, number fourteen, which is on the floor below. You're not planning on starting work now, are you?'

'We're going to have a quick debrief in the restaurant or . . . do you have somewhere less formal?' Noah asked.

'It's the first time we've met,' Hannah chimed in.

'Why not go to the snug?' Daniel pointed to a wide arched opening off the reception area. 'It's got a bar and you can order food, but it's more relaxed than the restaurant.'

'Great,' Noah said. 'Then perhaps tomorrow we could arrange a tour of the hotel?'

'Of course.' Daniel scratched his cheek. 'We've got the tree arriving, but not until later. How about ten o'clock?'

'Ten sounds good,' Hannah said. 'And you've got the tree arriving? The Christmas tree?' She couldn't keep the excitement out of her voice.

Daniel gave her a rueful smile. 'The first Saturday in December. I would have left it a bit later than that, but . . .' He shrugged. 'Sometimes I'm not as in charge here as I think I am.' There was a glimmer in his eyes as he spoke.

'You're in partnership with someone?' Noah asked. 'Your questionnaire didn't mention that. If it's a company who have a say over any changes you're planning to make—'

'No, no,' Daniel cut in, looking slightly embarrassed. 'I meant that my girlfriend sticks her oar in, especially when it comes to festivities. She'd start Christmas in October if she could.'

'I see.' Noah set his jaw, clearly annoyed at misreading the situation.

'I think the first Saturday in December is perfect,' Hannah said, and Daniel grinned at her.

'I have a feeling Charlie's going to be saying "I told you so". And I'd just like to point out that it's a sustainable tree. In a pot, rooted, with a rehoming arranged for it up near Bodmin in the New Year.'

'That's good to hear,' Noah said.

Hannah gave an exaggerated yawn. 'I'd love to see my room now, if that's OK? Noah, shall I meet you in the snug in twenty minutes?'

'Sure – good to meet you, Daniel.' He walked off towards the archway.

Daniel took Hannah's suitcase and led her to the lift. 'New colleague?' he asked evenly as the doors opened and they stepped inside.

'He's one of the freelancers our company works with,' Hannah said. 'Gerald likes to have someone with local knowledge on each project where possible, and Noah's got a lot of experience.' She didn't want to tell Daniel that this was her first case, and Noah was here to hold her hand.

'Does he get more cheerful than that?'

Hannah shrugged. 'I have no idea. Hopefully he's just tired because I kept him waiting.' She had to give Noah the benefit of the doubt. If she anticipated the whole week stretching ahead of them like this, then she might lock herself in her room and refuse to come out again.

Once Daniel had given her a quick tour of her sumptuous hotel room and wished her goodnight, Hannah sank onto the pale green bedcover and ran her hand over it. It was a perfect space. She had opened the curtains that ran the length of one wall and exposed the view and, with all but one lamp off, she could just make out the faintest glimmer of waves, like ghosts.

She got up and washed her face, hastily reapplied her eye make-up, sprayed on a waft of perfume to disguise whatever smells had accumulated over the course of her mammoth journey, and went to meet Noah. She would have to save the drench shower until later.

The Crystal Waters snug was beautiful and, as the name suggested, cosy. It had an array of low chairs and benches covered in grey and slate-blue fabrics, with scatter cushions in bolder colours. The tables were a mixture of wood and hammered metal, and long curtains were drawn across what Hannah assumed was another wall of glass facing the hotel's gardens and the sea beyond. The bar was small but well stocked, with a gleaming silver top and a mirror behind the optics that made the space seem bigger.

Hannah sought Noah out among the room's few occupants and found him sitting on a bench against the far wall, a mug in front of him.

He looked up as she approached, and for a moment she thought she saw real emotion – anxiety or uncertainty – in his eyes, before he gave her a brisk nod and gestured to the seat opposite him.

Hannah took it, inhaling the smell of coffee. She'd had enough caffeine on her train journey to last her until next Christmas.

'All sorted?' he asked.

'Yes thanks. The room is glorious, as you'd expect. I've not done a full recce, but it looks as if the toiletries are already environmentally friendly.'

Noah put his hand on the table, his fingers inches from hers. 'We don't need to do any of that now. Have a look at the menu.' He handed it to her and she glanced at it, choosing halloumi fries and sweet potato wedges. Once the waiter had taken their order and she had declined a glass of wine in favour of lemonade, a heavy, uncomfortable silence descended.

Before she could break it, Noah spoke. 'Gerald says you've not been working at Green Futures long.'

'I started in the summer,' she said. 'So I'm still finding my way around. This is my first client meeting – I'm sure he told you.'

'He did. He said you were one to watch.'

Hannah narrowed her eyes. 'As in, one to watch for the future, like they say about young nominees who fail to win at awards ceremonies, or as in, you'll need to keep a constant eye on me so I don't ruin the project?'

Noah's grin was so sudden and overpowering, it was as if Hannah had been blinded. It knocked dimples into his cheeks, revealed white, even teeth and crinkled the edges of his blue eyes, making them seem softer. He looked completely different.

'I think the former,' he said, 'even if failed nominee is a little harsh. He clearly thinks a lot of you, in that proprietorial sort of way where he imagines all your knowledge and talent is down to him.'

'That is *not* the impression I had.' Hannah thought back to Gerald's initial reluctance to let her take the case.

Their drinks were brought over – Hannah's lemonade and another coffee for Noah: black, with thick foam on the top. She wondered if he ever slept.

'Why not?' Noah asked, stirring his drink.

'He took a bit of convincing to let me have the case. Your involvement, to be precise. But I am new, so I need to prove that I'm an invaluable member of the team.' She smiled, keen to keep hold of his friendlier mood. 'You said you live in Mousehole. That's a fishing village isn't it?'

'That's right, down near Penzance.'

'How long have you lived there?'

'All my life. Dad's a fisherman and Mum runs a café except now it's called the Mousehole Deli, just to meet all the outlandish expectations of the second-homers.'

'Ooh really?' Hannah's stomach rumbled on cue. 'I love a good deli. All those cheeses and meats from far-flung corners of Italy, olives with unlikely fillings, like sausage meat or beetroot. I've lost big chunks of my salary to a couple of delis in Edinburgh.'

'You'll have to visit while you're here. Though I'm not sure it'll live up to your expectations.'

'Why not?' Hannah asked as their food was brought over.

'Because of your face,' Noah said, accepting his bowl of mac and cheese. It looked delicious, the top perfectly golden and crunchy, tiny cherry tomatoes sliced and studded throughout, like rubies. She pushed down the urge to point out how hot they would be, to make sure he didn't burn his mouth on their molten middles.

'My face?' she repeated.

'You spoke about delicatessens as if they're on some kind

of higher plane, and your eyes went huge, which was faintly alarming because they're already pretty big. You were reverent.'

'Good food deserves reverence,' Hannah mumbled. He'd gone from monosyllabic to grinning and noticing her eyes? They were one of her better features, according to her family and friends, large and deep brown, complementing her pale skin and naturally blonde hair. Like toffee pudding and custard, her mum had said once, knowing how much Hannah liked food analogies. She picked up a halloumi chip and dipped it in the spicy mayonnaise. 'How's your mac and cheese?'

'Great,' he admitted.

'Good-oh.' If he was going to be personal, so was she. 'So, Noah, why aren't you a fisherman? That's quite often a generational thing, isn't it? Dads handing down their boats and expertise, taking their children out to sea to learn the ropes, wearing yellow macs and wellies.'

She could see the tightness in his shoulders as he shrugged. 'It didn't work out that way. I love the water, I'm Cornwall through and through, but – when it came down to it – I realized it wasn't how I wanted to spend my days. My skills are more observational, analytical. I'm not cut out for the fishing life.'

It didn't seem to be a practised answer, which surprised her. She had assumed he must have been asked that question many times before. 'Did your dad mind?' she wondered.

'At first.' He ran his fork around the edge of his dish. 'But it's much harder than it was. Hard to scrape by, let alone make a good living, so I think he's relieved I got out before it all went down the pan.'

'But you stayed in Mousehole?'

'It's a great place to live.' Now there was a slight defensiveness, as if this life choice *had* been questioned.

25

'I'm looking forward to exploring it. Cornwall, I mean. When we're not working.' She flushed under his piercing blue gaze. 'I'm here to work hard, first and foremost.'

Noah's smile was soft. 'I don't doubt it. But I'd be disappointed if you didn't want to get out and see some of the county in any spare time, as moreish as Crystal Waters is. I'd eat here again.'

'We're going to be spending most of our week here. We could have breakfast meetings, debriefs over lunch and end the day with a light dinner.' She sighed happily, and Noah laughed.

'And in between all those meals, do a bit of consulting on the side, see if we can get this place scoring top marks at its next environmental impact assessment.'

'Oh that too,' Hannah said. 'I knew there was a reason I'd come all this way.'

Noah put his fork down and fiddled with his napkin. 'What made you become an eco-consultant? You're newly qualified, but I'm guessing it's not been a straightforward path?'

'Is that a kind way of saying I look older than twenty-one?' She grinned, showing she wasn't offended and Noah nodded. She didn't go for the obvious answer: that she wanted to save the planet. Somehow she knew it wouldn't wash with him, and she could never make it sound genuine anyway. 'My dad, he . . . he's always been a keen environmentalist.'

'Oh? Is he a consultant?'

Hannah pictured him the last time she'd seen him. Long, unwashed hair in a straggly ponytail, jumper with holes in the elbows, that energetic restlessness, as clear a sign as any that he was just passing through.

'No, he's a campaigner.' She shrugged. 'I've always felt

strongly about it too, but I wasn't sure which direction to head in.' She had wanted to make her dad proud, but the thought of drifting, like him, filled her with a cold dread. 'So I did a few admin jobs after school, worked in cafés and a couple of amazing restaurants, then went to university when I'd found the right course. Still, I don't think twenty-eight is too late to have found your calling.'

He stared at her for a minute, then shook his head. 'Not at all. Sometimes people don't realize what they want to do until much later in life. Some don't ever settle to one thing. We're all different.' He glanced at his watch and drained the last of his coffee. 'I'd better head off, it's getting late. I'll settle up.'

'You don't need to.'

'It's fine. You can get the next one.'

'Sure. Thank you, then. For coming to get me, and for this.'

'I'll see you tomorrow. I'll aim for half nine, so we can go over Daniel's questionnaire again before he shows us round.'

'Sounds good.' She watched as he went to the bar and paid the bill, then he gave her a quick salute and walked purposefully in the direction of the exit, towards his swanky hybrid Land Rover and a journey over dark, winding roads to home.

She wondered whether he had anyone waiting for him in Mousehole, and why, if he hadn't wanted to discuss work, he'd suggested they meet this evening. Had he wanted to make up for his initial frostiness, realizing they needed to be on friendly terms if they were going to work well together? He had certainly warmed up once they'd started chatting, and she was feeling much more comfortable with him; less worried she'd be coming up against a brick wall every time she tried to communicate. A solid but impressive brick wall, she reasoned, remembering the way his shirt had hugged his slender but well-defined body.

Back in her room, Hannah lingered under the drench shower, then got into her pyjamas and slipped into the wide bed, pulling the cotton-wool soft duvet up to her neck. She felt drowsy and content, ready to make the most of her time in Cornwall. After all, Noah had said he would be disappointed if she didn't get out and explore. And Noah, she had realized almost from the first moment she met him, was someone you didn't want to disappoint. Or, at least, *she* didn't want to disappoint him. As she drifted towards sleep, she wondered exactly why that was.

# Chapter Three

After the best night's sleep Hannah could remember having, she had sat back on her bed, clasping a cup of tea and watching the diving sea birds she couldn't name, thinking how different it was to the monochrome view of Edinburgh's rooftops she had from her city flat. At Crystal Waters, she felt almost as if she was on the edge of the world.

Arriving in the restaurant for breakfast, she gazed through the picture windows, wide-eyed at the stretch of Cornish coastline. The sea was grey and tumultuous beneath a sky where the dark clouds chased each other, full of rain and ready to spill. The restaurant was half full but she managed to get a table by the window, a bowl of fruit and yoghurt in her hand. There were several couples, a table of four – three women and a man in their fifties or sixties – who, judging by their thick jumpers and weather-worn faces, were seasoned walkers. She marvelled at anyone who wanted to walk at this time of year, but thought that with the reward of a cosy, fire-warmed bar and a mulled wine at the end, it might be worth it. There was a family of five, the youngest child in a high chair, the father patiently feeding his son food that was ending up everywhere but in his mouth.

When a waiter came to ask for her hot order, Hannah opted for smoked salmon and scrambled eggs on granary toast, then watched as the woman from last night's check-in – Audrey – walked into the room. She was wearing black trousers covered in white daisies, and a burnt orange jumper that slipped lazily off one shoulder. She picked a table and sat down, opening a leather-bound journal before she even looked at the buffet table of cereals, juices and fruit. Hannah couldn't help being intrigued by her, as well as a little envious of her bold style which, while slightly eccentric, definitely worked.

Hannah's own outfit was burgundy wide-legged trousers and a black jumper, her blonde hair tied away from her face. She wanted to be professional but had thought, in this environment, a suit would be too formal. She wasn't sure how the guests would react to suited and booted people walking around with iPads while they were on their way to the spa.

Hannah was glad when her breakfast arrived, and even happier when she tasted it. If all the food at Crystal Waters was like this then she would be reluctant to leave at the end of the week.

Noah met her in the snug at half past nine as arranged. She thought he looked slightly more relaxed today, a dark grey jumper over his shirt – perhaps he felt the same about not wanting to alarm the guests – and his dark curls not so severely waxed.

'Sleep well?' he asked, sitting down and pulling the bowl

of sugar cubes towards him, twisting it round in what had to be an unconscious move.

'Very,' Hannah said. 'Give me Crystal Waters beds and the sound of the sea outside my window every night. And then that breakfast, the buttery toast and those perfectly light, golden eggs—'

'Stop,' he groaned. 'I should have taken your suggestion of a breakfast meeting seriously.'

'It *was* serious,' Hannah said, laughing. 'What did you have?'

Noah wrinkled his nose. 'I had to cut the edges off the bread to get rid of the blue bits.'

'Noah! That is tragic. And your mum runs a deli, too.' She shook her head. 'We can get you something here.'

'I'm fine, honestly. Let's get going.' He got out his iPad, and Hannah moved next to him so she was able to see the screen. 'This is the questionnaire Daniel filled in. You've read it?'

'I have.' She scooted even closer, peering at the document. Noah smelled wonderful, a fresh scent like a mix of newly washed linen and something sharper, some exotic fruit. 'He's already doing pretty well, isn't he?' she added, to show she had taken in the details. 'And he seems willing. Not a reluctant client.'

'He's on the right track,' Noah agreed. 'But there's always room for improvement.'

Hannah nodded. She wondered if that was a standard line he used. She would have to learn all these, get herself thinking and speaking like a Green Futures champion.

Noah turned towards her. 'If you were doing this by yourself, what would your first suggestions be? What could Daniel and Crystal Waters be doing now to reach their sustainability goals? The quick wins, and then the bigger, longer-term jobs. We should pool our ideas, then see what else we can add after the walk-round.' He gave her a quick smile.

This was exactly what Hannah had hoped for. Noah seemed to get their unusual partnership: that she was the corporate face of Green Futures for this project, but also that she had so much to learn from him. Maybe her first impressions of him had been way off the mark.

The tour was enlightening, and Hannah felt privileged being allowed into every nook and cranny of the beautiful hotel. Daniel was an easy, relaxed guide, pointing out where they collected rainwater to use in the gardens, and the new range of spa treatments they were using after a course he'd been on earlier that year suggested them as an eco-friendly alternative.

'If you've been on that, then why did you want to employ consultants?' Noah asked. 'Not that I'm suggesting you shouldn't have: I think you've made the right decision. I'm just interested.'

'I got a lot of useful information from the course,' Daniel said. 'But I felt that if I launched into the changes they suggested – and some of them are pretty huge, like solar panels and an entirely new air-filtration system – it'd be too piecemeal. I can't see it as one big project by myself – I need you to give me an action plan, tell me where to start. There's no point doing it more than once.'

Noah folded his arms. 'You've got the right attitude, you've already taken steps and, along with the fact that this is a new hotel – four years?'

'That's how long it's been open,' Daniel confirmed. 'There was a building here before Crystal Waters, a Victorian place called the Clifftop Hotel, but there was so much wrong with it that I basically had to start again. Built it up from the ground, dug extra foundations. It was a lot of work, but it was worth it.'

'I'm not sensing any kind of Victorian vibe,' Hannah said. 'Not that there's anything wrong with that. It feels modern, but also classic, somehow. It's not sterile like some of those new business hotels, is it?'

'Sterile wasn't a theme on my mood board.' Daniel looked amused.

'We're starting in a good place,' Noah reiterated. 'Shall we move on to the kitchens?'

Hannah wouldn't announce it to either of her companions, but the kitchens of any building were her favourite place, and after the breakfast she'd had, along with the halloumi chips and wedges the night before, she'd been particularly looking forward to this part of the tour.

'This is Levi.' Daniel introduced them to a wide-chested man with a shock of white-blond hair, wearing chef's whites. 'He's our head chef. We tailor our menu around what's available locally and seasonally – but I don't want to steal Levi's thunder.'

'Great to meet you,' Levi said, his Cornish accent much broader than Noah's, his huge hand swallowing Hannah's as they shook. His grin was equally expansive, and Hannah found herself warming to him as he took them through his domain, showing them where they'd made small changes, asking what they could do on a larger scale, while Daniel stood back and watched. Hannah liked the way he let his employees shine, allowing them to show off their expertise.

By the time their tour of the hotel was over, Hannah's head was full of all the delicious dishes she wanted to try, rather than all the things she needed to add to her report.

'Shall we take an hour for lunch and then meet back here?' Noah asked as they stood in reception, the reversing beep of a lorry cutting through the serenity.

'Sounds good. I'm going into the village – did you want to come?'

Noah shook his head. He seemed distracted, his eyes alighting on her and then drifting off, his tight focus of earlier gone. 'I've got to make a few calls – nothing to do with this project,' he added, perhaps worried Hannah would think he was reporting back to Gerald. 'I'll see you in an hour.'

'OK,' Hannah said, the time opening up with possibilities. She would have lots of opportunities to eat in the hotel's restaurant, and Daniel had told them that the food markets she'd seen on the website for the Cornish Cream Tea Bus took place even in December. There was no way she was missing that.

She filled her lungs with crisp, cold air as she strode down the hill into Porthgolow. The cove was spread out below her, the slate of the sea and sky contrasting with the vibrancy of the beach, a section of which was packed with food trucks, marquees and vans and, at the centre of it, the gleaming red double-decker bus. Bunting, strung around the top floor, flapped madly in the wind, and as Hannah got closer the chatter and laughter got louder, the occasional scent wafting through the air to meet her.

The seafront was quaint and pretty, a convenience store called the Pop-In looking like a relic from the past, its windows crammed with seaside treasures: buckets and spades, fishing nets and postcards, brightly coloured flip-flops that wouldn't be her first choice of footwear in

December. The bed and breakfast next door looked cosy and inviting, with a poinsettia in the window and the gleaming brass knocker crying out for someone to give it a smart rap.

The aromas from the market were delicious, and Hannah had a moment of panic that she wouldn't possibly be able to choose from all the delicacies on offer, but her panic subsided as she realized how Christmassy everything was. The familiar strains of Wizzard's 'I Wish It Could Be Christmas Every Day' reached her, waking up a familiar, deep-rooted excitement, and twinkling lights or drapes of tinsel adorned every vehicle. An illuminated Santa Claus sat precariously on top of a tiny Citroën van selling coffee, and she could smell the spice of mulled wine, the tang of frying onions, her senses fully, happily overwhelmed. But nothing was drawing her attention as much as the Cornish Cream Tea Bus.

Inside, it was both simple and inviting, the crockery, teapots and vases red and blue, a tiny but smart kitchen area at the front of the bus, cake stands in the windows full of appetizing treats. Fairy lights winked round the ceiling, above tables that were all full, the chatter from the top deck suggesting it was the same up there.

A woman in the kitchen was putting pots of jam and cream on a plate alongside a golden scone, her red hair pulled back in a short ponytail, redder apron on over a sky blue jumper. Hannah hovered, wondering whether to look for a table upstairs, and the woman caught her eye.

'Give me two secs – I've just got to serve these.' She gave Hannah a warm smile and slipped deftly past her, carrying her tray up the narrow staircase.

Hannah stayed where she was, feeling awkward, until the woman returned.

'How can I help you?' she asked. 'We're full at the moment, but if you're happy to wait five minutes we should have a table free. Or I can get you something to take away?' She looked at her expectantly while Hannah dithered. Her hour was ticking quickly away.

'I think . . .' She was at a loss as to what to do.

'Are you OK?'

'I am!' Hannah said quickly. 'Just trying to make a decision. I don't want to miss out on one of your cream teas, but perhaps I should come back when it's quieter.'

'Do you live nearby?'

'I'm staying up at the hotel – Crystal Waters. I'm on my lunch break, so I can't wait too long for a table.'

The woman glanced behind her, then returned her attention to Hannah. 'You're staying at Crystal Waters, but you're on a lunch break? Is it a working holiday, or are you just very strict with yourself?' She smiled.

'Sorry,' Hannah said, laughing, 'I can see how strange that sounds. I'm working at the hotel. The owner, Daniel Harper, has . . .' She hesitated, unsure if she should tell this woman why she was there. Being environmentally minded wasn't something to hide, but it was Daniel's decision if he told the villagers what he was planning. 'It's not important. What *is* important, is that—'

'You're one of the green guys!' the woman said delightedly. 'Amazing! I wondered when I'd get to meet you.'

'You know about us?' Hannah asked.

'Daniel said you'd checked in last night, that you were doing a tour this morning. It's going OK?'

'It is, but—'

'Oh, sorry! It's my turn to confuse you. I'm Charlie Quilter. I own this beautiful bus, and I'm also Daniel Harper's other half. I know more than most about what happens at Crystal Waters.'

'Ah!' Hannah grinned as things slotted into place. 'You've insisted on the tree going up today.'

Charlie laughed. 'I have. And Daniel's got this beautiful net of gold lights to hang over the large window in reception, too. He needs a bit of encouragement, and he'll draw a firm line at anything remotely tacky, but he's learning to appreciate the sparklier things in life.'

'I can't wait to see it,' Hannah said. 'I'm Hannah, by the way. Hannah Swan. And the tour was great. I think we're going to work well together; that's me, Noah – my colleague – and Daniel.' She hoped she sounded professional.

'I'm glad,' Charlie replied. 'And you *should* come back when it's quieter. I'll treat you to a full cream tea, but food market days are always busy – which I'm not complaining about!'

'I'd love that, thank you. I'd better grab something and head back.'

'It's not Daniel setting you a strict time limit, is it?' Charlie folded her arms. 'If so, I'll have words.'

Hannah laughed again. 'No, it's Noah. But it's actually more sensible than he realizes, otherwise I'd spend hours down here, eating my way through the entire market.'

'The choice is pretty mind-blowing. I hope you find something to your taste, and maybe I'll see you at the hotel later, when I come to help decorate the tree?'

'Not leaving that up to Daniel, then?' Hannah grinned.

'Not a chance. Lovely to meet you, Hannah.'

'You too.'

She left the bus with a spring in her step. So the hotelier and the owner of the Cornish Cream Tea Bus were together.

Porthgolow was already proving to be charming and intriguing, and Hannah had been here less than a day. She wanted to fully immerse herself in all the things that made it different from home. She couldn't imagine visiting two Edinburgh businesses in one day and discovering that one owner was going out with the other: keeping secrets in Porthgolow must be a nightmare.

Wandering through the stalls, she eventually decided on a burrito, watching as the shredded beef, bean and rice mix was topped with generous dollops of sour cream, salsa, guacamole and grated cheese, before being expertly wrapped and encased in foil. She held it in both hands, relishing the heat radiating from it as she made her way to the quieter part of the beach.

The water was grey and choppy, foam bubbling where it spilled onto the sand. A man was walking a Dalmatian in the shallows, but other than that the activity was behind her, the cold kept at bay with burgers, cups of tea and the shelter of the vehicles.

Out here, it was exposed but beautiful. To her right the beach curved gently, Crystal Waters sitting like a gleaming lighthouse on top of the cliff. She wondered if the golden Christmas lights Charlie had mentioned would be visible out at sea; whether fishing boats like the one Noah's father must own covered this part of the coastline.

To her left the beach also curved – it was a perfect, crescent cove – but the run of the shore was interrupted by a stone jetty, two speedboats tethered there. Beyond that, where the cliffs cut off the sand, there was a low promontory stretching out into the water, and a building sitting right on the edge. It was a tiny yellow house, quaint and precarious, like something out of a fairytale. Hannah forgot about her delicious burrito, because something about that house was tripping up her thoughts.

It wasn't that it was yellow, or that it looked incongruous propped on a thin sliver of rock, as if it could be knocked straight off by a careless wave. There was something familiar about it. Something that sparked a memory in the recesses of her mind, that made her think of ice creams and sand-castles and the sharp sting of sunburnt shoulders. Hannah was sure, in that second, that she had seen the little yellow house before.

# Chapter Four

Hannah didn't remember finishing her burrito. She was vaguely aware of glancing at her watch and realizing her hour was almost up, turning away from the sea and threading her way back through the food market. It was the sight of Charlie's bus that returned her to her senses, reminding her what she was supposed to be doing. She peered behind her, but the yellow house was out of view. She needed to get back to Noah.

She turned abruptly and almost bumped into a man clutching a bag of fudge. Hannah loved fudge. She tracked down the stall and bought three packets – coconut for Saskia, chocolate orange for herself, and clotted cream for Noah. She had no idea what he liked, whether he was a fudge person at all, but it seemed wrong to return from the market with news of the burrito and the bus and Charlie, and not take him anything.

The walk up the hill was hard, but halfway up Hannah

was rewarded because, when she turned to look back towards the sea, she could see the yellow house again. There couldn't be many buildings like that, and she was convinced she wasn't inventing her recognition, piecing things together wrongly from a picture she had seen on the internet. The feelings that went with it were stronger than that, something shifting deep inside her.

She walked into Crystal Waters' reception with five minutes to spare. Two men were adjusting the position of the low sofa in front of the giant window, presumably to make space for the tree.

Hannah hurried to her room, flung her coat on the bed and took her diary out of her suitcase. It was a pink, fake snakeskin Filofax that her mum had bought her over a decade ago, at a time when she'd been desperate for a means of organizing her life, a place in which she could write all her secrets, hiding notes and photos between the pages. Now it was mostly defunct because of her phone, but she couldn't bear to part with it.

She took out the photos that lived in the slip at the back. There was one of her and her dad, just before he'd gone off on one of his eco-warrior trips to some far-flung part of the world, his frame thinner than Hannah's, his blond hair unruly and his face tanned. Hannah thought her eyes looked slightly haunted, her smile fixed, but that could simply be hindsight: there had been so many absences since then. He had sent a message, via her brother Michael, that he might be in Scotland for Christmas, but she knew to take those nuggets of possibility with a pinch of salt – he hardly ever stuck to his plans. Even so, she hoped that she would see him at some point, not least so she could tell him about Green Futures.

The second photo was of a group of her friends at their

favourite bar in Edinburgh. Saskia was grinning at the camera, Seth's arm slung lazily around Hannah's shoulders, oblivious to the effect he had on her. She dropped the picture onto the bed and dug her fingers inside the tight pocket, pulling out the third and final photograph.

It was her, her mum and Michael on a beach, and it was faded, the colours leeched to pastel hues. She had been about six, Mike eight, her mum's hair curly and flyaway in an invisible breeze. Hannah was crouching at her mum's feet, guarding the sandcastle she had built. Behind them, the sand stretched into the distance, the sea sliding into view on the right of the photo. Then, in the top corner of the picture, so small as to be almost unnoticeable, a yellow house sat proudly on a rocky foundation.

Hannah let out a long, slow breath. It was the same house. It had to be. And she knew that, when she was the age in the photograph, they'd had summer holidays in Cornwall. She needed to hold the photo up against the house to be sure, to find the exact spot on the beach so she could compare the captured memory with reality.

Her phone pinged with a message from Noah:

*Coming? N.*

*On my way*, she tapped out. She left the photograph on the bed and picked up her iPad, her room key and Noah's fudge. As she made her way upstairs, another thought struck her. It had always been just the three of them on those Cornish holidays – her mum, Mike and her. She remembered that much, despite being so young. So who had taken the photo?

'OK?' Noah asked, when she reached the snug. He was frowning, tapping his fingers on the table.

'Fine.' She gave him a bright smile as she sat opposite

him. 'A present from the food market.' She proffered the bag of fudge, which was tied up with red and green ribbon.

'For me?' Noah looked startled, picking up the bag as if it was full of diamonds rather than sugar. 'Why? I mean . . . thank you. Thank you, that's very kind.'

Hannah thought he looked genuinely perplexed, and felt a mixture of amusement and pity. Did nobody buy him spontaneous presents? 'I couldn't go there and not come back with something. It was amazing. I had the most delicious burrito.'

Noah leaned towards her, his face serious. 'Careful,' he murmured. 'You don't want Crystal Waters to know you've been cheating, and after less than a day, too.'

Hannah laughed. 'Good point. We will only talk about the food market in whispered tones. But did you know that Charlie, the woman who runs the Cornish Cream Tea Bus, is Daniel Harper's girlfriend? She's the one making him put the Christmas decorations up today. She's coming here later to help.'

'If you want to get involved in that then we'd better get on with this.' He tapped his iPad and it opened up the music app and started playing a song, male voices and a guitar, at full volume. 'Shit.' He fumbled at the screen, his cheeks reddening, and closed the app down. 'Not *that*, obviously. We'd better get on with *this*.' He swiped to the right app and brought up his notes.

Hiding her smile, Hannah ordered a pot of Assam tea for them both. Noah seemed softer, vulnerable almost, when he was embarrassed, and she felt herself warming to him a little more.

After several hours and two more pots of tea, Hannah sat back in her chair and blinked furiously. The curtains had been pulled across the huge window, indicating that while they'd been listing all the ways Crystal Waters was excelling as an eco-hotel, and the actions Daniel and Green Futures could take together to improve on it, the daylight had faded. It was after four, and both her and Noah's focus was waning. There were only three bits of fudge left, for one thing.

'We've made good progress.' Noah took his glasses off and rubbed his eyes. 'And we've definitely done enough work for a Saturday.'

'Agreed,' Hannah said. 'Do you want to carry on tomorrow?'

He shook his head. 'I can't – I hope you don't mind? I know you're only here for a week, but we've got a head start, so Monday should be fine. As long as you don't feel you're wasting time?'

'Not at all.' Hannah thought of what she could do with a whole day to herself. There was the spa and the swimming pool to visit, for starters, then the rest of the village. The Cornish Cream Tea Bus would be on the beach even though the food market was over, not to mention the small matter of the yellow house that she was almost certain was in the background of her photograph. 'I'm sure I'll find some things to amuse me.'

'Good. And well done,' he added, 'if that doesn't sound too patronizing. You've got some great ideas about how to improve the sustainability of this place. I'm impressed.'

Hannah grinned. 'I'm glad I'm stepping up to the mark.'

'I'd better get going.' His gaze lingered on her face, and for a moment she thought he was going to say something else, but then a loud 'whoop' went up from reception, and Hannah was up and out of her chair in a second.

She stopped in the doorway, gasping as she took in the sight of a large Christmas tree being carried horizontally by two men, its vibrant green branches reaching like tendrils into every corner, brushing the screens that scrolled through a slideshow of the hotel's highlights, fingering the pebble-shaped coffee table. The light-wall that Charlie had mentioned was covering the window, but it wasn't switched on, the glass bulbs shimmering like diamonds rather than gold.

'Is it definitely going to fit?' asked a familiar voice, and Hannah spotted Charlie behind the tree, her hands clasped together in front of her.

'I've measured it,' Daniel said. 'It's going to fit.'

'OK then.' Charlie gave him a smile that suggested she didn't entirely believe him.

There was a high-pitched yelp from somewhere and Hannah jumped, pressing a hand against her chest.

'This looks like it might be entertaining.' Noah stopped beside her, his arm lightly brushing hers.

'It's going to look magnificent,' Hannah sighed.

The tree was manoeuvred forward, revealing the source of the yelp. A small black and tan dog was positively vibrating with excitement, its lead wrapped around Charlie's arm, forcing it to stay close to her.

Charlie noticed Hannah and smiled. 'What do you think?'

'Very impressive,' Hannah said. 'It's going to look wonderful when it's decorated.'

'That's the theory.' Daniel folded his arms and watched as the two men nudged and cajoled the tree into place.

'Charlie,' Hannah said, 'this is my colleague, Noah. Noah, this is Charlie. She runs the Cornish Cream Tea Bus.'

'Nice to meet you.' Noah held out his hand for her to shake.

'Daniel said you were local,' Charlie said. 'Mousehole?'

'That's right. Not too far.'

'Far enough when it's dark and miserable outside. Do you want to stay for some spiced apple – if you're driving – and mince pies? There's going to be Christmas music too, while we decorate.'

'I'm sure Hannah and Noah don't want to help you decorate the tree,' Daniel said. 'They've been working all day.'

'Yes, Daniel,' Charlie replied, squeezing his arm as he joined them, 'but some people love Christmas: being festive and silly, putting up baubles and tinsel. They don't see it as work.' Daniel gave her a sideways look.

'Who's this?' Hannah asked, crouching to greet the dog, who pawed at her enthusiastically. 'He's adorable.'

'This is Marmite,' Charlie said. 'My barmy Yorkipoo.'

'Who is *not* going to help decorate the tree,' Daniel added. 'He'll derail the whole thing.'

'I can't miss that,' Hannah said. 'And I never say no to a mince pie.'

'Of course you don't,' Noah murmured. She turned to glare up at him, but he was smiling and she couldn't bring herself to tell him off – not when those blue eyes held hers so completely. And she *was* a self-confessed foodie.

'Are you staying for a spiced apple?' she asked.

'I might be persuaded,' he said.

'Excellent.' Hannah hoped her delight wasn't too obvious. 'I'll just go and put my iPad away. Back in a couple of minutes.'

Hannah couldn't remember the last time she'd enjoyed anything as much as she was enjoying decorating the Crystal Waters Christmas tree with Charlie, Daniel, Noah and Marmite. The decorations were in varying shades of gold and blue, which proved to be a beautifully elegant colour combination, and completely in fitting with the design and

46

furnishings of the hotel. The tree suppliers had checked the large Scots Pine was secure before giving Daniel an invoice and leaving him to it, and he'd seemed much happier since they'd gone and he could climb up a ladder and start working from the top down.

'He likes being in charge,' Charlie said to Hannah as they watched him place a glittering golden star on top of the tree, Mariah Carey singing about what she wanted for Christmas in the background. 'He's a doer rather than a director.'

'I get that impression about you too,' Hannah said.

Charlie laughed. 'And you'd be right. But heights aren't my thing. I'm happy for Daniel to be up there.'

Noah also had a special role, which was keeping Marmite out of trouble. The dog was enamoured with him, and from the way Noah was tickling Marmite's tummy and playing tug-of-war with an edible stick, his spiced apple forgotten, it was clear the feeling was mutual. Hannah could see the cracks in his armour: the smiles, the humour, the affection for furry creatures, all of which had seemed entirely unlikely when he'd picked her up from the station.

Every time a hotel or spa guest walked into the foyer, Daniel invited them to hang a decoration, and most of them were delighted, a few clearly nervous about getting it right. Hannah felt like an insider. She wasn't sure if it was her role as eco-consultant, or the fact that Charlie had been so friendly towards her at the food festival, but whatever it was, it meant she could help decorate one of the most impressive Christmas trees she'd ever seen, so she wasn't going to complain.

'Oh goodness,' said a voice, 'I am *so* sorry!' Hannah turned to see Audrey step hastily away from the ladder, then change her mind and lunge forward, grabbing hold of it. 'Are you OK? I haven't unsettled you?'

'No harm done,' Daniel said smoothly, though the look on his face suggested it had been a close call. 'Are *you* OK?'

Audrey rubbed her shoulder. 'Yes, fine. I didn't mean to . . . I should watch where I'm going.' She waved the book she was holding, and Hannah caught sight of the title: *A History of West Cornwall: Shipwrecks and Stagecoaches in the Victorian Era.*

'Are you a historian?' Hannah asked.

Audrey smiled, her eyes crinkling at the corners. 'I am, of a sort. I'm a research associate, and I'm writing a book about England's most haunted hotels. Actually, no,' she corrected, as Daniel made a noise – a grunt or a gasp – from the top of the ladder. 'I'm finishing a book, on behalf of a friend.'

'You're writing about haunted hotels?' Charlie asked, clearly intrigued. Even Noah had stopped playing with Marmite to listen.

'That's right.' She pushed her glasses up her nose. She seemed nervous now all the attention was on her.

'But not this one,' Daniel said, coming down the ladder. 'This building's only been here a few years.'

'Yes, that is a shame.' Audrey looked around, as if surprised by the modern surroundings. 'But there's still potential.'

'What do you mean, potential?' There was an unmistakable edge to Daniel's voice.

'The Clifftop Hotel that stood here before Crystal Waters,' Audrey continued. 'It was reputedly haunted, and that's what my friend, Richard, was working on. I didn't realize the old hotel would be entirely gone when I booked. I thought some of the original building might remain.'

'It was falling down,' Daniel said. 'It was unsafe. I had to get rid of it and start again.'

'I do understand that, Mr Harper,' Audrey replied, unruffled.

'And in fact, it might well not matter. I hadn't intended to do it this way,' she added, glancing at each of them in turn, 'but I would love to sit down with you all at some point, to find out about your experiences here, if there's anything unusual you've witnessed.'

'Oh, we're just guests,' Hannah said reluctantly. 'We've only been here a day.'

'There's nothing,' Daniel said firmly. 'No unusual experiences.' He was being polite, but Hannah could see it was an effort.

Charlie squeezed his arm, and he turned to look at her. 'Daniel?' She said it softly, but he shook his head, as if warning her not to say anything else.

A chill – part excitement, part terror – ran down Hannah's spine. In Edinburgh she was surrounded by history, the past right on her doorstep, and sometimes shoved in her face. There were at least a million ghosts in the city, if all the stories and nightly walks were to be believed.

She didn't discount the idea that ghosts existed, that tragic moments in people's lives sometimes played over and over, like a recording stuck on repeat, but she had never explored the idea, or how she really felt about it. She'd never been on a serious ghost hunt, never seen anything spooky herself, hadn't done more than laugh and squeal in the appropriate places on a tour that ended in Edinburgh's underground vaults. However, the thought that this glimmering, plush hotel might have dark secrets and voices whispering in corners was highly appealing. Ghost stories at Christmas were obligatory, but she had never imagined stumbling on one that might be *real*.

'OK then,' Charlie said, her gaze not leaving Daniel's.

'I haven't seen anything,' he reiterated. 'The occasional

flickering light is expected in a building this size, especially when the storms kick off. It's not paranormal.'

Charlie didn't say anything, and Daniel shifted uncomfortably.

'And I imagined those voices in my office. It was late, I was alone apart from the night staff, and I was tired. The hotel buzzes with activity so much of the day, it makes sense that my mind would play tricks on me. It didn't mean anything, Charlie.'

Audrey had tucked her book under her arm and opened a notebook. She was trying to scribble notes while the pad did its best to snap closed on her. Hannah wanted to point out that she could lean on the pebble-shaped table, but was reluctant to interrupt the conversation. She glanced at Noah and he raised his eyebrows, which gave her no insight into how he felt about the possibility of sharing their up-and-coming eco-hotel with some ghosts.

'This is very interesting,' Audrey said. '*Very* interesting. Would you be happy to go through your experiences with me in detail? When did they happen, exactly?'

'No.' Daniel shook his head. 'I'm sorry Ms Benson, but there is no chance this hotel's haunted. It's less than five years old!' His laughter sounded forced.

'What about the footsteps?' piped up a voice, and everyone turned to the reception desk, and the young, freckled woman who had checked Hannah in the previous evening.

'Chloe,' Daniel said. 'Now is not—'

'They happen every night,' Chloe continued, wide eyes showing that she was loving the drama. 'Eleven thirteen on the dot. I've been on lates recently, so I know. And they *run*. Right across the room, from over there.' She pointed to the corner where the shimmering Christmas tree stood. 'All the way over here, then behind us. It's like whoever it is goes *through* the desk, as if it didn't exist. It stops when it gets to your office, Daniel.'

'Where you heard voices that time,' Charlie said gently.

'And sometimes,' Chloe went on, 'there's this draught as the footsteps go past, you know? Like *whoosh.*' She swiped her hand past her face. 'It's why Kevin wanted to swap with me. He didn't want to do lates because it scared him.'

'This is *wonderful*,' Audrey said.

'I thought Kevin wanted to swap because the bus timetable changed and he couldn't get home if he did lates.' Daniel was sounding increasingly exasperated, and Hannah's heart went out to him. Clearly, a haunted hotel was not as appealing a marketing strategy as an eco-hotel.

'That's what he told you,' Chloe said boldly, 'because he didn't want you to think he was a wuss.'

'I wouldn't have . . .' Daniel started, then sighed. He rubbed his hands over his face and Hannah heard him mutter, 'For fuck's sake.'

'This is all a bit unexpected,' Charlie said, her tone soothing but authoritative. 'Audrey, what are your plans for the book? I assume you'll write about the history and any present-day . . . hauntings.' She glanced at Daniel, then slipped her hand into his. 'Will that make up one part of the book?'

'One chapter,' Audrey confirmed, looking up from her notebook. 'I'm very encouraged by this promising activity.'

'I'm not,' Daniel murmured.

'But I do appreciate this may not be ideal for you, Mr Harper,' she continued. 'I'll be discreet. Would you be happy for me to speak to your employees? Kevin and . . .'

'Chloe!' Chloe gave a little wave. 'You can always hang

out with me until eleven thirteen this evening and hear them for yourself.'

'Oh, I will undoubtedly be doing that, if Mr Harper sanctions me to run a low-level investigation.'

Daniel didn't reply immediately, and everyone turned towards him. Hannah realized she was holding her breath. She wanted him to say yes. She wondered if Chloe would let *her* stay in reception until eleven thirteen. She supposed she couldn't stop her.

'Ms Benson,' he said eventually. 'Please, call me Daniel. Perhaps we could have a chat over coffee tomorrow. You can tell me your plans while you're here and I can see how best to . . . accommodate you. How does that sound?'

'That's most generous of you,' Audrey said, beaming. 'And please call me Audrey. Now, I must dash. I don't want to miss my reservation in the restaurant – I can't wait to try the hake!' She wished them all good evening and strode away, her history book under her arm, her notebook still open in her hand, as if she might need to write something down any second.

Once she had gone, Daniel spun to face Charlie. 'Ghosts? *Ghosts*, now? She can't be serious.'

'We've all heard it, Daniel,' Chloe said. 'Sorry, but it's true. And you said yourself you've had some stuff happen, so you can't *totally* disbelieve us.' Hannah wished she had the same unfiltered confidence as the young receptionist.

'I don't disbelieve you, Chloe,' he replied. 'I could just do without this right now. And please, all of you, don't mention it to anyone else. I don't want it going further than the staff and . . . Hannah and Noah – you're happy to keep it quiet, too?'

'Of course,' Hannah said.

'I won't breathe a word,' Noah agreed.

'Good. Thank you. Not everyone loves the idea of their holiday destination being haunted.'

'You were very nice to her, eventually,' Charlie said. 'And wouldn't you like to hear a bit more of the history of the old hotel? See what might be causing all this . . . stuff?'

'Other than tired minds, faulty light fittings and dodgy air-conditioning units?' Daniel shrugged. 'Hopefully nothing. And fingers crossed, the changes Noah and Hannah are going to help us make will get rid of them for good.'

'Better an eco-hotel than an *ecto*-hotel, right, Daniel?' Chloe called.

Daniel gave her a bemused look.

Chloe rolled her eyes. 'You know, ectoplasm? You have seen *Ghostbusters*, haven't you?'

Daniel shook his head, but his mouth was lifting at the corners. 'That, Chloe, was a terrible joke. Beyond terrible.'

Chloe gave a little curtsey.

'Come on everyone,' he said. 'Back to the tree, otherwise we'll still be doing it when our invisible occupant makes an appearance. I hope he doesn't knock it down, that's all I can say. If people who died centuries ago start interfering with Christmas at this hotel, after all the effort we've put into it, then Audrey is going to have to do more than write about them in her book – she's going to have to find us a bloody exorcist.'

He climbed the ladder again, tension visible in his shoulders.

Hannah exchanged a glance with Noah and then looked at Charlie, who had her fingers pressed over her lips, her gaze on Daniel. Hannah thought that whatever the couple had prepared for in the run up to Christmas, it was unlikely to have been this. But as much as she felt sorry for Daniel, she wasn't entirely disappointed at the turn of events. She dropped to a crouch and buried her face in Marmite's warm fur, hiding her smile.

# Chapter Five

It was late when they all declared the tree fully decorated, and after standing for a moment in reverential silence and staring at it, the gold fairy lights fading on and off and making the whole thing sparkle magnificently, Noah reluctantly handed Marmite back to Charlie and said goodnight. Hannah walked him out to his car.

'That wasn't exactly in our remit,' she said, hugging herself. It was so cold, but the air was crisp and sea-scented, and the densely scattered stars winked mesmerizingly above them. 'It was fun, though.'

'You should go in.' Noah reached out and touched her arm, as if checking her temperature, then leaned against the bonnet as if he had no intention of leaving immediately. 'You'll freeze to death.'

'So will you,' she pointed out. 'That jumper looks thin.' She didn't add that she'd come to that conclusion because of the way it hugged his muscles, and that the effect was quite distracting, especially when it was a choice between looking at them, and looking at graphs on an iPad. 'Marmite's great, isn't he?' she added.

He nodded. 'I love dogs. Mum and Dad have got three: Albert, Rodney and Del Boy. No prizes for guessing where the names came from.'

Hannah laughed. 'What kind of dogs are they?'

'Pointers,' Noah said. 'They take up most of the house and need about three walks a day, so they sort of belong to the village. Neighbours are always pitching in, taking them to the beach or further afield.'

'Communal pets! Are they affectionate?'

'Very.' The smile Noah gave her was pure indulgence. 'If you make it to Mousehole you'll need an introduction.'

'I'd love that,' she said sincerely, overjoyed that Noah had thawed enough to *almost* invite her to his village. 'What do you think of the ghost stuff?'

He gave a short laugh. 'I think that Daniel's in for a tough ride if he's assuming he can sweep it under the carpet. Audrey and Chloe alone are a force to be reckoned with.'

'And . . .?'

'And I'm going to make sure that one day this week I'm here late enough to experience those footsteps for myself. I'm tempted tonight, but I've got an early start tomorrow and I won't be popular if I'm not at my brightest.'

'Oh,' Hannah said, 'then I'd better let you go. But I'd be up for ghost hunting with you whenever you fancy it. As long as we don't let on to Daniel that we're buying into the whole thing.'

'Of course not.' Noah opened the car door. 'But a word of warning, Hannah,' he said, turning back to face her. 'Client visits don't usually involve Christmas-tree decorating and impromptu hauntings. Just in case you were thinking that every project with Green Futures was likely to be this interesting.'

'Understood.' She nodded, matching his faux-serious tone. 'It must be something about Porthgolow. I'll lower my expectations for future cases.'

'Good idea. But obviously . . .' he paused, looking at her closely, as if he could gauge her response to what he was about to say before he spoke.

'Obviously what?' she asked with a laugh.

'Make the most of everything while you're here.'

She nodded, unsure how to reply. There was something about the way he'd said it that made her skin prickle. 'Oh, I intend to,' she said, with more gusto than she felt.

'See you on Monday, Hannah.' He climbed in and shut the Land Rover door, gave her a final wave and drove out of the car park.

She went inside, grateful for the hotel's blast of warmth, and said goodnight to Chloe.

'You're welcome to hang about for another half an hour if you want?' Chloe said. 'You know, to hear the ghost? I think we should give him a name. The more real we make it, the more likely Daniel is to believe it.'

'I'm not sure Daniel is ready to embrace the ghost,' Hannah replied. 'Maybe once he's talked to Audrey he'll change his mind. I'm off to bed now, but I'll take you up on that offer another night.'

They said their goodbyes and Hannah went back to her room. Once there, she found she couldn't sleep. Her mind kept replaying her last exchange with Noah. Not just the softening of his demeanour, the jokes and the puppy love, but the suggestion that he believed the stories. He was eager to experience the ghostly goings-on for himself. She realized that was why she'd turned Chloe down: she had been half an hour away from a possible ghostly encounter, but she didn't want to have it without Noah.

The week ahead no longer felt like a simple work trip, but one with huge potential. She wasn't sure she believed Chloe's story, and Daniel was convinced his own experiences had a mundane explanation, but she was determined to keep an open mind. If there was going to be a ghost hunt at the hotel, she wanted to be part of it.

Her eyes fell on her Filofax, and the photographs she hadn't put away. The yellow house had slipped from her thoughts, but there it was, sitting perched behind her family in a faded picture from her past. Audrey wasn't going to be the only one looking into the history of Porthgolow over the coming days: Hannah had some investigating to do herself.

She had a light breakfast on Sunday morning, eschewing the various cooked options because of where she was headed next. She had warmed instantly to Charlie, had loved helping to decorate the Christmas tree, and was keen to spend time getting to know the owner of the fabulous Routemaster while she was here.

When she stepped outside the hotel, the wind was flinging rain in every direction, as if falling straight to the ground wasn't dramatic enough. Hannah pulled up her hood and hurried down the hill to the soundtrack of waves crashing against the shore.

She stepped onto the bus, subtly festive with its twinkling fairy lights, and Charlie grinned at her.

'Hannah! It's lovely to see you. You and Noah aren't working today?'

'Noah had somewhere else to be,' Hannah said. 'A family thing, maybe.'

'You shouldn't be working on a Sunday anyway.' Charlie gestured to a table. Hannah could see Marmite in the driver's cab, scrabbling to get out now there was someone else to stroke him.

'You are,' Hannah said, laughing. She waved at Marmite and he barked.

'But I'm in the tourist industry. Sundays are one of our busiest days.' She looked around the deserted bus and shrugged. 'Except when it's freezing cold and pelting it down. Do you want a cream tea?'

Hannah paused, the 'yes' on the tip of her tongue, then changed her mind. 'Could I have a coffee and a scone with jam?' She took off her coat and put it on the bench beside her. 'I'd love a full cream tea, but I'm going to wait and bring Noah here.'

'What coffee do you want? We've got some special Christmas flavours.' Charlie handed Hannah a menu, and she scanned the options.

'Cinnamon latte please. How long have you run the bus?'

'Coming up to two years. I inherited it last February; there were a couple of false starts, and then I launched the Cornish Cream Tea Bus on this very beach last May. It's done pretty well for itself.'

'*You've* done well for *your*self,' Hannah said. 'I doubt the bus could have managed it all on its own.'

Charlie patted the wall. 'Maybe not, but Gertie is pretty special.'

'Gertie?'

'My uncle's name for her. He left her to me in his will.'

'I'm so sorry,' Hannah said, but Charlie waved her away.

She thought of the photograph, nestled inside her purse now, in case there was an opportunity to talk about it. 'Did he live in Porthgolow all his life?'

Charlie laughed. 'Oh no, I'm not from here. I'm from Cheltenham originally. My friend Juliette moved to Porthgolow and invited me for a holiday, and I brought Gertie with me and never went home.'

'You fell in love with Porthgolow?' Hannah glanced out at the swirling rain. Even in such bleak weather, the cove and the neat village rising up the cliff was attractive, enticing. 'I'm not surprised.'

'Porthgolow has a lot going for it. To me, it . . .' Charlie looked away, biting her lip. 'It feels like it's sprinkled with some kind of magic, and I'm not the only resident who feels that way. There are so many things to love about it.'

'I can see that,' Hannah said, then thanked Charlie as she brought over a steaming mug that smelled of spice, sugar and Christmas. 'And one of them is up at the hotel, slightly disgruntled about his unusual pest problem?'

Charlie shook her head. 'Poor Daniel. I can't remember the last time I saw him so ruffled – he's mostly unshakeable. When I first met him, he used to infuriate me with his unflappability, watching coolly while I got myself into a state over something.' She bent down to peer at the scone in the oven, then stood and leaned against the counter.

Hannah sipped her latte foam. 'Why do you think he's so upset about Audrey's revelation, if he usually takes everything in his stride?'

Charlie sighed. 'I don't know. Maybe it was just a shock – the idea that his hotel might have some unwanted guests and, in turn, attract some unwanted attention. He's worked so hard to get Crystal Waters to where it is, and he's always trying to improve it – as you know because he's brought you and Noah in. He cares about it, and maybe he feels this is out of his control.' She shook her head. 'I tried to talk to him last night, but he was still a bit put out. Then he texted me this morning to say that the Christmas tree was still standing, so the ghost hadn't got the better of it.' She rolled her eyes. 'If he starts waging a war on spirits that probably don't exist, I'm going to have to intervene.' She turned away, and Hannah watched as she took the scone out of the oven and put it on a plate, along with a tiny dish of butter and another of jam.

'It might not come to anything.' Hannah gratefully accepted her scone, took a moment to smell it, then cut it in half and liberally spread it with butter and jam. 'Audrey will do her research and go home, then by the time the book comes out, things will have gone back to normal. And even if it does get a bit of attention, tourists love the idea of haunted hotspots, don't they? Who doesn't love a ghost story? It can't do any harm to the hotel's reputation.'

'That's very true.' Charlie said, suddenly brighter. 'I don't want him to get stressed. We've got a lot going on this Christmas: my cousin and her boyfriend are coming back from LA in a few days to stay at the hotel, though Delilah hasn't told me exactly when.'

'Oooh LA,' Hannah said. 'Fancy!'

Charlie grinned. 'Sam's finishing a film role out there and Lila's with him. They're both actors now, which I'm trying to get my head around. They met when Sam was filming *Estelle* in Cornwall and Gertie ended up being part of the on-set catering.'

Hannah almost choked. 'I *read* about that – you being part of the filming. I had no idea your cousin ended up—'

'Getting in the middle of everything?' Charlie finished. 'She does tend to do that. But she's brilliant and I love her, and she and Sam are *so* happy. I can't wait to see them.'

'I bet,' Hannah mumbled through a mouthful of scone. 'This is delicious, by the way. I'm already looking forward to a proper cream tea.'

'You're welcome here any time I'm open, though that won't be every day during the week – not when the weather's so bad. I'll let you know.'

Charlie busied herself in the kitchen while Hannah ate. She heard her murmuring affectionately to Marmite, and it reminded her of the way Noah had softened the previous evening, the fond way he'd spoken about his parents' pointers. She wondered what he was doing today. It was obvious that he was close to his family, so maybe they had Sunday lunch every week. Hannah felt a pang of envy, wishing she was as close to her mum, that she'd had the chance to be close to her dad. She thought of the photograph in her purse.

'What's that yellow building for?' she asked casually. 'The one right on the edge of the water.'

Charlie smiled. 'Believe it or not, it's a house. My friend Reenie lives there.'

'Isn't it dangerous?'

'It can be, I think, especially when the weather is wild, but Reenie's been there for years, and she won't move now.'

Hannah wondered if Reenie had been living there when the photo was taken. She drained her coffee. 'Thank you so much for that, Charlie.'

'My pleasure. What will you do with the rest of your day?'

Hannah looked out of the window. The rain had eased, but it still looked fairly inhospitable. 'I might be brave and go for a walk, or I might go straight back to the hotel.' She got out her purse to pay, the edge of the photograph peeking out of the notes section. It was on the tip of her tongue to ask Charlie to look at it, to confirm that it *was* the same house, that Hannah wasn't seeing things that didn't exist, but there was a burst of voices behind her.

'Careful, Flora. Slow down. You don't know how slippery it is!'

'Can I have a cake?'

'I'm having a hot chocolate.'

Hannah turned to see a woman with dark curly hair and three children, two young girls and a teenage boy, step on board.

'Thanks so much, Charlie,' she said hurriedly and, pushing the photo further into her purse and smiling at the family, slipped past them and onto the sand.

# Chapter Six

Hannah was disappointed with herself for not plucking up the courage to ask Charlie about the photograph, but there was one person who would know for certain whether their childhood holidays had included Porthgolow. She had been vague when Hannah had mentioned it before, but then she'd only been asking whether her mum knew the part of Cornwall she was travelling to, and hadn't realized there might be a deeper significance.

The sight of the festively decorated hotel reception buoyed her, the light wall like a gentle, golden waterfall, the baubles, birds and snowflakes on the tree shimmering in its glow.

In her room Hannah put the kettle on and, standing at the window and looking out at the churning sea, dialled her mum's number.

'Hello?' She always answered as if she didn't know who was calling, even though she must have seen Hannah's name appear on the screen.

'Mum, it's me. How are you?'

'Good thanks. Busy. You know what it's like.' Hannah's mum worked in the office at Harvey Nichols, managing the security, and the run-up to Christmas was one of her busiest times. 'How's Cornwall?'

'It's beautiful, if a bit windswept, which is entirely understandable of course, but . . .' She took a deep breath to stop herself from babbling. 'The hotel is great. It's an interesting project, and the local consultant I'm working with, Noah, is . . . we're getting on OK. I'm enjoying it.'

'That's good, Han. Glad your first foray into the field is going well. How long—'

'The thing is, Mum,' she said, cutting over her, 'are you *sure* we didn't come to Porthgolow when we were little? I know we stayed in Newquay, but they're quite close together, and it's a really pretty village with a great beach.'

'I said before that we might have,' her mum replied. 'How do you expect me to remember where we went on day trips? Cornwall has hundreds of beaches.'

'There's a photo of you, me and Mike, and there's this yellow house in the background. I found it yesterday – the house – when I went to the beach. I don't know if—'

'If it's the same one? It's unlikely, don't you think, that a house so close to the water would still be there after twenty years? It would have fallen into the sea by now.'

Hannah hadn't thought of that. 'You're right. Sorry, I just wondered.'

'Why does it matter, anyway – you shouldn't spend all your time thinking about it. Enjoy the place, get your work done and show them what you're capable of, then come home. I need to head off now, love. Someone's at the door.'

'Bye then,' Hannah said, as her mum hung up the phone.

There had been nobody at the door. Her mum had a loud, ostentatious doorbell, and Hannah would have heard it in the background. She lifted up the photo, peering at the tiny house behind the three figures. It was close to the water, but there was a few feet of rock in front of the building that Hannah didn't think was there now. The cliff had eroded, but the house was still safe.

She pressed her hand against the side of the kettle, decided it didn't need reboiling, and poured hot water into her mug. She was about to add milk when a thought struck her: she had mentioned that the house was yellow, but had she said it was near the cliff edge? How had her mum known it was so close to the water – unless she could recall Hannah's photograph perfectly? She closed her eyes, trying to remember her exact wording.

Why didn't her mum want to admit they'd spent time in Porthgolow? She had asked Hannah why it mattered, and Hannah didn't know. Except that she had this strange feeling about being here, a feeling that it held some significance for her. Since she'd seen the yellow house she'd had a tightness in her chest, as if she couldn't fully relax. If her mum wasn't going to help, then she would have to rely on the locals. Hannah was going to have to get to know the people of Porthgolow.

She spent the rest of the day revisiting her and Noah's report, reading in her room and, in the evening, talking to Saskia on the phone, telling her about Noah and the hotel, giving her all the details of the Cornish Cream Tea Bus and the possible hauntings, but leaving out the connection between the village and her photo. She wasn't ready to share it with anyone else yet, not when the conversation with her mum had left her so unsettled.

Confusing thoughts kept Hannah awake into the night, and she woke on Monday morning with gritty eyes. Now she knew her mum wasn't telling her the truth, it meant there was something here to find. Hannah would look into it, but she couldn't let it take over. She had a job to do, too.

After breakfast, Hannah went to meet Noah in the snug. He was wearing a russet-coloured jumper over his shirt, the dark frames of his glasses unable to hide the blueish smudges under his eyes. He had already ordered a coffee.

'Hi,' she said. 'Did you have a nice Sunday?'

'Fine, thanks. How was yours?'

'It was good. I had a scone on Gertie.'

'Gertie?' He wasn't looking at her, instead fiddling with something on his iPad, and Hannah felt a surge of irritation.

'That's what the bus is called. It's like she's formally the Cornish Cream Tea Bus, and affectionately known as Gertie. Charlie's scones are delicious, you should really—'

'We should really be getting on with this, Hannah, if we can. There's a lot to get through.' He tapped the table.

'Sure. I didn't mean to—'

'No problem,' he said quickly. 'This is where we got to on Saturday afternoon.'

With her heart sinking, Hannah took her seat next to him. It seemed that Noah the frosty snowman was back.

Their progress that morning was focused, because Noah didn't give Hannah any choice. They discussed the different air-filtration systems they could offer Daniel, and how they could make the spa and swimming pool more eco-friendly. The financial and environmental costs of the work had to be weighed up against the savings they would make when they were complete.

Noah had an almost-encyclopaedic knowledge of green

solutions, and he'd worked on several local projects: the Eden Project, a hotel near Tintagel, a spa in St Austell that had been renovated with sustainability in mind. Hannah was learning a lot; she just wished it was happening in a less chilly environment. He was a different person to the man who had been playing with Marmite and sharing details about his family on Saturday night, and she wondered what had happened to affect his mood so completely.

'Right then.' He flung the cover of his iPad closed as if it had personally offended him, and rubbed his hands over his face. 'Lunch.'

'Shall we get something together?' Hannah asked.

He stood up. 'I have to make some calls.'

Hannah shot to her feet, too. She didn't know what she was going to say until it came out. 'No, not right now. You're coming with me.'

'I have things to do – unrelated to Crystal Waters.'

'They can wait. You've been like a bear with a sore head all morning, and I'm going to cheer you up.'

He clenched his jaw. 'I don't need you trying to make me feel better.'

'Tough. I've got to work with you, so it's self-preservation, really. I've made the decision, and now I'm going to get my coat: wait there.' She stormed out of the snug, wishing she didn't have to leave him, certain he wouldn't be there when she got back, but when she returned he was standing in exactly the same spot. She thought he looked sad rather than angry, and her irritation faded.

'Come on then,' she said, checking he was following as she walked out of the hotel.

'Where are we going?' he asked.

'Wait and see.' She would have thought it was obvious

now they'd left the hotel, but she didn't say that in case it upset the delicate balance of the situation.

They were halfway to the cove before he spoke. 'I'm sorry, Hannah. Yesterday wasn't particularly great, but you don't deserve my anger. It isn't aimed at you at all, I hope you realize that.'

'I guessed there must be something else wrong,' Hannah said. 'Unless you were offended by my outfit, and I picked it specifically for its inoffensiveness.' She flashed him a smile, and he almost returned it, his gaze flicking down to her long tan boots and up again. His hands were buried deep in the pockets of his coat, his shoulders hunched against the cold. 'You can offload on me if you want,' she added. 'It might help to talk about it.'

He shook his head. 'I shouldn't be bringing this stuff anywhere near work. I promise I'll make more of an effort. You're taking me to the Cornish Cream Tea Bus, I take it.'

'What do you have against scones?'

'Nothing, I just really fancied a sandwich.' He sounded genuinely upset.

'A full Cornish cream tea on Gertie *comes* with sandwiches. Charlie will do whatever it takes to lift your mood – she's that kind of person.'

'Honestly, I'm fine. I'm going to discard my dark cloud – look.' He waggled his shoulders, as if shaking something heavy off them, and Hannah laughed. This time when he smiled, it reached his eyes.

They were about to step onto the beach when the door of the Pop-In shop opened and a grey-haired woman came out, her arms tightly folded. She glanced in their direction then looked towards the sea. 'Storm's comin' in,' she said. 'Forecasts haven't spied it yet, but I've lived here all my life and I know when there's a big'un on the horizon.' She turned her full attention on them. 'What are you doin' here, grockles? You don't want t'be holidaying when it hits.'

'I'm not a grockle,' Noah said, his Cornish accent suddenly more pronounced. 'Mousehole born and bred.'

The woman looked him up and down. 'Fine. But you can't tell me this maid is local. Not wi' those clothes on, and those wide eyes as if everythin's new and shiny.'

'I'm from Edinburgh,' Hannah said, her curiosity outweighing her annoyance at the way she'd been spoken about. 'We're helping Daniel at the hotel, and are just on our way to see Charlie, on the bus.'

Her mention of the two locals had the desired effect, and the woman's eyes softened. 'Well then, enjoy it. You'll be stranded up at Daniel's place soon enough.'

'I'm Hannah.' She held out her hand. 'And this is Noah. Do you fancy having a cream tea with us?'

The woman paused, glancing between them. 'Rose is behind the till for the next hour, and I suppose a break wouldn't do any harm. I need to tell Charlie about the storm, too. Give me two secs to let Rose know, and I'll be wi' you. I'm Myrtle. Everyone knows me here.' She shuffled back inside and Noah turned to Hannah, his brows lowered in confusion.

'Why did you invite her?'

'The more the merrier,' Hannah said lamely. She couldn't tell Noah that she wanted to pick Myrtle's brains, that she hadn't missed the older woman saying she'd lived in the village all her life and, from the looks of things, was keen on knowing everyone else's business.

'*She* didn't approve of your outfit,' he said, and it took Hannah a moment to join the dots back to her earlier, pathetic joke.

'No,' she replied. 'It picks me out as an intruder, apparently.'

Noah raised an eyebrow. 'Well, just to make it clear, I think it's great. Especially the boots. Don't let her make you feel bad.'

'Oh.' Hannah's cheeks flamed. 'Thank you.' With her mind completely blank after his compliment – his *flirtatious* compliment – they waited in silence for Myrtle to come back out.

'Well I must say,' Myrtle said once they were settled at one of Gertie's downstairs tables, 'this is pretty cosy.'

Charlie had welcomed them on board, admitting they'd caught her just in time. The squally weather meant that customers were scarce, and she'd decided she would be more productive shutting up and focusing on Gertie's Christmas plans.

'So cosy,' Hannah agreed, clutching her mug of tea close to her body so she could absorb its warmth. 'Tell us more about your Santa tour, Charlie. Is Gertie basically the sleigh?'

'Sort of,' she called from the kitchen, where she was arranging mini sandwiches on cake stands. 'I thought I could bring some festive cheer to a few Cornish villages, and Hugh, the pub landlord, has agreed to be my Santa Claus.'

'You're giving out presents?' Noah asked. He was already more relaxed, and had listened to Charlie's description of her Christmas Cornish cream tea with increasing interest. Hannah thought she'd heard a quiet moan escape his lips at the mention of the brandy clotted cream that would accompany the mince-pie-inspired scones.

'Only tiny ones,' Charlie said, bringing cake stands laden with finger sandwiches and mini cakes to their table. 'I can't afford to be too generous, but the wholesalers I use do a few nice gifts, and meeting Santa is the most important thing. Dig in.'

'The problem when you've got someone like Charlie, is that people start to expect things.' Myrtle took a sausage and caramelized onion sandwich off the stand and separated it into two halves, a blob of sauce plopping onto her plate.

'What do you mean?' Hannah asked.

'Locals and visitors alike start to expect food markets an' tours an' fireworks on the beach when it's solstice. An' it's all well an' good, and I'm not sayin' I don't enjoy it, because I do. *Now*, anyway,' she added pointedly, leaving Hannah to believe that there had been a time when she and Charlie hadn't seen eye to eye. 'But there's folk who come to rely on it, for entertainment and company, to encourage visitors.'

'So Charlie's holding up the whole of the Porthgolow economy,' Noah said. 'And you're worried she'll leave?'

'I have no intention of leaving!' Charlie screeched. 'Myrtle, why didn't you tell me you felt this way? Gertie may have wheels, but I'm pretty sure Crystal Waters hasn't got a hidden pair of wings. Daniel isn't leaving his hotel, and I'm not leaving him – or anyone else in Porthgolow. My life is here.'

It was an impassioned speech that made Hannah feel a little emotional. She was relieved when Marmite broke the tension, waking up from his nap and barking at them.

Myrtle muttered something under her breath, and Charlie dropped into the remaining seat at the table. 'Has someone been spreading rumours?'

Myrtle shook her head. 'It's just . . .' she gestured outside. 'Storms. Winter. I don't like it. Always feels like it's threatenin' our little community. Ignore me.'

'Did you say you've always lived here?' Hannah asked softly.

'Been in Porthgolow all my life,' she said proudly. 'Seen a fair bit o'change, I can tell you.'

'You've seen lots of tourists, I expect.'

'On an' off. Not as popular as other places, mind. Porthgolow is unassumin'. Charlie's brought the life we need – Daniel too, if I'm bein' fair. But we've no arcades or amusements or any o' that rubbish. Stella and Anton are seeing the benefits, too.'

'They run the bed and breakfast on the seafront,' Charlie said, pointing. 'It's got beautiful views, and they're both such stylish people so their house is, too. It's a lovely place to stay.'

Hannah chewed her nail. 'You don't have any old photos, do you? I'd love to see what Porthgolow looked like years ago – before Gertie and Crystal Waters. Ooh, imagine if there were photos of the Clifftop Hotel. Wouldn't that help Audrey? Myrtle, if you've got any—'

'Who's this Audrey?' Myrtle asked warily.

Charlie tapped Hannah's hand. 'She's a guest at Crystal Waters, interested in history.' She didn't elaborate, and Hannah remembered Daniel's insistence that the spooky turn of events shouldn't be mentioned to anyone who didn't need to know.

'As is this lass.' Myrtle jabbed a finger at Hannah. 'I can have a look, I s'pose. See what I've got.'

Hannah smiled. 'That would be wonderful.'

'Give me a couple o' days – my spare room's a bit of a 'mare – an' I'll see what I can come up with.'

Hannah nodded enthusiastically as Charlie got up to check on the scones. The sandwiches had been delicious and, despite it being a Christmas cream tea, had no turkey in sight; instead they were filled with salmon, sausage and onion, and goat's cheese with a spicy, fruit-rich chutney that Hannah assumed was local.

She glanced at Noah, who was holding a mini doughnut in front of his face. It had a swirl of cream and a red jelly sweet on top.

'You do realize every doughnut is going to pale into insignificance after this one,' he said to Charlie.

She laughed. 'You've not even tasted it.'

'I've tasted the sandwiches, and anyway, if you're giving me themed cakes, you're already halfway to winning my affection.' His cheeks were slightly flushed, his blue eyes alive in a way they hadn't been that morning.

'Is it really that easy to gain your affection?' Hannah asked. 'Give a cake a hat?'

He glanced at her, his smile faltering. 'Just a hat isn't really trying, though. This one's clearly a Santa hat. No ordinary beanie will do.'

'Got it. An *identifiable* hat. I'll remember that next time I bring you something to eat. I can see why the fudge wasn't up to scratch.' She sighed dramatically to show she was joking.

'Hey.' He rested a hand on her forearm. 'The fudge was delicious, and generous, and unexpected. Spending time in Porthgolow with you is going to damage my waistline.'

'It's cheering you up, though,' she said.

His smile disappeared completely. 'It is. It *has*. Thank you, Hannah. I don't know how you—'

'Mince pie scones!' Charlie said, placing the cake stand on the table with a flourish, and Noah's sentence remained unfinished as he, Myrtle and, after a moment, Hannah, put one on their plates, the smell of brandy butter and spiced fruit filling the bus with Christmas promise. Hannah was far from disappointed, but she wished she knew what Noah had been about to say.

'Why do you want to see Myrtle's photos of the village?' Noah asked. He didn't sound out of breath, even though they had reached the steepest part of the hill. 'When Charlie said she'd also ask Reenie, whoever she is, if she had any albums, you looked happier than I've ever seen you. What's going on?'

Hannah glanced sideways at him. The wind was too strong for his hair wax and dark curls were trying to escape. 'I'm just interested. Audrey has got me thinking about the history of this place, the old hotel that used to be here—'

'That was an afterthought. You asked if Myrtle had any photographs and *then* you remembered Audrey. Don't think you can sneak this past me.'

'I'm not trying to sneak *anything* past you,' she said. 'I was trying to distract her. She seemed anxious, and—'

'That's not it, either. Have you found out something else about Porthgolow?' He stopped and turned to face her, and Hannah was forced to stop, too.

'It's not related to what we're doing at the hotel, or Audrey, though I do think she'd love to see old photographs of the village. It would really help with her book, don't you think?'

Noah folded his arms.

'Can we please go back to the hotel?' she said. 'It's so cold.'

'It's not that bad. Wait until the storm really ramps up.' There was a glint in his eye, and Hannah took the opportunity to change the subject.

'Have you ever been out on the water during a storm? You see it on those programmes like *Deadliest Catch*, where they're facing waves that are twice as tall as the boat. I can't imagine being out there when it's like that – it's scary enough from here.' She pointed out to sea, where the waves were cresting all the way to the horizon.

'It's magnificent though, isn't it?' He turned so that he was standing next to her.

Hannah silently agreed: It was nature at its wildest, and she was lucky she could stand here and watch it, but even so, she felt unnerved being so exposed to it.

'Hannah?' he prompted, looking down at her. 'Are you OK?' The back of his hand brushed against hers and she jolted. It had felt like a burn, the only point of heat when the rest of her was so cold.

She swallowed. 'It's spectacular, but I still wouldn't want to be out there.'

'Let's get back in the warm,' he said softly, and they started walking. 'Why do you want to see the photos?' he asked again, after a few minutes of silence.

'Why did you turn up in such a bad mood today?' Hannah countered, recovering some of her composure.

He sighed. 'There's just something I'm dealing with, at home. It's . . . difficult.' He paused in front of the hotel doors and ushered Hannah through. She stepped into the glittering reception. Once the doors had closed behind them, the gathering winds were a memory, the choppy sea beyond the glass as unreal as a silent video.

'I'm sorry,' Hannah said. 'Are you sure you're OK to be here, then? Working on this project?'

'Absolutely,' Noah replied quickly. 'It's good to have something to take my mind off it. And look, Hannah, it's none of my business why you want to see those photo albums. I shouldn't have pressed you. Back to the snug?' He gave her a weak smile, the earlier warmth gone from his eyes as if it had been blown away by the weather. Hannah nodded, her throat tight.

She followed him into the cosy room, feeling as dejected as he looked. It seemed she'd undone all her good work in one fell swoop.

## Chapter Seven

Over the next few days, Hannah and Noah built up a comprehensive plan of how Daniel could turn Crystal Waters into a top-performing eco-hotel. He was a constant presence, which meant they could run ideas past him, return with him to areas of the hotel where they thought a new innovation could make a difference, or where their plans would involve significant remodelling.

Hannah liked the methodical way Noah worked, and he always consulted her, treating her as an equal, listening to her ideas and debating them seriously. After their walk back to the hotel on Monday afternoon, he hadn't mentioned his difficult situation again, or asked about her interest in Porthgolow's past. He had been courteous and friendly, occasionally teasing, but sometimes she had noticed him staring at his phone or out of the window with a furrowed brow, his mind somewhere other than Crystal Waters.

Time had slipped away and Hannah was coming to the

end of her week in Cornwall. Although Myrtle had agreed to hunt down her old photo albums, Hannah found that she didn't have the confidence to follow it up. Besides, it was so unlikely that they would show her anything relating to her own past. She had asked the older woman on the spur of the moment, and now she felt silly for doing it.

As Thursday afternoon turned into evening, Hannah and Noah wrapped up the first draft of their report.

'What do you think?' Noah sat back on the bench and picked up his coffee – Hannah thought it must have been his fifth of the day, at least. 'Happy with what we've done?'

'Very,' she said. 'But I guess clients aren't always this involved in the early stages. Do you usually just present the report and see what they say?'

'It depends on the client, and the way they want to do things. Daniel is one of the most hands-on I've ever worked with. We already know he approves of our suggestions, and he's aware of the scale of changes we think he should make. Once I've costed it all, he'll have the complete picture.'

'Will you send me the report when you've added the costs?'

'I'll run everything past you,' he said. 'It won't go to Daniel without both of us – and Gerald – signing off on it.'

'Great.' She smiled, hoping he wouldn't see how sad she was about leaving. It felt like a missed opportunity. Porthgolow had so much potential and she hadn't had the time to explore it. 'Fancy a last sausage roll on the bus, if it's still open? I'll check – hang on.' She got out her phone to text Charlie, but Noah put a hand on her arm.

'I don't think you should go out in this.' As he spoke, the wind rattled the window at the far end of the room, the view of the gardens and the sea beyond obscured by heavy rain.

'There go my hopes of a hot-tub session before I leave. What about you? I don't like the thought of you driving all the way to Mousehole when the visibility's next to nothing.'

'I'm used to it,' Noah said. 'And my car is basically a small tank.'

'But even tanks are dangerous if you can't see where you're going.'

'I'll give it a couple of hours, then make a decision.'

'As we're not going into the village, I suggest we order a whole host of starters here and work our way through them. What do you think?' She raised her eyebrows and Noah laughed.

'Everyone knows starters are the best part of a meal. You have my full approval.'

'I can gain your affection with starters as well as themed cakes, then?' She was desperate to get the teasing Noah back one last time before she left Cornwall.

'Hannah,' he said, lowering his voice, 'you have no idea—'

'*Seriously?*' The angry voice they heard wasn't inside the room, but it was loud enough to break into their conversation.

'That doesn't sound good,' Noah said, giving her a questioning look.

'Nope. We should find out what's going on.'

They hurried to the doorway, to see Daniel standing next to the reception desk, facing off with a young man – a boy, really. Hannah felt a glimmer of recognition: she'd seen him with his family on Charlie's bus. Whatever he'd done, Daniel wasn't happy about it.

'I can't believe you would go into my office without authorization, Jonah!' Daniel turned away from him and began pacing, his hands on his hips. 'Who told you?'

80

The boy, Jonah, stared at the floor. He was holding something protectively, both arms cradled around it. 'Charlie mentioned it the other day. She told me not to say anything to anyone and I haven't, but she didn't say I couldn't *do* something.' He looked up defiantly.

Daniel stopped walking. 'So Charlie told you that some people believe there are . . . ghosts, here at the hotel, and you took it upon yourself to plant a fake one in my office?' His dark eyes were shining with anger.

Jonah shrugged. 'It's on a motion sensor, like an outdoor light, but it's a speaker so it plays the recordings I've created.' He held up the device and Daniel took it and turned it over. Hannah and Noah hovered next to the Christmas tree. Hannah didn't want to interrupt, and she was too intrigued to leave them to it.

Daniel nodded, his shoulders dropping. 'It's very clever,' he admitted, grudgingly. 'God help the rest of the world when you get going, Jonah, but I really don't appreciate you doing this. I've agreed that our guest, Audrey, can investigate certain areas of the hotel, and . . .' He glanced behind him, gave Hannah and Noah a quick, grim smile and then dropped his voice. 'How do you think she'd react if she discovered we'd faked the activity? And what about the hotel's reputation if your recordings led her to believe we really did have ghosts, and we got a write-up as one of the most haunted hotels in Cornwall when, in fact, there's nothing here? Pranks are all well and good, but you need to think of the consequences, OK?'

'It would have been so funny,' Jonah said, unperturbed.

'No doubt.' Daniel ran a hand through his hair, the glint of amusement back in his eyes. 'It's not happening, though. I'm going to circulate a memo to the staff along with your photo, and make sure nobody lets you go *anywhere* in this hotel alone. You're on Crystal Waters' "most wanted" list.'

Jonah sighed dramatically. 'Charlie won't get into trouble for telling me, will she?'

'I haven't decided what to do with her yet,' Daniel said ominously. 'Did you walk up here by yourself? It's rough out. Do you need a lift home?'

'Nope. Got my technical parka.' Jonah zipped the blue coat up to his neck, pulled on the hood and popped the poppers so it was tight round his head. Hannah thought he looked like a Smurf.

'Can I keep hold of this, just for today?' Daniel waggled Jonah's fake ghost device. 'I'll give it back next time I see you. Besides, you'll ruin it if you take it with you. It's biblical out there.'

'It's calmed down actually,' Charlie said, slightly breathless as she walked through the door. 'The rain has, anyway. Hi Jonah, what are you doing here?'

'Sabotage,' Daniel answered. 'For which you're partly responsible.'

Charlie stopped, her expression immediately guilty. 'What did you do, Jonah?'

'Something he won't be repeating,' Daniel said. 'Get off home while there's a lull in the storm.'

Jonah did as he was told, hurrying out with his head down.

Daniel turned to Noah and Hannah. 'Are you guys OK? Need anything from me?'

'Our report's all done bar the budget,' Noah said. 'We just came to see—'

'Why I was losing it? Fair enough. Thankfully, that particular disaster has been averted.' He gave them one of his winning smiles, and Hannah could see his anger was gone already. 'If you've finished your report we should have dinner together.'

'When you said you lost it, Daniel, what did you mean?' Charlie asked.

He turned to her. 'I shouted at Jonah because you told the entire Kerr family about Audrey and the ghosts, and Jonah decided the best thing he could do with that information was to plant some spooky sounds in my office to up the ante.'

Charlie closed her eyes. 'Shit. I'm so sorry. I didn't think any of them would do anything with it.'

'You expected Jonah to leave something like that alone?' He gave her a quick kiss. 'No harm done. I do want to hear this, though.'

He fiddled with the device and, a moment later, Hannah heard voices: urgent whispering that got more and more unnerving as Daniel turned the sound up. The words were indistinguishable, but Hannah felt the distress and anguish in the voices all the way to her bones. She shuddered.

'God,' Charlie said, eyes wide.

'Fucking hell,' Daniel murmured. He switched the recording off, plunging the room into silence. 'That boy is an evil genius and I'm glad I sprang him before he had a chance to plant this and give someone – probably me – a heart attack.'

'Did you say something about dinner?' Noah was two shades paler and Hannah bit the inside of her cheek. It wouldn't be fair to laugh when they'd all been scared by Jonah's handiwork.

'I did,' Daniel said. 'As the storm's eased off I suggest we go to the pub in the village. Marnie, are you OK if I head out for a couple of hours?'

He turned to the dark-haired receptionist who had

remained quiet throughout the exchange. 'As long as you take that thing with you, or destroy it on your way out.' She pointed at Jonah's device. 'It's creepy as hell.'

'No arguments there,' Daniel said. 'Coats, everyone. Meet you back here in five. As much as I love my hotel, I suddenly feel like a change of scene. And the Seven Stars does a mean fisherman's pie if you're interested.'

Hannah nodded eagerly. When it came to fisherman's pie, she was always interested.

The wind wasn't as extreme as Hannah had expected, but she still felt bullied by it as the four of them strolled down the hill. Porthgolow was lit up ahead of them, lights twinkling in the dark, the beach and sea a black void untroubled by moonlight. Charlie and Daniel walked ahead, hand in hand.

'OK?' Noah asked, as a particularly feisty gust pushed Hannah into him.

'Yeah. I was glad to get out, too. I love the hotel, but I'm looking forward to something different.'

'You've probably worked your way through the Crystal Waters menu now, anyway. As long as pub grub isn't a step down for you.'

'I'm not a food snob,' Hannah said, laughing. 'As long as it's delicious, it doesn't matter where it comes from or where I eat it.'

'And yet you're pretty trim,' Noah replied. 'How do you manage that? I have to go running to stay in shape, and that was before I started spending time with you.'

Hannah concentrated on placing one foot in front of the other. She didn't think it would be a good idea to compliment him on that shape, because then he'd know she'd been admiring it. 'I'm a fidgeter,' she explained. 'Mum says that's the root cause of our slimness, but I also go swimming a lot, and in Edinburgh it's easy to walk everywhere, but you don't manage it without a lot of hills, so there's that. Also, when I worked as a sous chef I was on my feet for long shifts, expending lots of energy. I don't know.' She shrugged. 'It's just one of those things. I'm lucky, though, because I could never stop enjoying food, regardless of how my metabolism processed it.'

'You were a sous chef?'

'While I was studying,' Hannah clarified. 'It was meant to pay my way through university, but it ended up being much more. The Whisky Cellar is this tiny, beautiful restaurant, and some of the food is pretty niche, but it's so delicious. You should come!' She turned to him, careful to keep her footing on the steep hill. 'Have you ever been to the Green Futures office? Visit Gerald and then I'll take you out, show you all the places only a local would know about.'

Noah laughed. 'It sounds great. And if you're passionate about this Whisky Cellar place, I definitely need to go. Better than Crystal Waters?'

Hanna chewed her lip. 'Possibly. But only because I used to chef there. If Crystal Waters let me cook for them, I might change my mind.'

Noah didn't reply, and despite the darkness she could tell he was staring at her. She could almost feel the weight of it.

'What?' she asked.

'It's just . . .' he started. 'Nothing. It's nothing, Hannah.'

At the bottom of the hill, she could hear that the waves were pummelling the sand with force, and the darkness suddenly felt threatening. She thought of Jonah's ghosts and gave an involuntary shudder, then had to keep her pace steady and not rush inside when Charlie pushed open the pub door and warmth and light engulfed them.

'Charlie, Daniel!' called a man from behind the bar. He was in his fifties, Hannah guessed, with dark receding hair and a cheerful face. 'I wasn't expecting many customers on a night like this. Just Jeb and Cliff, who I can always count on.' Two men who looked like stereotypical Cornish fishermen were sitting on wooden bar stools, heavy beards emphasizing their beady eyes as they tracked the newcomers.

'We thought we'd brave the storm for your pie, Hugh, if you're serving it tonight?' Daniel looked around the bar, and Hannah did the same. It was rustic but well appointed, the kind of pub she could spend hours in. An open fire crackled in the fireplace, and gold and red metallic paper chains did loop the loops above the bar. She had a sudden memory of her and Mike making them when they were younger, tongues and fingers smarting from the endless licking and inevitable paper-cuts. She only realized she was grinning when Noah gave her a strange look.

'Have you ever known me *not* serve my pie?' Hugh said, mock sternly.

'Course not,' Daniel replied easily. 'Let me introduce you to Hannah and Noah. They're helping me make Crystal Waters more sustainable. Hannah, Noah, this is Hugh, esteemed landlord of the Seven Stars and architect of Cornwall's best fisherman's pie.'

'Lovely to meet you,' Hannah said, shaking his hand. 'I love fish pie – I often make it for my friends.'

'So you're a proper connoisseur, eh?' Hugh smiled at her. 'And Noah, good to meet you too.'

'Likewise,' Noah said. 'Nice pub.'

'Said with usual Cornish enthusiasm.' Hugh laughed. 'Where're you from?'

'Mousehole. Porthgolow's great, though. What I've seen of it.'

'Which until tonight has been the hotel and the bus,' Hannah added.

'The Harper and Quilter empire,' Hugh said, grinning. 'And we're very happy to have it. I'm surprised, though, that you two are green experts and not exorcists.'

Daniel's smile vanished. 'How do you know?'

'Anton at the B&B,' Hugh said. 'No idea where he heard it from, but finding the original source of gossip in this place is near impossible once it's already doing the rounds. This pub is pretty old, you know. I've got a story or two I could tell.' He patted the bar top lovingly. 'Get your ghost lady to pop down here and have a gander.'

'I might do that,' Daniel said, before turning to Charlie and shaking his head slowly. She gave him a winning smile and asked Hannah to pick a table.

She chose one close to the fire and Daniel ordered a bottle of red wine, which seemed appropriate on such a miserable evening. As he poured, Hannah wriggled into the cosy bench enthusiastically, and realized she was wriggling against Noah.

'Sorry,' she murmured, moving away.

He gave her an amused glance and picked up his wine glass.

'Do you want to see the menu or are you going for the pie?' Daniel asked.

'Pie,' was the resounding chorus, and he returned to the bar.

'I'm going to miss this place,' Hannah admitted. 'I love

your bus, Charlie, and the hotel, and I know I'm supposed to be professional and not admit to having enjoyed myself, but even when the weather's like this, your village is beautiful.'

'Who says you can't enjoy yourself while you're working?' Noah said. 'I hope I haven't given you that impression. Or . . .' he chewed his lip. 'Don't answer that.'

'Of course you didn't give me that impression. I'm fairly new in the role,' she explained to Charlie, 'so I'm still finding my feet, and it's been good working with Noah, who's a total pro.'

'What made you become an eco-consultant?' Charlie asked.

Hannah shrugged. 'My dad's always been very active as a . . . green champion. I wanted to make him proud, to do something that really mattered to him.'

'You must be close, then?'

'Not really. He's not around much. He's always fighting the good fight somewhere, trying to make a difference. He's very passionate.' She wondered if they would be able to read between the lines: absent father; protestor; a bit nutty. 'This wine is delicious. What is it? A Côtes du Rhône?' She turned the bottle round so she could read the label.

'I'm surprised you're not a food critic,' Noah said lightly. 'That's something you're passionate about.'

'You can have more than one passion,' Hannah said, giving him a look. 'What are yours, other than sustainability, Cornwall, Santa-themed cakes, your incredibly posh Land Rover and your parents' dogs? Oh, and running.'

Noah grinned. 'You've been paying attention.'

Hannah's cheeks heated. 'Charlie, how are your Christmas plans for Gertie coming along?' Before Charlie could answer, she turned back to Noah, indignant. 'Anyway, Noah, you only just told me about the running, and I could hardly forget about your dog adoration after you spent that evening at the hotel rolling about on the floor with Marmite.'

Daniel returned from the bar and gave Hannah a bemused smile. 'OK?'

'Fine.' She folded her arms and stared at the table. 'So that's Hugh, who's going to be Santa on your tour?' Christmas seemed like much safer territory.

'He's such a kind soul,' Charlie said, nodding. 'The villagers are all lovely, really. It's one of the best things about this place, its sense of community. I can see how Edinburgh would be completely different. I used to live near Cheltenham – it's where my parents still are – and while it's a beautiful town, I never felt at home there the way I do here.'

'Edinburgh's great,' Hannah said. 'It's always busy, your senses never get bored, but . . .' she was about to say she felt at home here too, but that was ridiculous when she'd only been here a few days and had spent most of the time with her head buried in an iPad screen.

'But what?' Charlie asked.

'I think I came here when I was little,' Hannah rushed. 'On holiday. But I don't know. I *didn't* know, until . . .'

Charlie leaned towards her. 'Really? What makes you think that?'

Hannah glanced at Noah and Daniel. They were locked in a discussion about exercise, treadmills versus road running, so she took the opportunity to get her photo out of her purse. As she did, the wind battered against the thick windows, the fire spitting as the storm made its presence known. Daniel stopped mid-sentence and glanced around the room, his brows lowered.

'Better keep an eye on that,' he murmured, then went back to their conversation.

'This is one of my favourite photos,' Hannah said quietly. 'It's me, my mum and my brother on holiday. We used to come to Cornwall, and we always stayed at a self-catering place in Newquay. But look at the house behind us.'

Charlie picked up the photograph by the corners and scrutinized it. Hannah held her breath.

'That's Reenie's house,' Charlie said. 'No way it could be anywhere else. How amazing is this?' She was suddenly animated, her eyes wide. 'You came to Porthgolow when you were little, and so did Daniel. He loved it so much he built his hotel here, and now you've been sent here for work. Have you spoken to your family?'

Hannah nodded. She felt both relieved and uneasy after Charlie's confirmation. 'I spoke to Mum, but she says she can't remember coming here. Perhaps we beach-hopped all the time and she doesn't recall the names of the villages.' Hannah wished she could believe that, but she couldn't ignore the sharp way her mum had dismissed the subject.

'You used to come on holiday here too?' Daniel asked.

'It couldn't have been anywhere else,' Hannah said. 'Charlie agrees with me. Look.' The photo was passed around, Daniel and Noah as intrigued as Charlie had been.

'Is that why you wanted to see Myrtle's photo albums?' Noah asked.

Hannah shrugged. 'I wondered if seeing old photos would bring back any memories. I just have this feeling . . . but then that's all it is. We came here on holiday when I was little, which is amazing, but I shouldn't read anything else into it.'

'Other than that Porthgolow is a really special place, and people keep returning for one reason or another.' Charlie handed her back her photograph. 'Wow though, Hannah. To have only just discovered this and be heading home on Saturday. You'll have to come back next spring when the weather's better.'

'Oh, I'd love that!' Hannah said, exchanging a smile with her. And suddenly it was that simple. There was nothing strange that her mum didn't want her to know; they'd been here years ago, her mum had forgotten, and Hannah had decided there was some mystery to be uncovered, inspired by talk of ghosts and old buildings and the past.

Hugh arrived with their fishermen's pies and they tucked in, the chatter stalling while they ate. The pie was as delicious as Daniel had suggested, and reminded Hannah of nights with her friends, when she would spend the whole day cooking, lovingly preparing the fish and the sauce and the buttery, crispy, cheese-topped mash. In fact, it tasted like her own fish pie, down to the capers and chunks of fresh tomato, but a far superior version, as if it was infused with something uniquely Cornish, the essence of the sea, that she wouldn't be able to recreate in Edinburgh however hard she tried. It was perfect.

'What do you think?' Daniel asked.

'Bloody brilliant,' Noah murmured.

'The best,' Hannah confirmed. She cleared her plate and pushed it away from her, full and content. Daniel ordered another bottle of wine and Noah chose an alcohol-free beer appropriately named Ghost Ship, and as the drinks flowed, so did the conversation.

The four of them got on well: Daniel was laid back and charming – when his hotel wasn't being challenged on its spectral inhabitants – and Charlie was instant friend material, warm and easy to talk to. Noah, she discovered, was really funny when he let himself relax. He wasn't as horizontal as

Daniel, but the uptightness she'd seen earlier in the week was gone. Hannah wanted to capture it somehow, take this night back home with her so she didn't forget a single minute.

She was heading to the loos, her cheeks warm from the fire and the red wine, when she came to a sudden stop. On the door of the ladies' was a white ceramic tile decorated with a line drawing of a woman in a long dress and bonnet, a basket over her arm. She glanced at the men's door, where the sketch was of a man in a tailcoat and trousers, a pipe in his mouth.

Hannah felt a flash of nostalgia strong enough to make her catch her breath, like when a song playing in a shop transported her back to a night out with Saskia, or a waft of someone's perfume reminded her of a particular summer. She was sure she'd seen these tiles before. Of course, it was possible that she'd been in any number of pubs and bars with these same door signs. But it was also possible that she was remembering being here as a child.

She reached up to touch the tile, the crack that led from the bottom corner to the woman's booted foot. Blinking herself out of her trance, she pushed open the toilet door, registering her wide-eyed expression in the mirror above the sink as she did so.

As she returned to the main bar she heard raised voices, and found Charlie, Daniel and Noah with their coats on, Charlie's features pinched with worry.

'What is it?' Hannah asked.

'We need to go,' Daniel said. 'The storm's getting worse.'

Hannah could hear the wind flinging itself around the building, the rain battering the windows. At least she hoped it was the rain, and not the sea, advancing on the pub like some malevolent army while they drank wine in front of the fire.

Noah handed her her coat, and she put it on and zipped it up to the neck.

'Only goin' t'get worse,' said either Jeb or Cliff. They were still sitting at the bar, showing no signs of getting up themselves.

'Better be off 'ome,' the other one added. 'This is a rum'un, tha's fer sure.'

Hannah followed the others to the door. When Daniel opened it, it was as if all Cornwall's might was throwing itself at them in a single, desperate hit. Charlie gasped and Daniel shut the door again, wiping his face.

'OK,' he said calmly. 'Now we know what we're up against. Getting back to the hotel isn't going to be much fun.'

'You don't need to come with us,' Noah said. 'Hannah and I can go on our own.'

Daniel shook his head. 'I need to be up there. We might have power outages or damage to the building. I can't leave this to the night staff. Besides, I wouldn't feel comfortable leaving you to get back by yourself. And Noah, I know you're used to Cornish winters, but you might want to stay at the hotel tonight. You'll have a room, free of charge, if you don't want to risk the drive to Mousehole. Charlie,' he turned to his girlfriend, and kissed her, 'what do you think? Go back to yours and check on the dogs? I can't imagine Jasper's enjoying this, even if Marmite's fine. Call me the *second* you're home.'

'I'll get there before you do,' she protested. '*You* call *me*. You're the ones having to go up the cliff.'

'Done. But I want to see your missed call on my phone when we reach Crystal Waters.'

Noah and Hannah said goodbye to Charlie, the situation calling for hugs that Hannah didn't mind in the slightest. She loved this village with its friendly residents, its sandy cove and its beautiful bus; she would have liked to talk to Audrey more about her investigation, and to have spent more time sampling the food at the hotel, the Cornish Cream Tea Bus and – now that she'd tried the fisherman's pie – the Seven Stars. She may have read too much into her mum's forgetfulness, but Porthgolow was still a place she wouldn't forget in a hurry.

She glanced at Noah, and he gave her a warm smile. 'OK?' he said. 'We'll be fine.'

She returned his smile. She couldn't admit to him that she wasn't worried about the walk back to the hotel; in fact she was exhilarated at the thought of being out in such a raw, powerful storm. If he'd seen reluctance on her face it was because she didn't want to go home. And, if she was going to be entirely honest with herself in this precarious moment – they might not make it back, after all – a big part of that reluctance was leaving Noah.

She had spent the week with him and, grumpy moments aside, she'd loved being in his company. The glimmers of humour and warmth he'd let slip through had left her wanting more. She could have stayed in front of the fire, talking and drinking red wine, occasionally brushing his arm or his thigh with her own, until the storm was long gone.

The thought that he might be staying at the hotel tonight sent a rush of electricity through her, even though they barely knew each other. The prospect of returning to Edinburgh for Christmas, spending time with a newly single Seth, didn't burn as brightly as it had done before she'd arrived in Porthgolow.

'Right,' Daniel said, once he and Charlie had had a whispered conversation that Hannah hadn't been paying attention to. 'Ready, folks? Let's do this.' He gave a pointed nod and opened the door again.

Hannah took a deep breath and, keeping close to Noah, stepped out after Daniel into the midst of what felt, after the first couple of seconds, like Armageddon.

# Part Two

## Let Jingle Buns Ring!

# Chapter Eight

Cornwall was angry about something. That was the first thought Hannah Swan had as she stepped out of the Seven Stars with Daniel Harper, Charlie Quilter and her new colleague, Noah Rosewall, and into the storm. They had enjoyed their evening in the pub, a celebration of sorts after Hannah and Noah had spent the week at Daniel's clifftop hotel, Crystal Waters, preparing a report on how to enhance the hotel's green credentials. Hannah was beginning to regret that she hadn't had more time to get to know the Cornish village of Porthgolow, or her attractive, Cornwall-based co-worker, but now those thoughts were on hold because there was no room for anything else but the storm.

Porthgolow's usually placid cove roared with the sound of wave after wave crashing onto the sand, as if they were fighting each other in their desperation to reach land. Hannah was worried about Gertie, the Cornish Cream Tea Bus, but a quick glance told her that the vintage Routemaster was far enough above the tideline to survive even an extreme assault. Charlie was also looking at her bus and Hannah wanted to say something reassuring, but the ferocity of the wind and rain made keeping their eyes open – let alone talking – difficult.

The streetlights flickered, adding to her unsteady feeling, and something was banging repeatedly somewhere nearby, as if a board or door had come loose. She moved closer to Noah and he put his arm around her shoulder, anchoring her to him. They followed Daniel and Charlie along Porthgolow's seafront, until they came to the road that cut up through the centre of the village, sea-facing houses in neat rows on either side. Charlie clasped Hannah and then Noah's hand, gave Daniel a quick, tight hug, and then began striding away from them, her long legs making short work of the climb. Daniel watched her for a moment and then turned and gave them a thumbs-up.

Hannah wanted to laugh, the gesture wildly comical under the circumstances, but she and Noah returned it, and they started walking again.

Soon Hannah was soaked, chilled to the bone and struggling to drag in a full lungful of air. It was as if the storm was stealing her breath, and it was starting to feel less exhilarating and more exasperating. They hadn't even reached the end of the seafront, and somehow they had to get all the way up the cliff.

Something small and white darted across in front of her, a bright streak in the dark, causing her to trip and Noah to tighten his hold on her. She peered past him, trying to see what it was.

'What?' Noah said, almost shouting to be heard.

'Hang on!' she shouted back, and shrugged out of his grasp.

All the buildings on the seafront, apart from Myrtle's Pop-In, had three stairs leading up to their front doors, the houses tall with high windows. Hannah cupped her hands around her eyes to shield them from the rain, and was rewarded when she saw the white shape huddled against the steps of the bed and breakfast.

She crept towards it, keeping her movements small. She was only a few feet away when she saw what it was: a small, bedraggled dog. It looked up at her with large eyes, its ears drooping, its whole body vibrating with fear and cold.

'Oh my God,' Hannah murmured, and reached a hand out. Rather than cringe from her touch, the dog shuffled towards her. She unzipped her coat, picked the creature up and hugged it against her chest, covering it as best she could. It was about the size of Marmite, solid and heavy in her arms, mostly white with a few dark patches of fur.

'Hannah?' Noah and Daniel had followed her, and when she turned and pointed at the dog's nose sticking out of her coat, they stared at her as if she'd gone mad. But the wind was stronger than ever, shrieking its fury, and the raindrops were like pebbles, so there wasn't time for explanations. Noah held his hand out and Hannah took it, clutching the dog against her with her free arm.

They heaved themselves up the hill, Daniel's pace relentless, Hannah's legs aching before they were halfway up. The roaring of the wind got louder and the clouds churned above them, releasing an occasional glimmer of moon, like a spotlight behind curtains. She had been excited in the pub, but now she could almost taste her fear. Despite staying on the side of the road furthest from the sea, they were still close enough to the cliff edge that a strong gust could sweep them to unforgiving rocks and deadly undercurrents far below.

Hannah adjusted her hold on Noah's hand, lacing her fingers through his.

After what seemed like hours, they reached the familiar brick wall of the hotel. They hurried across the car park, the automatic doors opening for them and, just as quickly, shutting behind them, dulling but not eliminating the sounds of the storm.

Marnie, the receptionist, stared aghast as they caught their breaths, dripping water onto the polished floor. She disappeared as Hannah pushed her hood off her face.

'Who's this guy?' Noah asked, taking off his own hood.

'I don't know, but he was getting drowned.' The dog stared up at Hannah, Noah and then Daniel, his dark eyes intelligent. 'I know he's probably not allowed in the hotel, but I couldn't leave him there.'

'Of course not,' Daniel said. 'I've never seen him before, and I would have thought that if he belonged to someone in the village, I'd recognize him.'

The dog pulled a leg free from Hannah's coat and pawed Noah's arm. Now he was out of the storm, he seemed curious rather than frightened. Hannah unzipped her coat all the way, and the dog turned and licked her cheek.

'He's very cute,' she said, 'but I don't know what to do with him.'

'He can stay here for now,' Daniel replied. 'He can't go back out in that.' He took his phone out of his pocket and his expression softened. He pressed a button and held it to his ear, grinning when his call was answered. 'Charlie, you made it home OK?' He walked away from them as Marnie appeared with large, fluffy towels. She handed them out and then stopped, her eyes fixed on the dog.

'We found him out in the storm,' Hannah explained.

'Daniel said it's fine to keep him here for the moment. He doesn't recognize him – do you?'

Marnie held out a hand and the dog sniffed it. 'I've never seen him before. There's no collar, either.'

'He doesn't look like a pedigree,' Noah said. 'Just a good old mutt. No offence, dog.' He said it affectionately, ruffling the fur under its chin. When he unzipped his coat, Hannah could see his dark shirt was soaked, the cotton clinging to his torso.

'Can I put the dog down?' she asked Marnie, turning away from Noah.

'Sure. He's no more bedraggled than most of the guests this evening. I'll make sure the floor is dried before anyone else walks on it.'

Hannah could see they'd all tracked in a fair amount of water, the stone even shinier than usual. She set the dog down gently and he started exploring, Marnie keeping a watchful eye on him. Hannah took the opportunity to dry her hair with the fluffy towel which, she realized with glee, was also warm. She took her time, running it over her hair and face, imagining the hot shower she would have when she got back to her room.

'Better?' Noah asked, when she emerged. He'd also dried his hair, and for the first time his curls were unleashed. They were thick and dark and unruly, and so gorgeous that Hannah didn't know why he ever tried to hide them. He gave her a tentative smile, and she felt a surge of pure lust.

'Much better,' she managed. 'You?'

He nodded. 'We've survived one of Cornwall's more impressive storms. The waves sounded immense, but I didn't think it was wise to stop and take a look on our way back.'

'There's a great view from the snug,' Marnie said. She was

following the dog around the space, presumably making sure he didn't wander – or relieve himself – anywhere he shouldn't. He was sniffing the Christmas tree, his short tail wagging. 'We've been turning all the lights off, so you can really see what the sea's up to,' she continued. 'You should go, get properly dry. I can make you a couple of hot chocolates.'

'That sounds like a good idea,' Daniel said, joining them, his own towel slung around his shoulders.

'Did Charlie get back safely?' Hannah asked.

'She did, and the dogs are fine too. I pity any poor bastard who has to be out in this – twenty minutes was enough for me. Are you both all right?'

'Is that all it was?' Hannah asked, astonished. 'It seemed like hours.'

Daniel laughed. 'Afraid so. It did feel a bit Herculean. But well done for rescuing the dog; I didn't see him.'

'He shot across in front of me. I thought it was a ghost for a moment,' she added, then bit her lip.

To her relief, Daniel grinned. 'Escaped from here, you mean? If that was the case then the Crystal Waters ghosts are stupid. Nobody would go into that voluntarily. Speaking of which, Noah, are you going to stay here tonight?'

Noah shoved his hands in his pockets. 'If that's OK? Not sure I want to risk it when you're offering a more attractive alternative. I'll just have to make a call.'

'No problem,' Daniel said. 'I'll make sure there's a room ready for you.'

They disappeared in different directions, leaving Hannah alone. She took her sodden coat and her towel and went into the snug. There were a few people in there, the lights low and atmospheric, the bar top shimmering invitingly. She went to the long bench in front of the huge window:

there was a couple at one end, talking softly while they shared a bottle of wine. Hannah put her coat and towel on the opposite end and kneeled on the seat, pressing her hands against the glass.

Marnie had been right: the sea was a gargantuan monster, giant waves reaching like thick arms up to the sky before crashing down, bubbling foam gleaming in the intermittent moonlight. The wind screamed around the outside of the building, as if desperate to get in, and Hannah shuddered. She tried to think of pleasant things, like whether she should have cream and marshmallows on her hot chocolate, but her mind skipped quickly to Noah. She wondered who he was phoning; who was waiting for him in Mousehole. She sighed, and felt a gentle pressure on the bench next to her. The dog had joined her, and was looking up at her expectantly with his soulful eyes.

Hannah laughed and sat properly on the seat, scratching the fur between his ears. He lay down and put his nose on her thigh, his gaze never leaving hers. 'You're adorable,' she said. 'Where did you come from? Who's missing *you* tonight?' She swallowed. Who was missing *her*? Who would have been worried if they'd known she was out in the storm?

Saskia was enjoying her updates from Cornwall, but was busier than ever at work; her mum had been impatient with her the last time they spoke; a call with her brother, Mike, was long overdue, and her dad was god knows where. Even Seth was unaware how much Hannah had cared for him. She paused. *Had?* She couldn't stop being interested in Seth because she'd spent a week with an often irritated, occasionally teasing man who, after Saturday, she would only communicate with via phone and email. She put her head in her hands and the dog whined gently.

'Hannah? Goodness, are you OK? You look positively bedraggled.'

Hannah looked up to see Audrey staring down at her. Her words were full of concern, but her expression was curious. She was a researcher, Hannah remembered; she was probably intrigued by everything.

'I'm OK,' she said. 'We got caught in this on the way back from the pub.' She waved a hand towards the window. 'I'm just warming up.'

'May I?' Audrey gestured to the chair opposite.

'Of course. I think Marnie's bringing us hot chocolates. Noah will be here in a moment, and maybe Daniel, too.' She knew she was wittering, but she found Audrey's gaze unnerving, as if she could tell that Hannah had been thinking about Noah and was quietly amused by it.

'And your furry companion?' Audrey asked, as she placed a large glass of red wine on the table. 'I didn't realize dogs were allowed at the hotel.'

'I found him on the way here,' Hannah said. 'He came from the beach, I think, though I have no idea how he ended up there.'

Audrey turned her hazel eyes on the dog. 'A little mystery, then.'

Hannah swallowed. 'Have you found out any more about the hauntings?'

Audrey gave her a warm smile. 'Are you interested?'

'Yes,' she said, realizing she meant it. Maybe it was the storm adding to the atmosphere, but it felt like the perfect night for a ghost story. 'I really am. It's not a typical haunted hotel, is it?' She laughed, and Audrey joined in.

'No, but in some ways that makes it more fascinating – more worthwhile. Sceptics can easily discount strange noises

106

in a centuries-old building: the creak of floorboards, timbers shifting. Here, there are fewer places for the ghosts – and the explanations – to hide.'

Marnie carried over a tray with three hot chocolates on, each one topped with a cream and marshmallow mountain. 'Would you like one?' she asked Audrey.

'No, thank you.' Audrey gestured to her wine glass.

'Are Daniel and your friend joining you?' Marnie said to Hannah. 'I don't want these to go cold.'

'They should be,' Hannah murmured, glancing towards reception as she took one of the mugs. She didn't know where either of them had gone. Was Noah still having to deal with his difficult situation from afar?

'Great!' Marnie grinned and left them to it.

'You know, there's a theory that storms increase paranormal activity,' Audrey said. She took a sip of her wine, watching Hannah over her glass. She was very pretty, behind the ostentatious glasses, the frizzy hair and concentrated frowns.

'There is?' Hannah asked. 'Why?'

'Because storms stir up the energy in the atmosphere, and that in turn agitates whatever spirits, or souls, are here with us.'

'I haven't heard that on any of the Edinburgh ghost tours,' Hannah said. 'Mind you, I think they work off a script.'

'Edinburgh's a wonderful town. *Full* of history. So you don't live in Cornwall? Noah does, I presume?'

'He's a freelancer and I'm from head office.' Hannah explained their strange work setup, Audrey's intense focus ensuring she spent more time staring into her drink than meeting her gaze. She was clearly a wonderful listener, but Hannah didn't trust herself to speak casually about Noah any more. She was so aware of him all of a sudden; of the way her thoughts, and her body, had started responding to him.

'And you're going home on Saturday?' Audrey asked gently, as if she could sense that Hannah felt conflicted about it.

'We've finished the report,' Hannah said, 'so there's nothing keeping me here. But I would have loved to be part of your investigation, and I just feel—'

She was distracted by the appearance of Noah, who stood for a moment in the doorway and then, spotting her, gave a brief wave and came to join them. He sat next to Hannah, his hand going immediately to the dog's soft fur.

'Hi, Audrey,' he said.

'Hello, Noah.'

'All OK?' Hannah asked. 'Sorted for staying here tonight?'

'Yup. I had to reassure Mum and Dad that I was fine, can you believe?' He ran a hand through his thick, dark curls and a droplet of water landed on Hannah's cheek.

'They must be pleased you're staying here, rather than driving home in this,' Hannah said. 'I would have been worried if you hadn't taken Daniel's offer, and I've only known you a few days. Here, have a hot chocolate.' She pushed one of the full mugs towards him, but he didn't take it.

'You would have been worried?'

'Of course! I'd have been left to do all the costings for the report if anything happened to you, and I'm not sure that would please me *or* Daniel.' She grinned at him.

'Oh, like that, is it?' His mock annoyance made Hannah's pulse race.

'Possibly,' she said coyly. 'But I would have worried about you, too. Not just the report. Now you're safe *and* we get to spend the night here together, so it's win-win.' The words were out before she'd thought them through. She *should* have thought them through. The silence hung heavily over the table, Audrey seemingly content to let it stretch.

After several unbearable seconds, Hannah risked a look at Noah. She wished she hadn't. She couldn't deal with that level of intensity.

'There's lots to be grateful for, then,' he said, his voice slightly rough. 'Cheers.' He held up his mug and, relieved, Hannah clinked hers gently against it. Audrey joined in with her wine glass, and the dog looked up from his cosy position between Hannah and Noah on the bench.

With the tension broken, Hannah settled back, getting comfortable. The storm, in all its terrible glory, had given her the chance to have one perfect night before she went home. She would drink up the ghosts and the atmosphere and being with Noah, and then she would feel less sad about leaving. In fact, she told herself, she would be fine about it. Just this one night, and then she'd get Cornwall and Noah out of her system and look forward to going home for Christmas.

# Chapter Nine

With the soft lighting and the storm raging outside, the three of them sitting round the table with their faces half in shadow, it could have been a scene from an Agatha Christie novel. They had their faithful canine companion, the bar was well stocked, and the plush furnishings added to the cocoon-like effect.

Daniel hovered on the threshold between the snug and reception, his phone pressed to his ear and a hand on his head. Hannah wondered whether the weather was already causing him problems. She held up the remaining mug, offering it to him, but he shook his head and gestured at her, as if to say, 'You have it.' Hannah nodded and turned her attention back to the table.

'So it's going to plan, then?' Noah was asking Audrey. He had his hands clasped round his mug, and Hannah noticed that his fingers were long, his nails short and neat – smart, like the rest of him.

'Things are looking promising,' Audrey said. 'From my research so far and the accounts I've been able to glean from the staff here.'

'Daniel let you speak to Chloe?' Hannah asked.

'And Kevin. And they're not the only ones who have heard the footsteps, or experienced other, possibly paranormal events in the hotel. Daniel has been very accommodating, though I know he's not entirely comfortable with the idea of Crystal Waters being the focus of this sort of activity.' She pushed her blue-framed glasses up her nose. 'Of course I won't be able to verify any of this until I run a proper investigation, with the right equipment.'

'Do you have the equipment with you?' Noah asked. The dog was now sprawled across his lap, its back paws digging into Hannah's thighs.

'Richard said to always have the basics with you, so I make sure I do.' There was something about her smile that made Hannah feel sad.

'Who's Richard?' she asked gently.

'He was my colleague. This is all his – the book, the research. I'm simply picking up where he left off. He wouldn't have wanted it left languishing, I'm sure of that.'

'He wasn't able to complete it himself?' Hannah could tell what was coming, and hoped she was being sensitive enough.

'No.' Audrey took a sip of her wine. 'No, he died. It wasn't unexpected – he'd been ill for a while – but it was still a shock. I decided that the worst thing would be for his book to go unfinished. Of course, when you die lots of things *do* get left undone, you can't tie everything up in a neat bow, but this was the one thing – something that was very important to him – that I could do.'

111

'It's very generous of you,' Noah said. 'I'm sure Richard would appreciate it.'

'I'm fascinated myself,' Audrey went on. 'That's why I was happy to be his associate, to help him with his paranormal interests alongside my more mainstream work. It feels right that this book is completed.' The lamp in the corner of the room flickered as a violent gust of wind rattled the window.

Hannah glanced at Noah, only to find he was already looking at her, a hint of a smile on his lips. Was he silently asking her the same thing: *Did the storm do that, or was it the ghosts?*

Hannah looked away, bending down to unzip her boots. She pulled them off and tucked her legs up beneath her. 'Do you have any idea who the ghosts might be?' she asked. 'Who's still haunting this place, even though it's Crystal Waters and not the Clifftop Hotel?' This was what she wanted: the classic, whispered ghost story, full of death and heartbreak, that would thrill her to her core.

'I've got Richard's original research,' Audrey said. 'It's actually very detailed, so I know some of the history of the Clifftop Hotel and who could be lingering.' She looked first at Hannah, then Noah, prolonging the silence until it became unbearable.

'And?' Noah asked, a fraction before Hannah did. They exchanged another glance.

'It was one of those tragic love stories, as it so often is.' Audrey gave them a sad smile, and Hannah's gut twisted. 'The Clifftop Hotel was quite grand, by all accounts, and with its exquisite sea views it attracted a lot of wealthy visitors from London. A newly married couple, Edward and Anna Purser, booked to stay here for an extended period, but the young gentleman was more interested in his business dealings than his new bride, and she was often alone.'

'That's sad,' Hannah said. 'Especially as they'd only just got married.' She found it slightly unsettling that the woman's name was a variant of her own.

'What do you do when you have to spend long swathes of time alone?' Audrey asked.

'Dream up recipes,' Hannah said, and Noah shot her a curious look. 'What about you?' she countered.

'Go for a long run.' He shrugged. 'Walk the dogs. Nothing quite so creative.'

'It was actually a rhetorical question,' Audrey said, her eyes alight with mischief.

'Oh.' Hannah felt herself blush. Noah remained quiet beside her.

'Our London bride didn't go running or make up recipes,' Audrey continued. 'Instead, she went looking for company. And she found it in the arms of one of the fishermen who launched his boat from the jetty. An H. Medlin – I want to confirm his full name while I'm in Cornwall. The two of them had a passionate tryst, and unfortunately Edward found out.'

'Oh God,' Hannah said. 'Really?'

'What happened next?' Noah asked. His gaze was intent, his fingers pressed to his chin.

'He was furious, of course. But instead of exacting revenge on the fisherman – as would have been expected; blaming the cuckoo in the nest, rather than his dearly beloved – he took it out on her. She was, I'm afraid, discovered on the beach at low tide, pummelled rather severely by the sea.'

'Fucking hell,' Noah whispered.

'That's *awful*.' Hannah had been musing on the similarities

113

between Anna and Hannah, and how Noah had connections with the fishing trade, but she suddenly felt less inclined to draw parallels.

'It's certainly a tragedy,' Audrey said.

'But how did they—' Noah started, but was interrupted by his phone buzzing loudly on the metal tabletop. Hannah glanced at it and saw a photo of Noah and a beautiful, dark-haired woman, their faces pressed close together as they smiled at the camera, the sea just visible behind them. *Beth*, the screen announced.

'Sorry.' Noah snatched up the phone and stood. 'Hey, babe—' He paused, taking a breath. 'Beth. What is it?' He walked over to an empty corner of the room.

Hannah felt a hand on her arm and turned back to the table, where Audrey was looking at her with kind eyes. 'I'll wait for him to come back,' she said. 'Fancy something a little stronger?' She gestured towards Hannah's empty mug.

Hannah nodded, unable to speak through her mortification. She had been openly staring at Noah, her mind processing the cosy selfie, the *babe*, the *Beth*. Of course Noah had a girlfriend: of *course* he did. How could a man like that possibly be single? She watched the broad line of his shoulders, the hair curling at his nape. Longing and envy curdled with the hot chocolate inside her.

'A night for brandy, I think.' Audrey placed three glasses on the table, the amber liquid glinting in the lamplight.

'Thank you.' Hannah took a grateful sip, letting the silence stretch between them, and a moment later Noah returned to the table.

'Everything OK?' Audrey asked. She gestured to the glass. 'This is for you.'

'Thanks,' he said, sounding surprised. 'And everything's

fine – sorry I interrupted the story.' When Hannah caught his eye, he gave her a warm smile. Had Beth been saying goodnight, whispering sweet nothings into his ear? She turned her head away, her embarrassment deepening.

'So, Edward Purser,' Noah continued, clearly oblivious to her unease. 'How did they know he'd pushed Anna, that she hadn't just fallen – or taken her own life when she realized her husband knew about her affair?' He winced, as if even talking about such horrible things pained him.

Audrey sighed. 'When Anna was found, she was clutching a large button, her fingers cold and stiff around it.' She reached over and took Hannah's hand, turning it over so it was palm-side up. Hannah stared at it, part of her expecting the button to materialize. 'It was the button from a man's overcoat,' Audrey continued. 'Beautiful and expensive, and much more suited to the businessman than the Cornish fisherman.'

'They discovered that Edward had a button missing?' Noah asked.

'Not quite, Noah.' Audrey paused, her plump lips parted. Hannah could see that Noah was hanging on her every word, but all she could think about was Beth. *Babe*.

'What then?' Hannah whispered, trying to focus on the story.

'His overcoat was examined, of course, and all the buttons were there. But the policeman looked again, because something had caught his eye – something bright on the sombre black coat. One of the buttons, at chest height, was sewn on with a different coloured thread to the rest. Blue rather than black. And on looking more closely, he saw that the button itself was unique, with five holes instead of four.'

'Was that enough to accuse him of murder?' Noah asked. He brought his glass to his lips and took a long swallow.

Audrey shook her head. 'Nobody could prove *when* the button had been changed – that it hadn't been in London, months before Anna's death. It wasn't conclusive evidence, and in those days there were no forensics, events weren't recorded as rigorously, and of course a wealthy, influential businessman was much more likely to be believed than a fisherman. Edward Purser didn't want the matter pursued, choosing to put his wife's appalling death down to a tragic accident rather than foul play which, in itself, was rather telling.'

'Too right,' Noah murmured.

'It wasn't until months later, when Mr Purser had gone back to London to rebuild his life, that other evidence came to light.'

'What was that?' Hannah asked.

'A chambermaid at the hotel admitted that Edward had sought her out, asking for a sewing kit. Apparently his wife's had been left at home. He said he had a rip in his shirt, but he wouldn't let the chambermaid do the work, instead wanting to borrow the needle and thread. She gave it to him and agreed not to mention it – it was unheard of for a man of such high standing to be doing his own repairs in that way. Once Anna's body had been found, she was too afraid to say anything.'

'So he did it then,' Noah said, leaning back with a loud exhale.

'And Anna's the ghost?' Hannah asked. 'Thrown to her death on the cliffs just outside the hotel? It's her footsteps in reception, running away from Edward again and again. Oh!' She gasped. 'Or perhaps she's trying to run *to* her fish-erman? God.' Emotion burnt in the back of her throat.

She felt a warm pressure on her ankle – her feet were still

up on the bench – and thought it was the dog, but when she looked it was Noah's hand. Her heartbeat thudded double time. What was he doing?

'You OK?' he asked gently.

She nodded, and slid her feet off the bench. 'It's just so sad. Anna still wandering around here, unable to get back to her fisherman or be at peace.' She turned to Audrey. 'This is heartbreaking. Are you going to try and communicate with her? See why she can't let go?'

'I'm hoping to. Daniel has agreed to me running an investigation while I'm here. And through his research, Richard also discovered that, while some of the paranormal occurrences lean towards it being Anna Purser, who met her end on these cliffs or in the hotel, our lovelorn fisherman is also reputedly still around.'

'Hang on,' Noah said, frowning. 'What do you mean, Anna might have died in the hotel? Wasn't she washed up on the beach?'

'Yes.' Audrey held up a finger. 'But there was speculation that Edward had killed her in the hotel after discovering her affair, then thrown her off the cliff to cover it up. A body damaged by rocks and tides could certainly disguise the battering of fists.'

There was silence while Hannah and Noah took it in.

'Does Daniel know all this?' Hannah asked. 'He must have been upset by it.'

'It's a very sad chapter in Porthgolow's history,' Audrey said, 'but it's all in the past, Hannah. It won't do you any good to take on Anna's pain. I will tell her story as best I can.'

'When are you running your investigation?' Noah asked.

'In the next couple of days,' Audrey said. 'I'm waiting for

Daniel to confirm it. Of course, the storm might disrupt things: he has to put the welfare of his guests first. I will need a couple of additional people to cover certain areas of the hotel, and Daniel has said he'll find me some. If either of you are still here, you're very welcome to help. Excuse me a moment, will you?' She got up and strode out to reception.

Hannah stared at the brandy in her glass. She felt a heavy sadness for Anna's tragic life and, selfishly, it mingled with her own. She had only one night left in Cornwall after tonight, so she wouldn't be able to take Audrey up on her offer. She would go home to twinkly, busy Edinburgh, her friends' Christmas, Saskia and Seth, Mike and her mum. So why didn't the thought of leaving the hotel and getting on the train on Saturday morning fill her with delight? She pictured Noah going home to beautiful Beth, to his fishing village and his parents and his dogs, and swallowed down a sigh.

'There's no chance of you extending your stay, I suppose?' Noah turned towards her, holding the sleeping dog on his lap so it didn't fall off.

He sounded hopeful, which only deepened Hannah's confusion, but she answered honestly. 'I would love to do that. I know our report's almost finished, but there's so much more I could do in Porthgolow. Work my way through the Cornish Cream Tea Bus menu, have a pamper session in the spa. I haven't had a chance to try out the hot tub because of the weather, and now I'm going to miss out on a ghost hunt, too.'

'You never know, the weather might force your hand.' He leaned back and pulled the edge of the curtain, exposing glass that was so completely covered with rain splatter there was no longer any inkling of the view beyond.

'Trains are pretty solid things,' Hannah said. 'I expect I'll be OK.'

'Which is a shame,' Noah replied. 'Still, it doesn't stop you from planning another trip. And if Daniel goes ahead with the work we're suggesting, Green Futures will want to continue the relationship.'

'It would make sense for you to be the on-site consultant, though. The upgrade will take months.'

'That doesn't mean Gerald won't want visits from head office to make sure everything's going smoothly. And you should be that person.' He touched a finger lightly to her chin, then tilted her head up so she was forced to meet his gaze. 'Everything will still be here when you come back.'

Hannah held her breath. The moment felt overly intimate. The look he was giving her now, as if she was the only thing worth smiling at in the whole world, made her unsteady even though she was sitting down.

'The ghosts won't be here.' It came out as a scratch, and she bent down to tug at her sock, breaking contact with him.

'If they're here now, then they're probably here to stay. Unless Daniel gets a priest in to get rid of them, and I don't think he's the type to buy into it quite so wholeheartedly.' Noah seemed perfectly composed, as if the face-touching had been completely normal.

'You'll have to tell me how it goes,' she said, forcing lightness into her voice.

'I'll call you the moment it's over.'

The dog stirred and Hannah looked down at their scruffy rescue mutt, making the most of his comfortable surroundings.

'Dogs are very intuitive,' Audrey said, making Hannah jump. She hadn't heard her come back in. 'They often pick up on presences that we can't see.'

'He's pretty chilled right now,' Noah pointed out. 'Maybe there's nothing here.'

'Do you think we should give him a name?' Hannah said. 'Even if it's temporary?'

The dog raised his head, then jumped up to standing, his paws landing in a delicate area of Noah's lap. Noah's face creased in pain, and he lifted the dog's front paws, moving him slightly. 'Umph. He knows we're talking about him.'

'What shall it be?' Hannah asked the dog, biting back a laugh. 'Something appropriate, obviously. Storm? Crystal?'

The dog stared at her impassively.

'Midnight,' Audrey tried. 'Christmas. Marshmallow. Chocolate.' Still the dog didn't react.

'Maybe this isn't going to work,' Hannah said.

'No, look at his eyes.' Audrey pointed. 'He's listening.'

Hannah peered closely at the dog, and Noah groaned as it shifted its weight again. 'You should probably do it quickly, while I still have all the vital parts of my anatomy.'

'Ghosts are a bit of a theme,' Hannah said. 'And he's sort of ghostly, isn't he, with his scruffy white fur and the way he appeared out of nowhere?'

'What about Spirit, then?' Noah suggested, and the dog barked.

'He's only done that because he's standing on you,' Hannah said.

'Spirit,' Audrey tried, and the dog barked again. Noah grinned.

'Spirit *is* a good name,' Hannah admitted. 'He definitely has spirit.'

'Perhaps a bit too much.' Noah lifted the dog off his lap and put him back on the bench.

'OK?' Hannah asked.

'No permanent damage.'

'With that, you young things, I'm off to bed.' Audrey stood up.

'Goodnight,' Hannah said. 'Thank you for telling us about Anna and her fisherman.'

'If you want to be part of my investigation, just let me or Daniel know.' She wished them goodnight and walked out, passing Daniel on the way.

He placed a key on their table. 'I put you in the room next to Hannah,' he said to Noah.

'Thank you.' Noah slid the key off the table and put it in his pocket. 'Is everything OK with the hotel?'

Daniel nodded. 'So far. We've got power backups in place, I just need to keep a close eye on it all. Have you two got all you need?'

'We're fine, Daniel,' Hannah said.

'Let me top these up for you.' He took their glasses and went behind the bar, returning with replenished brandies.

'Do you want to join us?' Hannah asked.

'Thanks for the offer, but I've got to stay focused. I've set up food and water in my office for the dog, but if either of you want him in your room, just shout.'

'I'll have him,' Noah said.

'Sure?' Daniel asked. 'I'm going to check the outside of the hotel for damage, so I can take him out with me now. You'll still be here in twenty minutes?'

Noah held up his fresh drink. 'Yup.'

'We're calling him Spirit,' Hannah said.

Daniel glanced at the dog, an eyebrow raised. 'Very apt. I'll start making enquiries in the morning, see if he's been missed. Come on, Spirit.' The dog jumped straight off the bench and followed him out.

Then it was just the two of them, with nothing except the storm's squeal beyond the window, and thick, silky quiet inside the room. Hannah picked up her glass and swirled the amber liquid around.

'Hannah, I . . .' Noah started, but the end of his sentence never materialized.

'What is it?' she asked quietly.

'I know I've not been the easiest person to be around this week.'

'I've had a good time,' she said truthfully.

'You strike me as someone who sees the best in everyone, and I appreciate your kindness, but I'm not sure I deserve it. I haven't behaved as well as I could have. I'm sorry.'

'You don't have to apologize,' Hannah said. 'I've learnt so much from you, and besides, nobody can be upbeat all the time. Life has a habit of throwing unexpected things our way.' She glanced at her watch. 'Oh bugger.'

'What is it?'

'Eleven thirty-two. We missed Anna – or the fisherman. Whoever's making the footsteps.' The lights in reception were low, Daniel still on his perimeter walk.

'We might hear something if we sit here for long enough,' Noah said. 'I don't expect many people use this room in the middle of the night. One of the ghosts could be waiting to reach a chilled finger out from behind the curtain, or blow air on the back of our necks, or materialize as a shadowy, indistinct figure in the corner.' He pointed to the darkest part of the room, and Hannah shuddered.

'Oh my God.'

'What?' Noah whispered. 'Don't tell me you've seen something. If you have, I'd be inclined to say it's the power of suggestion.'

'No, but you are so good at being creepy. Do you really think we might have a ghostly encounter?'

'There's only one way to find out.' He took his phone out of his pocket, and Hannah saw that his screen was full of WhatsApp notifications – from Beth? – but he cleared it without reading them, then opened the voice recorder and put the phone on the table in front of them.

'Is that going to pick them up?' Hannah asked, resisting the urge to giggle.

'Maybe,' Noah said. 'Now, we have to be as still and quiet as possible. Get comfy.'

Hannah did as she was told, sitting cross-legged on the cushioned bench. She was bubbling with anticipation, but trying her best not to show it. Anna and her fisherman might not make an appearance, but Hannah was going to enjoy every moment of sitting here with Noah, the brandy making her glow from the inside out, every sense heightened. Even though, now, she knew nothing could happen between them, she couldn't bring herself to go to bed. They were still working together after all, so it wasn't as if she could avoid seeing him altogether. What was wrong with spending a little down time with him? She tried not to listen to the voice inside her head telling her that was a very dangerous thought indeed.

# Chapter Ten

The first thing Hannah was aware of was a sharp pain in her neck, which was unusual, because the bed in her hotel room was as soft as clouds. She shifted, trying to get comfortable, and realized she was in a particularly awkward position. She frowned, still not ready to open her eyes, and then something finger-like touched her hair. *Ghosts*, she thought, and sat up abruptly, the top of her head connecting with something solid and, it seemed, with pain receptors.

'Ow!'

It took her a couple of seconds to get her bearings, registering the Crystal Waters snug, remembering being with Noah and their impromptu ghost hunt. The lights were still low, she could hear the storm hadn't even begun to abate, and her empty brandy glass was on the table next to his. Spirit was asleep at their feet, but she couldn't recall Daniel bringing him back inside.

She glanced sideways. Noah was rubbing his chin but, thankfully, looking amused.

She opened her mouth, and her stiff jaw protested. She must have fallen asleep *on* Noah. On his lap? She'd felt his hand in her hair, hadn't she?

'Are you OK?' she croaked out. 'I'm so sorry, I was disoriented. Did I hurt you?'

'No, it was just a surprise. I was beginning to nod off myself.'

'Why didn't you wake me? Why did you let me . . . slump, like that? Have I got drool on your trousers? Oh God.' She covered her eyes with her hands, her face on fire.

'It wasn't the most thrilling ghost hunt,' Noah said. 'Hopefully Audrey's will be a bit more interesting. And don't be embarrassed: it's been a long day. We're well into tomorrow, now.'

'You should have poked me the moment I started dropping off,' Hannah said. 'Then we could have called it quits and gone to our rooms. Now it's far too late and I'm all stiff.' She circled her shoulders, trying to loosen them. 'No doubt you are too, what with me falling asleep on you, and I bet we didn't catch anything anyway.' She pointed at Noah's iPhone, which was still sitting on the table and, presumably, still recording.

'I have no idea. I'll have a listen, but I'm not holding out much hope. It felt peaceful in here. There'll be a couple of gentle snores, obviously,' he added, grinning.

'Please don't say that.'

'Don't worry, they were pretty adorable.' He stood and stretched his arms to the ceiling.

Hannah put her boots back on and slowly pushed herself off the bench. Had she heard him right? She felt simultaneously exhausted and wired – she was blaming ninety per cent of the wired on Noah – and wondered if she'd be able to sleep.

'I hope you don't mind me saying,' she started cautiously,

'I'm surprised you're so interested in this paranormal stuff. When you picked me up from the station last Friday, I—'

'You thought you were working with a dickhead? That's totally understandable.'

'That's not what I was going to say.' Hannah laughed. They had paused on the threshold between the snug and reception, the lights on the Christmas tree set to a slow fade, the gold and blue decorations sparkling gently. Noah walked to the door that led to the stairs and held it open, ushering Hannah, then Spirit, through. The little dog followed obediently, as if he understood exactly what was happening.

'What *were* you going to say?' Noah murmured, as they walked down the stairs side by side.

'I was going to say that I would never have picked you as someone who believed in ghosts.'

'Why not? How do you think you could spot a believer?'

'If they were wearing a *Ghostbusters* T-shirt?' Hannah shrugged. 'You just came across as the kind of person who wouldn't have time for ghosts. You didn't even have time for small talk, then.'

'As I said, dickhead. It wasn't – isn't . . .' He sighed. 'I have no excuses. But at least you've changed your opinion of me, even if only slightly.'

'Significantly,' she corrected, then wondered if she'd been too forceful. They had reached their corridor, Noah's room next to hers. 'Well, goodnight then. Or morning. What's the plan for our last day?'

He leaned against the wall and smiled at her, his eyes crinkling at the edges. 'We can have one of your much-loved breakfast meetings, then I thought we could find somewhere quiet to call Gerald and update him. After that, the day is ours.'

'I might need to spend tomorrow afternoon snoozing.'

'You had a solid nap upstairs. Quite a pleasant one, too, from the sounds you were making.' This time his smile was pure mischief.

'Trying to scare me with all that ghostly hair-stroking wasn't exactly soothing,' she shot back, and two points of colour appeared on Noah's cheeks.

'That wasn't . . .' he started, then shook his head. 'I wasn't trying to scare you. Look, we'd better . . .' He pointed at his door.

'We should. Night, Noah.'

'Sleep well, Hannah. I'll see you at breakfast.'

She waited until he'd taken Spirit into his room and shut the door, before unlocking her own. She sat on the bed and stared out at the sea, the waves churning wildly, the wind like a battering ram against the walls of the hotel. Eventually she pulled the curtains across, got ready for bed and climbed under the duvet. When she drifted off, she thought she could still feel Noah's hands sliding gently through her hair.

She was sitting in the restaurant, staring at her phone, when he found her the following morning. He was wearing a dusky-blue round-neck jumper and jeans, neither of which she had seen before, and his hair was a riot of dark curls instead of the carefully tamed style she was used to. The more casual, natural version of Noah was so distracting that for a moment she forgot the worrying news she'd had.

'What's up?' he asked.

'Your clothes,' she murmured.

'I had some extra stuff in the car,' he said, sitting down. 'Long story. But you were looking pissed off before you noticed me, so I don't think it can be that *my* outfit is offensive this time. What's happened?'

The two-person table was arranged so that both seats faced the window, and Noah was at right angles to her. This morning, however, the Cornish coastline was more nightmare than dreamy. The sky was a Turner painting with every conceivable shade of grey, and the waves mirrored the clouds, angry and unsettled. It wasn't raining at that moment, but she could see, above the horizon, the slate-grey haze that signalled another imminent downpour.

'Hannah?' Noah prompted.

She turned away from the view. 'All the trains over the next couple of days are going to be delayed. They're running a slower service on big chunks of the line because of the high winds, so even if I get the earliest train tomorrow, I might have to stay somewhere overnight. It's going to be a long and rubbish journey.'

Noah was frowning at her phone screen. 'Shit. How long does it usually take?'

'Between eight and ten hours depending on the route, but on the way down there was that signalling problem even before the weather interfered.'

'You'll have to play it by ear,' he said. 'And if there's a chance you could get on a quicker route, then I'm happy to take you to a different station. Truro – or Plymouth, even.'

'That's very kind, thank you. I'm sure it'll be fine. Now, what are you going to pick off the breakfast menu? I can recommend the haddock and poached eggs, or the pancake stack with bacon and maple syrup, if you're up for abandoning calorie counting. Mind you, we've both had very little sleep, so we probably need the extra energy.'

'Is that what you're having?'

'I think so. The maple syrup is calling to me.'

'That's what I'll have, then. You know what you're talking about when it comes to food.'

After Hannah had devoured her breakfast with gusto and Noah had made even shorter work of his, he suggested they go to his room to call Gerald. She agreed: they couldn't have a phone conference in a public area of the hotel.

Noah's room was a mirror image of hers, but still Hannah felt strange being in it. It was the fact that she knew he'd slept there, showered under the drench shower that morning, or maybe he was more of a bath person . . .? She shook the thought away, refusing to let her mind wander.

'Where's Spirit?' she asked.

'Daniel's taking some photos of him to put on local Facebook groups, to see if anyone recognizes him. Want one of these?' He loaded a capsule into the coffee machine.

'Sure.' Hannah sat in the desk chair, waited until he'd made their coffees, then took her phone out and scrolled to Gerald's number.

'Green Futures, Gerald Hawes speaking.'

'Gerald, it's Hannah Swan, and I've got Noah here with me.'

'Noah! Hannah! I was just thinking about you. Apparently the weather down there is even worse than it is here.'

'The storm's hit, and shows no sign of leaving just yet,' Noah said, glancing at Hannah.

'My journey home might be disrupted,' she added. 'But I'll make it back in time for Monday.'

'Don't take any unnecessary risks,' Gerald said. 'You must stay safe – that's the main thing. Now, how is Crystal Waters? I've read your updates, Hannah, and it sounds as if it's going well.'

'It's been great,' she admitted. 'I think I've been lucky with my first case.' She didn't add that she felt that way because she'd made new friends, found excellent food, possible hauntings and a stray dog, and developed a potentially massive crush on her colleague.

'Excellent,' Gerald said. 'Come on then, let's have all the details.' She heard the tapping of a keyboard through the phone, and knew he was opening up a blank document to make notes on.

It took them over an hour to run through everything, Gerald showing his usual interest and insight. Noah took a back seat, letting Hannah lead the conversation, only chipping in when there was something more he could add. She was grateful, but a small part of her wished he'd be less chivalrous and more egotistical or, better yet, revert back to the near-silent, permanently irritated version of himself – anything that would make her feel less sad about leaving.

Once they'd hung up, Noah leaned back on his elbows on the bed, twisting his neck from side to side. 'There we go, then.'

'He seems happy,' Hannah said, trying not to notice the hem of his jumper sliding up above the waistband of his jeans. The waves, she told herself, turning her gaze to the window, were much more interesting.

'I hope Gerald realizes what an asset you are to Green Futures. You're tenacious, you ask all the right questions, and you've already got a good level of knowledge.'

Hannah laughed. 'I like knowing the answers to things – I hate being left in the dark.'

'Is that why you wanted to see old photos of the village?' He leaned forward, resting his elbows on his knees.

Hannah sighed. 'I just think it's so strange that I used to come here on holiday. That the first case I work on, I discover it's somewhere I visited as a child. But then I was partly drawn to the project because I *do* remember having some happy times in Cornwall. Maybe if the case Gerald had touted at that meeting had been in Lancashire, I wouldn't have put myself forward so readily? It feels like a coincidence, but perhaps it isn't: just a series of events and decisions which *seem* coincidental. I used to come here when I was little, but so what?'

It was a moment before Noah replied. 'Did you come here with your mum *and* dad? He wasn't in the photo, was he? Did he take it?'

Hannah was surprised that he'd noticed. 'No, I . . . he was pretty much out of the picture by then. He's always been passionate about his causes, and caring about the planet is no bad thing. But it meant he didn't have time for us. Me and Mike, or Mum.'

'I'm sorry,' Noah said. 'That must be hard.'

Hannah nodded. 'It is. It has been. I've come to accept that's the way things are.'

'Are you close to your mum?'

Hannah rubbed her forehead. 'We get on OK. She's not a warm mumsy type, though. She's been *brilliant*, looked after me and Mike so well, and we were a tight unit. I can talk to her about most things, but it's as if she's been so hurt by what Dad did, her heart stays firmly locked away. But that's OK – she shows her love in other ways. She puts on these *amazing* Christmases. They're like something out of a catalogue, but . . .' She bit her lip. He didn't want to hear all this.

Noah stared at the floor for a moment, and when he looked up, his eyes were bright and clear, seeing right into her. 'I don't quite believe you, you know.'

'About what? My mum's Christmases?'

'About the "so what?" I think that *you* think there's more

131

to it. You said you mentioned Porthgolow to your mum, and she was vague?'

Hannah nodded. Part of her mum's efficiency, her always-on-the-job attitude, was that she was icicle sharp. She could parrot Hannah's exact words back at her whenever they got in a fight and Hannah tried to deny she'd said something; she never forgot a name or a face, and she often came out with picture-perfect memories: *Do you remember that boat trip out on the Forth, when a seal followed us all the way back in, and we got chips and chilli sauce and sat outside the pub? It was just after your eleventh birthday, because you insisted on bringing your pink Polaroid camera with you, and you wanted to take photos straight down into the water and I was convinced you'd drop it and lose it for ever.*

And yet she couldn't remember if, in all the years they'd been to Cornwall, they'd ever visited Porthgolow. Even though there was a photograph – one that Hannah had always treasured – proving exactly that.

'She's never vague,' Hannah said. 'And I do think there's more to it. But I can't . . . I mean, what could she be hiding? And do I want to uncover it? She'd have a good reason for holding something back from me, I think.' She thought of the times her mum had kept things from her. They were mostly to do with her dad and his whereabouts, and were always done to save her from hurt.

'Then you need to decide,' Noah said, 'whether you want to find out for yourself, or whether you'd rather accept your mum's version of events and allow her to curate your life in that way.' He said it calmly, not dropping his gaze.

Hannah felt a flash of irritation. 'She's not curating my life.'

He shrugged. 'I saw how keen you were to see Myrtle's photos, and you haven't got long left. I could come with you, if you want? I'm not sure even the walk to the village is safe when it's like this. We could take my car.'

'Why are you helping me? I was ready to let it go, to accept what she's told me, but now you've brought it all up again.' She stood and walked towards the door.

'I didn't mean— it's just that I want you to be true to yourself. If you want to find out what's going on, if you think there's some piece of your past connected to Cornwall, then hunt it down. Don't let other people dictate what you should and shouldn't know.'

'What, like you're doing to me now?' She folded her arms and glared at him.

He stood up, his mouth lifting at the corners. 'I'm not saying you *should* do this. I'm saying it's up to you. Don't listen to your mum if you think she's shutting you down unfairly, don't listen to me if you'd rather forget it. Do what *you* want to do.' He ran a hand through his curls and they sprang back around his face.

Hannah stepped towards him. She held her breath as she reached up and put her hand on his arm, his bicep tensing beneath her touch. His eyes widened, and she wondered what he would do if she told him that what she *really* wanted to do, more than anything, was kiss him. She felt giddy – with exhaustion, and with the unreality of the situation, standing in a hotel room with a man who, a few days ago, she had thought colder than the ice rink at Winter Wonderland. A man who, she reminded herself, had a girlfriend.

'Thank you, Noah,' she said instead. 'I really appreciate you looking out for me. I—'

'Hannah,' he cut in.

'Yes?' The look in his eyes made her shiver. 'What is it?'

Noah's ringtone and the BBC Breaking News alert sounded

simultaneously, making her jump and him step back. Hannah saw the photo of him and Beth on Noah's phone screen as he picked it up.

'Hey,' he said, turning towards the window. Hannah tapped him on the shoulder and pointed to the door, but he shook his head and held up a hand, asking her to wait.

She leaned against the door and took out her own phone, wondering idly what was so important that the BBC were alerting everyone, her stomach twisting with a strange mix of anxiety and excitement when she saw what it was.

'It's best if I stay here for now,' she heard Noah say. 'Because of the storm, and because . . .' He stopped, waiting, a muscle moving in his jaw. 'Of course, that's yours . . .' He turned fully away from Hannah, his shoulders squared. She just made out his next words, murmured towards the glass. 'I don't know yet, but it makes sense, doesn't it? Doing it like this?' Another long pause. 'But I'll see you when I get back? Good. OK. Bye.' He took his phone away from his ear, but it was a few moments before he turned round. 'Sorry about that. I just—'

'No problem,' she rushed.

'What is it?' he asked. 'Something's wrong.'

It was a statement rather than a question. How was it that he could read her so easily, when they'd only known each other a few days? 'The train line at Dawlish,' she said, exhaling. 'It's collapsed in the storm. It looks like I won't be going home tomorrow after all.'

## Chapter Eleven

'So you're trapped, then,' Noah said.

'I'm not getting a train back home yet, that's for sure.' Hannah sat on the edge of Noah's bed, her earlier reticence gone in the face of the sudden change of events.

He frowned. 'Travelling in this kind of weather isn't a great idea, anyway. Maybe it's a good thing that you have to stay for a couple of extra days.'

'But it says in the news report that a section of the track has collapsed, so it's going to be longer than a couple of days. I'll have to find another way of getting home.' She chewed her lip, knowing she couldn't use this as an excuse to extend her stay in Cornwall. She wanted to, but it wouldn't be professional.

'How?' Noah asked. 'There won't be any flights, and you can't hire a car.'

'Why not? There must be companies that will let me pick up in Truro and drop off in Edinburgh.'

135

'Hannah, have you seen what's happening outside?' He flung an arm towards the window. It looked like a particularly dramatic scene from *Poldark*, all tumbling clouds and frothing water. 'Driving short journeys will be hard enough. Regardless of the environmental concerns, you can't just pick up a car and drive all the way to Edinburgh, solo, even if this corner of the country is bearing the brunt of the storm.'

'I just need to get out of Cornwall, then it will be plain sailing.'

Noah shook his head. 'It's not safe.'

'And yet you're going to drive back to Mousehole along the coast road.'

'Not right now, I'm not. I'm staying here. But, even if I was, my car is equipped to deal with this sort of weather, and I've been driving on Cornish roads since I was seventeen. It's completely different. You can't drive back to Edinburgh, there are no trains or flights. You need to stay here until the storm's blown itself out.' He was glaring at her, his tone not to be argued with.

Hannah swallowed. 'I'll phone Gerald and see what he says, then I'll talk to Daniel.'

'Let me know the outcome,' Noah said. 'I'll be here.'

Hannah walked to the door, then turned to look at him. He was staring out of the window, his hands on his hips, a portrait of frustration. She wondered what he'd been talking to Beth about. She closed the latch quietly behind her and returned to her room.

'Hannah,' Gerald crowed, 'phoning again so soon? I hope nothing's wrong.'

She explained the situation, wondering whether he would have the same concerns as Noah, or if his priority would be getting her back to the office.

'You must stay until it's safe, and less than a two-day return trip,' was his firm assessment. 'You can work on the budget with Noah, rather than having to do it remotely.'

'It's not going to be a problem me not being in the office?'

'The sensible thing would be to work from Cornwall for the time being, so that's what you must do.'

Hannah kicked her shoes off and sat cross-legged on the bed. 'Next Friday is supposed to be my last day at work before Christmas – I've booked the week after that as leave.'

'And if you're not back here by the end of next week, I'll drop your Christmas gift round to your flat,' Gerald said calmly. 'It's only a bottle of something I get for all my colleagues, but I don't want you missing out. There's no need for you to fret.'

'I really appreciate this, Gerald.'

'As long as Crystal Waters isn't about to fall into the sea too, then I'd much rather you stayed put – tell Daniel to put your extra nights on our account. And you're in safe hands with Noah.'

'Oh yes,' she said enthusiastically. 'He's been really good to work with. Knowledgeable and encouraging.'

'That's great to hear. I'm pleased with what you've done, Hannah. Keep up the good work.'

Once the call was over, Hannah allowed herself a glimmer of excitement. Of course, she couldn't extend her stay at the hotel if there weren't any rooms available: she was only booked in until tomorrow.

'Do you know where Daniel is?' she asked Chloe on reception, just as the phone rang.

'He's in his office. Hold on a second while I answer this, and I'll get him for you.'

'Thanks.'

Hannah stared at the screens embedded in the walls, showing all the delectable things on offer at Crystal Waters: the views, the spa treatments, the food and the luxurious bedrooms, while Chloe dealt with a customer who, it was clear from the bits of conversation Hannah could hear, was cancelling their booking due to the railway collapse. Chloe was the epitome of professionalism, but her shoulders sagged as she tapped at the keyboard, commiserating with the guest and suggesting they rebook sometime in the New Year.

'Right, sorry about that,' she said, once the call was over. 'Let me get Daniel.'

'Have you had lots of people cancel?' Hannah asked.

'A few. It's understandable with what's happened at Dawlish, and I think some of our guests are reluctant to travel when it's like this. It's something we have to face in the winter, but I can't remember the last time we had a storm this bad. Daniel's worried the power will be cut off.' She disappeared through a door behind the desk, and reappeared with him in tow.

'Hannah, hi, how are you?' He had dark smudges beneath his eyes, but the smile he gave her seemed genuine.

'I've had a change of plan, because of what's happening with the trains.'

His smile was replaced by concern. 'How are you planning on getting home?'

'I've spoken to Gerald, and we've decided I should stay on for a few days, until the storm dies down and the trip home is easier. But I wanted to check if I can extend my stay? Gerald said to put it on our account.'

'Absolutely,' Daniel said. 'We're getting cancellations for the same reason. Please stay as long as you like.'

'Thank you.' She grinned. 'How's everything here? Are Charlie and the dogs OK?'

'They're fine. Charlie's at home, but she'll be here later.'

'Any luck with finding out about Spirit?'

Daniel shook his head. 'I've sent an email to my local contacts to see if anyone's aware of a missing dog, but no luck so far. He's going to be with us until the storm passes, at the very least. Noah's happy to keep an eye on him, and he's already confirmed he'll be staying another night, which is only sensible.'

Hannah's heart lifted at the news. So he'd meant it about not driving back to Mousehole right away. 'Another happy captive,' she said, and Daniel laughed. 'Thanks again, Daniel. I'll see you later.'

Hannah knocked on Noah's door, nerves fluttering in her stomach.

'Hey,' he said, beckoning her into the room. 'What's the verdict?'

'The verdict is that you and Cornwall have got me for another few days.'

'I'm glad. You shouldn't be going anywhere in this.'

'You're staying put too, Daniel said.'

'I've no reason to go back, and it actually . . . helps things if I'm here for a few days. I'm paying for the room.'

'Why does it help?'

Noah glanced out at the storm, then looked back at Hannah. 'I've been staying with my folks, and while their hospitality is second to none, it does feel a bit as if I'm a teenager all over again. Staying at the hotel suits us all.'

'You haven't got your own place in Mousehole?'

'I have, but I'm not there at the moment.'

Hannah waited for him to elaborate, but he didn't. Was

this to do with the difficult situation he mentioned? Did he have an infestation of rats, or bats, or squirrels? Was his house about to fall into the sea, and someone was trying to sort out the subsidence? She wondered why he was reluctant to tell her and why, on this occasion, she felt she couldn't ask. The photo of him and Beth flashed into her mind, reminding her that he was just a colleague.

'What will you do with your day?' she asked instead. 'We could meet up later, in the snug? Perhaps start on the costings.'

'Good plan,' he said, but the brightness had left his eyes. 'Let's get together this afternoon.'

'Sure. Great.' She edged towards the door, gave him a quick, idiotic wave and then returned to her room. The day stretched ahead of her, full of possibility. What, she wondered, should she do first?

The swimming pool at Crystal Waters was beautiful, with a wall of windows that looked out on the most sunken part of the gardens and the outdoor pool – covered at this time of year – then the sea beyond. Currently the view was obliterated by rain, the wind unrelenting, but it somehow made the blue-tiled interior even more of a sanctuary: spotlights in the ceiling, loungers lining one wall and a water cooler in the corner, the space with a gentle, welcoming humidity. Hannah stepped to the edge, then lowered herself to the tiles and slipped into the water, feeling a shock of cold before warm currents pooled around her legs and middle.

There were only three other people in there: a man with greying hair doing laps and a couple on adjacent loungers, the woman reading a Kindle and the man flicking through a Christmas catalogue. Hannah wondered just how badly the weather had affected Daniel's bookings.

She started her first length, quickly finding her rhythm, even though the pool was much smaller than the one she was used to. She had spent the morning in her room, had left a message on her brother's voicemail asking him to call her back, had scanned through her and Noah's report, recapping in preparation for the next stage, but she had found it difficult to concentrate. She had wondered what Noah was doing. Was he lying on his bed with Spirit next to him? Had he ventured into the grounds to walk the dog, despite the wind and rain? Eventually she had snapped out of it. It wasn't a productive way to spend her extra time in Cornwall; she should be taking advantage of the facilities on offer.

She'd finished her fifteenth length when she saw that she wasn't the only one who'd had that idea: she'd just got there first.

Noah's trunks were royal blue and came to midway down his thighs, like surf shorts. He had one of the hotel's fluffy towels slung around his shoulders, but other than that, it was all Noah. She saw those strong arms, the muscles fully on show; his legs looked equally powerful, and his chest and stomach were toned, with a smattering of dark hair. Hannah's thoughts might have already wandered into what he looked like under his clothes, but they hadn't done him justice.

She was at the far end of the pool from him, and she sank down until only her eyes were above the water, self-conscious in her watermelon-print costume. It was the nicest one she owned, but it was far from new.

Noah draped his towel over a free lounger, folded his glasses on top of it and strode to the pool edge, crouching and sliding into the water in one smooth motion. He swam towards her and Hannah wondered how bad his eyesight was, whether she could glide past him without him noticing.

But it was irrelevant, because she was suddenly unable to move. She pressed herself against the side of the pool as the dark curls got closer, and then there he was, beside her.

He pushed his hand against the tiles, was halfway through a turn when their eyes locked. He did a double-take, pulled himself up short and splashed her fully in the face.

'Shit, Hannah, sorry. Sorry, I . . .' he reached out, his hand hovering inches from her cheek.

Hannah wiped her eyes and smiled at him. 'It's fine. Hi, Noah. Fancy seeing you here.'

'It's not exactly running weather, so.' He hitched a shoulder up, and she dragged her gaze away from his collarbone, the smooth skin covered in tiny water droplets. 'You said you swam a lot, back home?'

'I try to go at least three times a week. It's good for my head space.'

'Running's the same for me: it's as much about my mental health as my physical. It feels like the ultimate freedom, as if I could keep going forever if I wanted to.' He was looking at her intently, and she wondered if that was because he didn't have his glasses on.

'I love that freedom,' she replied. 'Though of course you run out of pool after a bit. Have to turn round and come back the other way.' She smiled, and Noah returned it. 'Perhaps I should take up running.'

'There are a lot of hills in Edinburgh.'

'Cornwall's not exactly flat,' Hannah laughed, gesturing out of the window.

Noah turned and leaned his arms on the side of the pool, then rested his chin on his shoulder, looking at her. 'Do you ever want to keep going for ever?'

He said it casually, but she could hear the weight behind

his words. She copied his posture, their elbows grazing, legs treading water behind them. 'No, not really. But coming away always makes you reassess everything, doesn't it? It's like hitting the reset button. You can see your life from a distance, so you can see more of it, somehow.'

'And you don't like what you see? With Green Futures?'

'Oh no it's not . . .' she started, but realized she had replied automatically, not considering his question. 'I'm still finding my feet, I guess.'

'From where I'm standing, you've found them. You're good at it, Hannah, but that doesn't mean it's what you want. You can be brilliant at something and never want to touch it again, or you can be shit at something and want to dedicate the rest of your life to getting better. Just because you can do it, doesn't mean you should.'

'I didn't realize my swim session came with a talking motivational poster.' She smiled, showing him she was teasing.

Noah rolled his eyes. 'I'm too serious, I get it. I just want you to be happy.'

'Why?' she asked softly.

'Being happy is all that matters. Anyway, that's it.' He blinked, rubbed his eyes. 'I've exhausted all my life lessons, and I've only done one length.'

'How many are you aiming for?'

'Twenty.'

'I've done fifteen, so I'm going to get to thirty and then I'm going to the steam room. Bye.' She grinned and then, before he had a chance to respond, turned and kicked off from the edge of the pool. She knew he was behind her: she could hear him in the water, feel the ripples that his movement created. But she was a fast swimmer and, despite

143

his powerful, *amazing* body, she knew she could match him.

The third length they swam together. She reached the end of the pool a couple of seconds before him, and as she turned their gazes snagged. Noah's eyes were so blue, his wet lashes inky black, and Hannah faltered. Her hand brushed against his under the water, and she tried to think back to their first meeting, to his complete lack of warmth, but it was no good; mid-swim Noah was a potent image to try and replace. By the time her brain had finished processing he was ahead of her, and she had to put all her effort in to catching up with him again.

She kept up her pace all the way to her last lap and then put her arms on the side, levered herself up and out, picked up her towel and walked to the door. She allowed herself one glance back. Noah still had a few laps left, and she could see the muscles in his back, his strokes easy and elegant. She poured herself a glass of water, downed it and went to the steam room, where the thick air smelt of eucalyptus.

Hannah sat on the bench and rested her head against the wall. She had said she was going to the steam room, but she hadn't invited him to join her. Would he come? She closed her eyes, breathed in the scented air and let her limbs relax.

She heard the door open, heard the soft pad of bare feet on the tiles, felt the presence beside her. She opened her eyes.

'Hey,' she said.

'Hi,' Noah replied.

'Good swim?'

'Sort of. I had my ass whooped by a girl.'

'Woman, thank you very much. And yes, you did. Obviously.'

Noah's eyes flickered down the length of her body, and

Hannah wondered how he was seeing her, whether he was appraising her the way she had him, if he liked the watermelon costume. She was thankful for the thick steam, even though it seemed to be getting steadily hotter.

'I feel hustled.' He was still breathing heavily, his chest rising and falling. 'I didn't know I was going up against a pro.'

'I'm not a pro, and anyway, if we went running, you would leave me in your dust. Take the loss like a man.'

He glanced at her, his lips pressed together. 'I can do that,' he murmured.

'Can you?'

'As it's you.'

'Because you want me to be happy?'

His lips twitched. 'I didn't mind following you in the water. If we went running, I'd probably lag behind then, too.'

'Oh?' It was definitely getting hotter in here. 'Why's that?'

He turned slightly towards her, and Hannah tried not to gaze at his firm chest, the trail of dark hair that ran down the centre of his stomach, his abs defined under the skin. 'A beautiful view always keeps me motivated, and if I had you ahead of me—'

'Noah,' she cut in, thinking of the photo of him and Beth, the one that appeared on his phone screen when she rang him.

'What?' he whispered.

She wanted him to keep going, to tell her she was beautiful and that he liked her as much as she liked him. But did he really think it was OK to flirt with her so openly? And it wasn't as if Beth could be his sister – he'd called her *babe*. It was all sorts of wrong. 'I'm overheating,' she said quickly. 'It's hot in here, isn't it? Too hot. I think I'm just going to—'

'OK,' he said, suddenly concerned. 'Do you want me to get you some water?'

'No, I'll be fine. I'll just . . . see you later.' She stood quickly and pushed open the door, the cool air a balm on her flushed skin. She picked up her towel and hurried back to the changing rooms, her heart pounding.

# Chapter Twelve

When Hannah drew back the curtains the following morning, she had to squint against the bright shards of light breaking through the cloud. The wind still howled, the waves were still ferocious enough to swallow her whole, but there was a glimmer of sun. Sunshine wouldn't fix her train line, but it would make her extra time in Cornwall more pleasant – she might even be able to go outside.

She showered and dressed, then picked up her phone. She'd texted her mum the previous evening, when she'd been hiding like a coward in her room, to let her know she'd be delayed for a few days.

*Are you sure?* her mum had replied. *There must be other routes.*

*Not without taking 2 days. Best to sit tight for a bit. Gerald knows – he encouraged me to stay.*

*I don't like you being there, Han. I miss you. Get back here ASAP! :) Love Mum. Xx*

The signs of affection that she'd dropped into the short message – I miss you, love, kisses, smiley face – were about as common as Hannah turning down a dinner invitation to her favourite restaurant. This was not usual Mum behaviour. But what could she say? *Why are you suddenly being so affectionate? Is it your way of getting me to come home sooner and not dig into whatever it is you're hiding from me?*

Pushing the thought from her mind, she went to find breakfast.

As she was coming out of the restaurant, her stomach full of delicious sausage sandwich, she almost bumped into Daniel coming in the other direction. He put his hands on her shoulders to stop them colliding.

'Hannah, just the woman. Did you sleep well?'

'I did, thanks,' she said. 'Your rooms are well insulated against storms.'

'They have to be, being so close to the sea.'

'It's not causing you too many problems?' she asked, seeing the pensive look on his face.

'We've had a few cancellations, and we're constantly checking our contingencies in case the power goes out or there are supply issues. It's not how I wanted to spend the run-up to Christmas, but the storm was anticipated, even if we didn't realize how bad it would be. But that wasn't what I wanted to talk to you about.'

'Oh? Is anything wrong with my booking?'

'No – that's all fine. Charlie's canvassed her food market regulars and around half of them can make it, despite the weather, so it's still going ahead, would you believe? She asked me to tell you, as she knows you're keen on the market.'

'I am! I'd love to go.'

'OK, well, be safe if you do. I think I'm going to stamp

that on my forehead: *Be Safe.* You honestly don't want to mess with weather like this.'

'Understood. I promise I'll be careful.'

As Daniel walked away, Hannah felt a swell of relief that she had an excuse to get out of the hotel rather than sneak around trying to avoid bumping into Noah.

'Maybe I should have cancelled it,' Charlie said, sliding her arms along the table and resting her forehead on them. 'It's pretty bloody miserable, isn't it?'

Hannah looked out of the window. There was still a good collection of trucks and vans, making a marked impression on how cheerful the beach looked, but awnings were being battered, some shutters were half-closed to prevent the wind from destroying the food preparation areas inside, and the offerings significantly outnumbered visitors. 'You did what you thought was right, and that's all you could have done.'

'The problem is everyone's so nice, so when I asked them whether they were happy to come today, I'm sure some of them said yes just because they didn't want to let me, or the other members of the market, down. I should have been bold and made the decision to cancel it.'

'But you would have had some visitors turn up anyway, because they hadn't gone on social media and seen the announcement, and then they would have been annoyed. I think with something like this, it's very hard to please everyone.'

'You're right. Another?' Charlie took Hannah's mug and went into the kitchen, the coffee machine whirring to life.

Charlie made an excellent cappuccino and, even though Hannah was now about seventy per cent festive-flavoured coffee, she couldn't resist. The bus was a warm haven, the fairy lights fading softly in and out and Christmas hits playing in the background. There was a box of Christmas cards and crocheted snowmen and robins for sale on the corner of the kitchen counter, next to the contactless payment machine. A sign on the front of the box said: *Local and hand-made.*

'You don't have to spend your day here, you know,' Charlie said, bringing over their drinks and a plate of warm sausage rolls that smelled utterly tantalizing. Hannah was going to put on all her extra Christmas weight before Christmas arrived at this rate. 'The hotel is much cosier.'

'I've spent a lot of time at the hotel over the last few days and, lovely as it is, I wanted a change of scene.' *And a change of company.* 'And it's not a day for walking the coastal path, even if the views would almost make it worthwhile. Has Marmite minded being cooped up?'

Charlie laughed. 'He did laps of my house yesterday, and managed to destroy a cushion and break a vase, so I took him and Jasper on one of the most bracing walks of my life. Jasper was done after five minutes, but we got all the way down here to the beach before Marmite changed his mind and started whimpering.'

'Careful what you wish for, little guy,' Hannah called to the driver's seat, where the dog was curled up. An ear-twitch was all the reaction she got.

Her gaze tracked a couple wearing waterproofs; they were running from the car park towards the fudge stand, holding their hoods tight to their heads. The rain had started again, the earlier chink of sun long since hidden behind a wall of cloud. Reenie's little house was obscured by spray as wave after wave hit the cluster of rocks it sat on.

'Is Reenie in her house at the moment?' Hannah asked. 'It must be terrifying.'

'She's mentally tough,' Charlie said. 'And I'm keeping in touch via WhatsApp and Skype. She's well stocked up, and she's working her way through the *Walking Dead* box set.' She laughed. 'I'm more worried than she is, but she ignored Daniel's entreaties to stay at the hotel for a few days before the storm broke. Reenie won't do anything she doesn't want to.'

'She's braver than I am,' Hannah admitted. 'I'm much more frightened of the storm than I am of Audrey's impending ghost hunt.' *And seeing Noah again*, she added silently, although 'frightened' was a bit strong. 'Uneasy' was a better word for how she was feeling.

When a bedraggled couple appeared, seeking out a Christmas cream tea, Charlie busied herself in the kitchen and Hannah was left alone with her thoughts. She should ask Noah what was happening, instead of avoiding him. But what if she was misreading the situation, seeing too much in his actions because it was what she *wanted* to see? The last thing she needed was to call him out on his flirting only to discover that she'd got it wrong, and end up with their tentative friendship in tatters. Part of her wished she'd never gone to the swimming pool.

The weather continued to worsen over the morning, as if it had lulled them into a false sense of security with the glimmer of early morning sunshine. As lunchtime neared, Charlie decided that, with no more customers and the trucks exposed on the beach, it was time to close. Hannah agreed to help, and between them they visited all the vendors, telling them to go home, shouting over the crackle of wind as it buffeted the awnings, wiping rain out of their eyes. By the time they made it back onto Gertie they were soaked to the skin, and Hannah couldn't feel her hands, nose or ears.

Charlie passed her a towel, and she was running it over

her sodden face when she heard footsteps. She dragged the towel away to see Daniel in the doorway, dressed in an expensive-looking waterproof coat, only his eyes, nose and mouth free from the confines of its hood. Behind him, his black coat covered in water droplets, was Noah.

'Charlie, this is madness,' Daniel said. 'You have to close up.'

'It's done.' Charlie planted a kiss on his nose. 'I realized how futile it was. I'm just going to turn everything off and lock up. Hi, Noah. Are you OK?'

'Good, thanks,' he said. 'I bumped into Daniel on his way out, and offered to drive him down here.' He turned his gaze on Hannah, and she gave him a weak smile.

'Hey.'

'Hi.' He sounded wary, and Hannah cringed again at the way she'd run out of the steam room.

'I think we should all go to the hotel,' Daniel said. 'I need to be there anyway, and the forecast says the storm's going to worsen again. I want you there too, Charlie. You, Marmite and Jasper.' His dark eyes were devoid of their usual amusement.

'You don't mind the dogs being up there?'

'We've already got Spirit,' Daniel explained. 'It's fucking grim, and there's talk of power cuts and more travel disruption. I'd feel much happier if you were with me.'

'Of course,' Charlie said, but Hannah saw the worried look in her eyes.

'What's wrong?' she asked.

'Reenie's still out there, in her house. If the storm's going to get even worse, then—'

'I know,' Daniel said gravely. 'I'm not happy about her being there. She needs to be up at the hotel with us.'

'How are we going to do that?' Charlie asked. 'How will we get out there?'

Daniel sighed and put his hands on Charlie's shoulders. 'Very, very carefully,' he said, and in the quiet that followed, all Hannah could hear was the roar of the sea as it crashed against the shore and the rocks, its assault on Porthgolow unrelenting.

# Chapter Thirteen

The last of the food trucks had driven off the sand, leaving the beach empty but for the Cornish Cream Tea bus. Waves raced angrily up the shore, shattering and frothing, then receding to start all over again, while the wind whipped the sand up, twisting it into shapes – almost like ghosts, Hannah thought wryly.

Marmite was asleep, oblivious to the drama unfolding outside the window, but Hannah and Charlie stood, transfixed, watching Daniel and Noah struggle across the beach, pushing into the wind as they made their way towards Reenie's fairytale cottage.

'They'll be fine,' Charlie said with a determined nod. It sounded as if she was trying to convince herself as much as Hannah. And it wasn't Hannah's boyfriend out there, but that didn't stop her wanting to run outside and bring them back, bring *Noah* back into the warm, with an almost feverish desperation.

'They're stubborn, egotistical men,' Hannah replied, trying to lighten the mood. 'Of course they'll be fine.'

When Daniel had explained his plan, Charlie had protested, saying she made the journey more frequently than the others, that she should go with Daniel and Noah should stay, but she'd been overruled. She'd told Hannah she'd only conceded so as not to prolong their journey.

'At least Noah's used to Cornish terrain,' Hannah continued. 'He goes running a lot. He's probably as nimble as a mountain goat.' She was watching their progress like a hawk, her phone in her hand, ready to call for help if they got into trouble, or if they couldn't get Reenie back easily.

'You're worried about him,' Charlie said, shooting her a glance.

Hannah kept her eyes on the window as Daniel and Noah reached the narrow, precarious path that wound its way along the rocks to Reenie's house. 'He's my colleague. A friend. I'm worried about Daniel, too. I want them all to get back safely.'

'They will,' Charlie said. 'And when they do I'm going to give Daniel hell for playing the "man" card.'

'And I'm going to . . .' *Apologize to Noah. Try my hardest not to put my arms around him.*

'What?' Charlie prompted.

Hannah shook her head. 'Nothing.'

She was holding her breath as they neared the house. The huge waves crashed against the rocks, and she knew that even without the rain they would have been soaked through. But they made good progress, their heads down, determined, and after what seemed like hours – days, even – they reached Reenie's cottage. Hannah saw them huddled against the front door for a moment, then they disappeared inside.

She let out a long breath and exchanged a smile with Charlie. They were safe, for now.

'You said before that you were close to Reenie,' Hannah prompted, wanting a distraction while they waited.

'She's amazing,' Charlie replied. 'Forthright and blunt – sometimes too blunt – but she has a big heart. Knowing that she cares about you, that she's got your back, is the best feeling.'

'She sounds wonderful,' Hannah said, her fear increasing. If anything happened to the three of them on the way back, Porthgolow would never recover.

'Her determination will get them through this, if nothing else.' Charlie took Hannah's hand and squeezed it. 'Noah will be fine. They all will. Here – look.'

Hannah turned back to the window, and saw that Noah and Daniel had reappeared. Daniel's hand was wrapped around the arm of a slight woman wearing a bright red raincoat, a rucksack on her back. Hannah squinted; it looked as if the woman was shaking his hand off. There was a moment when the three of them stood outside the house, heads bowed, then the older woman – presumably Reenie – was stepping over the rocks, Daniel and Noah behind. Reenie seemed the most sure-footed of them all, moving easily over the uneven ground.

The second they were safely on the road, Hannah and Charlie flung their arms around each other, Charlie laughing, Hannah's heart feeling as squeezed as the rest of her. Marmite lifted his head sleepily to see what the fuss was about.

Soon the three of them were back on the bus, Daniel shaking water off his coat, Noah leaning against a table and wiping his face. Reenie lowered her hood and glared at her rescuers.

'Good Lord, you two,' she said sharply. 'What on earth possessed you?'

'You couldn't stay there, Reenie.' Daniel stood up straighter.

'You don't even know if the house is going to survive,' Charlie added, stepping forward and pulling Daniel into a hug.

'You put them up to this, did you?' Reenie turned to her. 'It's weathered worse storms than this, and these two have just risked their skins. I don't even know who this young man is!'

'I'm Noah,' Noah said. 'Hi.'

Reenie glared at him, then turned back to Charlie.

'Why didn't you pick up the phone? I have a plan for severe weather, and I would have told you that, currently, there is nothing to worry about, but that if you were concerned I would come – by myself – to the hotel, and stay for a few days. You didn't need to enact a precarious and pointless rescue, and drag this poor Noah into it. Honestly, it was like something out of *The A-Team*. Gung-ho and crazy.'

Hannah bit her lip. She felt as if she was being told off, even though she wasn't the object of Reenie's wrath. Charlie's cheeks were pink, and Daniel's gaze was fixed on the floor.

'At least we're all safe now,' Noah said.

'More by luck than judgement,' Reenie replied. 'You looked like blundering elephants clambering over those rocks. What would have happened if you'd been swept into the sea? I was much safer coming on my own.'

'I had my phone, ready to call someone if it went wrong.' Hannah waggled her mobile.

'Who are you?' The older woman had a handsome face, her features sharp, her eyes piercing. She sounded half accusatory, half curious.

'This is Hannah,' Daniel said smoothly. 'She and Noah are the eco-consultants who've been working at the hotel.'

'Noah and Hannah,' Reenie repeated, holding out her hand to each of them in turn. Her grip was strong, bony and, unsurprisingly, cold. 'I would suggest you're a bad influence on Charlie and Daniel, but I'm inclined to think it's the other way around.'

'Help me pack up the cakes,' Charlie said quickly. 'If everyone's going to be up at the hotel for a while, then these won't go to waste.'

'Are you going to infiltrate my hotel with your baking?' Daniel raised an eyebrow at her.

'Of course,' Charlie said. 'Did you expect anything else?'

Hannah helped Charlie box the cakes and pastries, aware of Noah standing close to the stairs, wiping his glasses with the edge of his jumper. When the last lid was secured, she walked up to him.

'Are you OK? It looked horrible out there.'

'I'm fine,' he said. 'Better now it's over, but it wasn't too bad.' Hannah glanced out of the open doorway as a particularly large wave hit the rocks and Reenie's house disappeared from view. She turned back to him. 'OK,' he conceded, 'it was fucking scary. But we had to get Reenie, and we did. We got her, so . . .' His breath came out in a long exhale, and it blew out Hannah's last bit of resolve.

She put her arms around him, her hands pressed to his shoulder blades, his soaked coat against her cheek. After a second he hugged her back, bringing them closer, and her relief faded as desire took over, as she felt the solid shape of him, his strong limbs, the muscles she had seen in the pool. She breathed steadily and closed her eyes. He was safe: that was all that mattered.

'Come on you two,' Reenie said, 'he's not just come back from Dunkirk. We've got to go out in the storm again, so wait until we reach Crystal Waters before you hug it out.'

Hannah let go and stepped away from Noah, her cheeks flaming, and Daniel rolled his eyes and gave her a conciliatory smile. It seemed nobody was spared Reenie's sharp tongue.

Despite Noah's comfortable Land Rover taking them back up the hill, it was a bedraggled party of five people and one dog that arrived at Crystal Waters that afternoon. Hannah had had limited time outside herself, but she still felt as if she'd been on an emotional journey, and had to stop herself hugging the Christmas tree, she was so relieved to see it.

'Golly,' Chloe said. 'Are you all OK?'

'Nothing a hot bath won't fix,' Charlie said brightly. 'Where shall I put these?'

'We'll take them to the kitchen.' Daniel turned to the receptionist. 'Chloe, will you book Reenie into one of the suites, please?'

'Of course.' Chloe tapped quickly on the computer keyboard.

'I don't need any special treatment, Daniel,' Reenie chided.

'You may not *need* any,' Daniel said, 'but that doesn't mean I can't give you any. You need to stop fighting everything and let the people who love you look after you.'

For the first time, Reenie didn't have a comeback. She gave Daniel a distinctly watery smile, then crouched to pat Spirit and Jasper, who had come padding out of Daniel's office.

'Who's this?' Reenie asked, as the scruffy white dog nosed his way towards her.

'This is Spirit,' Noah said, crouching next to her. 'Hannah found him on the beach in the middle of the storm.'

'Let me take those.' Charlie held out her hands for the cake tins Hannah had carried in from the car.

'That's OK,' Hannah said. 'I'll come with you.'

She left Reenie and Noah fussing over the dogs, and followed Daniel and Charlie down the plushly carpeted corridors to the kitchen. She'd already seen it on the tour, but that didn't stop the wave of happy nostalgia as she stepped inside. The clank of metal against metal; the shouts, steam and sizzling; the familiar aromas of mouthwatering food – roasting meat and chips; the base notes of different sauces bubbling away; the glare of stainless steel. The Crystal Waters kitchen was smaller than that of the Whisky Cellar, but after the unease she'd felt watching Noah and Daniel rescuing Reenie, Hannah found it comforting being somewhere so familiar.

'Put them over here,' Daniel said, sliding his tower of cake tins onto a counter. 'I'll get them on plates and lay them out in the snug.'

'This place is so nice,' Hannah said, putting her tins down. 'And it's very state-of-the-art.' She took in the heavy-duty ovens and hobs, the shimmering utensils, the short man in chef's whites chopping carrots and courgettes with lightning speed. It wasn't Levi, whom she'd met on her second day, but presumably one of the sous chefs.

Daniel gave her an amused look. 'You're into commercial kitchens? You didn't say anything when I showed you around.'

'I worked in a restaurant while I was at university. It was the maddest – and best – job that I've done.' The words slipped out before she had a chance to modify them. 'Best job until my current one, I mean.'

Daniel's expression changed from amused to interested. 'You were a chef?'

160

'A sous chef. In a restaurant called the Whisky Cellar. It was all wooden beams, oak barrels and backlit shelves with bottles of rare single malts: a glowing amber haven in the middle of the city. And the chef, Cedric, was a weird genius – proudly Scottish, so everything we cooked had its roots in the Highlands or Glasgow or Aberdeen. Whisky creams and haggis balls, and tattie scones crafted into towers. I love that your menu is full of fresh fish.'

'It would be criminal not to make the most of what's here, and Levi is almost military in his quest to use fresh local produce. I leave him to it most of the time, though of course he runs everything past me. It's a different world from all this,' he added, gesturing towards Charlie's mouthwatering morsels. 'But both are of the highest quality.'

'What's the highest quality?' Charlie asked, appearing beside them. 'Sorry, I got sidetracked.'

'We were talking about your cakes,' Hannah explained, 'while simultaneously trying not to eat them all.'

'Speak for yourself,' Daniel said, laughing. 'Help me put them on plates, Charlie. Hannah, go to the snug and we'll bring them up.'

'I can't help?'

'I know you're a bit more than a paying guest, but this isn't in your remit.'

'I don't mind, though.'

Daniel hesitated for a second and then, shaking his head, took some plates out of a cupboard.

'What's all this then?' Levi came over and peered into the tins as they started taking lids off.

'We've brought in contraband, Levi,' Charlie said, grinning at him. 'I had to abandon my food market, and there's lots of stock left over. Daniel won't let me go home, and even if

I had I wouldn't have known what to do with all this.' She gestured to the tins full of sausage rolls, cream doughnuts and gingerbread biscuits in the shape of Christmas trees and snowmen, the scents of sugar and well-seasoned sausage meat making Hannah's stomach rumble, in spite of the snacks she'd already eaten. She wondered if it was the cold making her so hungry, or the stress, or simply that, everywhere she turned in Porthgolow, there seemed to be more and more delicious food.

'What's all this I'm hearing about a ghost hunt?' Reenie's question rang out as Hannah followed Daniel and Charlie into the snug, carrying plates laden with Gertie's leftovers. The room was fuller than Hannah had ever seen it, and she wondered if word had got out that they were bringing the contents of the Cornish Cream Tea Bus to the hotel.

The room had a small Christmas tree in the corner that hadn't been there yesterday, decorated in red and silver, the lights reflecting off the metal tabletop it stood on. A deep, mellow voice crooned about a white Christmas in the background, just loudly enough to tip the atmosphere into festive perfection.

Noah was sitting next to Reenie, wearing jeans and what looked like a traditional fisherman's jumper in sky blue. His curls were dishevelled, as if he'd dried them with a towel and left them to it, and his cheeks were pink. Someone – Hannah was willing to bet Reenie – had ordered whiskies, and there were five on the table, presumably for the four returning rescuers and the rescuee. Hannah didn't feel entirely deserving as she hadn't been in any danger, and it was only mid-afternoon, but it was gloomy enough to pass for evening, and the cosy scene, featuring a safe, slightly rumpled-looking Noah, Christmas lights and music, the dogs at their feet, was impossible to resist.

Daniel hurried to the table and Reenie took a sausage roll off his tray before he'd even put it down.

'Reenie, keep your voice down,' he hissed.

'How can I, when faced with such incredible news? I wouldn't have believed it, but Chloe was so animated, and Noah here didn't exactly deny it when I asked for confirmation, so I'm inclined to believe it's true.' She patted Noah's knee, and he gave Daniel an apologetic look.

'She's too cunning for me,' he said. 'Sorry.'

'We've all been there,' Daniel replied. 'Don't worry. Reenie, we've got a researcher staying here. She's following up on some work done by a colleague of hers about the Clifftop Hotel. He thought it was haunted, and that some of the . . . ghosts were still around, despite the original building being demolished.'

'The Clifftop Hotel was most definitely haunted,' Reenie said. 'And I'm sure there's something lurking in the Seven Stars, though of course Hugh is best placed to give you those details.'

'You know about the hauntings?' Hannah asked, sitting next to Noah and taking a gingerbread snowman from the tray. She would have to limit herself to porridge and salads in the New Year. Noah took a doughnut.

'No hat,' she mouthed.

He shook his head, his eyes alight with amusement.

'Anyone who's been in Porthgolow longer than a few years knows about the hauntings,' Reenie continued. 'Footsteps, bangs, cold spots. I know a woman who used to clean here, when it was the Clifftop, and she was aware of more than one visitor who'd curtailed their stay because they'd found it too unsettling.'

'I haven't had any cancellations like that,' Daniel said, folding his arms. Charlie held up the last glass of whisky and he shook his head. 'I can't now. Later, maybe.'

'Have you asked, Daniel?' Reenie probed. 'Or would you prefer not to know? I have to say that I'm astounded you're entertaining the idea of a ghost hunt in your luxury clifftop castle.'

'It's not going to do any harm,' he murmured, looking uncomfortable.

'No, certainly not to your publicity. Haunted hotels are all the rage these days. Everyone runs *towards* ghosts, not away from them. You should learn to embrace it.'

'I think I'll wait and see what happens tonight.'

'Tonight?' Hannah squeaked.

'I've agreed Audrey can run her investigation later today.' Daniel said. 'You and Noah are still here, and you seemed interested, so—'

'We'd love to help out,' Hannah rushed. 'I mean, I would.'

'Me too,' Noah added, around a mouthful of doughnut. 'I could do with a bit of excitement after the boring day we've had.' He smiled, and everyone laughed.

When Hannah caught his eye he gave her a quick, entirely flirtatious wink and, try as she might, she couldn't help the swell of happiness that filled her chest. The storm had unleashed something in Noah Rosewall and, complications or not, Hannah couldn't help responding to it.

## Chapter Fourteen

The reception of the Crystal Waters spa wasn't large, but it was sleek, and it had the same air of luxurious calm as the rest of the hotel. It was on the building's lowest level, behind the swimming pool, so there were no sea views. In fact, it had no windows at all. The storm could have been hundreds of miles away, for all Hannah could see and hear it. She sat on one side of the corner bench and Noah sat on the other, their knees touching. She could imagine arriving here for a massage, facial or pedicure, but didn't think she would be as excited as she was now.

'We're supposed to turn the lights off,' Noah said in a low whisper.

'OK. Although how are we supposed to see anything if it's pitch black?' Her laughter betrayed the fact that nerves mingled with her excitement.

'Standard ghost-hunt rule,' Noah went on. 'Always do it in the dark if you can. Maybe they only come out at night, or maybe they're always here, but you can only see them when there's no light source.'

'Maybe they're always here,' Hannah echoed, shuddering. 'Thanks for that.' She got up and walked to the door, checked it was closed and then flicked the switches.

She was plunged into a world of black velvet. There was no light anywhere, not even a soft glow from the computer or the red dot of a smoke alarm.

'I can't . . . how do I get back to the bench?' She took a tiny step forward.

'Follow my voice,' Noah said. 'This way.'

Hannah did as she was told, her arms out in front of her, following Noah's soft, calm voice until she bumped into something.

'Got you.' He put his hand on her arm. 'You just need to move round here.' He manoeuvred her gently, Hannah shuffling until she could feel the bench against the backs of her legs. She sat down and realized she was even closer to him than she had been before, their knees squashed against each other. But it would be awkward if she moved away.

'Settled?' Noah asked.

'Yup.'

'Righto.'

Slowly, Hannah's eyes adjusted to the darkness. She was able to make out the curve of the reception desk, the shape of the computer monitor sitting on top of it, the cabinet on the wall opposite, full of high-end scrubs and lotions. She looked to her left, and there was Noah. Just the shape of a man to begin with, but then, moment by moment, his features materialized: curls, glasses, strong jaw, the thick-weave, entirely huggable jumper. He was a John Lewis catalogue model; intelligent and pensive, his smoulder not immediately obvious, but – from the second you saw it, and forever afterwards – completely devastating.

A devastating John Lewis catalogue model on a ghost hunt. Hannah suppressed a laugh and took a long, steadying breath.

'I can't hear anything, can you?' he asked. 'Not the storm or the buzz of equipment, or water in the tanks. This whole place is cushioned by insulation.' Daniel had told them about it on the tour: it meant the spa was as calming as it could be for the guests, but also ensured that heat retention was high and energy use low. It was one of the biggest clues for Hannah and Noah as to how eco-conscious he already was.

'Good for being green, good for hunting ghosts,' Hannah murmured. 'Maybe those two things are compatible, and we could become paranormal experts on the side. What would we be called? "Green Futures, Hidden Pasts", or something.'

'That's very clever.'

'But? I can sense there's a "but".'

'Are you nervous? I'm not criticizing, just asking.'

'I'm wittering, aren't I? We're not going to hear any ghosts if I keep spewing out nonsense.'

'I wasn't going to put it that way, exactly.' She could hear the smile in his voice.

'Right. Quiet, then. Let's listen for Anna or the fisherman – except, should we ask questions, like Audrey told us to do at her briefing?'

'Sure. You go.'

'All right.' Hannah cleared her throat. 'Anna Purser, are you here with us? Did you lose your life inside the Clifftop Hotel, or outside, on the rocks? Why are you still here?'

The silence seemed to thicken as they listened for a response. Hannah wondered how long to wait before saying something else. Audrey had told them it would come naturally once they were in their locations, but it didn't feel natural at all.

'Have you started the recorder Audrey gave us?' she asked in a loud whisper.

'As soon as we sat down,' Noah replied.

'Yay!' Hannah said lamely. And then, after a moment, 'Do you want to have a go?'

'OK. Mr Medlin, do you still mourn Anna's loss, all these years later? Did you try to see justice done for her murder? Do you regret falling for a married woman?'

Hannah sucked in a breath at that last question. It seemed to echo around her as the silence persisted.

She leaned her head back and closed her eyes. The room was warm, comfortable and entirely unthreatening. Audrey had talked about cold spots, the sensation of being watched or someone standing behind you, lights flickering, strange smells – lavender, unexpected perfume or burning – which were all apparently signs of a presence. Hannah felt nothing. The only charge was inside her and, specifically, where her knee touched Noah's.

'Did you think,' Noah said, his voice making her jump, 'at the end of last week, when you arrived at the station and got into my car, that we'd end up doing this?'

'Are you asking me if I have premonitions? The answer is definitely no. I thought I'd work hard on preparing a report for the hotel and maybe, in my spare time, visit the Cornish Cream Tea Bus. I did not anticipate storms or ghost hunts or stray dogs or any of this, but I am glad it's happened. How about you?'

'You don't mind being stuck here, not making it back to Edinburgh when you'd planned to?'

Hannah shrugged. 'I was worried at first, but now I'm embracing it. Gerald is far more relaxed about it than I thought he'd be, and that was my main concern. My friends and family – and Christmas – will all be waiting for me when I get back.'

'Your mum's show-home Christmas?'

'That's the one. It's lovely, though, despite – I mean, it's not chaotic at all, and sometimes that's what you want, isn't it? Except if my dad turns up, and then it will be the wrong kind of chaos.'

'Why?'

'Because he doesn't get it,' Hannah said. 'He doesn't get how much he hurt my mum, even though she divorced him. He thinks he can come back whenever he feels like it and play happy families, that Mum will accept him being in her house for the sake of me and Mike, that we won't resent how little he's been around, or how he thinks it's OK to waltz in for five seconds and then leave again.' She was shocked at how angry she sounded.

'Shit, Hannah, I'm sorry,' Noah said softly. 'You said you trained to be an eco-consultant for him?'

She dropped her head, even though he wouldn't be able to see her expression anyway. 'Partly. He was absent so much of the time, but that meant that – when I was little, at least – seeing him was a treat. He's such a gregarious person, full of life and laughter, and because he was never around to do the parenting, he didn't have to be responsible.'

'He was the fun guy while your mum had to put her foot down.'

'Exactly,' Hannah said, swallowing. 'And I bet Mum *hated*

that, but she never said anything to us. So I guess I wanted to get my dad's attention. To prove to him that I was worth more of his time. I wanted what I did to matter to him, so that *I* would matter to him.'

'Hannah, that's—' he cleared his throat.

'What about you?' she asked, before he could go on. 'Will you be with your mum and dad?'

He didn't reply immediately, as if he wanted to spend more time talking about her, but he relented, saying, 'Yup. They would never forgive me if I didn't have Christmas with them. That's why it's good that I'm here for a few days. I'll be back in my own house before Christmas Day, but the less we're on top of each other in the mean time, the better.'

He hadn't mentioned Beth, or what he'd said to her in the steam room. But then the day hadn't exactly been a quiet one. 'Why aren't you—' she started, then shivered. 'God, can you feel that?' The icy blast appeared at the same time as she saw the light: a thin strip of yellow under the door. 'Is there a window open somewhere?'

'You're cold?' he asked.

'You aren't?'

His hand came over hers. His skin was warm, and she heard his sharp intake of breath. 'You're like ice.'

'Is someone in the corridor?'

Why could she feel it when he couldn't? Was Anna communicating with her because she identified with her – because Hannah wanted someone forbidden? Was this Anna's way of telling her to back off?

'I don't think so,' Noah murmured. 'The corridor only leads to the spa, so unless a guest has managed to get seriously lost . . .' He stood up slowly, releasing Hannah's hand, and stalked towards the door. Hannah followed him as quietly as she could, stopping behind him as he reached out to grasp the handle and slowly, *slowly*, pushed it down and pulled the door towards him.

Hannah stepped back and, with her heart in her throat, peered around the opening door. Her pulse was racing, as if already trying to escape whatever was beyond it: a shadowy figure; a woman in white, ethereal and wispy; a hellhound like the one she'd seen in a Netflix drama not that long ago. What she found was an empty corridor.

'Fuck,' Noah said under his breath.

'You can't see anything either?'

'Nope, just a corridor.'

'Just a corridor,' Hannah repeated, but it felt as though something had changed. The light and the sudden cold meant that, despite its neutral carpet and unadorned walls stretching towards the main body of the hotel, it didn't quite seem the straightforward, unassuming space it had when they'd walked down it.

'You OK?' Noah squeezed her shoulder, concern in his blue eyes. 'Still cold?'

'I'm fine. I'm sure the light's just one of the others: Charlie or Daniel coming to check on things, or one of the dogs has escaped from the office and triggered the sensor.'

'Charlie and Daniel know we're here and would have called out, and we would have heard Spirit or Marmite haring down the corridor. Neither of those dogs have it in them to be stealthy.'

'No.' Hannah chewed her lip. 'So, something else set off the sensor.'

'And dropped the temperature, but only around you. Let's sit back down and start concentrating.'

He gestured towards the bench and only let the door close

once she was seated. Then he pushed it firmly, so the latch hit home. He came to join her and, apart from the thin sliver of light still showing under the door, reminding her that they had already experienced something they couldn't quite account for, they were in darkness once more.

# Chapter Fifteen

'Is there something keeping you here?'
Pause, to listen to the silence.
'Do you need to tell us something?'
Pause, followed by another achingly long period of nothing at all.
'We want to communicate with you,' Noah said. 'Are you in here with us?'
'One knock for yes, two knocks for no,' Hannah added.
'What?' Noah whispered.
'That's what they do on *Most Haunted*. You know: are you here, knock once on the floor for yes and twice for no.'
'If the ghost isn't there, then how are they supposed to knock twice on the floor?'
'Don't be such a smart-ass,' Hannah said, her cheeks burning.
Noah's teeth were white in the dark as he grinned at her. 'At least the light's gone off now.' It had flicked off five minutes

after it had come on, and hadn't bothered them again since. Hannah was disappointed. She *wanted* something else to happen. She wanted to return to the snug with Noah as triumphant ghost hunters, with tales of bravery and intense paranormal activity to recount.

She wondered how Audrey and Reenie – who, despite all her cynicism, had turned out to be an eager would-be investigator – were getting on in reception, where the footsteps had been heard, or how Charlie and Daniel were faring down by the indoor swimming pool. She thought it would be creepy, being in such a big room with the still, silent pool and the storm raging outside. But Audrey had said that was where the Clifftop Hotel's grand dining room had been, so it might well be a good place to capture activity.

'If Anna and her Mr Medlin are still here,' Hannah mused, 'then what can Daniel do about it? I assume that once Audrey's got what she needs for her book, he'll want to get rid of them. If you can, I mean. I've never really believed in exorcisms.'

'Me either,' Noah said. 'It all seems very far-fetched. More far-fetched, even, than sitting in a hotel spa in the dark, calling out to people who died hundreds of years ago.' Hannah caught the movement of him running his hand over his face.

'I thought you were up for this?'

'I am. I'm just impatient for something to happen.'

'And you must be tired after earlier. All that adrenaline from being in such a dangerous situation, then the comedown when you reached safety.' She swallowed the lump in her throat. She wondered how the sea had looked from his point of view; those giant waves so close, their roar unbearably loud.

'I'm fine,' he said, but it wasn't entirely convincing. 'Anyway, I'm not leaving here without getting something.'

Hannah laughed. 'What if there's nothing?'

'We've already had the light and your cold spot. We need to keep asking questions.'

'OK.' Hannah pushed away her embarrassment at speaking into an empty room. 'Are you still here, Anna? My name's Hannah – it's so similar – and I just want to talk to you.'

She paused, listening hard. She could hear her breathing, and Noah's. There was nothing else.

'What was your fisherman's name, Anna? We just have an initial. Did you love him, or was it just a crush, an infatuation? How did you know?'

She sensed Noah straightening, his head turning towards her. She looked resolutely ahead. She was on a roll now.

'Didn't you realize it was wrong, when you were already married? Or didn't you care? Was your love for him too strong to deny?'

The silence this time seemed heavier, but Hannah didn't know if it was something in the room adjusting, or simply her imagination.

'Did Edward kill you, Anna?' Noah asked. 'Or did you fall?'

'These are some weighty questions,' Hannah whispered. 'Do you think we should be asking all this?'

'We're more likely to get a response to this kind of thing than if we ask what her favourite colour is.'

'True,' Hannah conceded. There was no obvious response to Noah's stark questions, and Hannah wondered if they would get back to the snug, listen to the recording and hear answers to everything they'd asked amongst the white noise. 'What's your favourite colour?' she asked, suppressing a shudder.

'Hannah,' Noah laughed.

'I'm asking you, not the ghosts.'

'Oh. Yellow, then.'

'Yellow? I would have guessed blue.'

'Why?'

'You wear it a lot; it brings out the depth in your eyes, which you already draw attention to with those black-framed glasses.'

'So you think blue is my favourite colour because it's the one that plays to my vanity?' His chuckle told her he thought the idea was ridiculous.

'There's no denying you keep yourself fit,' Hannah said, and then wished she hadn't, because it conjured up images of him in the swimming pool.

'I like being healthy,' he said. 'I've only got one body, and I choose to look after it. You swim a lot; you make sure that, despite your food obsession, you stay in shape. Is your favourite colour gold because of your hair?'

'My hair's blonde not gold,' she countered. 'Nobody has golden hair except in romance novels and fairytales. And my favourite colour's orange.'

Noah laughed again. 'All right then, Goldilocks.'

'Shush, we're supposed to be concentrating.'

'Is this bench too big for you, or too small, or is it *just right*?'

'Shut up, Noah,' she said, grinning.

'How do you like your porridge?'

Laughter bubbled out before she could stop it. 'You're being entirely inappropriate. This is a very serious, very important ghost hunt, and we're filling the recording up with—'

'What would your ideal bed look like?'

'It would have you in it and a big mound of—'

A loud crash shattered the quiet and both of them jumped, Hannah letting out a pathetic squeak.

'Holy shit,' Noah whispered. 'What the fuck was that?'

'Hello?' Hannah said, her voice trembling. 'Is anybody there?' She felt cold again, but that might have been fear. She tried to sense if anything else felt different, but her heart was pounding and she couldn't focus.

'What's on the other side of the wall?' Noah asked. 'It's a treatment room, isn't it?'

Hannah nodded. 'We should go and check it out. There's probably an obvious explanation.'

'Probably.'

Hannah stood and, with her eyes as adjusted to the gloom as they were going to get, made her way slowly round the desk, past the cabinet on the wall, and through a door at the back of the room. It opened onto a small, square hallway, and Hannah could just make out three other doors leading off it. The one to her left must lead into the room next door, where the bang had come from.

Hannah tried the handle. It pushed down easily and she felt the door swing away from her, her heart in her mouth as the dark space revealed itself inch by inch. The treatment bed was a hulking shape in the middle, the far wall covered by an elaborate cabinet, the ghostly shapes of various lotions and jars laid out on the shelves, waiting their turn. It smelt heavenly; of vanilla and lavender and something rich and deep like cocoa.

'It doesn't look as if anything's fallen,' she whispered, taking two tentative steps inside, Noah's warmth behind her. She turned and leaned against the high bed. 'There's nothing against this wall,' she continued, 'and I can't see anything on the floor, although I suppose something could have fallen off the shelf and rolled under the bed.'

'The cabinet in reception actually rattled,' Noah murmured. 'I don't think something falling off a shelf in here would have done that.'

'Maybe it came from the floor above?' she tried, but Noah didn't reply. She was sure he was thinking the same thing she was: that the hotel was so well insulated, sounds rarely travelled between one room and the next. 'It would have to be something big. What if the storm's damaged the hotel? The winds have got up and blown in a window, or—'

'Hannah, stop. It'll all be fine.' Noah stepped in front of her and put his hands on her shoulders.

'How do you know?' she whispered.

He laughed softly. 'I don't. I'm just trying to reassure you. You're not meant to question it, you're just meant to feel better.' He was speaking so quietly, every word thrumming through her, as if she was a tuning fork attuned perfectly to Noah's frequency.

'That would be a lame response,' Hannah whispered back. 'If you've got no evidence to back up your statement, how am I supposed to believe it?'

'Shush.'

'*You* shush.' His hands were warm and solid against her shoulders; it should have been comforting, but her senses had gone into overdrive. 'Noah?'

His lips parted. She thought he was about to reply, but he tucked a strand of hair behind her ear. She could feel his breath on her forehead, could sense his intent even though his eyes were in shadow. She tried to put some space between them and the edge of the treatment bed jabbed into her lower back.

'Ow!'

'What is it?'

'Sharp edges,' she said. And then, hoping to break the tension, added, 'This particular bed is not my ideal bed, just so you know. Especially not if it's in a haunted room.'

'You said your ideal bed would have me in it,' he murmured.

'Yes,' she whispered loudly. 'And then I was going to add, with a big mound of pillows so I could smother you.'

'Really?' She saw his eyebrow lift, even in the dark.

'Really.' She nodded, but it was as if she was nodding in response to something else, an unasked question.

Everything else shrank away: the dark room and the ghosts, the fear that had whistled through her when the quiet had been broken. It was just her and Noah, his features indistinct but also, somehow, completely clear to her. She leaned forward, into his personal space and his warmth, and tilted her head to look up at him. He bent his towards her, until they were inches apart.

'Noah,' she whispered, her voice choked, because of course this couldn't happen. He paused, and she could feel the tension radiating off him.

Then he kissed her.

Hannah tingled from head to toe. She wanted more than anything to deepen the kiss, to lace her fingers into his dark curls, but she couldn't. She couldn't enjoy it, couldn't lose herself in the moment when she knew about Beth, about their phone calls and their photograph and that she was playing a part in his betrayal of her. She stepped back, not caring that her spine was pressed painfully against the bed.

'We can't do this,' she said. 'Can we? I mean, we just can't.'

'Hannah, I'm sorry. I didn't—'

'We should go back to reception. There's nothing here, is there? I mean, it smells of lavender but that's because we're in a spa.' Her laugh sounded strange. 'The bang was probably just the wind, echoing around the hotel. I don't know why Audrey thought it would be a good idea to hunt for ghosts during a storm, anyway.'

She slipped past him and walked out of the room, back to the spa's reception, and found her place on the bench again, putting her hands under her knees as she sat down. 'Was that you, Anna?' she muttered. 'Are you messing with our minds, making Noah act out of character? He's not a fisherman, you know – that's his *dad*. And my name's Hannah, not Anna. We're not destined to repeat your tragic love triangle.'

She stopped her whispered tirade when Noah appeared in the doorway. She wondered what he'd been doing in that thirty-second delay: berating himself? Sending Beth a guilty text? Clearing his head after a bout of ghostly possession? She rolled her eyes at that one. The whole thing was ridiculous.

'Hannah, I'm sorry,' he whispered as he joined her on the bench. 'I shouldn't have done that. I didn't mean to overstep.'

'It's fine. It's forgotten. We should . . .' she pointed at the recording device, not wanting the others to hear them picking over something that shouldn't have happened, but which had set her senses on fire. Ghostly intervention or not, that briefest of touches had shown Hannah that kissing Noah properly would be every bit as wonderful as she'd been imagining. She felt singed by it, dizzy, as if her body wouldn't be happy until she'd gone back to that moment and hit replay.

They sat in relative quiet, occasionally repeating their questions, but Hannah felt nothing else: nothing that could match the tension between her and Noah, anyway. Her thoughts were spinning. He didn't seem like a cheater: from what she'd seen, he had too much integrity for that. And yet she couldn't dismiss the evidence of her own eyes and ears. She wondered if the ghosts were laughing at them, delighted at having tied them up in knots.

After what seemed like a thousand awkward minutes, her phone vibrated in her pocket. She took it out and read the message from Charlie: *Audrey's calling it. Come back to the snug. Xx*

'We're done.' She let out a sigh of relief. 'Time to meet everyone back in the snug.'

'OK,' Noah said evenly. As she reached the door and flipped the light on, he put his hand on her arm. 'Are we all right?'

'Of course,' she replied. 'It's been a strange night, that's all.'

He nodded, and together they walked down the corridor.

The foyer was softly lit, the Christmas tree winking in the corner, reminding her that not everything was dead people and darkness and gorgeous men she wasn't supposed to kiss. She took a step towards the snug and a white streak shot past her. She pivoted, expecting the automatic doors to be locked for the night, but when Spirit approached they slid open and he raced through, just as a blast of wind howled inside, its chilling tendrils wrapping around her.

'Bollocks,' Noah said, and took off after him.

Hannah followed him outside, the shock of the storm instant. It wasn't raining but the air was like ice, the wind so strong that it caught her off balance. She tugged her hair back from her face, securing it as best she could as Noah turned right and jogged down the side of the building, into the gardens. Hannah kept close, relieved that Spirit hadn't gone towards the road, but not convinced he was out of danger.

'Where's he going?' she shouted, raising her voice above the wind.

'No idea,' Noah called back.

'Spirit!' she shouted. 'Spirit, come back!' The dog turned to look at them, and for a moment she thought he was going to behave, but then he trotted forwards again, weaving between bushes and shrubs that had been flattened by the powerful weather.

Hannah kept up with Noah, her teeth chattering and her fingers numbing, following the white streak as he ran further into the gardens.

'Spirit, come on!' Noah shouted.

'Here boy!'

'He's down this way.' Noah pointed, and they picked up their pace as Spirit pattered down the steps that led to the covered outdoor swimming pool. He ran round the side and stopped in the corner closest to the building, triggering the hotel's outdoor light sensor.

'Thank God.' She and Noah slowed in case he darted off again, but the dog seemed content to sit and pant, his fur tangled but his eyes bright.

'Come on Spirit,' Noah said breathlessly. 'Tonight is not the night for this sort of nonsense.'

Spirit barked up at him and pawed at a large rock that was part of the rustic border separating the flowerbeds from the concrete surrounding the pool.

'It's OK, boy,' Hannah cooed. 'Don't be frightened, it's just a bit of wind.' She took slow, gentle steps and crouched down, wishing they'd thought to grab a lead before they'd followed him. 'You don't need to be . . .' Her eyes fell on the stone Spirit was pawing, and her words stuck in her throat.

'What is it?' Noah crouched next to her, and she felt him

go still. 'Fucking hell. Does that say what I think it does?'

'*Anna*,' Hannah read out shakily, '*my heart is yours. I will see you again. H.*' It was crudely carved into the rock, an inelegant bit of graffiti. But the name and initial were right, the circumstances, the location.

'That is crazy,' Noah murmured.

'Did Daniel use some of the stone from the Clifftop Hotel for the landscaping?' Hannah asked. 'It's the kind of thing he'd do, isn't it?'

'It's not in any of the reports, but I bet you're right. Anyway, what else could this be?' He took out his phone and snapped several shots of the stone.

'I can't believe we've found evidence to back up Audrey's story,' she said. 'Anna, my heart is yours. I will see you again. H.' She shivered, and Noah took her hand and helped her up.

He carried the dog against his chest, his other arm around Hannah's shoulders, pulling her close as they made their way back to the warmth and comfort of the hotel while the sea raged behind them. Hannah wanted to find out if the others had any more pieces to add to the ghostly jigsaw they were putting together.

Since arriving in Cornwall, her plans had been consistently derailed, but she'd begun to embrace all the weird and wonderful things that were happening unexpectedly. Well, nearly all of them: there were some things she *shouldn't* be embracing, and she hoped she had the resolve to keep it that way.

But a dog had just shown her that answers were out there, often hiding in the least obvious places. It made her think that she should keep looking too; that she shouldn't give up on trying to find out more about her own past simply because it wasn't straightforward. As she went with Noah and Spirit back to the hotel, Hannah knew she had to make the most of the time she had left in Porthgolow. There might still be some secrets waiting to be uncovered.

# Part Three

## I'm Dreaming of a Hot Chocolate

# Chapter Sixteen

'I don't believe this. Where is it again?'

Hannah Swan chewed her lip as Daniel Harper stared at the photo on the phone, shaking his head while the others in the room – Charlie, Noah, Reenie and Audrey Benson, orchestrator of the night's ghost hunt – gathered round him.

The snug at the Crystal Waters Spa Hotel looked stark with all the lights blazing instead of the usual mood lighting, as if they were all craving brightness after spending so long sitting in the dark. The Christmas tree twinkled gently in the corner, and every time Hannah glanced at it, it lifted her spirits.

'Down by the outdoor swimming pool.' Noah answered Daniel's question. He was Hannah's colleague, a local free-lancer working with her on transforming Crystal Waters into an eco-hotel. Things had been going well between them until that moment, that *kiss*, mid-ghost hunt. Not that Hannah hadn't wanted to, but Noah had a girlfriend. 'On one of those pieces of rock that borders the flowerbeds,' Noah continued. 'Hannah and I thought you'd probably used some of the stones from the demolished Clifftop Hotel in the gardens.'

'I did, but . . .' Daniel exhaled. 'I would have noticed. It's not exactly subtle, is it?' He gestured to the phone, which was showing the photo Noah had taken of the scrawled graffiti they had found. Or, rather, Spirit the stray dog had led them to.

'But if you weren't looking for it,' Hannah said, 'you might well have missed it.'

'You didn't oversee the placement of every single pebble when the garden was constructed, did you?' Reenie arched an eyebrow.

'I wish you'd mentioned there were still pieces of the original hotel in the grounds,' Audrey said. 'This is a *fantastic* discovery.'

Daniel ignored the comments. 'So this proves the story is right? H telling Anna that she has his heart and he'll see her again. It could be anyone.'

'It fits so neatly,' Charlie said. 'And if it's true, then it's heartbreaking. It clearly wasn't just a fling for him: he loved her.'

'And we're absolutely sure that Jonah Kerr doesn't know about this story?' Daniel asked. 'Because if he does, if you've told him about the Pursers and the fisherman, Reenie, and he knew we were doing the investigation tonight, then I can easily see him planting something like this. He's far too creative for his own good.'

'I'm sure Jonah didn't do this,' Charlie said softly. 'It doesn't look freshly carved, and it would take some serious strength and patience to gouge the rock this deeply. It's not like it's sandstone or anything.'

'No, you're right.' Daniel ran a hand through his dark hair. 'Bloody hell.'

'And it was Spirit who found it,' Hannah reminded him, shooting Noah a look. 'He went straight to it.'

'Not a chance,' Daniel said quickly. 'That was a coincidence. I am not having psychic dogs as *well* as ghosts. He was looking for the most sheltered spot, end of discussion.'

'Did anyone else see or hear anything?' Charlie asked. 'Daniel and I saw zilch in the pool room, apart from a couple of the solar lights flickering outside, but I'm sure that was the storm.'

'It got cold at one point,' Daniel admitted. 'There was an icy blast that we couldn't explain. No vents nearby, nothing else that might have caused it.'

'Oh yes – there was!' Charlie nodded. 'That was so strange.'

'We had a bit of luck, actually,' Audrey said. Hannah saw that she was only just containing her excitement. 'But then I had, very selfishly, positioned us in the spot where activity had already been reported.'

'You heard the footsteps?' Hannah asked.

Reenie folded her arms. 'I'm not one for flights of fancy, but these were bold as brass. From the corner by the Christmas tree over to the desk. They faded when they reached Daniel's office.'

'Bloody hell,' Noah murmured. He was standing beside Hannah, their bodies close, and her hand tingled traitorously at the proximity.

'What were they like?' Charlie asked. 'Did they just sound like normal footsteps?'

'They were fast and determined,' Reenie said. 'Not someone who was worried about being overheard. It was peculiar listening to them, when Audrey and I were standing stock still and there was nobody else nearby. No wonder people find ghosts unnerving.'

Audrey smiled. 'It was someone with purpose, and it sounded as if they were wearing boots; something hard-soled. I haven't had a chance to check the recording device, but if they're on there – and there's no reason they shouldn't be – then it will be incredible evidence. I'll go through all the recordings tomorrow.' She pressed a hand to her chest. 'Right this moment, I feel quite giddy!'

'And I feel exhausted,' Reenie added. 'I'm off to bed, if none of you minds? It's already way beyond my bedtime, and I've had more excitement today than I've had in a long time.'

'Of course. Night, Reenie.' Charlie hugged her, and everyone wished her goodnight.

'What about you two?' Charlie asked, once Reenie had gone. 'Any strange things happen down in the spa?'

The silence held for a moment longer than was comfortable, before Noah answered. 'We heard a crash coming from one of the treatment rooms, but when we went to see what might have caused it, there was nothing.'

'Nothing,' Hannah repeated hurriedly. 'Nothing at all. But the recorder could have picked something up, couldn't it?'

'It might have done,' Noah said quietly, holding her gaze.

When Hannah tore hers away, Charlie was watching them curiously.

'I'm eager to have a listen,' Audrey said. 'Thank you so much, everyone, for taking the time to help me with this. I've got lots to work with, and finding that message is hugely exciting – I can't wait to look at the stone myself in the daylight. Now I suggest we all get off to bed. These investigations can be tiring.'

Goodnights were said and Noah picked up Spirit, who had stayed close at their heels since he'd come back from his enlightening foray into the gardens. Noah and Hannah went with Audrey to the lower floor, then stopped outside their adjacent rooms. Spirit scrabbled to be put down.

'I'd better . . .' Noah pointed at his door.

'Sure.' Hannah put her key in the lock, then looked up at him. 'I had fun tonight,' she said, giving him a warm smile. 'I'm glad I got to investigate with you.'

The look on his face was pure relief. 'Me too, Hannah. Goodnight.'

She went inside her room and closed the door, hoping she could put what had happened out of her mind and get some sleep.

The first thing Hannah noticed when she woke was the crack of light peeking through the gap in the curtains. She leapt out of bed and pulled back the heavy material. The sun was trying to assert itself, with patches of blue between clouds that were sparser, and less angry, than they had been during the night. The sea still danced and tumbled, the wind was still strong, but the storm was definitely abating.

She opened the Trainline app, knowing she couldn't take advantage of Daniel and Charlie's hospitality, or the Green Futures business account, any longer than was necessary. Having gone through every step of planning her trip home, however, she couldn't help feeling relieved when she discovered that, because of the Dawlish collapse and slower track speeds, the journey to Edinburgh would take two long days. She closed the app and put thoughts of going home to the back of her mind.

Even though it was late, the restaurant was still serving

breakfast, and she hovered in the doorway, wondering which table to choose when she saw Audrey waving her over.

'Come and join me.'

'If you're sure?' Hannah sat down and browsed the menu, knowing Audrey's choice of muesli wouldn't cut it. She decided on scrambled eggs and bacon, figuring she could use the protein. She wasn't used to staying up into the small hours, and exhaustion was tugging at her from all sides.

'Are you happy with how last night went?' she asked, once she'd given her order to the waiter.

'Very,' Audrey said. 'I can't thank you enough for your contribution. For Daniel to put his uncertainty aside and embrace what I'm doing is one thing, but for him to have allowed the investigation to go ahead, and recruited his friends and family to help, was beyond anything I deserved. I'm like a cat with an *extra* nine lives!'

'Have you listened to the recordings yet?'

'No, that's my task for today. I need to document everything, and with Reenie and me hearing the footsteps, and the discovery of H's message to Anna in the gardens, I doubt it could have gone better. If I can back up our experience with solid evidence then this will be a thrilling chapter of the book.'

'What will you do after that?' Hannah asked, wondering if she could add any more pieces to her own puzzle: the photograph, the strange feeling she had that Porthgolow was special, and the flash of a memory she'd had in the Seven Stars.

'I'm going into Truro to look at the local records,' Audrey said. 'Richard hadn't got round to making the trip down here, and there could be more to find.'

'Does it feel sad following in his footsteps, knowing that

192

he never got to complete his last project?' Hannah poured coffee, and then milk, into a mug.

Audrey's gaze flitted to the window, then back to Hannah. 'I am terribly sad that he died. He had a long-term condition that affected his immune system, and he knew he was on borrowed time for the last few years of his life. But, as you would expect from someone who was fascinated by what happens after you die, he wasn't scared of it. He was a brilliant man, a breath of fresh air, and I miss him very much. But,' she continued, her smile lighting up her eyes, 'I feel very proud to be continuing his work. It's a huge privilege that he trusted me with the research, that he believed I could fulfil his wishes. I want to do his book justice, which is why I'm so grateful to Daniel, and the rest of you, for your help.'

She spoke calmly, and it was Hannah who found her throat thickening with emotion. 'I'm so glad it's going so well, and that Spirit found that message.'

'Ah yes, wonderful Spirit. Daniel wasn't particularly pleased with that detail, was he?'

'I can see why it's hard for him to accept what you're doing,' Hannah said carefully.

'He's been a lot more understanding than most. I have met many, *many* people who think the whole thing is nonsense, and won't entertain me even for a couple of minutes. It's why I don't usually announce my intentions at a location until I'm sure I have enough to put in the book. And I often get no cooperation whatsoever, and have to limit the hauntings to our research files. Not everyone wants it known that their hotel or restaurant or shop is haunted.'

'I wonder if Daniel will fancy renaming this place the Haunted Waters Spa Hotel?' Hannah grinned.

Audrey's smile was mischievous. 'I doubt that very much,

despite all he's done for me. But what about you, Hannah? I get the sense that you're very much on the fence.'

'I have an open mind,' she said slowly, 'and that message is very compelling. But even if it's proof of the Purser tragedy, it's not proof of the ghosts.'

'You're right, but that's the joyful part of all this: the history is as interesting as the hauntings. They feed off each other, the unusual experiences sometimes corroborating what might only be snippets of a story, and the stories fleshing out – as it were – the ghostly activity. It's all about history and how we understand it; how it never really goes away.'

'It doesn't, does it?' Hannah murmured. Her scrambled eggs and bacon arrived, and she thanked the waiter and added a grind of pepper. 'And you think it's worth pursuing it – the history – even if you only have hints that something might have happened? Even if you're not certain there's anything major to discover?'

Audrey rested her elbow on the table, her chin in her hand. She appraised Hannah openly, and Hannah dug into her breakfast to avoid meeting her gaze.

'I absolutely think that,' she said eventually. 'You have to be tenacious, follow even the thinnest threads offered to you. And trust your instinct. If you believe there's something to uncover, then more than likely, there will be. It's just that sometimes you have to tread on a few toes to get there.'

Hannah returned to her room, full of buttery eggs and crispy bacon, and with a plan forming. She would not look at Trainline any more; she had a place to stay and permission to be in Porthgolow. She also had a few thin threads to start unravelling. She took out her iPad, opened a new note and made a list of everything she had so far: the photo of her,

her mum and Mike with Reenie's house in the background; the tiles in the Seven Stars; the feeling she had about Porthgolow; her mum's evasiveness.

They were wispy cobwebs, barely there, but Audrey had told her it was instinct, more than anything, that should guide her. She would speak to the locals she'd already been introduced to, find out a bit more about the village at the time when she would have been a visitor. There were also Myrtle's photo albums, and while it was unlikely she would find anything significant in them, she thought that talking to Porthgolow residents and seeing old pictures of it might trigger some of her own memories from those long-ago holidays.

While she didn't really know what she hoped to find, it was somewhere to start. And she was looking forward to delving into the history of a place for which, even in the midst of an unforgiving winter storm, Hannah felt a huge amount of warmth. She had been inspired by Audrey's words and Spirit's discovery. If a scruffy dog could uncover such an important piece of history, then surely she could find out a bit more about her own past. After all, what did she have to lose?

# Chapter Seventeen

'So, Reenie, what do you remember about the end of the Nineties?' It was a vague opening gambit, but Hannah didn't know how else to start.

'Goodness, child, that's a bit random, isn't it?' Reenie stopped and turned to her, strands of long grey hair whipping in front of her face. 'Is this your way of engaging me in small talk?'

Hannah dropped her gaze. She found it impossible not to feel embarrassed in Reenie's presence. She was a kind woman but, as Charlie had warned her, quite an exacting one. 'It's not, actually.' She stepped over a plant that had been uprooted, then turned and tried to right it. The wind knocked it straight back over.

'Leave that, Hannah. Daniel will have a plan for all this once the storm's gone; it's not up to you to fix it.'

'Of course,' she said.

'So?' Reenie pressed. 'What is all this Nineties business? What are you researching?'

'My life.'

They were walking in the hotel gardens, having found each other in the snug and deciding, over a cup of tea, that they would get cabin fever if they stayed inside all day. The storm was on its way out, the wind tugging rather than battering, and the view was breathtaking. Hannah could see the coastline to the north and the south, Porthgolow's bay looking freshly polished, the sea sparkling for all it was worth, even while white horses flecked the surface.

To the south the sky was a blistering winter blue, puffy white clouds the only remnants of what had gone before, while in the north a sheet of grey hung over the horizon, the powerful storm moving up the country, at last leaving Cornwall behind. Hannah inhaled, breathing in the air that was thick with sea salt and the earthy, rich smell of vegetation.

'You're researching your life,' Reenie said slowly, 'and yet you want me, a near stranger, to tell you what I remember from over two decades ago. Has your brain been addled by late-night ghost hunting?'

Hannah laughed. 'Not quite. I'm trying to find out about the time I visited Porthgolow before, when I was little.'

'I didn't realize this was a return trip. You've been working on Daniel's green project, haven't you?'

She nodded. 'I didn't realize it was a return trip either, not until I'd been here for a couple of days and noticed the significance of this.' She took the photograph out of her purse and handed it to Reenie. The older woman stopped walking to examine it. They were standing next to the covered hot tub, and Hannah wondered whether Daniel ever opened it in the winter. She'd been to a couple of spas with outdoor jacuzzis in Scotland, and they were always more enjoyable when the air was cold.

Reenie looked at the photograph for a long time before handing it back. 'How old are you there? About eight?'

'Something like that. I would have been eight in 2000.'

'That makes sense. I can't make out much of the detail, but it looks like the old paintwork, before we had the house redone with something better suited to survive the elements. You can see here,' she pointed, 'it's faded in some places. You probably can't actually, but I can tell. This was taken before 2002.'

'And the faces aren't familiar?'

She shook her head. 'I'm sorry. This is your mum and brother?' Hannah nodded. 'Porthgolow was quite a popular town back then, so there were always tourists. It's picked up again recently, of course, thanks to our interlopers. But my son is older than you are – he'll be forty next year, and so there isn't much chance we would have played with you on the beach.'

'I didn't think you'd be able to help, but I had to ask.'

'You don't remember much about your holidays?'

'A few bits and pieces,' Hannah admitted. 'Finding a tiny cove you could only get to down a really steep path, and how blue the water was; fish and chips that I couldn't rest on my knees because they were sunburnt; watching some surfers come back in and feeling so relieved because I'd been worried about them out there in the huge waves. We were always based in Newquay, and of course we would have visited other beaches, but I'd never heard of Porthgolow – or at least, it didn't ring any bells with me – until I got the job to consult on Crystal Waters.'

'Yet this photo is undoubtedly Porthgolow. No other houses like mine, that I know of.'

'No,' Hannah said, smiling. 'I don't imagine there are.'

Reenie gestured to a bench further up the sloping garden. Hannah followed, wondering when she could declare she'd had enough of their bracing walk and go back into the warm. But she didn't want to end the conversation prematurely.

'Your mum's memories must be better than yours,' Reenie said, once they were seated.

Hannah shrugged. 'I've called her a couple of times, but she won't tell me anything, and I think she's hiding something. I can't talk to her properly until I get home, and by then I'll have missed out on the chance to discover anything else here. When I was in the Seven Stars I recognized the signs on the toilet doors, but that doesn't prove anything other than that I've been in the pub – or somewhere else with those same signs.'

'In that case,' Reenie said, 'you should speak to Hugh. He's owned the pub for decades, and he's served food for as long as I can remember. A traditional pub serving good grub is a staple part of any British holiday, so if anyone has memories of long-ago tourists, then it'll be him.'

'Thanks Reenie, I hadn't thought about it like that. I'll speak to Hugh next.'

'You know, this doesn't surprise me,' Reenie said. 'You doing a bit of poking around.'

'What do you mean?' Hannah asked.

'Porthgolow's natural charms may be a bit rough and ready, but with Charlie's bus and this hotel to give it a bit of character, it really is something special.'

Hannah turned to look at her. 'Are you saying that I just want there to be a story linking me to Porthgolow, because it's such a lovely place?'

'Not at all – the opposite, in fact. Once you've been here, Porthgolow gets into your bones and stays there. If you think it holds an important part of your past then it's worth digging deeper.' She gave her a warm smile. 'I like you, Hannah. You've got a good head on your shoulders, and you're not afraid to ask for the things you want. Keep going like that, and you'll make progress.' She stood up. 'Should we go in? I fear if we stay out here too much longer we'll get sunburnt, so rare is that yellow orb in the sky.'

Hannah nodded. She didn't mind the sun at all – her problem was that she could no longer feel her fingers. 'Thank you for your encouragement, Reenie.'

'All I ask is that you keep me abreast of discoveries. It's important that I know what's going on in this village.'

'Because you want to look out for everyone?'

'There's that,' she said, then turned to Hannah with a wicked grin. 'And also I'm just impossibly nosy.'


Early that evening, after a restorative nap and a steaming shower, Hannah lingered by the Christmas tree on her way to the snug. It smelt of fresh pine and cinnamon sticks, its glittering decorations a feast for the eyes that she couldn't get enough of. She wondered what it would be like to spend Christmas Day somewhere like this, enjoying presents and roast turkey and tipsily watching the TV specials with the people she had come to know over the last few days, instead of the ones she usually spent it with.

Something nudged her foot and she saw that all three dogs were snoozing beneath the tree: a haphazard collection of unlikely Christmas presents. She hoped none of the other guests got the wrong idea and took Marmite, Jasper or Spirit home with them.

When she finally stepped through the archway into the snug, she was tempted to walk straight out again. Instead, she blinked twice and forced a smile to her face. Despite all her assurances to herself that there was no lingering awkwardness between them, she hadn't seen Noah all day, and she wasn't ready for him.

'Hey guys,' she said, approaching the table where he was sitting with Charlie and Reenie.

The others looked up but Noah shot to his feet, almost knocking over a glass.

'Hannah, hi,' he said roughly. God. No awkwardness here – not at all.

Reenie gave him a curious look and he slunk back onto the bench, his eyes on the floor.

'Are we just waiting for Audrey?' Hannah asked.

'And Daniel,' Charlie said. 'But he's been on the phone for the last half an hour. You know it's a difficult conversation when he asks them to hold the line so he can go into his office. He might be a while.' She grimaced.

'Audrey popped in ten minutes ago,' Reenie added. 'She told me she had half an hour of recording left to review, so she'll be here soon with the evidence.'

Hannah grinned. 'It's exciting, isn't it? Like an extra, early Christmas.'

'Except with dead people as the presents instead of perfume and socks,' Reenie pointed out.

'I'll just get myself a drink, then,' Hannah said, her cheeks burning. 'Do any of you want one?'

Nobody did, so she went over to the bar only to find Noah beside her a couple of seconds later. The barman was serving a man in a tweed jacket who seemed to have his table's order written on a piece of scrap paper.

'You didn't have to stand up when I came in, you know,' she said. 'That seems a *little* bit formal, even for you.'

Noah winced.

'It was a joke.' She squeezed his arm, realizing the moment she made contact that it was a mistake. The electricity buzzed between them, suitably undampened by the few hours they'd spent apart. 'I'm glad you're here for this.'

'Are you?' he asked. 'I'm not so sure.' He worried a hand through his curls, and Hannah wondered if – now he'd let them out of their waxy prison – he wouldn't bother to hide them again. Anyone with hair that gorgeous needed to share it with the world.

'You don't need to be restrained around me,' she assured him, trying to hide her smile. 'Obviously I'm not saying you should *throw* yourself at me—'

'I get what you mean,' he said quickly. He pressed his hands against his cheeks, his fingers sliding under his glasses to rub his eyes. 'Shit. I need more sleep.'

'You haven't given in to the urge to have a nap?' He did look exhausted, his blue eyes red-rimmed, a smattering of dark stubble along his jawline. She felt slightly guilty for teasing him, but she had thought it might dispel some of the tension between them.

He shook his head. 'I tried, but I couldn't seem to drop off. Anyway, I can't wait to hear what's on the EVP recorders.'

'EVP? Oh, that's right, electronic voice . . .'

'Phenomenon.'

'You're such a swot.' She smiled.

'And you clearly weren't paying attention,' he said. 'But that's OK, you've got me to walk you through it. Anything Audrey says that you don't understand, just ask me and I'll enlighten you.'

'Oh, how gallant of you! What would I do without you, Noah?'

'I dread to think. At least while you're in Cornwall it won't be a problem.'

'That's very reassuring. Thank you, from the bottom of my heart.' She pressed a hand to her collarbone and they grinned at each other.

They went back to the table, Noah's words ringing in Hannah's ears, and it wasn't until ten minutes later, when Audrey had started playing the first recording, that she realized she had failed to order herself a drink.

'Oh my God,' Charlie whispered.

Reenie gave a dramatic shudder. 'They sound fairly sinister when you play them back, don't they?'

'Do you want to hear it again?' Audrey asked. Everyone nodded their agreement.

She pressed play on her laptop and turned the screen round, so it was facing away from her. On it was a sound bar, the vertical lines showing the volume level of each noise they'd picked up. There was a row of staccato spikes with nothing in between; a visual representation of the footsteps that had been heard in reception even before Audrey had arrived at Crystal Waters.

There was the loud fuzz of recorded silence, then Hannah couldn't stop herself jumping when the first footstep sounded, even though she'd heard it several times already. The steps continued, loud and regular, for about fifteen seconds before silence fell again. Then there was a loud, exhaled breath, quickly followed by Audrey's voice saying, 'Goodness.'

'So, there we are,' Reenie said into the quiet that followed Audrey pressing stop. 'Crystal Waters is officially haunted. What do you think about that, Daniel Harper? Going to start offering ghost tours as well as luxury facials?'

'Not sure my guests are ready for that,' he admitted. 'And I know I'm not. It's bad enough having Charlie's influence on the place without allowing a couple of dead guys to throw their weight around as well.'

'I resent that!' Charlie said. 'You *love* all my Christmas ideas. The trees look great, and if you're not careful I'll source some Christmassy bunting to hang over reception.'

'I take it all back.' He squeezed her hand. 'You know I love your creativity.'

'And the rest,' Charlie said.

'And the rest,' Daniel repeated, his voice softening.

'What happens now, Audrey?' Noah asked.

She closed her laptop and clutched it to her chest. 'Now I go to the records office in Truro to fill in the blanks of the Pursers' story, have a serious think about how to write it all up for our book and, quite possibly, listen to this recording several hundred more times to believe that it really happened; that I really was witness to it. I only wish that Richard was here to share it.'

She said goodnight to everyone, her departure the first of many as Daniel went to check on something in his office, and Charlie excused herself to take the trio of dogs for a walk. Soon it was just Hannah, Noah and Reenie, the older woman eyeing them knowingly.

'I'm off to see what the restaurant has to offer this evening,' she said. 'I am entirely happy eating on my own, so it is *imperative* that you don't follow me.' It might have been Hannah's imagination, but she thought she saw the older woman wink at her before she left.

Hannah and Noah sat at the table with everything that remained unspoken between them, all the feelings that Hannah was holding back. For once, she didn't know where to start.

'I'm going back to Mousehole tonight,' Noah said, gazing sightlessly at the bar.

'Oh.' Disappointment swooped through her, even though she should feel relieved. It wasn't that she didn't like spending time with him; she loved it too much, and now she knew that he had feelings for her too, it no longer felt safe. 'Then you can't have one of those,' she said.

'Sorry, what?'

'You're eyeing up the fifteen-year-old Dalwhinnie. As a former employee of the Whisky Cellar, I can promise you it's delicious, but also that you'll need to keep hold of your room key if you start laying into it.'

He gave her a tentative smile. 'Another night, maybe.'

'We've not done any more work on the report.' Hannah knew they'd got to where they needed to, and that it would make more sense for Noah to work on the costings by himself and show them to her, rather than them try and do it together. It wasn't a collaborative process like the main body of the report, but she was worried that, if he left now, she wouldn't see him again.

'That doesn't matter,' he said, confirming her thoughts. 'But I was thinking, if you're going to be in Cornwall for another few days, you should come to Mousehole and have a look around.'

'I should?'

He nodded. 'It goes without saying that Porthgolow is not the only great Cornish village, and I'm fully prepared to be your tour guide for this particular trip.'

'That sounds good,' Hannah scratched out. 'I'd love to see it. Maybe I could meet your parents' dogs?' This felt like safer ground; dogs were always good for breaking any tension.

His face lit up, the worry lines gone in an instant. 'A trip to Mousehole includes an introduction to Rodney, Del Boy and Albert, don't worry about that.'

'Can't wait then,' she said, returning his smile. If Noah was offering to show her round his home town, he clearly didn't want to put any distance between them, despite what had happened. Perhaps he'd decided that they were both sensible adults and could move on from it. It was good, really, that they'd tested the boundaries and knew where they stood. There was no need for things to be uncomfortable.

They stood up, facing each other across the table.

'Goodnight, Hannah.' Noah gave her a tired smile, his eyes crinkling at the edges.

'Night, Noah.' She watched him walk out of the snug, leaving her in the soft, twinkling surroundings, warmth pooling in her stomach at the thought of spending more time with him, even if it was just as friends.

# Chapter Eighteen

Hannah grinned when she saw the Christmas decorations that Myrtle had chosen for the Porthgolow Pop-In. The place was already crammed and colourful, the shelves piled high with staples – tea bags, coffee, biscuits – and traditional holiday fare: buckets and spades, fishing nets for rock-pool trips and jelly shoes that went out of fashion in the Nineties, but were perfect for the beach because you could swim in them and not cut your feet to ribbons on pebbles on the way to the water.

Then there were the completely random things that Myrtle insisted on stocking. Hannah was tempted by the dust-covered Tropical Barbie that reminded her of one she'd had when she was little, with blue eyeshadow and a Day-Glo jumpsuit. There were packets of vacuum-cleaner bags for makes of cleaners that probably no longer existed, and a row of ceramic raccoons in different poses – with glasses, with hats; one sitting in a treehouse. Hannah couldn't begin to imagine how long some of these things had been here: she wouldn't be surprised if there was at least one genuine antique among all the clutter. It would be discovered one day and sold for thousands of pounds in a Christie's auction.

The Christmas decorations were entirely in keeping with the shop's personality. There was a row of metallic paper chains hanging from the ceiling – what was it with Porthgolow and paper chains? – that looked as though they were on at least their third outing. The old-fashioned till was wearing a Santa hat with an abundance of white fur around the brim, and the counter held a white fibre-optic Christmas tree, the tips of its branches twinkling through a rainbow of colours.

'Myrtle, how are you?' Charlie asked. 'Glad the weather's decided to calm down?'

'I did tell everyone.' Myrtle folded her arms. 'I said it was comin' and it did.'

'I've never seen a storm like that,' Hannah admitted. 'Edinburgh gets very cold and rainy, but I can't remember the wind ever being so fierce – you're so exposed here. It was very impressive.'

'Not so much of the "impressive", lass,' she said, tutting. 'It don't need encouragin', we don't want it back. Now, what can I help you with? You movin' here like the rest of 'em?' She eyed her suspiciously, and Hannah laughed.

'Not at all! And what do you mean, the rest of them?'

'Seems most people who come 'ere for a few days end up stayin' for ever.' Her attention turned to Charlie. 'Your Lila's comin' back with Sam soon, from all that la-di-da-ing over in America?'

'They're going to be shooting the second series of *Estelle*,' Charlie explained. 'So it makes sense for them to be based here. They won't need to stay in self-catering accommodation like the rest of the cast and crew. Anyway, Hannah is only here longer than she intended because the train line collapsed and her journey back to Edinburgh is going to take about a hundred days.'

'I can keep working here for the time being,' Hannah said, wondering whether Noah had started on the costings.

'On all that greenery stuff up at the hotel?' Myrtle asked.

'Exactly. And also . . .' she glanced at Charlie, and Charlie nodded. 'I was wondering if you had those photograph albums to hand?'

'I did wonder if you'd forgotten about that. Hold on a sec.' She disappeared through the doorway behind the counter and returned hefting two large square albums. One had a maroon leather cover, and the other was white and fluffy, like a cushion. 'Don't make that face,' Myrtle said, putting them on the counter. 'This was a present from my friend Rose, and it's the perfect size for all the old village photos, even if it does look like a yeti.'

'This is brilliant, Myrtle, thank you. When do you need them back?'

Myrtle waved the question away. 'As long as you don't go disappearin' off to Scotland with 'em, keep 'em as long as you need.'


'Oh look at these,' Charlie said, once she and Hannah were back at the hotel, installed on the sofa in reception. The fluffy photo album felt disconcertingly like a pet sitting on Hannah's lap. 'That's the seafront, you can just see the Pop-In sign – it's exactly the same. Myrtle must have had to repaint it since then, though.'

'Is that the other side of the bay?' Hannah pointed to a black-and-white photograph of a bench on a grass-covered clifftop, the white dots of daisies visible around the wooden legs. A small boy in shorts was sitting cross-legged on the bench, grinning broadly.

'It is – bloody hell! It shows how much the cliff has eroded. There's no bench any more – it's called Crumbling Cliff now and, well, it's not very safe at all.' Charlie shook her head, biting down on her bottom lip. 'How Reenie's house has survived for decades is beyond me.'

'Maybe the rock's more solid closer to the ground?' Hannah offered. 'It's not always being battered by the wind like the flat cliff face.'

'Or maybe Jonah wasn't far off and Reenie's some kind of witch,' Charlie mumbled, turning the page.

'Reenie's a witch?' Hannah laughed.

'Or a mermaid, depending on who you talk to. Ooh, look it's the Clifftop Hotel.'

It was a grand building with four floors, the stonework pale grey, columns on either side of the tall entrance where a man stood, unsmiling, in a dark suit. It was a much more traditional building than Crystal Waters, sitting on top of the cliff, rather than shaped around it. It looked imposing but forlorn, with cracks in several window frames, and Hannah could see why Daniel had made the decision to start again.

'If Audrey had pitched up to that hotel instead of this one,' Charlie said, gesturing around her, 'then the whole haunted thing would have been much easier to believe. It looks like something out of an old horror film.'

'Imagine all those long corridors, like in *The Shining*,' Hannah added. 'We should show this to her, and to Daniel. It might help him understand where she's coming from a bit more.'

'He's taking her much more seriously now, especially after that recording.' Charlie shuddered and picked up her coffee. Spirit, who had been sleeping under their feet, blinked lazily up at them. 'He wasn't blasé about that, just . . .'

'Just what?' Hannah prompted.

'He seemed deflated, which is very unlike him.'

'Deflated by the ghosts?'

'Maybe,' Charlie said. 'He's usually so full of energy, whether it's positive or angry or cheeky. He's hardly ever downcast.'

'There's a lot going on, I guess,' Hannah said, turning the pages of the album, past shots of the beach, the inside of the Seven Stars, the rows of terraced houses, bright in the sunshine. 'There's Christmas, and he's lost a lot of bookings with the storm and all the travel problems, then to have Audrey and her ghosts on top of that – maybe he's overwhelmed?'

'Maybe. I just wonder if there's something he's not telling me.' She tapped her fingers against her lips.

'Have you asked him?' Hannah said, scanning the photos. They were secured to the pages with sticky dots, so the edges still lifted from the thick paper. Her gaze snagged on a picture in the bottom corner and she had to look again, her breath catching in her throat.

'Ooh, is that—' Charlie started.

'That's us,' Hannah said quickly. 'Me, Mike and Mum. There.' She pointed to the image of the three of them sitting at a polished wooden table, benches and other people indistinct in the background. They looked the same age as in the beach photo; she and her brother had glasses of Coke with red-and-white stripy straws, her mum a small glass of white wine.

'Oh yes, look. You can tell it's you, even at that age.' Charlie appraised her, smiling. 'The same open expression. I bet people trust you easily.'

'I hope so,' Hannah said. 'I don't like hiding things.' She knew she sounded defensive, but this photo was yet more proof that her mum wasn't being honest with her. It hadn't just been one random, forgettable beach trip to Porthgolow when they'd had enough of Newquay.

'That's the Seven Stars,' Charlie continued. 'Recognize it? Hugh's done some polishing and painting, and I think he's had the chairs reupholstered, but it's still got the same character.'

'It's a lovely pub,' Hannah murmured. She was trying to force more memories forward, but they remained as evasive as her mum.

'What will you do now?' Charlie asked.

'Speak to Mum again. She *has* to talk to me after this.' Hannah took a photo of the picture on her phone, angling it so there was no glare on the glossy surface.

'What's that?' Daniel had stopped opposite the table, and was looking faintly disgusted.

'One of Myrtle's photo albums.' Charlie grinned at him. 'It's very cosy.'

'It looks like a dead animal,' he said, grimacing.

'There are photos of the Clifftop Hotel in here, which I think we should show to Audrey.'

'OK.' He folded his arms. 'What else?'

'My family in the Seven Stars,' Hannah said.

Daniel's eyebrows rose. 'Really?'

Hannah turned the album round and put it on the table. 'Here.'

He scanned the page. 'This is you?' He pointed to the

212

photo, and Hannah nodded. He flicked through a couple more pages, then froze.

'What is it?' Charlie asked.

Daniel laughed and swivelled the album back round to face them. 'Who do you suppose that is?'

Hannah and Charlie both leaned in. It was a picture of a small, dark-haired boy crouching on the sand and holding a net above his head, though there was no rock pool in sight. A pretty women kneeled behind him, captured in the process of tucking dark hair behind her ear.

'No way.' Charlie looked from the photo to him. 'That's you!'

'Very young me. I had no idea this was in here – no idea one of our family holidays was put in the official Porthgolow album.'

'They're not official,' Charlie said, 'but how amazing to have you *and* Hannah in here.'

'Porthgolow has always had a pretty small feel to it, even with the tourists.' He shook his head. 'I wonder who took the photos? How they ended up here?'

'I'll ask Myrtle,' Charlie said. 'Someone must have been responsible for collecting these – they're so eclectic, and they can't all have been taken by her.'

'You OK, Hannah?' Daniel asked, crouching down. Spirit got up and nosed his hand, seeking attention, and he stroked the dog absent-mindedly. 'You look a bit shell-shocked.'

'I'm all right,' she said. 'It's just . . . this is more than one photo on the beach. There must be more Mum can tell me. I just hope I get some answers this time.'

'No, but Mum . . .'

She had come outside, to a sky bleached of colour by the

winter sun, wind that was more exhilarating than destructive. Her spot, perched on the wooden bench that circled the outdoor hot tub, afforded her a beautiful view of white-topped waves stretching to the horizon. It was calming, which was exactly what she needed when it turned out that – even in the face of definitive proof – her mum wasn't prepared to meet her halfway.

'I don't know why you're pursuing this, Hannah. You should be sorting out your journey home. What am I meant to do without you in the run-up to Christmas?'

'Exactly what you always do,' Hannah said. 'We see each other at the weekends, we do the tree together, I know, but you never want any help getting Christmas dinner ready because you like to do it yourself.'

'What if I want some help this time?' Her tone was whee-dling, and it set Hannah's teeth on edge.

She shook her head: she would not let her mum distract her. 'What is it you're not telling me? Why won't you just admit that we spent time in Porthgolow? I *knew* there was something special about this place when I arrived. We came here a lot, didn't we?'

'So what if we did? What are you chasing? It's a perfect holiday destination, much quieter than the beach at Newquay, and not too far in the car.'

'So why didn't you say so before?'

A seagull swooped, circling above her and screeching, and Spirit sat up on his haunches and barked. When the seagull drifted out to sea, the little dog settled once more at Hannah's feet.

'Mum?' she prompted.

'I spoke to Mike last night. He's so looking forward to seeing you, catching up on all your news.'

Hannah closed her eyes. She couldn't take much more of this. 'I don't want to talk about Christmas, I want to talk about Porthgolow and photos of us, here. Who took them? Who else was there? And don't tell me it was Dad because I know it wasn't.'

'Hannah,' her mum sighed.

'You ask what I'm chasing? I wouldn't be chasing anything if you hadn't been so weird about this from the start. The moment I told you where I was coming on this work trip, it was like something switched off inside you. What can be so bad that you want to keep it from me, all these years later?'

'There's *nothing* to tell you! Why won't you just accept it?'

Hannah was shocked by her mum's raised voice. She couldn't remember the last time she'd seen her shouting – though no doubt it had been at her dad.

'I'm trying to talk to you about the present, about what's happening now,' her mum continued, 'and all you can go on about is this strange feeling you've got about somewhere we spent a few afternoons on a holiday years ago. Get a grip, Hannah, for god's sake!'

'Get a grip? Is that all you have to say? Just tell me what it is. I won't judge you, Mum. I just want to know.'

'I have nothing else to say. My soup's about to boil over. I'll speak to you again when you've calmed down.' The phone went dead.

Hannah stared at the screen for a moment, then slumped against the side of the hot tub. She felt like a small child throwing a tantrum, which, she realized, was exactly how her mum had wanted her to feel. She was still intent on putting her off, which made Hannah even more determined to find out the truth.

She didn't know how long she stayed there, staring out at

the ever-changing sea, but by the time she pushed herself off the bench, her backside had gone numb and the hand gripping the phone was an icy claw. She took Spirit to her room with her, glad to have the dog for company now that Noah was back in Mousehole, and lay on the bed, pressing her hands over her eyes. She couldn't allow herself to despair. She would not stay in her room, make endless coffees and eat the bag of fudge she'd bought for Saskia.

The sun was shining, she was in Cornwall, and there was a rascal of a dog who would enjoy a long walk on Porthgolow beach. She could cheer them both up, put Noah and her mum and secrets behind her, and spend the afternoon being as carefree as Spirit.

# Chapter Nineteen

'Oh wow, this is incredible!'

Hannah stepped onto Gertie and her eyes suddenly had too much to do. There were more fairy lights than there had been before, white strings and multicoloured strings, and a red and green set flashing above the coffee machine. There were little colour-changing snowmen on every table, and cut-out paper snowflakes stuck to the windows. The air smelled of cinnamon spice and marzipan. It was the most Christmassy place Hannah had seen so far, and completely in contrast to the elegant decorations at Crystal Waters. Charlie clearly knew what she was doing: one set of rules for the bus, one for the hotel.

'I know it's completely over the top,' Charlie said, 'but for me, that's what Christmas is about. And Gertie has never been a subtle bus.'

'I love it,' Hannah replied truthfully.

'I'm glad you're coming with me today,' Charlie continued.

'It's always better when I'm not on my own. I'm not discounting you, Marmite,' she added, stroking his ears, 'but you don't always keep the conversation flowing.'

'Where are we going?' Hannah asked, sitting down and resting her elbows on the table.

'We're going south!' Charlie turned to the coffee machine. 'I haven't set up in a different village for a while, and it's a good way to get people talking about Gertie. Besides, I want to promote my Santa Claus tour.'

'Sounds fun,' Hannah said, and it did, even if she wasn't entirely in the mood. Since the conversation with her mum, Hannah had struggled to raise her spirits. She had spent a lot of time on the Trainline app looking for return journeys that wouldn't be torture, but everything was still disrupted because of the track problems at Dawlish. Besides, she didn't need to be back in the office, and the thought of going home to her mum's denials and a Christmas that didn't involve the seaside or the Cornish Cream Tea Bus no longer felt that appealing.

Charlie had called her the night before, asking if she was at a loose end and wanted to accompany her on a trip. It was almost as if, Hannah thought wryly, Daniel had mentioned to his girlfriend that she'd been mooching around the hotel in a lacklustre sort of way, taking Spirit for walks and reading in the snug, not quite managing to lift the pall of sadness that hung around her.

'Are you OK?' Charlie asked now.

'I'm fine,' Hannah said, accepting a frothy cappuccino that smelt of gingerbread.

'Good start.' Charlie sat opposite her. 'But how are you really?'

Hannah scrunched up her face. 'How did you know?'

'I have a number of spies in this village, and most of the time I'm not asking for gossip – I can't avoid it even if I want to. You seemed fired up after we discovered that photograph, so what's happened since?'

'My mum's still not having any of it,' Hannah admitted. 'She got angry, which is so unlike her. I got angry back, and . . .' She sighed. 'Now I've caused a rift between us, and I'm even more convinced that she's hiding something.'

Charlie stirred her drink. 'And you think it's something you need to know?'

'You think I should let it go? Leave whatever it is in the past?' Hannah didn't mind Charlie challenging her; she relished talking things through rather than leaving them to stew.

'If you usually get on with your mum, and she's clearly against telling you what's going on, then maybe it would be best, for now at least, if you accepted it. She might tell you further down the line.'

Hannah nodded. She had considered this, too. She wasn't good at letting things go once she got an idea in her head – it was how she'd gone from wanting to make her dad proud to researching, training for and then getting a job as an eco-consultant. She was naturally determined, but sometimes it wasn't the wisest approach. When she'd told her dad she'd qualified with honours – on the phone, because he wasn't on the same continent – his reply had been a distinctly crackly: 'That's great, love. Listen, I've got to head off.'

'I just hadn't expected any of this,' she said. 'I thought I'd have one week here, meet a few new people, get my first case under my belt and go home. But it's so much more.'

'Is that what's making this hard to let go?'

Hannah shrugged. 'I'm here right now. And I know that

Porthgolow is special. Not just because you and Daniel have told me, but because I can feel it. And believe me, I'm not usually a fanciful person – maybe Audrey is rubbing off on me.' She smiled.

'You don't believe that.'

'No, not really.'

'So,' Charlie said. 'More detective work?'

'I'm going to speak to Hugh next.'

'He'll help if he can, for sure. Is that the only thing that's been worrying you?'

An image of Noah popped into Hannah's head and she pushed it out. 'That's all,' she said.

Charlie looked at her for a beat longer, then nodded. 'Right then, time to get our Christmas show on the road!'

She stood and scooted Marmite off the driver's seat, and he immediately came over and sat on Hannah's lap. He was warm and solid and affectionate, and Hannah petted him and cooed at him, feeling slightly disloyal to Spirit who had been curled up in his basket when she left the hotel, and hadn't been enticed by the promise of a bus trip – even one that might include a bit of sausage roll.

She sat hugging the dog, watching the winter landscape pass while Charlie drove. It was a beautiful morning, the low sun painting everything with gold, and mist hanging over the fields. They travelled south, towards the tip of the country, the sea on their right.

'Not long now,' Charlie called. 'It's a lovely day for it.'

'It's stunning,' Hannah said, her eyes drawn to the way the sea shifted from slate grey to glistening blue as the sun rose higher.

Charlie slowed the bus as they approached a roundabout. A couple of car horns blared, and she returned the greetings with a toot and a wave. Hannah thought how nice it must be to work somewhere that was always viewed with affection. Her most recent jobs, sous chef and eco-consultant, weren't flashy. The food at the Whisky Cellar was, but she had always been in the kitchen, keeping her head down. Eco-consultant was an increasingly important role, and some of the transformations that Green Futures instigated were spectacular, but most of the changes were internal, and anything architectural was done by someone else. They were only consultants, after all.

Charlie lived in a world of bunting and fairy lights, satisfied diners and chocolate-smeared children. She met everyone who came on board the Cornish Cream Tea Bus, and she was proud of it. Hannah wished she could have that confidence, that absolute certainty that what she was doing was appreciated. A picture of her dad, scruffy and entirely at home in the battered leather armchair in their old living room, appeared in her head. She shook it away and looked out of the window, her heart skipping as they passed a sign:

*Welcome to Mousehole.*

She stayed quiet as the bus crept along impossibly narrow streets with buildings crammed together on either side, painted blue and grey and clotted-cream yellow, the sun just beginning to hit their roofs. Seagulls screeched around them, and the streets were busy with people rugged up in woolly hats and gloves, nobody here fooled into thinking that the sunshine meant it would be warm.

Hannah was on high alert, her body rigid as she scoured the streets for Noah's tall frame and purposeful walk, that inner confidence that had only shown signs of cracking after their exchange in the steam room. She realized that she knew so much about him: about the way he moved and held

221

himself, his tendency to splay and curl his fingers when his arms were by his sides. Subconsciously, Hannah had been taking it all in, everything rushing to the surface now she was on Noah's turf.

Charlie drove Gertie past the houses, the village's busy harbour to their right, fishing boats bobbing on the water, a car park a little way ahead. The turning looked far too narrow for the bus, but Charlie slowed Gertie down and made the turn gracefully.

'It looks beautiful here,' Hannah said, once the engine was quiet. 'A bit busier than Porthgolow, with the harbour.'

Charlie turned, resting her arm along the back of her seat. 'It's a lovely village. I don't get here often, but the council are always welcoming when I ask for a temporary licence.'

Hannah nodded. She couldn't help examining every face that went past, checking for dark-framed glasses and brown curls. 'Gertie's already getting a lot of interest,' she pointed out. People were staring at the Routemaster and, in some cases, slowing their pace. A few had stopped completely, taking out their phones to snap photos.

'Gertie always gets lots of attention,' Charlie said. 'She's the extroverted part of me. Come on, let's get these cakes and pastries laid out, then we can open the doors and let them on board. It looks like we picked a good destination for our pre-Christmas trip.'

Gertie was busy within minutes of the door opening. Charlie asked Hannah to greet customers and direct them to tables, then take their orders when they were ready. She enjoyed being a part of the hubbub, and while she was fully versed in the inner workings of a kitchen, she wasn't used to being front of house. She wrote as quickly as she could, writing

222

down requests for cappuccinos and sausage rolls; Danish pastries and Americanos with a splash of milk; a Christmas Cornish cream tea with a pot of Earl Grey.

From their accents and general demeanour, Hannah thought most of the customers were locals. Cornwall was more a summer than a winter destination, though her time at Crystal Waters had shown her that a luxurious Cornish break was possible even when the weather was raging – just add a hot chocolate, a twinkling tree and a crackling fire, and you could enjoy the beauty of the coastline from the comfort of your indoor retreat.

'Can I have *two* gingerbread men, Mum,' asked a small boy, his younger brother mesmerized by the colour-changing snowman on the table.

Their mum narrowed her eyes in response. The boy giggled, but the woman held her pensive expression expertly, and by the time she eventually said yes, even Hannah was on tenterhooks. She took the family's order and hurried down the stairs.

Charlie was in the kitchen, chatting to a woman wearing a thick blue scarf over a red padded gilet, her dark curly hair pushed messily away from her face.

'It truly is remarkable,' the woman was saying, her Cornish accent mild but noticeable. 'I heard about your bus very recently, but never thought I'd see it in Mousehole. It's one way to brighten up a chilly day.' Her laugh was loud and hearty.

'I'm glad you like it.' Charlie was putting sausage rolls on a plate, no doubt for the big, burly men who had made the whole bus shake as they stomped up to the top deck and smiled at Hannah through their well-cultivated beards. 'I don't want to step on anyone's toes, but part of the fun of running the Cornish Cream Tea Bus is bringing it to new places, spreading the joy throughout Cornwall.'

Hannah hovered with her order, wondering whether to interrupt.

The older woman waved a dismissive hand. 'Oh, don't worry about that. I'm more about cheeses, meats and olives, though I do make the occasional Scotch egg or brie and cranberry slice when I've got time, but the crossover's tiny. No toes being stepped on here, and these're steel toe-capped wellies so I'd barely feel it anyway.' She laughed again and Charlie grinned, then gestured for Hannah to swap her order with the tray.

Hannah blinked as she replayed everything she'd just heard. Something about it made the tiny hairs on the back of her neck stand up.

'So sorry, my love,' the dark-haired woman said. 'I'm totally in the way here. I'll take myself to one of the tables and order like a normal person.' She turned around and Hannah tried to slip past her to collect her tray, but as their eyes met, the woman gasped and grabbed Hannah's arm. 'Are you . . .?'

'Am I . . .?' Hannah repeated stupidly.

'Long blonde hair, big brown eyes like Bambi, fan of the Cornish Cream Tea Bus. You're Hannah, aren't you?'

'I am,' she murmured. 'And are you—?'

'Scratch that last idea,' the woman said, flapping her hand. 'I'm going to go and get Noah, bring him down here. He'll be made up to see you. He needs a bit of brightenin' up, my poor son. Back in a jiffy!' She hurried off the bus, her dark curls flying recklessly behind her.

'Was that . . .?' Charlie started. 'Because if so, then . . . golly.'

Hannah nodded. 'That must have been Noah's mum. And she's gone to get him, and bring him back here.'

Charlie laughed. 'Isn't that a good thing? You two get on, don't you?'

'Of course we do,' Hannah said. 'It'll be lovely to see him.'

*Too lovely.*

She was sure she hadn't said it aloud, but Charlie's eyes widened in surprise, then softened with understanding. 'Are you and Noah—'

'No, absolutely not,' she cut in. 'We're friends. Nothing happened on Audrey's ghost hunt.'

'I didn't ask about Audrey's ghost hunt,' Charlie said gently.

'Oh.' Hannah looked away, wondering if the heat in her cheeks would set the cakes on fire. 'I'd better take these sausage rolls up. We wouldn't want them to get cold, would we?' She took the tray before Charlie could say anything else, but she could feel her friend's amused, interested gaze on her all the way up the stairs.

# Chapter Twenty

In the following ten minutes, Hannah got two of the three orders she took wrong and dropped a cheese twist on the floor in the kitchen, which had Marmite whining as if he'd been starved for weeks and the fallen pastry had his name on it.

'She might not come back with him,' Charlie tried.

Hannah gave her a straight stare. 'Did she look like the kind of woman who doesn't do what she says she's going to?'

Charlie laughed. 'Maybe not. Anyway, just because she wants Noah to come here, it doesn't mean Noah will agree.'

This time Hannah's glare wasn't accompanied by words.

'Fair enough,' Charlie said. 'He'll be here any minute. But that doesn't mean it needs to be awkward. What exactly happened between you anyw—' From the look on Charlie's face, it seemed Hannah had run out of panic time.

She turned round slowly.

Noah was standing at the threshold of the kitchen, his mum's arm slung around his shoulders even though she was a couple of inches shorter than him. Standing next to each other, Hannah could see how alike they were, with the same blue eyes and curly hair, his mum's face slightly more rounded – though still with prominent cheekbones. Hannah's breath stalled, as it did now every time she was faced with him anew.

He was wearing a thick waxed jacket above jeans, his hair glossy with product but not restrained, so the curls were tighter. 'Hi Hannah, Charlie,' he said. 'I expect Mum has forgotten to introduce herself.'

'Oh God, I did forget! Jill Rosewall.' She held out her hand to Hannah, then Charlie.

'Hi Noah,' Charlie said. 'It's lovely to meet you, Jill. Are you going to have a seat?' She was peering over Jill's shoulder, clearly wary of neglecting any customers.

'I'm staying here,' Jill replied. 'I thought Noah could give Hannah a tour of the harbour.'

'Oh I can't.' Hannah spoke just as Noah said, 'That would be great—'

'Nonsense, Hannah,' Jill cut in. 'Dave's covering the deli and I can help Charlie here – it's not as if I don't know what I'm doing – and that'll free you up to get some fresh air with Noah. Aren't there some *costings* you need to discuss?' She raised an eyebrow.

Hannah wouldn't have thought it was possible to make the word 'costings' sound dirty, but Jill Rosewall had managed it.

'Charlie, are you sure it's OK?'

Charlie looked as if she was trying hard to tamp down her glee. 'I would be upset if you *didn't* go with Noah.'

'Oh wonderful!' Jill clapped her hands. 'Go on, then.' She pushed Noah forwards, towards the kitchen and Hannah.

'We need to go the other way if you want us to actually get off the bus,' Noah said.

Jill grinned at him. 'Of course, darling. Don't listen to your silly old mum. Off you trot, Hannah. It may seem a bit crabby on the outside, but Mousehole's a wonderful place when you get to know it well.'

They strolled along the harbour front with reusable cups full of steaming coffee that Charlie had given them before they left. The moulded red plastic fitted snugly between Hannah's gloved hands, steam curling up towards her face. The morning had matured into a bright but blisteringly cold winter day, the air making her nose tingle. Marmite trotted between them, weaving easily between other people, Noah holding his lead.

'Your mum's lovely,' Hannah said, after the silence had stretched from companionable to strained.

Noah chuckled. 'There's a difference between lovely and wildly overbearing.'

'I don't think the two have to be mutually exclusive.'

'I was working on the Crystal Waters costings when she hammered on the door of my room and told me there was a family emergency. She has no scruples about lying to get me to do what she wants.' There was scorn in his voice, but Hannah didn't believe it.

'You didn't want to leave your work behind and come and see Gertie?' she said softly. It was easier to think he hadn't wanted to see the bus, rather than her.

'I disagreed about leaving my desk because I didn't believe Mum's wolfish cries of emergency. If she'd told me Gertie had rocked up in the car park with you and Charlie on board,

228

along with this guy,' he pointed at Marmite, 'I would have happily left my spreadsheet behind. This was one occasion where she didn't need to make things more complicated.'

'Are you still staying with your parents?'

Noah stopped next to a bench, the seat in sunshine, and pressed his palm to the wood. 'It's not too cold,' he said. Before Hannah had sat down, Marmite bounded onto it, and she sat on one side with Noah on the other, the dog a bolster between them. 'Just for a couple more days,' he added, answering her question. 'I should be home by the end of the weekend.' He leaned back and rested his arm along the bench, looking out at the harbour, and Hannah's gaze followed his. Boats of all different sizes and colours bobbed up and down on the gentle swell. The thrashing, destructive waves of a few days ago had gone.

Hannah swivelled so that she was facing him. He had a great profile, bold and proud like a Roman god's, the glasses and curls softening it. 'How are you getting on with the costings?' she asked.

'OK. I can show you what I've come up with later, if you like. How are your plans for getting home? Are things looking easier?'

'Not so far,' Hannah admitted. 'And I'm torn about whether to go back or not.'

Noah sat up straighter. 'At all?'

Hannah coughed down a mouthful of coffee. 'No, I didn't mean that. I will have to go back at some point, seeing how my family and my friends, my job and my flat are all there. But Daniel and Gerald have both been generous, and I found something else – in the hunt for answers about my past.' She raised her eyebrows dramatically, being deliberately over-the-top, but Noah seemed genuinely interested. So Hannah

229

told him about Myrtle's photo album, about finding the picture of her family in the pub, and then about the argument that had followed with her mum.

Noah leaned forward, his elbows on his knees, his expression serious. 'You don't know that this thing – whatever it is that she's refusing to tell you – isn't something she wishes she could forget, for both your sakes. Or maybe she wants to talk about it face to face, rather than over the phone?'

'She does keep asking when I'm coming back,' Hannah murmured. 'But then why not just say that? *I'll tell you when you get home*. Why keep on insisting there isn't anything to say?'

'I've no idea,' Noah said. 'You're going to speak to Hugh?'

'It's the logical next step.'

'But you discovered the album on Monday, and you don't know how long you're going to be here, and now it's Thursday.' He said it carefully.

She sighed. 'I know, I'm stalling. But what if you and Charlie are right, and that once I find out what it is, I'll wish I hadn't?'

'If you decide to forget about it and walk away, will you really be able to, or will it always be there, hovering?' He tapped the side of his head.

'Oh, it'll hover for sure.'

'Then you need to speak to him, but you don't have to go alone. I'll come with you, if you want? I'm sure Charlie would too, if you asked. She knows Hugh well, doesn't she?'

'Thank you, Noah.' She let out a breath that misted in the cold air. 'Now, what about this tour? I want to know all the ins and outs of your village.'

He grinned and stood up, holding out his hand. He wasn't

wearing gloves, and as Hannah let him pull her up, she wished she'd taken hers off too. She shouldn't think about being skin on skin with Noah; she should put all those fantasies into the junk folder in her mind and then hit 'delete'. But she had already come to realize that was going to be impossible.

After dropping Marmite back with Charlie, Noah showed Hannah round Mousehole, focusing on the places that were special to him, rather than the tourist highlights: the convenience store where as a child he'd bought neon beach toys, new buckets and spades, and the inflatable ring that his mum wouldn't let him use unless she was in the sea with him, and where he now sometimes got an energy drink on the way back from a particularly gruelling run. He pointed out his favourite spot on the harbour wall, where he stopped on clear mornings and watched the sun raise its head above the sea, Mousehole facing east rather than west; the tiny fish restaurant where he could get a bowl of fresh mussels with whichever sauce the chef had concocted that day.

With every step, every new place, Noah warmed up, his gestures expansive and his smile wide, and that made Hannah warm up, too. She was wholly focused on him, the cold forgotten.

'I used to hang off these railings with my friend Jamie,' he said, grabbing hold of the metal bars, the drop down the sheer brick wall to the water below about fifteen feet, though that probably changed with the tide. 'We'd swing over, lower ourselves down, and people walking past wouldn't notice our hands, so whenever we heard anyone we'd hoist ourselves up and shout boo.' He laughed.

'It sounds dangerous,' Hannah said, but she couldn't help laughing with him.

'We both fell into the water more than once, but our parents never found out because we just claimed we'd been playing on the beach.'

'Is this your running route then?' Hannah asked as they walked, his story reminding her that, beneath the buttoned-up appearance, he was actually very physical.

'It is. There's nothing like running by the sea to wake you up in the morning, or blast your thoughts away in the evening.'

'How far do you go?'

He shrugged. 'Depends how I'm feeling. Sometimes five k, sometimes ten. I can come out every day for a month and see thirty different skies, thirty different seas.'

Hannah leaned on the railings, watching seagulls bob alongside the boats. 'It's a magical view. I can't imagine ever taking somewhere like this for granted.'

'I have no desire to live anywhere else: Cornwall can have me until the day I die. But you don't feel that way about Edinburgh? When did you move there? I've been trying to work out your accent, and it's not Scottish, but there are occasional words or phrases that are.'

'We moved there when I was nine, from Oxford,' Hannah said. 'That's when the holidays to Cornwall stopped and we started going north instead: up to Aberdeen, the east coast of Scotland. But it wasn't like down here. In Cornwall the sky and seas always seemed so blue; we often ended up walking around with no shoes on, even though the pavement was hot and gritty under our feet.' She laughed. 'I remember having to put them on when we—' One of Myrtle's photographs popped into her head: the Clifftop

232

Hotel, with its imposing structure and the man waiting outside. Except it wasn't the same because Hannah was there, carrying her jelly shoes, and a woman in a neat red skirt and white blouse was talking to her mum, telling her they couldn't come in unless they put their shoes back on. 'Oh my God.'

'What is it?' Noah asked.

'I went to the Clifftop Hotel! I remember it. We went for a cream tea, and Mike and I weren't wearing shoes, and we had to put them on before we could go in and Mum was mortified. I don't remember much . . .' She closed her eyes, trying to picture the hotel's interior, but all she got were glimpses of large windows that looked out over the coastline, bunches of elaborate flowers on the tables and a glass of lemonade with beads of condensation running down the outside. 'I've definitely been there, though. That didn't come from Myrtle's album.' She spun round to face him, gripping his arms. 'I need to speak to Mike. He's a couple of years older than me, so he'll remember more. I left him a voicemail a few days ago, but he hasn't got back to me.'

'Do you want to call him now? I can always leave you . . .'

She shook her head. 'I'll do it later.'

'This is great, Hannah. You're getting closer. Maybe you needed a bit of distance from Porthgolow to let the memories come?'

'I was trying too hard.' She was still holding onto him, and she realized how easy it would be to slide her hands up his arms and shoulders and around his neck, bring his face down to meet hers. She stepped back and pulled her ponytail tight. 'Where now, then?'

Noah was smiling at her, his blue eyes bright. 'Do you

want a drink to celebrate? The Ship Inn does a great local lager.'

'Sounds perfect.'

They sat at a table outside with pints of Korev and packets of cheese and onion crisps. The sun glimmered above them, sprinkling white-gold light onto the water, the sea on the horizon a murky grey. Shades of cold, Hannah thought, and wrapped her rainbow scarf more tightly around her neck.

'Are you sure you're OK with this?' Noah asked after he'd taken a sip of his drink, beads of foam lingering on his top lip before he licked them off.

'What, beer and crisps? I've already told you I'm not a food snob. And cheese and onion is the best flavour. None of your weird flavours like Marmite, or Brussels sprouts.'

'You don't like sprouts?'

'I love sprouts, but not as crisps. Last year for my friends' Christmas, I deep-fried the sprouts and they were *utterly* delicious. You wouldn't believe what a bit of well-seasoned batter could do to the humble sprout – I'll have to make them for you sometime.'

Noah laughed, and when Hannah turned away from the view, he was scrutinizing her.

'What?' she asked.

'Why aren't you a chef, running your own restaurant and working your way up to your second Michelin star?'

'Because I'm an eco-consultant,' she said, grinning. 'Food is my favourite hobby. Would you run for a living?'

'If I was good enough, then sure. You have to do something you're passionate about, something that makes *you* happy.'

Hannah kept her smile firmly in place. 'This job does make me happy.'

'Not just your dad?' he asked softly. 'You didn't do it *just* to make him proud? To remind him that you're worth so much more than he's offering you? And what about Porthgolow? Are you so intent on finding answers about your past in Cornwall because you don't feel things are right in Scotland?'

Hannah swung her leg over the side of the bench so she was no longer straddling it, and turned fully to face him. She pressed her palms into the rough wood of the picnic table. 'Why are you asking me this? I just told you I remembered being in Porthgolow. Once I've spoken to Mike I'm sure he'll confirm it. Mum won't, for whatever reason, but he will.'

'But why does it matter to you so much?' Noah frowned, exhaled. 'You're using up all this emotional energy, as if you're desperate to find *something* down here. You don't care if it's a horrible skeleton that should stay in the closet, you just need to find it. It's as if you're missing something where you are.' He reached his hand out so it was mirroring hers, the tips of their middle fingers touching on the table.

She couldn't look at him, and instead of pulling her hand away, she found herself pressing her finger more firmly against his. She had taken her gloves off to eat the crisps, and was soothed by the warmth of his skin, even if his words weren't comfortable. 'I don't know,' she admitted. 'This trip has been so much more than I expected. And I have enjoyed the work, but once I'm home and I look back on it, it won't be what I remember: checking out Daniel's air conditioning and researching water filtration systems.'

'What will you remember?'

She forced herself to look up at him. 'Our cream tea on the bus, the storm, finding Spirit. Hearing Anna and her

235

fisherman's story in the Christmassy snug with Audrey. The views, great breakfasts, ghost hunting with you in the spa. This.'

'What do you think that's telling you?'

'That holidays are more fun than work?'

He rolled his eyes. 'Hannah—'

'That those are the things I care about,' she said. 'And you're in almost all the memories. No, not almost. All of them.'

'I wasn't trying to—'

'No, I know you weren't. But you asked, and I'm just being honest. I know that nothing can happen, that it's not . . .' She shook her head. 'I'm going home in a few days, hopefully. So even if – if we could, then, it's not really . . . it's not right.'

'What are you saying, Hannah?' His lips lifted in a tentative smile.

'I'm saying that, despite what there is between us, I know we can't—'

Noah's phone jingled with a message. He stared at it for a moment, his brow crumpling, and the name *Beth* echoed through Hannah's thoughts.

'What is it?' she asked.

'It's Mum,' he said, sliding his thumb up the screen.

'What about her?'

'You know I mentioned that she has a tendency to be wildly overbearing?' Hannah nodded. 'Well, she's sent Charlie and the bus back to Porthgolow.' He gave her a sheepish grin and ran a hand through his hair, sending the dark, glossy curls into disarray. 'Apparently you're coming for dinner, and she won't take no for an answer.'

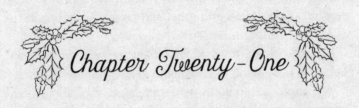

# Chapter Twenty-One

The sun was starting to sink as they set off, dipping out of sight behind the houses. Hannah's breath misted in front of her, the cold burning her cheeks and fingers. She hadn't had time to fully consider the sudden turn of events: she was going to spend the evening with Noah's parents. She had wanted to see the dogs, but being welcomed into the bosom of the Rosewall family was extremely intimidating. And it didn't help that Noah seemed equally nervous, unable to meet her gaze since telling her what his mum had done.

'Here we go then.' He stopped outside a stone house. The front door, painted glossy black with a brass knocker, opened straight onto the narrow pavement; the window frames were duck-egg blue, and light glowed from a skylight in the roof. It looked homely and inviting. Noah didn't take out a key or knock on the door, he simply pushed it open, gesturing for Hannah to go in ahead of him.

The dogs greeted her first, racing down the corridor to

angle their proud noses into her hands. Two of them were mottled brown, the other grey with white patches. They struck a balance between being scruffy and elegant, their temperaments gentle and affectionate. They spent a few moments fussing over her, but their reaction to Noah was something else: they barked and yipped and bounded up on their hind legs, until he was forced to crouch and put his arms round them, a tangle of legs and arms and paws and hair and fur, his laughter filling the narrow hallway.

'Hannah, Noah, my sweets.' Jill's arms were outstretched, glasses of fizzy wine in each hand. 'Here you are at last.'

'We came as soon as you messaged me,' Noah said, extracting himself from the dogs. He took Hannah's coat and scarf and put them on a hook, then shrugged out of his own.

'Ah yes.' His mum handed them each a glass. 'It's just that I concocted this little plan the moment I met Hannah, so subconsciously I've been waiting for you all day.'

'I'm not drinking, Mum,' Noah said. 'I've already had a pint, and I'll drive Hannah back later.'

'No you won't, my darling,' Jill replied. 'I am the instigator, so I'll do the driving. You relax, because God knows there's not enough of that in your life right now. Hannah, never mind these incorrigible mutts – come through.'

'Which one is which?' she asked as she followed Jill down a corridor with a thick, pea-green carpet. She was already very fond of the incorrigible mutts: Noah had been right about them.

'Del Boy's the grey,' Noah said, 'that's Rodney, and this one here is Albert, because he's always had a tuft of white fur between his ears.' He patted the dog, who was walking loyally at his side.

The corridor opened up into a kitchen and dining room

that looked as if it ran the entire width of the house. The kitchen to the right was farmhouse style, with pine counter-tops, cream doors and a spacious island in the middle, hosting bowls of crisps, a flourishing poinsettia, and a packet of Christmas cards, some already addressed in envelopes, some waiting to be written. To the left was a large rustic dining table and eight chairs, and straight ahead was a pair of French doors, the curtains open to reveal a tiny courtyard garden. A string of simple white fairy lights twisted along the rail, suggesting the curtains were never closed, at least not at this time of year. The smell of herbs and roasting potatoes made Hannah's stomach rumble.

'All right, Noah,' said a voice from behind them, and Hannah turned to find a man filling the doorway, his thin-ning hair a shock of white, his skin weather-worn, his eyes a shade lighter than Noah's. Noah shook his hand, and Hannah noticed him straighten his shoulders in a subcon-scious squaring-up.

'Dad,' Noah said, 'this is Hannah, my colleague from Green Futures.'

'Hannah,' Noah's dad boomed. 'Champion to meet you. I'm Gerens. Heard a lot about you – second-hand, mind. Noah talks to his mum, not me, about affairs of the heart.'

Hannah shook his hand; his grip was warm and solid. She wanted to ignore his last comment, and not cling desper-ately onto it as if it was a cliff-edge keeping her from falling to her death.

'Lovely to meet you too. I'm just a work colleague, though, not—'

'Come and take a pew,' Jill cut in. 'Drink your fizz, tell us all about yourself. I want to hear about these ghosts up at the hotel you're consulting on. Noah was tight-lipped when we asked about the investigation, and he'd been so looking forward to it.'

'You're talking as if I'm twelve and didn't like the monkeys at the zoo.' Noah gestured for Hannah to take a seat on the far side of the table, and once she'd sat down he sat next to her, pulling in his chair and moving it a little closer to hers, so that when he put his elbows on the table their shoulders brushed. His jumper was speckled blue, cobalt mingling with azure, and it did frankly indecent things to his eyes. It took her back to their conversation in the spa, about favourite colours and Goldilocks.

'Well, you behaved like you were seven, all folded arms and "don't want to talk about it",' Jill said, pushing her hair away from her face with the heel of her hand. 'Just because you're staying with us doesn't mean you can revert to being a child. So now I'm going to ask Hannah, and you're not going to interrupt.'

Noah glared at her and she blew him a kiss. He rolled his eyes.

Gerens brought a bowl of crab mayonnaise and a plate of crusty, warm baguette chunks to the table. The aromas of pepper and lemon wafting up from the crab made Hannah want to weep with joy – that, and the atmosphere. 'Dig in, you two,' he said, sitting opposite them. 'I can't let my wife take all the credit for the cooking. We've got our own specialities.'

'And fish is yours?' Hannah asked, taking a piece of bread and spreading a spoonful of the crab mixture onto it. 'This smells wonderful.'

Gerens gave a loud, unbridled laugh, which reminded her of Noah, the few times she'd seen him completely relaxed. 'Doesn't hold back, your girl, does she? That's what I like to see.'

Noah appeared to be as stumped by the "your girl" as Hannah was, but she soon learned that silence wasn't a common occurrence in this house. She also discovered it was impossible not to get swept up in their good humour; the laughter and gentle ribbing the family seemed to run on. Noah took a while to warm up, but then he was joking along with his mum and dad, the stiffness in his shoulders loosening. The dogs nudged into legs and licked hands, seeking affection, while Jill moved around the kitchen, lifting pot lids and crouching in front of the oven, swearing and grinning in equal measure.

'What is it?' Noah asked, as he slid another slice of bread onto Hannah's plate.

'What do you mean?'

'You were shaking your head.'

'Was I?'

'Yup.'

'Your family are lovely.' She said it quietly, so Gerens wouldn't hear. He was fussing with one of the dogs – Rodney, she thought – and wasn't paying attention.

Noah gave her a lopsided smile. 'They're all right. They have their good sides and bad sides, as all families do.'

'You're so lucky.' She hadn't meant to sound emotional, had definitely not wanted her voice to crack on the last word. 'It reminds me of my friends' Christmases, all the good-natured bickering. But we don't have any dogs at ours. Saskia keeps threatening to get a chihuahua, but so far her handbag is dog-free.'

'Will you still get to do it this year, now you've been delayed?'

'It's not until the twenty-third, so I should.'

'And you do *all* the cooking?' He raised an eyebrow.

241

'I get someone else to do the pudding, but I pick what it's going to be. Because I want it to go with the rest of the menu,' she explained, when he laughed. 'This year I'm thinking of a chocolate and mallow log, with a bitter cherry sauce. The log is so sweet, but you add biscuit pieces to give it some texture, and then if you make the sauce *really* bitter, it cuts through the sweetness and the whole thing is just—' She hummed with pleasure, closing her eyes at the thought.

When she opened them, Noah was staring at her, his lips parted.

'What?' she asked, feeling the blush rise up her neck.

'That is some reaction,' he whispered. 'And to think you were only *talking* about it.'

'Sorry, I—'

'Do not apologize for that,' he said. 'I'm almost tempted to have a go at making it myself, if it provokes that kind of response.' His lips flickered into a smile, and warmth pooled low in Hannah's stomach.

'Five minutes, chaps,' Jill said, and Noah blinked and looked away. 'In the meantime, a top-up.' She brought over the bottle of sparkling wine, the gold script on the label glistening under the spotlights in the ceiling. 'Local vineyard, this one. They do the most wonderful tours, and you can get involved in the harvesting and bottling if you have several hundred pounds to join their club. It's tempting, but not as much as the wine itself.' She filled both their glasses, then returned to the hob, calling over her shoulder. 'What about this haunted hotel, Hannah? You must have wondered what you'd done to deserve a project that involved my son *and* several spooks.' She bent to take plates out of the oven.

Hannah laughed, took a deep breath and then, acutely aware of Noah watching her, told them everything they'd learned from Audrey about the hauntings, the story behind it, and what had happened during their temporary foray into paranormal investigating. She left out the events of the spa treatment room, moving swiftly on to the recording of the footsteps. She watched their reactions – Gerens's was easier to gauge because he was sitting opposite her, while Jill was dishing up the main course. She didn't think either of them was laughing at her.

'Sounds exciting,' Gerens said, scooping up the last of the crab meat.

'You don't think it's rubbish?' Hannah was taken aback. He seemed like such a grounded person that she had assumed he would be sceptical.

'Course not. Cornwall's full of ghosts. These seem a bit more upmarket than our usual fare, but then it sounds like they're interlopers, stuck here after their untimely ends. Do you know what piskies are?'

Hannah shook her head.

'They're mischievous sprites that roam throughout Cornwall. I've seen 'em, more than once, just as dawn breaks.'

'Darling,' Jill chided softly.

'She's the one who doesn't believe.' Gerens pointed at his wife. 'Though she would if she'd seen 'em. Noah knows they're real, don't you?'

Noah pressed his fingers over his mouth. He glanced at Hannah before replying. 'I've never seen one.'

'But you know they're real.' His dad raised a white eyebrow.

'I think there are too many stories – of piskies and ghosts and hauntings – to discount them all. There has to be something to them. What that is, I'm not sure.' He shrugged.

'Well, we don't need to solve that mystery round this table tonight,' Jill said, bringing over plates of roast pork and crackling, roast potatoes, broccoli, carrots and parsnips, a rich-looking gravy draped over the whole thing. 'Now, we need to eat.'

'This looks wonderful,' Hannah said, her taste buds rejoicing all over again. 'Thank you so much for having me.'

She waved a dismissive hand. 'No problem, my love – I couldn't believe my luck, you coming into the village with Gertie and Charlie. I thought you'd be a fair maiden I'd only ever hear about, and would always regret not meeting.'

'Mum,' Noah mumbled through a mouthful of potato.

'It's true! From the way Noah talked about you, I knew you'd be special, and I was right. We both were.' She leaned over the table and tapped Noah's hand. He deepened his focus on the food in front of him.

After that the atmosphere lightened, Gerens and Jill keeping Hannah entertained with stories about working in the deli, the customers and the stories they brought with them, and about fishing. Noah's dad painted it in an almost mythical light, skirting round how hard it was, how demoralizing it could be. He told her about heading out to sea with dolphins alongside the boat as the sun turned the world pink; the strange catches he'd had – giant sunfish in the warmer months; the times he'd seen whales, occasionally getting closer to them than was entirely comfortable.

The food slid down easily and time slipped away. The local fizz was replaced by a mellow red wine, the roast pork followed by a warming berry crumble with a hint of Christmassy cinnamon. All the while, Hannah sensed Noah at her side, felt him relax as the conversation turned away from him, joining in with the stories he must have heard a hundred times before.

At some point during the evening, Jill lit the open fire

and the dogs gathered around it, slumping down on the rug as if world-weary, their tails wagging lazily. Hannah felt inclined to join them. Her cheeks were red from the flames, she was full of food and wine, and she could easily have curled up with Rodney, Del Boy and Albert.

'I really should be going,' she said, stifling another yawn. 'I've had a lovely time, but it is . . .' she glanced at her watch and saw it was almost midnight. 'Wow.'

'Oh dear lord!' Jill jumped up from her seat. 'I *always* do this. I'll drive you back now. Noah, find Hannah's coat.'

'It's not you,' Hannah said, laughing. 'I mean it is, but only because you're such good hosts. All of you.'

'It's been great to meet you, Hannah.' Gerens pushed his chair back and stood up.

'Don't include me in this,' Noah said. 'I'm nowhere near as hospitable as them.'

'Still trying to maintain the grumpy, aloof eco-consultant façade?' Hannah asked, emboldened by the wine.

'He loves it,' Jill said, coming back into the room, car keys chinking. 'He was born to be the put-upon son, the tortured hero, dealing with his eccentric parents and misunderstood by everyone.'

'Maybe not everyone,' Gerens corrected, pulling Hannah into an unexpected hug.

'No,' Jill said thoughtfully. 'Maybe it no longer is everyone, after all. You'll need to adjust your view of the world, my son.' She ruffled his hair, provoking a scowl. 'I'll go and get the car – we have to park it on another street, Hannah, the roads at the front being what they are. Gerens, bring the dogs out with you, let them say goodbye.' She stood in the doorway while he gathered the instantly alert dogs and put their leads on. There was a whirlwind of barks, chatter and laughter, and then Hannah and Noah were alone, with only the crackle of the fire breaking the quiet.

'This has been wonderful,' she said. 'And I know your mum invited me tonight, but I don't just mean tonight. Seeing Mousehole, finding out why you love it so much. I've had a great day.'

'So have I,' Noah replied. 'Whatever happens after this, whether we get to work with each other again, I'm glad we ended up on this project together. And I'm still happy to come and see Hugh with you, if you want me to?'

Hannah swallowed. She had forgotten all about that. She had been so busy sinking herself into the middle of Noah's family, she'd managed to forget about the gaps in her own. 'I'll have a think over the next couple of days.'

'And you'll let me know if you book your journey home?'

'Of course. I wouldn't want to leave without . . .' What? Kissing him goodbye? 'Without telling you,' she finished lamely.

He nodded. 'I didn't show you the costings.'

'Email them to me. I'll be at the hotel, I can take a look at them there.'

'Sure.'

'Great.'

'So, then—'

'I'd best go. Your mum will be waiting.'

'Blocking up the road, probably.'

They exchanged smiles.

'Night then,' Hannah said.

'Goodnight, Hannah.' He stepped forwards and wrapped his arms around her, pulling her tightly against him. She felt the softness of his jumper, the warmth and strength of his body beneath and, after a beat, she hugged him back, his steady breathing tickling the top of her head. She closed her eyes, let her senses soak him up, then moved reluctantly away when a car honked outside.

'I'd better go.' She turned and hurried down the corridor, pulled her coat off the peg and stepped into a night that was shrouded in mist, fragments of moisture dancing in the car headlights. She climbed into the passenger seat of a Land Rover that was what Noah's would become after twenty years and several rough journeys. As Jill beamed at her and put the car into gear, Noah appeared in the doorway, the light of the hall behind him.

Hannah waved, unsure for a moment if he could even see her, but then he raised a hand in return. They watched each other until Noah was no longer visible, the car turning a corner onto the harbour front, the sound of the boats' clinking masts like phantom ships lost in the mist.

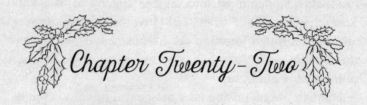

# Chapter Twenty-Two

The landscape was obliterated by darkness and fog, and Noah's mum was a cautious driver: much more cautious than Noah would have been in his upgraded Land Rover. But Hannah didn't mind. Jill was telling her about how nice it was having Noah staying with them, and how they always teased him, but he usually gave as good as he got.

'I understand why he chose to stay at the hotel, though,' she said, glancing over at Hannah. 'Obviously there was the storm to consider, and I wouldn't have been happy with him driving this route when it was at its worst, but he's a grown man and there's only so much mothering he can take.'

'Why has he been staying with you?' Hannah found it was easier to ask Jill than Noah, and not just because Jill seemed to be an open book.

'He didn't say?'

'No, he just mentioned something difficult he was dealing with.'

Jill tapped on the steering wheel and shook her head. 'Good god, my boy. So he hasn't told you about Beth?'

'His girlfriend.' It was an effort to get the word out.

Jill sighed. She didn't reply immediately, and when Hannah glanced over her face was pensive. 'Ex-girlfriend,' she said quietly.

Hannah's stomach turned over. '*Ex?*'

'He really hasn't told you?'

Hannah shook her head, her lips dry.

'It hadn't been working for a while,' Jill said. 'That was obvious to see. Beth's a lovely girl, but they want different things. Noah has Cornwall written all the way through him, like a stick of rock. Beth has wanted to move to London for as long as I can remember. Noah takes pains to recycle everything, Beth works for an exclusive travel company that sends rich people round the world in private jets. They loved each other, but the gap had got too wide.'

Hannah thought of the photo of the two of them on Noah's phone, the way he'd said *Babe* and then – what – corrected it? 'When did they break up?'

'The beginning of November. Noah's been staying at ours to let Beth have the house. She obviously had a lot of arrangements to make for moving to London: finding a flat, sorting the lease, packing her things up. It made sense for him to be with us and give her space to do that.'

'He's . . . I mean, he's—'

'Free as a bird?' Jill slowed to a snail's pace to take a sharp bend, her eyes never leaving the road. 'He is, and I can guarantee he didn't expect to fall for anyone else so soon. It's blown him sideways, meeting you. I'm sure, being Noah, he expected to stay unattached for a long time. He doesn't rush into anything.'

Hannah scrolled through all their previous interactions, everything tilting on its axis as she reconsidered it with this new information: the way he had been cold, sometimes miserable or distracted, during their first days together; how he'd started to tease her and she'd felt the charge between them, but had also noticed his reserve, as if he wasn't entirely comfortable about it. She'd thought it was because he was in a relationship, that he knew he shouldn't be flirting, but it was actually because he was newly single and testing out his feelings. She'd thought she had to step up to do the right thing – walking out of the steam room, not kissing him back during the ghost hunt. She'd got it so wrong.

'Why didn't he tell me?' she said. 'Why didn't I *ask* him?'

Jill sighed. 'Unlike me, my boy is discreet. He would have taken pains not to mention Beth or how he was feeling. And especially with a colleague, when he was supposed to be being professional. But it wasn't acrimonious; they're still in touch, while she's sorting her things out in the house, so maybe that's why you were confused.'

Hannah shook her head. 'I assumed he wasn't available.'

'You need to talk to him, Hannah. Since he came home after that first trip to Porthgolow, he's been dropping your name into every conversation. And it isn't rebound talk, not from Noah. I've been his mum for thirty years, so I know all his tells.' They were both quiet for a moment and then Jill said, 'When are you going back to Scotland?'

And there it was. The reason why, even though Noah was single, it still wasn't straightforward. They had a whole country between them.

They arrived back at Crystal Waters with the fog swirling around the clifftop, picking the hotel out in indistinct patches.

'Will you be safe getting back?' Hannah asked.

'Of course. Don't worry about me.' Jill unclipped her seat-belt and pulled Hannah into a hug, then pushed her back to look at her and said, 'Thank you for coming to our home tonight. You're welcome any time you want.'

When she got back to her room, the dog basket was empty. Spirit was probably in the hotel office as Hannah had been out all day. It was late, but sleep was the last thing on her mind. She had been acting under a misapprehension the whole time, believing Noah was in a relationship. But he'd only recently broken up with Beth, so even though he was attracted to her, perhaps he hadn't acted on it – apart from that one, aborted kiss – because it was still too raw. He wasn't ready for something else; he'd only known Hannah for a couple of weeks and she lived hundreds of miles away.

She sank onto the bed and pulled out her phone, reading the message he'd sent her:

*Hope you got home safely. Thanks for today. Nx*

She scrolled to his number, hovered over it for a moment and then changed her mind, finding a different contact and hitting call.

'Han?' the familiar voice said. 'What are you doing up so late?'

'Hi, Mike,' she replied. 'Long time no chat. How are things? Burning the midnight oil, like always? I did leave you a voicemail, you know.'

'I know, and I'm sorry. Things have been manic.' Her brother was a plumber, unable to turn down a job and constantly on the go. 'How are you? Mum said you were going back to Cornwall. How was it?'

'I'm still here. There were storms, train delays. The line

251

collapsed at Dawlish, so I've basically been stuck, and I found some things out and it's all been totally—'

'Are you *drunk*?' He laughed.

'Maybe a bit,' she said. 'I have had a *lot* of wine, but—'

'Are you OK?' His tone had changed. He could always tell when she was anxious about something.

'Porthgolow, this village in Cornwall – do you remember visiting it when we were on holiday here?'

'The place with that dusty old shop with all the knick-knacks, and that pretty crescent beach? Big spooky hotel on the top of the cliff?'

Hannah closed her eyes. 'Yup. That's the one.'

'Sure. We spent loads of time there once Mum discovered it. That's not where you are, is it?'

'It is.' Hannah sighed. 'Do you remember anything else about it?'

'Like what?'

'Like . . . I don't know. I've been trying to talk to Mum about it and she wouldn't even admit we'd been here.'

'She's in full-on Christmas mode. You know what she gets like: if it's not something on her agenda, then she doesn't want to listen. You'll be back here for the day, right?'

'Of course.' Hannah thought of Noah and Spirit, the Cornish Cream Tea Bus and the free pass Gerald had given her. 'But if, for any reason, I'm not, then—'

'Then we'll catch up soon,' Mike said easily. 'Don't stress, Han. Take some photos for me too. I'd love to see what that place looks like now.'

'You'd love the hotel I'm staying in – it replaced that spooky one, but it's kept all the ghosts!' She laughed.

'God, you're definitely drunk. Sleep it off, Han. Catch up soon.'

'Bye, Mike.' She hung up and threw her phone on the bed, then rubbed her hands over her eyes. She should have asked Noah about Beth sooner, and she should have called Mike the moment she'd spotted Reenie's house. So much for being organized. And still, nothing was resolved. Mike had no explanation for her mum's weirdness about Porthgolow, and she knew Noah was single, but he didn't know she knew. How should she bridge the gap? Should she even try, when she would be leaving Cornwall in the next few days?

She scrolled to the message Noah had sent.

*Back safe*, she typed. *I had the best time today, thank you. Sleep well. Hannah. xx*

She plugged her phone in to charge, got ready for bed and climbed under the covers, hoping that sleep would find her soon.

After a breakfast of good old-fashioned jam on toast, and half an hour spent with Spirit in the hotel gardens, the racing clouds peppering the land and sea with fast-moving shadows, Hannah conceded there was nothing stopping her going to see Hugh. All she needed to do was find some courage from somewhere. She had told herself she wasn't allowed to look at the Trainline app again, or even consider planning her journey back home, until she'd followed up this final lead.

She waited until lunchtime when the Seven Stars opened, and made sure she had her treasured family photograph and Myrtle's fluffy album. She put on her coat, searched every-where for her rainbow scarf and then, realizing she was just looking for an excuse to stall, slipped back out into the hotel gardens and walked to the gate that led out on to the road.

She didn't want to bump into Daniel or Charlie, and she hadn't told Noah that she was going, because there was a

253

whole other conversation they would have to have first. Her chest was knotted with anxiety. She didn't know whether it would be worse to realize there was nothing to find out, that she had misread her mum completely, or to discover that she had been protecting her from something less than welcome.

The panorama of sea, sand and clouds spurred Hannah on, and she filled her lungs with fresh, salt-scented air as she walked. Porthgolow's seafront was bright and festive, with a tiny Christmas tree twinkling in the window of the bed and breakfast and white fairy lights wound round the poles of the Victorian-style street lamps. A tree decorated with delicate gold lights stood outside the pub, and a wreath with dried orange slices and cinnamon sticks nestled amongst green foliage had pride of place on its wide door.

Hannah pushed it open.

Once inside, the brisk day left behind her, she felt less certain. The pub had only just opened and there was nobody to greet her, the only sounds coming from the kitchen. Clutching the photo album, Hannah hovered at the bar. She peered at her reflection in the glass behind the optics; her hair had been mussed by the wind, her mouth was pinched with nerves and her eyes were wary. She told herself there was nothing to be afraid of, and as she did, Hugh walked out of the kitchen and gave her a wide smile.

'Hannah! I didn't expect to see you here so early in the day. Charlie with you?' He put a box of snack-sized peanut packets on the floor and stood in front of her, obscuring her worried reflection.

'No, it's just me this time,' she said. 'And I'm not here for an early pint, or even for your delicious fish pie.' She put the photo album on the bar and smoothed her palm over the fluffy cover.

'What's this, then?' Hugh asked with a laugh. 'It looks vaguely familiar.'

'It's Myrtle's photo album,' Hannah said. 'She let me have a look at it.'

'Oh, right. For this ghostly business, was it?'

'No, not for that.' She lifted the pages and it fell open in the right place, as if willing her on. 'It's this, actually.' She turned it round so it was facing him, and Hugh glanced at it, his brows creasing. She was sure she saw him tense, his lips twitching, but it was half a second and then he smiled, meeting her gaze.

'What did you want to show me, Hannah love?'

'This picture,' she said softly, putting her fingertip just above her mum's dark hair. 'Do you recognize these people? Or . . .' she took her own photo out of her pocket, 'or here?'

Hugh looked at the pictures carefully, bending towards the weighty album, lifting her single photograph up to the light, his face blanching when he faced the winter sun head on. After what seemed like an age, he turned back to her. 'Are you hoping I recognize them? That one was taken in here, over there by the window, but I don't know the people in it. What's this about?'

Hannah's shoulders dropped as the tension left her body. She felt unsteady, as if she'd run too fast for too long. 'It's me, actually. Me and my mum and brother. We used to come on holiday here, and I'm just . . . I only remember a few things about it. I'm trying to fill in some of the blanks. It's a small village, so I thought maybe . . .'

'Lots of people pass through here, Hannah,' he said gently. 'We were always busy, back when you would have been small. I'm sorry you don't have many memories of the place, though while you're here you can create a few new ones. And we

255

have Gertie now, the markets too. Much more goin' on than there was back then, though you youngsters didn't need anything other than a beach and a bucket and spade to keep you entertained.' He chuckled. 'Bit different these days. Now, can I get you anything, seein' as you've come all this way and been disappointed?'

'I'm OK thanks. I need to get back.' She smiled and looked around her. Thousands of people must come in this pub every year: why had she expected him to remember a holidaying family from over twenty years ago? 'I did recognize the toilet signs though,' she added. 'Those pretty tiles on the doors. They sparked a bit of nostalgia when I was here the other night.'

'Oh yes,' Hugh said, laughing. 'You don't find those any more. Glad I've not needed to replace them – I'm quite fond of the posh lad and his bonnet-wearing missus. Seems ideal for this place, somehow.'

'They're great,' Hannah agreed. 'Thanks for talking to me, Hugh. Sorry to ask you something so out of the blue.'

'Not at all, Hannah. No ridiculous questions in my book, only ones I can't answer, and I'm truly sorry about that. You have a good day, now. And pop in before you head home – I expect your mum's longing to have you back.'

She nodded. 'I've got a date with a ticketing website later on today. Hopefully there'll be a way of getting home that won't take me until after Christmas.'

'Do come and say goodbye, won't you? You'll need to have one of my fisherman's pies for the road. Bet you can't find one like it anywhere in Edinburgh.'

Hannah thanked him again, and walked out of the pub and onto the beach. She looked up at Crystal Waters, solid and proud on its clifftop. She wondered if Spirit was sleeping under the Christmas tree, and what would happen to him now that Daniel had exhausted all the avenues for finding out where he came from. The dog seemed at home in Porthgolow, and Hannah hoped he would be allowed to stay.

She couldn't escape the obvious truth that, for her, it was time to go home. She had known it for days, really. She had wanted to find reasons to hold on, to be closer to Charlie and Daniel, to Noah and the shadows of her past, but she'd run out of excuses. Her life was in Edinburgh, and she needed to get back to it.

She strolled across the sand, trailing her hand along Gertie's red paintwork as she passed. The bus was closed today, but it would be open for the Christmas market tomorrow. And she had a date with Trainline, just as she'd told Hugh. She wondered if she'd get a chance to see him again before she left, which of the villagers she'd have time to say goodbye to, and which of them would remember her after she'd gone.

But now wasn't the time to be sentimental: she'd let Porthgolow tug at her emotions, and she had to put it all behind her. The intriguing photographs, the ghosts, Charlie and the bus – they'd been the best kind of diversions, but they weren't part of her future. But then she thought of Noah, the way they'd touched fingertips outside the pub the day before, and how he'd questioned what she was doing, burrowing under the surface of her thoughts in a calm, unapologetic way.

Even if she found a way to get home this afternoon, the weekend routes would be slower, so she was unlikely to be travelling back until Monday. That gave her one final weekend; two whole days to get in touch with Noah, to ask him to visit her and to tell him she'd got it wrong, to see what his response would be.

She might have only known him for a couple of weeks, but her feelings for Noah had been growing steadily since the first day. Could she have a sprinkling of Christmas romance before she went home? The idea put a spring in her step, and she barely noticed the slog up to Daniel's hotel as she thought about what she would say to him. Hannah Swan wasn't done with all Cornwall had to offer just yet.

# Part Four

## All I Want for Christmas Is Cake

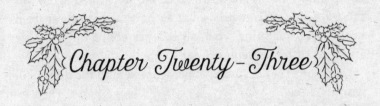

# Chapter Twenty-Three

Hannah Swan sat in the snug, the lounge-cum-bar of the Crystal Waters Spa Hotel, her eyes starting to cross as she stared at her iPad. She would happily pay a significant sum of money for someone else to organize her train journey back to Edinburgh, give her tickets and an itinerary of where she had to be and when. But there was nobody to do it except her, and she couldn't put it off any longer. She had been on borrowed time in Porthgolow long enough.

A hot nose gently nudged her knee and she looked down to see Spirit, the scruffy white dog she had rescued from the beach the night the storm hit. She patted his head and noticed he had something in his mouth, something that glittered in the light.

'What have you got there, Spirit?' She chucked him under the chin so that he lifted his dark eyes to meet hers. It was a biro, with hologram print on the outside and a plume of soft purple fluff at the end. It reminded Hannah of school, and the treasures she and her friends used to have in their pencil cases at the beginning of each term. 'Whose is this? Where did you get it?'

The snug was empty so early in the morning, only the Christmas tree with its softly sparkling lights keeping her company. Many of the guests would still be having breakfast, and the bookings were down since the storm had taken out the train line at Dawlish. Glad to have a distraction from her journey planning, Hannah left her coffee on the table and walked into reception.

'Hannah.' Daniel smiled at her from behind the desk. 'Still with us, I see.'

'Despite my best efforts,' she said, then realized how that sounded. 'I would happily stay here for ever, but I'm not one of those old Victorian ladies who can afford to live in a hotel, and I do have things to get back to.'

His smile faded. 'You're not having any luck with the trains?'

'The services are still disrupted, but I'm going to have to bite the bullet. It's only going to get worse the closer it gets to Christmas.'

'If there's anything I can do to help, please let me know.' As she approached the desk, he slid a piece of paper off it and into his pocket. It was a smooth, efficient manoeuvre, but she still saw it. She was going to say something, but then decided she'd had enough of trying to unearth secrets – especially ones that turned out to be in her imagination. Her theory that there might be some significance to the time she'd spent in Porthgolow as a child had proved to be even less substantial than Audrey's ghosts.

'I will, thank you. Oh . . . is this yours?' She held up the shimmering, fluff-topped pen. Daniel raised an eyebrow. 'Maybe Chloe's, or one of the other staff? Spirit had it.'

'He's a proper magpie dog,' Daniel said. 'Keeps nicking the stapler off my desk. I think it's because it's silver – he's not interested in the black hole punch. Or maybe he knows they're redundant. Who uses hole punches these days?'

Hannah shook her head. 'You've had no luck tracking down his owner?'

'No, and I've tried everywhere. All the online message boards and Facebook groups. I might have to take him to a shelter.' There was real pain in his eyes.

'You and Charlie can't have him?'

'We're just about managing with Jasper and Marmite. Marmite's happy on Gertie when Charlie's at work, but I already ask my neighbour, Lily, to look after Jasper a lot during the day. She's got two dogs of her own and it wouldn't be fair to add another mutt to her babysitting duties, however lovable he is.'

'And he *is* lovable,' Hannah said, tears stinging her eyes. 'Oh, poor Spirit. He's far too affectionate for a shelter.'

Daniel ran a hand through his hair. 'I'm going to hold onto him until after Christmas. There still might be a chance that . . . Hannah, are you OK?' He hurried around to her side of the desk and put a hand on her shoulder.

She bent her head and wiped frantically at her eyes. 'I'm so sorry, it isn't really about this. I know you've done all you can for Spirit.'

'What is it?' he asked gently.

She sniffed and looked up at him. 'A combination of things. I didn't mean to blub at you Daniel, I'm so sorry.'

'Please don't apologize. Give me five minutes to get someone to take over and I'll—'

'Hellooooo?' called a high, lyrical voice, and Hannah turned to see a couple walk through the door, wheeling

263

suitcases behind them. The first thing she noticed was how attractive they were. The woman was slim with long dark hair and a smattering of freckles across her pale skin, her eyes full of mischief. The man was tall, with a slightly unruly crop of dark blond hair and high cheekbones. His demeanour was easy, relaxed, while she was positively brimming with energy.

'Lila, Sam!' Daniel gave Hannah an apologetic glance, but her moment of sadness was gone. *This* was Charlie's cousin and her actor boyfriend, back from LA? 'I didn't realize you were arriving today.' Daniel stepped forward and drew Lila into an embrace, then exchanged a manly hug and back slap with Sam.

'The journey's been pretty shit,' Sam said, but he was smiling. 'The weather was awful, and I almost lost my kneecap on the flight over.'

'That's only because the turbulence was so bad,' Lila said, laughing. 'I needed something to hold onto. But we're here now, and this place looks wonderful. Wow.' She clapped her hands together. 'Look at that tree! Oh Sam, this is going to be magical. It's so good to be home. I texted Charlie and she said she'd come up in a bit, but we can always go down to Gertie. How's everything? How are you? Was the storm really bad here? Where are Marmite and Jasper?'

Daniel grinned. 'Steady on, Lila. Why don't you get settled in your room, and we can have a proper catch-up when Charlie's here.'

'Of course!' she said, her gaze landing on Hannah. 'I'm so sorry, I didn't mean to interrupt your conversation. I'm so rude, I'm just – don't you think this place is amazing? I mean, of course you do, you wouldn't have booked to stay here otherwise.'

'It's wonderful,' Hannah managed. She'd read all about *Estelle* and the Cornish Cream Tea Bus's role on set on her train journey down, and standing here with two of its stars – even if one of them was Charlie's cousin – she felt overwhelmingly starstruck. 'I'm so looking forward to *Estelle*,' she blurted.

Lila's eyes widened. 'Oh, thank you! The whole production is magnificent, but Sam really makes it. He's the complete package – a total superstar!'

'And you're not at all biased,' Sam said.

Lila rolled her eyes. 'I loved your acting *before* I loved you, remember?'

'Lila, Sam,' Daniel cut in, 'this is Hannah Swan. She's one of the eco-consultants I've brought in to help make this place more sustainable. Hannah, it seems as if you know who they are already, but this is Delilah, Charlie's cousin, and Sam.'

'I knew he wouldn't wait until after Christmas!' Lila said, shaking Hannah's hand. 'What do you think? Is it a lost cause?'

Hannah laughed nervously. 'Not at all. Daniel's already ticked a lot of the boxes, we're just helping him get to that next level.' She cringed at her awful business-speak, and tried to force herself to relax.

'Are you staying here for Christmas?' Sam asked.

Hannah shook her head. 'I'm trying to book a train home. Everything's been disrupted by the storm, but I'm hoping to get back to Edinburgh in time. I've got a few days yet.' She gave them a timid smile. They seemed so nice, so normal, but there was a definite aura around them. They actually *looked* like film stars, as if they were a slightly different species to the rest of them. She was saved from saying anything else deathly dull by the arrival of Audrey.

'Oh Hannah, my pen! Where did you find it?'

Hannah smiled brightly at Audrey, conscious of Sam and Delilah watching them while Daniel went to get their room key. 'It's yours?'

'One of my favourites. Bought at the station Paperchase when I was in a rush, but I've grown unaccountably fond of it. I'm sure I had it in my room earlier.' She shook her head, perplexed, as Hannah handed it to her.

'Could your room have been invaded by a dog at any point over the last couple of hours?' Daniel asked, emerging from his office. 'How on earth is he managing to get into other bedrooms? Is he opening doors now?'

'He sleeps in my room,' Hannah explained, 'but other than that, he's a bit of a law unto himself.' She shrugged, apologetic.

'Don't worry,' Daniel said. 'He seems to have adopted the hotel as his own, and I don't expect you to keep track of him the whole time.'

'Is this Spirit?' Audrey asked. 'Of course! He followed me after breakfast, but I was sure I hadn't let him in.'

'That dog might turn out to actually *be* a ghost, for all we know. A ghost with very light fingers. Lock up your precious jewellery, guys.' Daniel's smile fell, replaced with something close to alarm. 'If you'll excuse me, I just need to – will you be OK, Hannah?'

'I'm fine. Thank you, Daniel.' She watched him hurry into his office and close the door swiftly behind him.

'What's this about ghost dogs?' Lila asked. 'What's going on?'

'Uhm.' Hannah wasn't sure it was her place to tell them when Daniel was still slightly prickly about the whole thing.

'I'm investigating the hauntings at this hotel,' Audrey said boldly.

Delilah's mouth fell open.

'What?' Sam asked, laughing. 'Here?'

'We've already gathered some excellent evidence, and I—'

'Oh my God!' Lila grabbed Audrey's arm. 'Seriously? This isn't a wind-up because of *Estelle*?'

Audrey gave Lila a blank look.

'Sam and Lila are actors,' Hannah explained. 'They're in a drama series that's being shown on the BBC over Christmas. *Estelle*? It's a ghost story.'

'Goodness!' Audrey shook their hands in turn. 'It's lovely to meet you. You should have been here for the investigation.'

'I'm not sure how we could have helped,' Sam said.

'Oh, and Lila is Charlie's cousin,' Hannah added.

'This trip just gets more and more interesting,' Audrey said. 'How wonderful!'

'Perhaps we could meet up with you later?' Lila tucked a strand of long hair behind her ear. 'I'd love to hear about the ghosts.'

'We'd better get sorted first.' Sam gestured to their suitcases. 'We're filling up reception with our stuff.'

'I'm going to be in the hotel all day,' Audrey said. 'Do come and find me when you're ready.'

'I can't wait!' Lila beamed at them. 'It was lovely to meet you both. Hopefully we'll see you later.' They wheeled their cases across the polished floor, Sam calling goodbye over his shoulder.

'The drama never ends,' Audrey said, once they'd gone. 'Are you all right, Hannah?'

The question surprised her: she thought she'd hidden her earlier wobble well. 'Things are catching up with me a bit, that's all. Trying to get home, you know.'

267

Audrey nodded. 'What are you doing now? Fancy an exchange of information?'

'You've found more out about our ghosts?'

'Something fairly conclusive, I believe.'

'I'd love to hear it, but I don't have anything exciting to report in return.'

'I just thought you might like to offload. I'm quite a good listener. Come on, let's go and get a coffee.' Hannah followed Audrey back into the snug, where Spirit, coffee and, perhaps, the conclusion of the ghostly tale, would take her mind off things.


'Oh my God!' Hannah sat back in her chair and pulled Spirit's warm body more firmly onto her lap. This time her tears were for someone else, and it reminded her that, however much she had to deal with, she was incredibly lucky.

'I know.' Audrey smoothed her hand over the page of her notebook. 'Isn't it tragic?'

'He couldn't bear to live without her,' Hannah choked out. 'He scratched those words into the stone just before . . . before he jumped?'

'His body was washed up on the beach, just like Anna's. Only a few days later. Initial speculation was that Henry Medlin – it's good to finally have his first name confirmed – had gone out to fish as usual, but had fallen foul of particularly rough seas, but his boat was never found, so they couldn't be sure.'

'And the fact that he ended up below these cliffs,' Hannah added.

'And now we have the message he left, saying he would see her again soon.' Audrey shook her head. 'I feel both triumphant and desperately sad that we've found out what happened.'

'Wasn't his boat in the village? If he'd jumped from here, then shouldn't his boat still have been moored up?'

'In the report it says it wasn't, which was why it was thought it had been lost at sea. He may have cast it adrift himself, knowing he'd no longer have need of it, wishing that to be the version everyone believed.'

Hannah stroked Spirit's ears. 'So Anna and Henry both died here, and it could be either of them still haunting the hotel? Edward went back to London and carried on with his life, despite all the rumours about what he'd done?'

Audrey nodded. 'Remarried, had five children. Lived a good, long life, unlike the lovers he left behind.'

Hannah shook her head. 'It's so tragic. Poor Anna, poor Henry. I know they weren't necessarily in the right, having an affair like that, but they didn't deserve to *die* for it.'

'Sometimes the heart wants who the heart wants, regardless of logic or morals.'

Hannah looked up from Audrey's notes, and found the researcher watching her closely. She tried to swallow, but her mouth was dry despite the large latte she'd just had. Audrey held the silence, and Hannah began to squirm. 'You're not psychic like Spirit, are you?' she asked. 'I thought you weren't a medium, just a paranormal enthusiast?'

'You don't need to have special powers to see what's been happening between you and Noah.'

'I thought he had a girlfriend,' Hannah admitted. 'I couldn't help being attracted to him, but I thought he wasn't free. When he – we almost . . . when something happened, I was so confused.'

'But he's not in a relationship?' Audrey asked gently.

Hannah shook her head. 'I found out a couple of days ago. He's just come out of one, and he was discreet about it

269

because he's a careful person. He never told me he wasn't single, I just assumed. We're nothing like Anna and Henry.'

'Sometimes the present mirrors the past. Patterns repeat.'

Hannah laughed. 'When we were on our investigation, things got pretty . . . intense, and I thought maybe we *were* getting mixed up in their story. I'm Hannah, she's Anna. Noah's not a fisherman but his dad is. When he—' she took a breath. 'I thought maybe the spirits were manipulating our feelings.' Spirit whined and put his paw on her forearm, his claws gently scratching her skin. 'But they weren't. I mean, it was just *us*.'

'Sometimes it's easier to think there are other forces at work when you're not entirely comfortable with how you feel or behave,' Audrey said.

Hannah shrugged. 'And it turns out that we weren't doing anything wrong. I missed my chance, and in a few days I'll be back in Edinburgh and we'll each carry on with our own lives. It's a tale as old as time, but at least it's not going to end in tragedy for anyone. Tell me more about Henry and Anna.'

'There isn't much more to tell,' Audrey said. 'I'm delighted to have found out what we have.'

Hannah sighed. 'So what happens now?'

'Now I document it all. The love affair, the repercussions, the hauntings. The fact that the investigation here ended with your and Noah's discovery ties the whole thing up brilliantly. I couldn't have asked for a better, more rounded story for Richard's book.'

'Your book too,' Hannah said. 'You're writing it now.'

Audrey nodded, her eyes bright behind her glasses. 'I need to collect my thoughts and write it up for Daniel. I need him to know what I'm planning to say about his hotel.'

'I think he'll be OK,' Hannah said. 'Perhaps he's come around to the idea that his hotel is haunted?'

She and Audrey exchanged a smile. Hannah was pleased that at least one of them had found answers while they were here.

'Thank you, Audrey, I appreciate you telling us.' Daniel rubbed a hand across the back of his neck. Hannah was surprised he didn't look more relieved. Audrey had everything she needed: she could go away and write her chapter now.

Lila and Sam exchanged a glance. Sam looked anxious, but Lila was obviously trying to hide her excitement at being thrust into a drama so soon after arriving. Audrey had asked to speak to Daniel now she'd tied up the loose ends of the story, and he had suggested the hotel's private dining room. Hannah didn't know how Sam and Lila had got wind of it, but having had an introduction to Charlie's cousin, she wasn't massively surprised that she was there.

It was a beautiful room, windows on two sides giving an almost panoramic view of the sea and sky, the violet hues of one of Cornwall's subtler sunsets. Darkness wasn't far off, and it wasn't even four o'clock.

'Why aren't you jumping for joy about all this ghost stuff?' Lila asked. 'Don't you think it's amazing to have such interesting history connected to your hotel? It's tragic, for sure, but life sometimes is. You put this story about – is it Anna and Henry? –' Audrey nodded her confirmation – 'on the website and mention the ghosts, it won't *stop* people coming here. It'll have them flocking like zombies.'

Daniel gave her a sceptical look. 'I'm not sure zombies *flock*, Lila.'

'Delilah's right,' Reenie said. 'Most haunted hotels are

creepy. Sometimes cleanliness and comfort are sacrificed to enhance the spooky atmosphere. But if you offer hauntings *and* back massages, all in beautiful surroundings, you'll have your hand bitten off – just to keep to the zombie theme.' She grinned. 'You need to stop being so precious about your reputation and move with the times.'

'It wasn't ever how I imagined marketing my hotel,' Daniel said.

'So adapt,' Reenie countered. 'You're a smart man, Daniel. You can get into the spirit of it, as it were. As Lila says, once this book is published you'll likely get a whole new influx of visitors.'

'You could sell copies in reception,' Lila added. 'Along with DVDs of *Estelle*, once that's come out. There are *endless* opportunities here.'

'And the staff are bound to be reassured when you tell them the story,' Audrey continued. 'It's so often fear of the unknown that causes the most upset, and once they know about Anna and Henry, everything will fall into place.'

'I'm not sure Kevin will feel that way,' Daniel said. 'But I can talk to him about it, explain that there's nothing threatening here, even if—'

'Even if the ghosts really exist?' Audrey asked. 'Don't worry, Daniel, I've come across more sceptics than you can imagine, and everyone is entitled to their opinion.'

'So that's it then?' His shoulders dropped. 'We can get back to focusing on Christmas?'

There were nods and murmurs of assent, and then Lila spoke up. 'But shouldn't we do something? For Anna and Henry?'

'Do something for them?' Reenie said. 'They're dead, Delilah. I think they're rather beyond helping.'

She wrinkled her nose. 'Couldn't we help them be at peace? What happened to them was so heartbreaking, and now they're roaming around here, tormented. Isn't there something we can do?'

'If we get rid of them, then the hotel won't be haunted any more,' Sam said. 'And Daniel will lose his new marketing angle.'

'I don't think that would matter,' Charlie replied. 'Ghosts are never guaranteed, after all. It's the idea of a place being haunted that's most appealing. But can you really do that? Help spirits be at peace?' She shrugged, and all eyes turned to Audrey.

'There is one thing,' Audrey said softly. 'I know a few of Richard's contacts in the field, and I am sure one of them could help me with a cleansing spell. I could perform it down by the swimming pool, where Henry's message to Anna has ended up. I have no idea how successful it would be, but it would be a way for *us* to say goodbye to Anna and Henry, at least.'

'A cleansing spell,' Reenie repeated. 'Did you ever hear such nons—'

'That sounds perfect!' Lila said.

'You weren't even part of the investigation, Lila.' Daniel shook his head, but he was smiling. 'OK then, if everyone's up for it?' He glanced around the room and got nods in return, including from Hannah, who agreed with Lila that it would be good to do something to acknowledge the people she'd come to learn about, even if they were only notes on a page or footsteps on a recording. 'Let's finish this thing properly,' he said decisively. 'And *then* we can put all our efforts into Christmas. I have plans, and I don't want them to be derailed.'

Back in her room, Hannah took out her phone. She still hadn't booked her train ticket, but she had already decided

273

that she wanted to be there for Audrey's cleansing spell. She thought Noah would want to be there, too.

She scrolled to his number, wondering if she could speak to him without giving away what his mum had told her. She didn't want to have that conversation over the phone. With her pulse beating wildly, she hit call.

He picked up on the second ring. 'Hannah, how are you? Is everything OK?'

'Everything's good!' She took a deep breath. 'Except Henry Medlin committed suicide after Anna died, by jumping off the same rocks. Audrey's going to help them find peace with a cleansing spell.'

It was a moment before he replied. 'Shit. He killed himself?'

'Isn't it awful? I want to be there when Audrey says goodbye to them.'

'You're not going home yet?' She might have been imagining it, but she thought he sounded hopeful. 'You're running out of time, Hannah.'

'I've got a few days.'

'Any luck with Hugh or your brother?'

'I spoke to them both,' she said, pulling her legs up under her on the bed. 'Hugh didn't recognize us from the photos. Mike said of course we'd been to Porthgolow – he remembers it much better than I do – but that there wasn't anything strange about it. I think I created a story because I wanted to have some significance here, some connection with the village.'

'You wanted to belong,' Noah said, and she could almost hear the shrug in his voice. 'It's completely understandable. You know how I feel about Cornwall.'

'Yes, and you've infected me,' she replied, trying to lighten the tone. 'Perhaps this is all your fault, Noah Rosewall.'

'I didn't make you fall in love with Cornwall. If I did, then I can't claim any real credit, because it requires no effort at all.'

*Maybe it was the combination of you* and *Cornwall*, Hannah thought. 'I'd like to see you before I go,' she said. At the very least, she wanted to explain why she had backed out of their kiss. She didn't want him to think that she hadn't been interested.

'Monday?' Noah suggested. 'I'm tied up this weekend.'

'Moving back home?'

Hannah heard noises in the background, and imagined him sitting at the table in his parents' beautiful back room, with the fire crackling and the dogs at his feet. 'Yeah,' he said, after a moment.

'Monday's good.' Hannah pictured her train journey sliding further and further into the future, until it disappeared over the horizon just like she should be doing.

'Great,' he said. 'I'll be in touch.'

Once they'd ended the call, Hannah walked to the window and pressed her fingers against the glass, the darkness beyond almost complete. Maybe Noah was right, that all her interest in Cornwall – the ghosts and her old photos, hanging on to see Noah one last time – were excuses. Perhaps she was delaying her return yet again because her life in Edinburgh wasn't the one she wanted any more.

# Chapter Twenty-Four

The soothing wafts of Michael Bublé's Christmas album filled the bus, his voice crooning out 'Santa Baby'. Hannah sat opposite Charlie, Lila was alongside her, and Marmite and Spirit lay flat out on the benches at another table. The multiple strings of fairy lights twinkled around them, while Porthgolow beach, with its muted winter shades and blustery, frothing waves, provided a chilly-looking backdrop.

'Tell me more about the meal you cook for your friends,' Lila said, cradling her coffee. She'd made them all cappuccinos with gingerbread syrup that were Christmas in a cup.

Hannah couldn't quite believe that she was here, chatting to a bona-fide celebrity – one who had just made *her* a coffee. And it wasn't as if Lila acted like a diva: she was just simply, effortlessly shimmering.

'Do you really go to town on the menu?' she continued, when Hannah didn't answer immediately. 'Sam and I spent most of our evenings in LA with a group of friends – people he got to know on set who he introduced me to – but the cooking was pretty basic.'

'You mean you got chips from the local takeaway?' Charlie asked.

Lila looked aghast. 'Chips? In LA? Eaten by actors appearing on screen? It was all nutritionally balanced salads and hideous concoctions from the juice bar down the block. Ugh.' She shuddered dramatically. 'Even Sam was careful about what he ate, though he wasn't as paranoid as some of them. Imagine being *paranoid* about what you eat? Thinking that people are deliberately shoving extra calories into your food so you lose out on a role that they then get? It's nuts!' She shook her head and tore a large chunk off her chocolate twist. Charlie had just taken them out of the oven, the chocolate gooey and thick inside.

Hannah laughed and took a big bite of her own pastry, the bitter-sweet flavours infusing on her tongue.

'How many of you are there?' Charlie asked.

Hannah counted them off on her fingers. 'There's usually between eight and ten of us, depending on who's able to make it. We tend to swap venues, though I prefer cooking in my own kitchen.'

'Is your flat massive then?' Lila asked. 'One of those beautiful old houses with views across the park to Edinburgh castle?'

'God no,' Hannah said, laughing. 'If only! But that's part of the fun. I have to move all my furniture around, then scrounge additional chairs off neighbours. Some of my friends bring deckchairs. It's so much fun, always completely mad, and it's often the best part of Christmas.'

'And now you're going to miss it,' Charlie said. 'I'm so sorry.'

Hannah shrugged. After Audrey's revelation yesterday, the enticing promise of the cleansing spell, she hadn't booked her tickets home. It felt like the one task on her to-do list that would never get done. Somehow, December had slipped away from her. It was the twentieth, five days from Christmas, and she was hundreds of miles from home. It scared her how little she was bothered.

She had sent a message to her friends' WhatsApp group that morning, when she had realized that, even if she got a train home the following day, there was no way she could get everything ready for their dinner on the twenty-third. She used being stranded as her excuse – the trains weren't working, the storm had delayed her finishing her report on the hotel, it had all gone to hell in a handcart. Everyone had been sympathetic, saying they would get together at the pub instead and would raise a glass to her or, if by some miracle she made it back in time, would buy her dinner.

Saskia had messaged her separately.

*It sounds like you're having a tough time. Is there really no way you can get back? Miss you. S. Xx*

She had replied, feeling guilty about sending half-truths to her friend, promising herself she would tell her everything once they were sitting opposite each other in a familiar pub. *It's lovely here, just frustrating the trains are so bad. Hope to get back this week and will see you before Xmas! Say hi to Seth for me. :) Xx*

Seth had replied to her group message, saying he would be really sorry not to see her, but that they could have a New Year get-together. Usually, that sort of response from him would make Hannah giddy, but she hadn't been able to muster more than a brief pang of regret that she wouldn't get to see him. In a short space of time, her feelings had changed completely.

'Do you know what?' she said now, 'I'm not that sorry. My friends will still be there when I get back, and I wouldn't have changed my time in Porthgolow for anything. I'm happy to give up my dinner this year to come with you on your Cornish Cream Tea Bus Secret Santa Tour.'

'There's a tongue-twister if ever I heard one,' Lila said, grinning.

'I think it has a poetic ring to it,' Charlie countered. 'And I'm thrilled to have an extra elf to help me out. I have a feeling it's going to be a busy day.'

'We don't actually have to wear elf outfits, do we?' Lila asked.

'Says the actress.' Charlie rolled her eyes. 'No, just aprons. I mean, God, not *just* aprons – it's not that kind of tour – but you can wear your own clothes, then aprons on top. A pair of reindeer ears or deely boppers if you're feeling adventurous.'

'And how will it work, exactly?' Hannah asked.

'I've planned a route along the coast.' Charlie spread out a map on the table, moving mugs and plates out of the way. 'We've got an hour in each destination and I've already sold all the tickets, so we won't end up with a massive scrum.'

'Customers come on board,' Lila continued, 'each parent and child can have a hot or cold drink and choose a snack – a cookie or mince pie, gingerbread biscuit or sausage roll – then they go upstairs, one family at a time, and meet Santa.'

'Santa will do the "ho-ho-ho, have you been a good child?" bit, and give them a present.' Charlie gestured to the bags piled up on the tables behind them. There were also rolls of festive wrapping paper, spools of brightly coloured ribbon and packets of Sellotape. 'And they go off happy with their gift and a twenty-per-cent-off voucher for the Cornish Cream Tea Bus. Then, in the New Year, they come back – for a cream tea here, or on one of my tours, or anything else that I plan.'

'Charlie's got a booking for a wedding next spring,' Lila said. Hannah could hear the pride in her voice. 'Gertie will be at the venue for an older couple who are getting married, serving cream teas to the guests. She catered Juliette and Lawrence's wedding in the summer. Have you met them?'

Hannah frowned. 'I don't think so. I don't think they've been up to the hotel.'

'It was a lovely wedding,' Lila said. 'On this very beach.' She sighed, a dreamy look on her face.

'It was a wonderful wedding,' Charlie agreed, tapping Lila's hand. 'But today is not about weddings, today is about Christmas. And our first, and least entertaining job – depending on how you feel about present wrapping – is to get this lot ready for tomorrow.'

'Is Santa too busy to wrap his own presents, then?' Hannah asked. 'Where are all his elves?'

'We're his elves,' Charlie said, 'and Santa's probably getting ready to open the Seven Stars, so it's all down to us.'

'Oh yes.' Hannah bit her lip. 'Hugh's going to be Santa, isn't he?'

Charlie paused in the act of rummaging through one of the bags. 'Is that OK? Did you speak to him about—?' she glanced at her cousin, who was as quick as a bloodhound.

'About what?' Lila asked.

'We used to come on holiday here when I was young,' Hannah explained. 'My mum, brother and me. I've got a photo that I've carried around with me for years, and it turns out Reenie's house is in the background. There was another one, in Myrtle's photo album, of the three of us in Hugh's pub. I asked him about it, but of course he doesn't remember us. I thought there might be some story about why we ended up here. It seems like such a coincidence.'

'Of all the Cornish villages in all the world,' Lila said, doing an excellent impression of Humphrey Bogart, 'you had to come back to this one.'

'Exactly!' Hannah laughed. 'But I was trying to create a story when there isn't one.'

'It doesn't mean that Porthgolow isn't special to you, though,' Lila said. 'I knew it was, the moment I rocked up here. It has its own brand of charm.'

Hannah sighed. 'I just didn't expect my trip here to be so much fun. To be so . . .' She searched for the right word, one that would encompass meeting Noah, Audrey and the ghosts, being taken under Charlie and Daniel's wings, finding Spirit.

'Long?' Lila suggested, grinning. 'I think it's because you don't really want to leave.'

Hannah shrugged and returned Lila's smile. She almost admitted that it was true – that she was torn about going back home, which was why she kept returning to, but never completing, her Trainline booking.

'Do you want to do some stargazing from the bus later?' Charlie asked.

'I'm not sure the sky's going to be clear,' Lila said, frowning. 'Why?'

'Because if we don't get started on wrapping these presents, then we're still going to be here at midnight. Chop-chop.' She tapped Lila on the head with her roll of wrapping paper, then shot her a grin when Lila glared at her.

With four tables downstairs, they rearranged everything so they each had one to work on. Charlie placed a couple of boxes on the last table, where they could put the wrapped presents ready to be taken upstairs.

Hannah sat opposite Spirit, who was lying on his back on the bench, his tummy exposed. She marvelled at the thoughtful gifts Charlie had got: a set of Christmas-themed cookie-cutters, toy Routemaster buses as shiny as Gertie and sets of colourful bunting, the pennants small so they'd appeal to a child. There were snow globes with the Cornish coastline inside, teddy bears wearing 'I love Cornwall' sashes, and mini kaleidoscopes.

'These are great,' she said, cutting a sheet of wrapping paper, a miniature Gertie lying on its side in the middle.

'Snow globes,' Lila announced, 'are a joy to behold, and a devil to wrap. Couldn't you just have got a selection of CDs?'

Charlie laughed and replenished their coffees. 'Just think how expert we'll be by the end of this. Wrapping our own presents will be a doddle.'

'Haven't you done that yet?' Lila was aghast. 'At least I've got an excuse – I've only been in the country a day.'

'What have you got Sam?' Charlie asked. 'Or shouldn't I know? We're opening them all together on Christmas morning, aren't we?'

'Yup,' Lila said. 'So I'm keeping shtum. No sneak peeks or spoilers. What about you, Hannah? Have you done all your present buying? I except Edinburgh will be heaving the last few days before Christmas.'

'It will be so pretty and festive though.' She sighed.

She usually enjoyed the mad crush of last-minute Christmas shopping, and she only had a few bits left to get. She already had her mum and her brother's gifts, and she'd bought a rucksack for her dad, made from recycled materials by an eco-friendly company. Of course, it was unlikely that she'd see him, and then she'd have to get an address for wherever in the world he was, which was usually like drawing blood from a stone. Sadly, it was a post-Christmas ritual she was used to.

'It'll be fun,' she continued. 'And I don't have a boyfriend to buy for, so the pressure's off there.'

Charlie gave her a curious look, and Hannah shrugged. Once she got home, she would have to put Noah out of her mind. She was never going to be in a happy, successful relationship if she kept mooning about men who were out of reach.

She wondered briefly if that was something she did – go for guys she couldn't have so she wouldn't have to risk a real relationship. She even wondered if it had been easier to assume that Noah was unavailable; easier to keep that ambiguity between them because it meant she didn't have to commit. But that couldn't be true. She'd had boyfriends in the past, and they hadn't been with other people when she'd met them. And she *would* have let the kiss in the spa happen, had she known Noah's circumstances. The amount of time she'd spent imagining that scene playing out differently convinced her that her heart wasn't risk averse. It definitely wanted Noah.

By the time all the presents were wrapped, the sun was hanging above the sea like a chandelier, and Hannah's hands were covered in paper cuts. Lila offered her a tube of hand cream and she accepted it gratefully.

'Back here at seven tomorrow,' Charlie said. 'It's going to be a long day, but hopefully a fun one. Hannah, are you sure you want to be part of it?'

'I wouldn't miss it. I can't imagine anything more Christmassy than this tour.'

'And *then* you'll go home?' Lila said with a mischievous look. 'Not that I want you to! I'm just amused by how taken you are with Porthgolow.'

'I'm going to stay for this, and then Audrey's cleansing thing, and then—'

'And then it'll be Christmas Eve, and all the public transport will be reduced,' Lila cut in. 'Won't your family be sad if you miss Christmas with them?'

Hannah thought of her mum's pristine house, the precision with which everything would be done. The food would be delicious, the gifts generous, but there would be no room for silliness, no space for errors or spontaneity: Even Mike's easy-going nature seemed somehow restricted when they were together for Christmas. It was as if there was a secret camera on the ceiling, watching her mum's every move and giving her marks out of ten.

'They would be, I think,' Hannah said carefully. 'But it's only one year. They'd get over it.'

'It sounds to me like you're not sure you want to go back for Christmas.' Charlie leaned against a table, rubbing cream into her hands.

Hannah ran her fingers through her hair, pulling at the strands. 'God, I don't know. It's just . . . all this stuff with my mum – the arguments we've had on the phone. Mike will be there, and we always get on, but . . .' She thought of Noah's chaotic family home, full of love and noise and laughter, and envy twisted inside her. 'I'm not really looking forward to it. Is that the worst thing ever?'

'Nope,' Lila said. 'Relatives are hard work, sometimes. I should know, I'm one of the hardest.' She grinned at Charlie and they both laughed. 'You don't have to be with them just because you're family, or out of a sense of duty. That's why you organize dinner with your friends, isn't it? So you can celebrate with the people you love spending time with.'

'That's true,' Hannah said.

'If you don't want to spend Christmas with your mum and brother this year,' Charlie added, 'then don't.'

'But what do I do instead? I guess the hotel's still open, but—'

'Of course it is,' Charlie said. 'We're all going to be there. Me and Daniel, Lila and Sam, all having dinner together in the dining room. Quite a few of the villagers are coming too, Myrtle and Rose, and Reenie, because she's on her own. There's definitely space for you at our Christmas party, if you want to come?'

Hannah stared at her. Did Charlie want her to be there, or was she just being nice, as she had been from the moment they met? She looked at Lila, who nodded vigorously.

'Are you sure?' Hannah asked.

'Completely, one hundred per cent sure,' Charlie said.

Hannah laughed and stood up, hugging her then Lila. 'I can spend Christmas with you?'

'And you could do your friends' Christmas at the hotel, too, if you wanted?' Lila shrugged. 'Sam and I would come, and Charlie and Daniel obviously. You could invite the ghost lady, Audrey.'

'Lila,' Charlie said. 'You can't get Hannah to cook you an extra Christmas dinner.'

Hannah's heart thudded. 'Daniel and Levi wouldn't want me in the kitchen . . .'

'They wouldn't mind about that – I'm sure Levi would be happy to have you. But you don't have to cook for us. It's ridiculous.'

'I'd love to,' Hannah said. 'There's not much time to prepare, to get the ingredients, but . . .'

'You're serious?' Charlie asked.

'Very serious,' Hannah confirmed. 'If you're sure it'll be OK?'

'I'll speak to Daniel this evening.'

'Excellent!' Lila's smile was nothing short of smug. 'It wouldn't feel right if you left straight after the Secret Santa Tour, anyway. We'll have to celebrate our success. We'll be like the Three Amigos, or – oh my God!' She turned wide eyes on her cousin. 'We could be Charlie's Angels!' She held both hands up for high-fives.

Charlie and Hannah obliged, Charlie saying, 'Don't you want it to be *Delilah's* Angels?'

'God, no. I couldn't face the responsibility. You're the leader, for sure. We need to practise our poses.' She turned sideways and held her hands up in the shape of a gun, blowing on the finger-barrel and pouting dramatically. Charlie and Hannah joined in, copying Lila's poses as they got more and more elaborate.

By the time they'd finally stopped laughing, Spirit and Marmite had polished off the three mince pies that they'd carelessly left on a table, and were looking up at them with innocent expressions, pretending to be angels themselves.

## Chapter Twenty-Five

It was still dark when Hannah walked up the hotel stairs to reception to meet Lila for the Cornish Cream Tea Bus Secret Santa Tour. After the hilarious wrapping session the day before, which had warmed her to the core and ended with the promise of a Christmas full of laughter and fun, she had phoned her mum to let her know her plans had changed.

It was never going to be an easy conversation, but she hadn't been prepared for her mum's vehemence. 'There are *five* days to go, Hannah. You can't just tell me you're not coming – what will Mike and I do? What on earth could induce you to want to stay down in that place for Christmas?'

'Lots of things! I've made friends, Mum, and they've invited me. It would be easier for me to get a train back after Christmas now. It's better all round.'

She'd listened to the silence, a hand against her chest, waiting for it to be over.

'It's nothing more than that?' her mum had asked eventually.

'What do you mean?'

'You're not paying me back for not—'

'Not telling me the truth?' Hannah had said quietly.

'I'm not going over this again. It's obvious you want to punish me, and you've succeeded. We'll talk about it when I see you. *If* you ever make it back here, that is.' She'd hung up before Hannah had had a chance to reply.

She had known her mum wouldn't be pleased, and she did feel guilty about changing her plans so late, but had she also done it to get back at her? She hoped she was beyond behaving like that, but she couldn't entirely separate the two things: her mum had refused to help, so why should Hannah go through their usual festive performance when her heart wasn't in it? Of course, it would make things harder when she got home, but she wouldn't think about that now.

Hannah was going to live in the moment, and there were happier things to focus on now that she was looking forward to a Cornish Christmas. She had gone straight from the call with her mum to texting Noah:

*Don't worry about coming to Porthgolow in the morning – I'm going to be on Gertie most of the day. How about coming to my friends' Christmas on the 22nd? x*

Daniel had confirmed it was fine for Hannah to use the kitchen, but explained that Audrey was going home on the twenty-third, so if she wanted to include her – and Hannah did – she should have her dinner on the twenty-second. She had initially panicked at losing a day's preparation time, but Daniel had told her to leave a list of the ingredients she needed, and he and Levi would sort it out together.

Hannah had left her wording to Noah purposefully vague, and laughed at his prompt response.

*Very tempting, but not sure I'll be back in Mousehole in time for Christmas if I come to Edinburgh with you, and you know my folks will kill me. Nx*

*What about if it's at Crystal Waters?*

She'd watched the dots dance across the screen before his reply had appeared.

*Seriously? You'll still be here? Then I'm in, for sure! Send me the details. Nx*

She had done just that, then flopped on the bed, anticipation replacing the sadness of another difficult conversation with her mum. She would see Noah again. She tried to remember if there was any mistletoe hanging up in the snug.

Charlie greeted her and Lila at the door of the Cornish Cream Tea Bus, her red apron on over a black-and-white striped jumper and jeans. She'd added white fluffy edging to the top of the apron, and was wearing a headband with reindeer antlers on. She had to bend in the doorway so she didn't knock them off.

'Welcome! Come aboard! Find accessories!'

'Isn't Gertie dolled up enough without us having to make the effort too?' Lila asked.

Charlie put her hands on her hips. 'For someone whose actual job is playing make-believe, you've become very reluctant to dress up.'

'I really haven't,' Lila said. 'But it very much depends on *what* you want me to wear.'

'White fluff on your apron, which is non-negotiable because I've already added it, and some other adornment. Mistletoe earrings? Or you can be a reindeer like me. Or sparkly.' She held up some silver sparkly deely boppers with stars on the ends of the antennae.

'I want those,' Hannah said.

Charlie handed them to her. 'There you go. What about you, Lila?'

'I'm going to be a reindeer,' Lila said, with feigned reluctance. 'Come on then – let's get this Christmas party started.'

'We have to wait for Santa.' Charlie pointed in the direction of the pub.

Hugh was strolling across the sand wearing a Father Christmas outfit. He was a slim man, and he'd clearly added some padding. His coat was brilliant red, his boots and belt-buckle glossy black. He wasn't yet in the hat or the beard, and Lila made hurrying motions with her hands.

'What is it?' he asked, puffing as he joined them.

'You can't let anyone see you like that,' Lila said. 'You'll give away the whole Santa Claus thing! What if a family was driving past? You could ruin their Christmas.'

'Lila,' Charlie laughed.

'I'm serious,' Lila said. 'You have to be either full Santa or full Hugh. No in-between. Understood?'

Hugh nodded. 'Understood.' He pulled on the white curly wig, complete with beard, and then a traditional Santa hat, with fur round the brim and an oversized bobble. The result was impressive. He caught Hannah's eye and gave her a smile, his eyes crinkling at the edges. Hannah waggled her head in return, making the sparkly deely boppers bounce. She thought that, today, she might reach Peak Christmas.

Charlie drove the bus to Penzance and they parked in the harbour car park, which had a breathtaking view over St

Michael's Mount, the sun cutting through banks of grey cloud to set the castle aglow and make the sea shimmer. The three of them took it in turns to manage the queue outside, serve snacks and drinks inside, or be Santa's little helper.

Hannah soaked up the Christmas spirit: the festive tunes playing from the bus's speakers, the queue of eager families waiting to come on board, some of the children feverish with excitement at the promise of meeting Santa, their eyes wide with awe when they came back clutching their gifts. Hannah stood at the door, chatting to the people in the queue and helping tiny legs navigate the stairs. She got fresh air – which was at times a bit *too* bracing – and views over the harbour, and let the festivities consume her.

'It's nearly *Christmas*,' said a young girl at the front of the queue, her hands held above her head by her dad, who already looked exhausted.

'It is!' Hannah matched her tone. 'What are you most looking forward to?'

'*MEETING SANTA!*' she squealed, and her dad winced.

'And you're only minutes away,' Hannah said, crouching down so she was on her level.

'Have you met him?' the little girl asked.

'I work with him,' Hannah said. 'He's really, *really* nice.'

'Does he give you presents too?'

'Of course. Santa gives everyone presents on Christmas Day.'

'What about if you're on the naughty list?'

Her dad frowned. 'You're not on the naughty list, Maisie.'

'Aren't I, Daddy?' She tipped her head back to look at him. 'What about when I put Ben's toy in the toilet? Nobody was very happy with me then.'

Hannah watched Maisie's dad struggle not to laugh. 'That wasn't very kind, Maisie, but it's not enough to put you on the naughty list.'

'What would be?' she asked thoughtfully.

Hannah and the dad exchanged a look: *She's smart, isn't she? See what I have to deal with?*

He was saved from answering by the child before coming slowly down the stairs, his mum holding on to him and his gift. It was one Hannah had wrapped: she had used silver holographic ribbon to adorn her presents, and could tell from the shape that this was a snow globe. She wondered whether the boy would get to open it straight away, or would have to wait until Christmas Day.

'My turn?' Maisie whispered, after Charlie had given the boy and his mum their drinks and mince pies, and Hannah had said goodbye to them.

'Your turn,' she said. 'Come on board Santa's Christmas Cornish Cream Tea Bus! You get to go and meet him, then choose a cake on your way out. How about that?'

Maisie jumped up and down and clapped, then gave her dad an angelic grin.

'Thank you,' he said. Hannah watched as he made Maisie walk up the stairs in front of him, his hands out ready in case she missed her footing.

Charlie came to join Hannah. 'I did wonder about making them go up and down the stairs, but there's no way we could have had Santa down here. There's not enough room.'

'I think they like it,' Hannah said. 'It adds a sense of adventure and anticipation – what will they see when they get to the top? And most kids love stairs.'

'The parents won't thank me, but I did put it in bold font on the website.'

'It's all going swimmingly,' Hannah said. 'Don't worry.'

Above them, Lila laughed loudly. Hannah thought she was probably getting acquainted with Maisie.

'What about you?' Charlie asked. 'How was your mum when you told her about Christmas?'

Hannah wrinkled her nose. 'Cross. But I've texted her since, and she's replied without shouty capitals, which is a step in the right direction.'

'I didn't want to make trouble for you by offering.'

'And if I hadn't wanted to stay, or I thought it would cause too many problems, I wouldn't have accepted. You can't feel guilty because I'm changing my plans at the last minute – that's down to me, and I'm so happy I get to spend Christmas with you in Porthgolow. It's an extra silver lining to this whole experience.'


'Oh for God's sake,' Charlie called from the driver's seat. 'What's going on?'

Hannah hurried up to the top deck, where Lila was already peering out of the front window, trying to see why the bus had come to a halt at the end of what they could only guess was a long queue leading into Mousehole. They were on a narrow, steepish road that led down to the harbour.

'Can you see?' Hannah asked.

'Nope, not that far ahead,' Lila said. Hannah joined her, but the road turned too acutely for them to see what was happening further down the hill. 'This isn't just traffic lights. Something has gone seriously wrong.'

'And it's backing up behind us too,' Hugh called from the back of the bus. 'Whatever this is, we've no way of escaping it. We're stuck for the duration.'

'I'll walk down the hill and see what's happening,' Hannah

volunteered, hurrying down the stairs. 'Charlie, I'm going to go and have a look.'

'Thanks. Will you take Marmite with you? He could do with a leg stretch.'

Hannah attached the dog's lead and stepped off the bus. The air smelled of fish and cold, but there was also a tang of something else; something deep and rich and delicious, perhaps from a nearby coffee shop. She strolled down the hill, past the queue of vehicles. Some of the drivers were sticking their heads out of windows, and horns echoed up and down the line of traffic. As she got closer to the harbour, she heard raised, angry voices. Marmite sped up, forcing Hannah to tug on his lead and then, when that didn't work, pick up her pace to match his.

They rounded a sharp turn and she saw what had caused the problem. A van had clearly taken the bend too quickly and smashed into a bollard. The damage didn't look too bad – one of the angry men was wearing a high-vis and standing next to the open driver's door – but the shunt had caused the back of the van to open, and there was a lot of detritus. Detritus that, on closer inspection, Hannah saw was Christmas puddings.

There were hundreds of them, wrapped in red cellophane and spilling out across the road and pavement, and while the driver argued with whoever it was who was most annoyed about his accident, people were sneaking towards the puddings and taking them.

Hannah didn't know what to do. Should she alert the driver? It was unfortunate enough that he'd crashed, but now whoever these puddings were destined for would lose their order. She hovered, debating, but the job was taken out of her hands.

'Excuse me, lad,' called a man from the doorway of a gift shop, 'but your puddins aren't goin' to last much longer.' He pointed at a woman who had several in her arms and was scurrying away, a furtive look on her face.

The driver sighed, his hands on his hips. 'The stock's ruined anyway – no way my client can sell these now. Better they get used than wasted. Go on, help yourselves!' he shouted. 'I'm covered by the insurance, and I'll organize a new order ASAP.'

He turned back to his original conversation, his voice dropping as he placed a placatory hand on the shoulder of the older man, whose cheeks were red with anger. Hannah heard the 'whoop whoop' of a police car coming from the opposite direction. The situation would be taken control of, but Charlie and the bus might have a long wait before they could get near their car-park spot.

Marmite had wandered forward and was sniffing one of the puddings. Hannah resisted the urge to take one – she was sure that Levi up at Crystal Waters had already made his own for Christmas Day.

She started making her way back to Gertie to give Charlie the news, pausing to look up a side street before crossing. It took her a moment to process what she was seeing, her breath faltering as she did.

Noah was standing on a doorstep several houses up, looking gorgeous in a loose, biscuit-coloured jumper and jeans, his feet bare despite the cold. Marmite skittered towards him but Hannah held the lead tightly. Should she go and say hello now? The urge to was strong, but she needed to get back to Gertie and she didn't want a rushed conversation with him. It would be better to wait until tomorrow.

She was about to turn away when a car door slammed

and a slim, pretty woman with shining auburn hair walked up to him. Hannah recognized her from the photo that had appeared on Noah's phone when Beth had rung him. She was too far away to hear what they were saying – it was bad enough that she was watching – but she couldn't tear her eyes away.

Noah stepped off the step and Beth wrapped her arms around his waist, resting her head on his shoulder. His arms went around her in return, and Hannah turned her head away so fast she felt a stab of pain in her neck. She walked quickly, crossing the road without looking, desperate to get away. Marmite trotted alongside, keeping close to her heels, as if he could sense her mood change.

So, that was Noah's house. And that was Beth. Beth who was supposed to be in London, now that Noah had moved back home. Hannah felt winded, as if she'd run straight into a solid object – her chest tight and her stomach aching. Had Noah's mum been wrong about the break up, or had Noah and Beth talked it over and realized they'd made a mistake? After all, Christmas was a time of reconciliation.

It was a beautiful, romantic reunion for a gorgeous couple; all it needed was some snow to complete the scene and it would be Christmas-card perfect. Hannah should be happy for them. She would be, once she'd got over the shock.

Lila was waiting for her on Gertie's step, her dark brows knitted in concern. 'Are you OK, Hannah? We thought you'd got lost. What's happening down there?'

'Christmas puddings,' she managed, as Charlie joined them. 'There's been a Christmas pudding spillage.'

'But they're not *dead*, are they?' Lila asked, and Hannah stared at her, bemused. 'There have been no Christmas pudding fatalities? Only you look mortified. Oh, it's because you love food, isn't it? You can't bear to see that happen to something so delicious.' She grinned, and Hannah tried her best to return it.

'They've just been shaken up,' Hannah said. 'The fact that they've fallen out of a van wasn't putting people off, so they'll all find homes.'

'Disaster averted then,' Charlie said, narrowing her eyes at Hannah.

Hannah took a deep breath and pulled herself together. 'Disaster averted,' she confirmed, thinking that was an apt way of putting it. At least she wouldn't pour her heart out to Noah at her meal tomorrow night: she would avoid the crushing embarrassment of telling him how she felt, only for him to gently reject her because he was back with his girlfriend. The Christmas pudding spillage had been her saviour, but she wondered if she would be able to view them with as much fondness as she had done up until this moment, or whether they would always remind her of Noah and Beth, and leave a slightly bitter taste in her mouth.

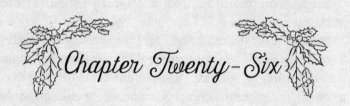

# Chapter Twenty-Six

Hannah wasn't sure exactly how long it took the Christmas pudding pile-up to be removed, but after what she'd seen, she wasn't thinking much about anything except for Noah and Beth.

'Whoop!' Lila called when, finally, the car in front of Gertie started its engine and got moving, and Charlie slid into the cab and moved the bus forward.

'Half an hour late!' she called. 'I'm sure we can make the time up and get through everyone. We'll just have to be super-efficient, OK?'

'Got it!' Lila said.

'No problem,' Hannah added distractedly. She knew she had to get through the rest of the day, focus on the joys of Christmas and giving the children the experience they had come for, despite the sadness that was seeping through her, making her listless. Her stomach gnawed with something other than hunger, and she pressed a hand to it, trying to wish the pain away.

There was no sign of the Christmas pudding van or the accident, apart from a slight dent in the solid-looking metal bollard that had borne the brunt of the van's bumper, but the air still smelled faintly of spiced fruit. Hannah took up position, this time at the top of the stairs, ready to lead their young guests to Santa.

'Doin' OK, Hannah?' Hugh asked. He looked red-faced beneath his hat and wig, even though Charlie had turned the heating on the bus to low so he didn't boil to death.

'I'm good,' she said overly brightly. 'Glad that little drama is over.'

'Oscar, *please* be careful on the stairs,' called a female voice as a small body careened into Hannah, knocking her into a table.

'Hello,' she said, to the small, stocky child with rosy cheeks and caramel-coloured hair. He was wearing a Batman costume, though the eared face-mask was nowhere to be seen. 'Are you here to see Santa?'

'Yes!' he shouted. 'Yes, yes, yes!'

'Sorry about that,' said the pretty woman appearing at the top of the stairs. She had the same red cheeks and thick brown hair. 'He is rather overexcited.'

'Sure Santa Claus will be a match for Batman?' Hannah asked Oscar.

He nodded, looking up at her with wide eyes. 'We're both goodies,' he said.

'That's very true.' She turned and smiled at Hugh, who leaned forward slightly.

'Ho-ho-ho!' he bellowed. 'Who do we have here? Come forward, young man.'

Hannah and Oscar's mother watched as, awestruck, the little boy stepped towards the Christmas magic.

By the time they got back to Porthgolow, day had turned to night.

'Lots of happy children,' Charlie said, stepping out of the cab and arching her back. 'And a few gifts left to give to any who come onto the bus over the next few days.'

'You're going to be open?' Hannah asked. She was exhausted. The effort of appearing cheerful had taken all her energy, even though the innocent wonder of the children and the twinkling Christmas atmosphere had buoyed her slightly.

'I'm running the last food market on the twenty-third – even though it's not a Saturday – so people can pick up any final bits. And I'm expecting a few regulars tomorrow, people on their way home after a hard day's shopping who might fancy a cream tea. When can you treat yourself, if not at Christmas time?'

'I'm going to treat myself to a very large glass of wine when I get back to the hotel,' Lila said. 'And see what's happened to my boyfriend.'

'Daniel said he was going to show the warm-up cricket match in the snug,' Charlie replied. 'So I expect that's where Sam is.'

'What's a warm-up match when it's at home?' Lila asked. 'Cricket isn't the most energetic sport at the best of times. What on earth do they need to warm up for?'

'It's the matches they play before the Tests,' Hugh explained, coming down the stairs. 'You know, against the B-teams and local sides. So they can get their eye in, get used to the pitches.' Three faces looked blankly back at him. He shrugged. 'It's India, I think. Should be a great series.'

Lila groaned. 'Are we going to be cricket widows, Charlie?'

'Not if I have anything to do with it. There's Christmas to be celebrating, and I will enunciate the word loud and clear when I next see Daniel. *Christmas* not *Cricket*.'

'Our slogan,' Lila nodded decisively. 'At least I know where to find him. What's left to tidy?'

'It's almost done. Another ten minutes and we'll have blitzed it.'

They worked quickly, while Hugh collected rubbish from upstairs. Most children had taken their wrapped gifts away with them, but a few had ripped them open there and then, and he came downstairs with a bin bag full of paper and ribbon.

'That's one thing I always find so dispiriting about Christmas,' Lila said. 'All the wasted wrapping.'

Hannah took the bag from Hugh and looked through it. 'You can recycle most of it these days – it's only the really fancy paper with velvet or sequins that's harder to deal with. I just give people presents in tote bags. If they want to use the bag again they can, if not then I take it back and reuse it myself. Newspaper also looks pretty cool – you don't have to use traditional paper.'

'Maybe in future I could wrap gifts up in scarfs,' Lila said. 'Nobody would mind, would they? It's about revealing the present more than anything, then they could just give them back.'

Lila's words reminded Hannah that she still hadn't found her scarf, the one with rainbow stripes that her dad had given her years ago. She would have to search her room when she got back to the hotel.

'We're all done,' Charlie said. 'I'm going to take Marmite home and pick Jasper up from Lily's.'

301

Lila slung an arm around Hannah's shoulders. 'I'll walk back to the hotel with you.'

'Actually, I was wonderin' if I could have a word with you, Hannah?' Hugh had discarded the hat and beard, but he still looked festive in his padded suit. His face, however, was serious.

'Sure,' Hannah said. 'Where—'

'Come to the pub with me. I can run you up the hill if you don't fancy walkin' up afterwards.'

As she followed Hugh off the bus, Charlie caught her arm. 'I'll be up at the hotel later. Come and find me if you want?'

'Do you know what this is about?' Hannah asked.

'No, but I've very rarely seen Hugh look quite so sombre. Whatever it is, don't be on your own if you don't want to be.'

With those words ringing in her ears, Hannah followed Hugh to the Seven Stars.

The pub was bright and warm. A young woman Hannah hadn't seen before was behind the bar and quite a few locals were already at the tables, including Jeb and Cliff who she'd seen on the night of the storm. Hugh got a round of applause, to which he gave a red-faced bow.

'When are we gettin' our presents?' Jeb called. 'I promise I've been a good boy!'

'Never knew Father Christmas ran a bar on the side,' someone else commented.

Hugh gestured to the corner of the pub, where it was quieter. 'Take a seat. I'm goin' to get changed and then – would you like a drink? We've got a new Malbec in, if you fancy it.'

'Malbec's one of my favourites,' Hannah said. 'Thank you.'

302

Once he'd gone, she sat down at the most secluded table in the pub. She got her phone out for something to do, and saw a message from Noah on the screen. Her mouth went dry: had he seen her watching him and Beth? She opened up his message, her fingers fumbling slightly.

*Really looking forward to tomorrow. Can I bring anything? Nx*

She frowned. He still wanted to come all the way to Porthgolow, despite his reunion with Beth? And *she* still wanted to see *him* again, despite the scene she'd witnessed. She shook her head as she typed her reply, the phrase *glutton for punishment* dancing through her thoughts.

*Just yourself and your Christmas cheer. Can't wait! H. xx*

She wondered if she'd be able to muster up any Christmas cheer herself. She switched the ringer onto silent and put her phone away. Whatever it was Hugh wanted to talk to her about, she didn't want to be interrupted.

'One large Malbec.' Hugh put the glass down and sat opposite her. He'd changed out of his Santa outfit into a pale blue shirt and dark trousers. 'Thank you for agreein' to this.'

'Of course. Though I don't know what it's about.' She laughed nervously.

'It's about those photos,' Hugh said hurriedly. 'The pictures you showed me, of you and Michael and Susie – Susanna.'

Hannah felt as if she'd been drenched in cold water. She never thought of her mum as Susie; she hardly ever thought of her as Susanna. She had definitely never referred to her by either of those names while she'd been in Porthgolow.

'You saw us?' she whispered.

'Susie brought you in the pub, your first time here. You'd been on the beach, and you and Mike both wanted chips. We got talkin'. She was – is – great, your mum. Is she keeping well?' His expression was hopeful and sad all at once.

303

Hannah nodded dumbly. 'She's fine. She lives near Leith, so we're not too far apart. Was it just that one time? I don't remember much at all.'

'You were too little. Mike was a bit older, but we – we were careful, your mum and I.'

'Careful about what?'

'It should really be her telling you all this, Hannah. But it hurt me, lyin' to you the other day. Seein' you come close to the truth and then leadin' you away from it. It didn't seem right.' He sipped his drink. It looked like tonic water. He was probably heading behind the bar after this.

'You and my mum were *together*?'

'It was a summer romance. I won't use the word fling, because that doesn't credit it with enough meanin'. I loved her, almost from the moment I saw her. She'd brought you on holiday while your dad was away. She told me the marriage was all but over. We clicked – it was as simple as that.'

Hannah pressed a hand to her mouth, as if that might keep her swirling emotions under control. Her mum, so polite and formal. So strait-laced. She'd had an affair with this friendly, slightly bumbling Cornishman whose presence Hannah found comforting, even though she didn't really know him. Was that some residual feeling from a time she didn't remember? 'Were you together for just one holiday? One fortnight?'

Hugh shook his head. 'You came back to Cornwall four years in a row. Susie and I – we saw each other every time. Only a few occasions – a couple of trips here with the three of you, then I'd come to your holiday home in Newquay in the evenings, once you and Mike were in bed.' His cheeks coloured. 'I know it was wrong, Hannah, but I hope you can appreciate the circumstances. I've never met your dad. I don't want to speak ill of him—'

'He was never there,' Hannah said. 'He still isn't. Our family – *his* family – we're not what he cares about. Not really. I just . . . even as I grew up, I guess I never realized how lonely Mum must have been, how hard it was for her to bring us up on her own.'

'She did a grand job from what I saw,' Hugh said softly.

'I was always so absorbed with not seeing my dad. I never really . . .' She held Hugh's gaze. 'Were you in touch between the holidays?'

'A couple of letters, here and there. We both understood that it couldn't really survive outside Cornwall, and to begin with, I thought it would be a one-off. But then Susie turned up the next summer, with you and Mike, and it was so easy to pick up where we left off. We talked about the future, about you all moving down here, but I think we both knew it would never happen. Then, one year, Susie wrote to me in spring and said you couldn't make it that summer. She didn't explain, just said she'd always remember our time together.'

'We moved to Scotland,' Hannah explained. 'I don't think it was possible for us to come all this way after that.' She could tell Hugh had truly cared for her mum, and must have been devastated when it ended. She wondered how her mum had felt. 'I'm sorry,' she added.

Hugh shook his head. 'We both knew it couldn't last.'

'What about afterwards?' She presumed Hugh hadn't been married during the years he'd been seeing her mum, albeit only for a fortnight every summer. Had Hugh spent his life pining for someone he could never have? Hannah thought of Noah and unease slid through her, slippery and cold.

'I've had other relationships since,' he said. 'I don't want you to think that, after Susie, I couldn't reconcile myself to seeing anyone else. But I find that, with this place to run,

I'm more suited to my own company. Your mum was very special to me, Hannah. Susie and I truly respected, and loved, each other. But maybe you can understand why she has been reluctant to tell you.'

Hannah took a sip of wine before replying. Her hands were shaking slightly. 'I'm still trying to prove to my dad that I'm worth his time. That's a big part of why I became an eco-consultant.' She shrugged. 'I can see why Mum wouldn't want me to know about you, what happened between you. She thinks I still idolize my dad, though I'm beginning to realize that my feelings are quite a lot more complicated than that.' She remembered how Noah had spoken to her so frankly about it, how he had seemed to get to the truth of it when she'd struggled.

'But now that you know . . .?' Hugh's eyebrows rose. There was a lightness to his expression that hadn't been there when he'd sat down; the relief of getting it out in the open, she supposed.

'I'm glad my mum had someone,' Hannah said. 'I'm glad she did something for herself, and I should . . . be kinder to her.' She ran her finger over a grain in the table, the whorls rough against her skin. 'Did you know, the first time I came into the pub?'

'You're not that different to when you were small, Hannah. Same blonde hair and those intense, clear eyes. The moment Charlie introduced you, I knew it had to be you, even though it seemed staggerin' that you'd suddenly turned up here, and especially since you seemed to have no idea about the connection. I realized Susie hadn't told you, and I understood why, which is why I didn't answer your questions to begin with.'

'But you relented.'

He smiled at her. 'I saw how pragmatic you are. I realized

306

I could tell you and that you would weigh everythin' up, see it from your mum's point of view. I can see what a kind, responsible woman you've become.'

Hannah blushed at the compliment. 'I wish Mum saw me like that, too. I wish she'd trusted me enough to tell me.'

'She's much closer to you, and has more to lose. If I'd misjudged your reaction . . .' He fiddled with his collar, and Hannah reached out and took his hand. It felt strange, doing something so intimate. He wasn't her dad, but he'd been her mum's lover. He had taken the photo she treasured.

'You didn't misjudge,' Hannah said. 'If anything, I'm at fault because I haven't made it possible for Mum to confide in me. I'll tell her that, too.'

'Let me call her first, Hannah. I need to let her know I've told you. Pave the way. If you're happy to give me her number?'

'OK. I'll wait for her to get in touch with me. I'm glad she had you and Porthgolow, when Dad deserted her.'

'So am I. And thank you, for bein' so understandin'. I loved spending time with you, you know. All three of you. Mike wanted to play games all the time. He'd pull out all the board games, spread counters and dice all over the floor.' He pointed to a haphazard stack of boxes piled on a shelf, the colours faded as if they'd been there for decades.

'What about me?' Hannah asked. She wanted to know how he'd seen her back then.

'Even when you were tiny, you were interested in food. You were desperate to go into the kitchens, and the last year you visited I took you in there and showed you how to make my fisherman's pie. It's a family recipe, passed down the generations, but by then you felt like family to me. I wrote it down for you, as a memento. You slipped it in the pocket of your dungarees, but—'

307

'Your fisherman's pie?' Hannah sat back in her chair. She'd thought his had tasted similar to the one she made. She pictured the large, blue-covered notebook that she'd filled with recipes over time, copying them from cookery books, some given to her by family and friends. She must have held on to Hugh's piece of paper – or maybe her mum had, slipping it inside one of her own cookery books for Hannah to rediscover later, when she'd forgotten where it had come from. All those years she'd been making it, oblivious to the fact that it had come from this tiny village on the Cornish coast where, it turned out, she *did* have a connection.

She refused Hugh's offer of a lift to the hotel – she needed time to think about what she'd found out, to let it settle inside her. But when she left the Seven Stars, she hugged him, tight. 'Thank you,' she said, 'for telling me. And for being there, back then. For making my mum happy.'

She walked back to Crystal Waters with her coat wrapped tightly around her and the moon shimmering on the surface of the sea, a feeling of calm settling over her like snow.

## Chapter Twenty-Seven

Her mum's phone call didn't come until later, when Hannah was in her room with the side lights on and the window cracked open, letting in a tantalizing waft of sea air. It had taken all her willpower not to make the call herself, but she had trusted Hugh to do as he'd promised, and instead stayed in her room, toying idly with the pages of a book before realizing she had too much in her head to take in anyone else's words.

She felt bad for not seeking Charlie out, but she didn't want to talk about what she'd found out until she'd spoken to her mum, so instead she'd ordered room service; a steak fajita made with local beef, with chilli sauce and chunky guacamole, and listened to the sound of people walking past in the corridor outside her room, footsteps appearing and then drifting into the distance, voices and laughter loud and hushed.

Christmas was four days away, and even in this slightly

dislocated hotel world there was a bubble of anticipation. The rule book no longer applied: chocolate could be eaten for breakfast and champagne drunk with lunch; pyjamas could replace work clothes – though she wasn't sure Daniel would react favourably if she wore them in the restaurant – and films could be watched all day. Hannah hadn't reached that state yet; the conversation with her mum was unfinished business, and she was awash with nerves.

When her phone lit up and buzzed gently on the duvet cover, Hannah snatched it up and stared at the photo of her mum standing on top of Arthur's Seat, Edinburgh's stunning backdrop behind her. She answered it after five rings.

'Hello?'

'Hannah?' Her mum's voice was thick with emotion.

'Hugh told me,' she rushed. 'I'm so sorry, I—'

'I shouldn't have kept it from you,' her mum said, interrupting her. 'I should have told you as soon as you said you were going to Porthgolow. I thought I could feign ignorance until you came back, but of course I should have known you would get to the bottom of it.'

'I didn't really,' Hannah said, tucking her legs under her. 'I'd given up, after talking about it with Mike. It was Hugh who came to me. You're not mad at him, are you?' She felt childlike all of a sudden, and wished she could see her mum, have this conversation face to face.

'No, Hannah. I was shocked, of course, but it was so easy to talk to him, even after all this time. I just wish I'd been brave enough to tell you myself.'

'I'm happy that he was there for you, when Dad wasn't. Hugh's lovely. You know, immediately, who he is. He's so straightforward.'

'He was a breath of fresh air,' her mum said softly. 'He

reminded me that I could be loved for me, that I could be more than just a struggling single mum.'

'So then why . . .' Hannah swallowed. 'Why didn't we move to Cornwall instead of Edinburgh? If Hugh was there and you loved each other, why did you choose to go in the opposite direction?'

She heard a loud sigh down the phone. 'So many reasons,' her mum said. 'And I still wonder if I made the right decision. I was going through the divorce, and I didn't want to put Hugh through that right at the beginning of a relationship. The work was in Edinburgh – there were so many more jobs than in Cornwall, and I thought you and Mike would thrive more in the city. But also, those holidays were magical, and I was . . . scared. Scared that it wasn't real, that if I took the plunge and tried to make it last, it wouldn't. I was still hurting from your dad, and in the end, I took the safe option.'

Hannah lay back on the bed. 'I'm so sorry. And I'm sorry I made it hard for you to talk to me. If you thought that you couldn't be open because of Dad.' She was realizing more and more that she had never made it easy for her; doting on her absent dad, being harsh on her mum because she was the one who was there, having to be the parent. Whereas she saw now that her mother had been the one who'd been working so hard to keep her and her brother safe and happy.

'I was worried you'd think less of me,' her mum replied. 'And really, you have every right to. I just hope you can forgive me for finding comfort with someone else, and for not telling you sooner. You've always had such a strong sense of right and wrong.'

'Of course I forgive you,' Hannah said. 'It hurt that you

didn't want to tell me straight away, but now I understand why. And with you and Hugh, there's nothing to forgive. I get it, completely. Dad wasn't there, and Hugh made you happy. I know that feelings don't follow any rules, not even the ones you set for yourself.'

Her mum sighed, and it sounded like static. 'I thought that you were punishing me – staying in Porthgolow for Christmas.'

'I was a bit,' Hannah admitted. 'After all our arguments, I wasn't relishing the thought of coming home. But it's as much about the people I've met here, and the fun I've had, as it is about us. I really want to do this, Mum.'

'Tell me about it,' she said eagerly. 'Tell me who you've met and what's happened.'

'Now?' It was nearly eleven o'clock.

'Unless you've got somewhere else you need to go?'

'No, I haven't. I'm just going to make a cup of tea.'

'Good idea. Do that and call me back.' She hung up and Hannah stared at the phone, wondering if her mum had been replaced by an imposter. She hadn't sounded that enthusiastic about anything for ages. Hannah made herself a peppermint tea and settled back against the pillows to return the call.

She ended up telling her everything. She hadn't intended to, but her mum – who she would never be able to think of as Susie – was receptive in a way Hannah wasn't used to. It was like slipping into a pair of comfortable old pyjamas, and she couldn't resist. She told her about Charlie and the Cornish Cream Tea Bus, about Lila and Sam – genuine celebrities – turning up at the hotel, and how down-to-earth they were. She told her about finding Spirit, about Audrey and the tragic story of Anna Purser and Henry

Medlin, and the dog finding the carved stone down by the swimming pool.

'Goodness,' her mum said after a moment's silence. 'Anyone would think you hadn't done any work at all! What about your contract, working with that local chap? Didn't you enjoy your first job away from the office? When you leave something out, there's usually a reason.'

And so, after only gentle prompting, Hannah filled in all the gaps she'd left empty because they included Noah. She told her mum about that first frosty drive to the hotel and the way he'd gently thawed; about the night of the ghost hunt, meeting up with him in Mousehole and spending time with his family. She tried not to sound too wistful about that, remembering her less than generous comparisons to her own family Christmases.

'So you see,' she said at the end, 'I can't be judgemental about you and Hugh, because even when I thought Noah was with Beth, I wanted something to happen between us.'

'You say that, Hannah, but you were the one who stopped the kiss. I don't believe you could have enjoyed being with him, knowing he was with someone else. You're not a cheater, and you wouldn't want him to be either, because if he could do it to Beth, then he could do it to you, too.'

'Do you think?' Hannah whispered.

'I'm certain of it,' her mum said. 'While it remains firmly in the "could have been" category, you can play out any fantasy you want. The feelings only hit you when you can't take it back.'

'Did you feel guilty, about Hugh?'

'Maybe a flicker at the beginning. But your dad and I – I knew by then that our marriage was over. He was away for

313

months at a time, and when he returned it was more like a bed and breakfast, with me as his unwilling host. It took longer than I'd hoped to finalize the divorce, because my solicitor couldn't track him down. But no, there wasn't much guilt with Hugh. I loved him.'

'You wouldn't consider revisiting it? Coming down here and seeing him again?'

Silence hung in the air for a long time before she replied. 'I honestly don't know, Hannah. It was twenty years ago.'

'He talks about you so fondly.'

'He does?' Hannah could hear the smile in her voice.

'It's something to think about, at least. Porthgolow's not *that* far away.'

'Says the woman who used a long train journey home as her excuse for staying in Cornwall weeks longer than she was supposed to.' Her mum laughed. 'Now I know why.'

'Yes,' Hannah said, sighing. 'But it's pointless, isn't it? All the time I thought he wasn't available and he was; then the moment I find that out and have the chance to tell him how I feel, he's back with Beth. I'm happy for him, of course, but . . . I'm gutted, too.'

'I'm so sorry it hasn't worked out with Noah, Han, but that doesn't mean you can't enjoy your Christmas there. With Charlie and the actors and Audrey. Focus on those things instead, and then come home – unless you're planning on moving to Cornwall?'

Hannah laughed. 'Of course not! I'll be back before the New Year. Maybe we could have our own Christmas a few days late? I could do all the cooking, to make up for bailing on you at the last minute.'

'I'd love that,' she said. 'Just the three of us.'

Hannah nodded, tears springing into her eyes. She should

have been this open with her mum weeks ago – perhaps years. 'I love you, Mum.'

'I love you too, Hannah. Now go and get some rest, it's almost tomorrow as it is.'

Even though it was late, and Hannah had got up so early – she could barely believe the Secret Santa Tour had been that day – she wasn't tired. She hadn't changed into her pyjamas and, having spent the whole evening in her room, decided she needed a change of scene. She took her key and pushed her door open slowly, not wanting to make too much noise, then crept along the corridor and up the stairs.

There was nobody behind the reception desk, though Hannah knew the night staff would be about somewhere, perhaps getting through paperwork in the office while it was quiet. The spotlights above the desk and front door were muted but welcoming, and the Christmas tree twinkled in the corner next to the snug, her favourite room for once in total darkness.

Unsure what to do now she was here, she sat on the sofa, her back to the window with its cascade of golden lights. The Christmas tree was to her right, its pine needles smelling of promise and presents. She'd been there a couple of minutes when she heard a scuffling sound, and a moment later Spirit came out from under the tree. He jumped on to the sofa and lay down beside her, his head on her lap.

'You're not supposed to be up here with me,' she said softly. 'I thought I left you sleeping. How did you sneak out behind me, without me realizing?' The way he behaved, she wouldn't be surprised to learn that he could open doors. She stroked his warm fur, felt the rise and fall of his small body under her hand.

She felt completely calm, as if the conversation with her mum had broken down years' worth of barriers between them. She also knew, now, that she hadn't been wrong about her mum keeping something from her. She had been right to trust her instincts. But then, she'd trusted them about Noah, too, and that had been a mistake. And now she'd lost her chance.

'Oh Spirit,' she said. 'I need to have a word with myself, don't I?'

He lifted his head off her lap, and she thought how intuitive he was, how alive to human emotions. But he wasn't looking at her: he was staring out at the dim reception, his body tense, his ears pricked up.

A cold wave of dread washed over Hannah, and she found she was pinned to her seat by fear. It was after midnight, so she'd missed the ghostly footsteps – unless Chloe had got it wrong and the time varied? Ghosts were the opposite of an exact science, after all. She closed her eyes, but that made it worse. She was here now: she had to face whatever it was.

She waited, eyes and ears alert, for the first steps. They came from the Christmas tree, supposedly, but she couldn't even turn her head to glance at it. She heard a whimper, and realized it had come from her. Spirit was standing now, his front paws digging painfully into her thigh as he glared ahead, his body vibrating. Fear was an acrid taste in her mouth, her tongue fat and useless. She dared not blink.

She didn't know how long she sat there, but eventually the dog relaxed. He turned his head and looked up at her, his eyes dark pools.

'Was that it, then?' Hannah said, laughing with relief. 'Has it gone?'

Spirit barked once, loudly, and as he did a waft of air

passed by Hannah's face, a cool breeze that had come, inexplicably, from the centre of the room. It moved past her, as if heading through the glittering window and out into the gardens. For a few seconds the scent of lavender was so strong that Hannah almost choked on it, and she felt an overwhelming sadness, as if not only would she never be able to kiss Noah or tell him how she felt, but she would never see him again. It was a deep, hollow ache that came upon her so suddenly that her breath lodged in her throat.

Then it was gone. The air was still and smelt only of pine needles, her intense misery felt instantly ridiculous, and she wondered if she had imagined the whole thing. Or she would have done if it hadn't been for Spirit, who had stepped over her lap and was standing with his front paws on the back of the sofa, his ears pricked and his tail wagging, staring out at the hotel gardens, looking intently at something, or someone, that Hannah couldn't see.

# Chapter Twenty-Eight

Coming into close contact with a ghost was bound to make sleep more difficult to come by, Hannah reasoned as she stared at the ceiling, shapes morphing out of the darkness as her eyes struggled to adjust. It also made her feel incredibly emotional about the prospect of Audrey's cleansing spell. She didn't understand why a waft of air – that any sceptic would explain away in a heartbeat – had made more of an impression on her than Audrey's retelling of the tragic love story.

When she made it upstairs the next morning Daniel and Audrey were standing close to the front desk, deep in conversation.

'Good morning,' she said.

'Hi Hannah,' Daniel looked up briefly then turned back to Audrey. His dark eyes were serious.

'Oh Hannah, I was just telling Daniel that I'm ready to cleanse the hotel. I've had a long, enlightening discussion with my friend, and everything's in place. We've agreed to do it this evening.'

'Before your meal, Hannah, if that's OK?' Daniel said.

'Sure.' Hannah was proud of the menu she had planned, and felt a thrill of excitement at the day stretching ahead of her in the kitchen, getting everything prepared.

'We can go outside as it gets dark,' Audrey said. 'At the liminal time.'

Hannah pictured a small procession of them, slinking out of the snug, through the winding paths of the gardens and down to the outdoor swimming pool, all holding candles. They would look like a cult, or a witches' coven. They only needed a couple of velvet cloaks for the effect to be complete – even a hoody might give the wrong impression. She could see why Daniel didn't exactly look over the moon.

'Let me know if there's anything I can do to help,' Hannah said. Once Audrey had gone, she asked Daniel if he was OK.

'I will be,' he said. 'Once this little chapter is finished and I can put all my effort into Christmas. I can't have anything going wrong on Christmas Day, not this year. Not phantom guests or wily dogs or storms that threaten to take out all the power. It sounds myopic, but that's my focus right now.'

'If karma has anything to do with it, you should be all right,' Hannah replied. 'You've had enough disruption to last you the next five years, at least.' She realized now was not the time to tell him about her experience the night before.

'I'm not taking anything for granted. It has to be perfect.' He was staring at his phone, full of nervous energy. It was so different to how he'd been when she first arrived – the coolest of cats, all charm and unwavering confidence. This wasn't just about Christmas. A thought struck her then, and it seemed so obvious that she couldn't help grinning.

'If there's anything I can do, Daniel, anything at *all*, please let me know.'

He narrowed his eyes. 'You're going to be busy enough in the kitchen today.'

She nodded. 'It was so kind of Charlie to ask me to stay, and of you to let me take over your professional kitchen. And I loved spending yesterday on Charlie's bus – she's brilliant, isn't she? You must be so proud of her.'

He nodded, watching her closely. He opened his mouth, as if he was about to say something, then seemed to change his mind.

'I'd better go and see Levi,' she said. 'I've got cod fillets to prep, dauphinoise potatoes to make.' As she walked away, she knew he was still watching her. But he didn't need to worry; even if she was right about what he was planning, his secret was safe with her.

In the kitchen, Hannah forgot about everything else. Cooking was the perfect activity; it engaged all her senses and took over her thoughts. She prepared her cod fillets, seasoned them and arranged them. She peeled potatoes, and selected the best stems of purple sprouting broccoli. Her friends' Christmas menu was never roast turkey, never anything too traditional, and being in Cornwall she had gone big on the fish: seared scallops and pancetta to start – a classic, but one of the best – and cod for the main course. There were vegetarian options for Lila, and she was making a version of her chocolate log with bitter cherry sauce for dessert.

That was the only part where she faltered. She could picture Noah's face when she'd described it to him, the way he'd looked at her so intently, flirted so obviously. And she hadn't responded instinctively because of Beth – Beth, who he hadn't been with then, but was with now. The irony was almost too much.

'Looking great, Hannah,' Levi said, nodding his approval. He had a sprig of holly in his chef's hat, and Hannah couldn't help grinning.

'It's going OK so far.' She wiped her hands on a tea towel and moved to a different work station. 'I want to marinate these for a bit longer, and add more mint to the pea purée. What do you think?' She held out her spoon and waited while Levi tasted it, his eyes closing briefly.

'Magnificent. Where is it you work again?'

'Green Futures,' she said, staring at her purée. 'I prefer this sort of green, though.' She gestured to the pan, to the fresh mint leaves and broccoli. 'Do you ever get bored of creating delicious food for willing customers?'

Levi laughed. 'Not for a moment.'

'No,' Hannah said. 'I didn't think so.'

Levi went back to preparing the restaurant's standard menu, leaving Hannah to her work. Noah would be there tonight, because she had invited him and he still seemed willing. Would he bring Beth with him? She couldn't imagine he would do that without asking her first, to check it was OK numbers-wise, if nothing else, but it was a possibility.

She had sent him another message that morning, letting him know Audrey's spell was happening before dinner, suggesting he come earlier if he wanted to be there, but she hadn't looked at her phone since. She didn't know what she would say when she saw him, or how she should behave.

But she couldn't think about that now: she had scallops to clean.

She was finished in time to freshen up before Audrey's gathering, and Levi had said he would oversee everything from that point onwards.

'I can't ask you to do that,' she said, undoing her apron. 'The scallops and cod need to be cooked last minute, and you've got your own menu to deal with. I'll be back soon.'

'And who's going to host your dinner?' he asked, folding his arms over his chest. 'You've been working all day, and it'll still be your cooking, your meal, if you leave the rest to me and my team.'

'I'm not worried about that,' she said, brushing a strand of damp hair out of her eyes. 'I'm worried about lumping a load of work on you when you've got enough to do.'

'So, accept this as my Christmas present to you. Go and say goodbye to your ghosts, then change into a sparkly dress and host your dinner party.'

Hannah grinned. 'I don't have a sparkly dress.'

'I'm sure you have something,' he said. 'Regardless. Your time here is done. Over. You're banished.'

'From my *own* menu,' Hannah protested, as Levi turned her round by her shoulders.

'At least you're getting it now,' he said, and pushed her gently through the door.

Before she went back to her room, Hannah stepped outside and took in large gulps of cold air. Working in a kitchen was always hot, sweaty work, as good a workout as one of Noah's runs, or fifty lengths in the swimming pool. She rubbed her eyes and blinked. The sun was the colour of apricots, hovering

322

above a gunmetal sea, and when Hannah tipped her head back she could see the first stars winking in the indigo expanse above.

Crystal Waters was lit up like a beacon, the bay tree lolli-pops either side of the front door draped in pinprick fairy lights. Excitement twisted low in her stomach at the thought of the next few days: Audrey's cleansing spell followed by her own event, the last festive food market tomorrow, then Christmas Eve and Christmas Day spent in this beautiful location, with Porthgolow Bay just beyond the glass. She had been so caught up with thoughts of Noah, worrying about her mum and the photographs, that somehow the reality of where she was had passed her by.

'Hannah!'

She peered around the nearest car to see Lila and Sam, laden down with bags. They had obviously been Christmas shopping, but Lila looked immaculate in jeans and a leather jacket, her dark hair falling around her shoulders.

'Wow, you look like you've been busy,' Lila said.

'I look a wreck,' she laughed, glad she couldn't see herself next to Lila's effortless glossiness. 'But I'm on my way to get changed. Levi's very kindly going to oversee things in the kitchen while we're saying goodbye to Anna and her fisherman.'

'What are you wearing?' Lila asked as Sam put his bags down and stretched his arms above his head.

'I have this black skirt and quite a nice polka-dot blouse . . .' Hannah stopped when Lila shook her head at her. 'I was only meant to be here for a week,' she added. 'And with no parties on the itinerary.'

'It's a good thing I've packed for lots of parties then, isn't it? Come with me.'

Hannah let herself be led back into the hotel by Lila, Sam grinning behind them.

'Now, I don't need you to do anything other than focus on what I'm saying and, if it's amenable to you all, hold hands in a circle. We can sort that out once we're down there.' Audrey gave the gathered group a warm smile. The room was thick with anticipation, the guests having a pre-dinner drink in the snug looking on with interest. Audrey was wearing a black blouse with gold embroidered detail, her tightly curled hair as wild as ever, her lips red. Hannah didn't know whether the effort was for her spell, or the dinner afterwards.

She felt unexpectedly glamorous herself in the navy dress Lila had lent her: it had shimmering silver thread detail on the bodice that winked in the light, and she'd complemented it with eyeliner and a bold pink lipstick that she'd brought with her on a whim and had never expected to use.

'Don't we need to chant along with you?' Lila asked. She was wearing a cream jumpsuit with dusky pink flowers on it, and even though her heels were low – probably due to their impending trip out into the dark hotel gardens – she looked red-carpet ready.

'Chanting?' Reenie said. 'Good lord! There won't be any of that, will there?'

'No chanting,' Audrey confirmed. 'I'll just be reading out some words from this book.' She held up her trusty notebook, and Hannah wished she could take a look at all the stories it held; what other places she'd visited, chasing the shadows and ghostly trails that her friend had left for her to follow. 'It's not a ritual, as such. We're simply opening up a channel for Anna and Henry to walk through, so they can be at peace.'

Hannah thought she heard Reenie snort, though it could have been a cough. She realized she hadn't told anyone about her experience in reception. After tonight, would it all be gone? Had she had the last ever paranormal experience at Crystal Waters? She was desperate to tell Noah about it, but he hadn't responded to her message, and he hadn't appeared. Perhaps now that he was back with Beth, he wouldn't turn up at all.

'Shall we get going?' Daniel asked, glancing at his other guests. 'Best to do it before the temperature drops too much more.' He gestured to the doorway and, after a flurry of everyone putting their coats on over their finery, Audrey led the way, the others following, Lila whispering excitedly to Sam.

Outside, the cold was all-pervasive. The sun had taken the last of the warmth with it, and Hannah zipped her coat up to the neck, heard the rustle of others tightening scarves and pulling on gloves. She still hadn't found her rainbow scarf, and wondered if she'd left it on board Gertie – she would have to remember to ask Charlie later.

Spotlights at the edges of the path marked their way through the gardens, and ahead of them the moon was star-tlingly white, reflected on water that was, for once, almost as flat as glass. Stars sparkled above them, bolder than they ever were in Edinburgh, and Hannah was awed by it. It felt as if this was a special night; the perfect time for Audrey to set Anna and Henry free.

She followed the others down the steps that led to the outdoor swimming pool. The tiles surrounding it gave them ample space to stand in a circle, next to where Spirit had found the graffiti'd stone.

'I can't hold hands,' Audrey said, 'as I need to hold my notebook open, but I'll still be part of the circle. If you could all join hands please.'

Hannah took hers out of her pockets. She had Charlie on her right, and Reenie's thin, bony grasp on her left. The hotel was behind Charlie, the sea beyond Reenie, and the covered pool ahead of her, past Lila and Sam. Audrey had her back to the sea with Daniel next to her, his eyes cast downwards. Hannah thought he must be relieved that it was almost over, so he could get back to his celebratory plans. She dropped her head too, hiding her smile.

Audrey cleared her throat twice, and then spoke: 'Anna Purser, Henry Medlin, we are here tonight to release you to the other side. To bring you peace, to take away the guilt and fear, the regret and blame that leaves you here, in the space between life and death.'

Her voice rang out clearly, and there was something about the way she spoke that reached Hannah's heart. Audrey cared about these people who had died all those years ago; she wanted their story to be known, the details of how they had lived and died as important as the possibility of a haunting. She was interested in their history. Perhaps she thought that cloaking it in spectral footsteps and unexplained cold spots would make more people pay attention.

Hannah closed her eyes and let Audrey's words wash over her, her thoughts returning to the strange breeze, the strong smell of lavender she'd experienced the night before.

'Use our energies,' Audrey said. 'Take strength from us one final time. Be at peace. Be free.' She fell silent, and Reenie strengthened her grip on Hannah's hand, as if afraid Anna or Henry would whisk her away when they went, carrying her out to sea. The quiet remained, and in it Hannah heard distant sounds; the shushing of the waves, a dog barking somewhere, raised voices and laughter from inside the hotel.

'Are we done?' Lila whispered.

'That's it, everyone,' Audrey said. 'Thank you.'

Hannah lifted her head just as Spirit barrelled into the centre of the circle, jumping up at each of them, his tail wagging frenziedly.

'Aw, he's gutted he missed it,' Lila said, trying to catch hold of him.

'Do you think it worked?' Sam asked Audrey.

She looked at him with clear eyes and said, 'I honestly have no idea.'

Daniel clapped his hands together. 'But it's done. It's over. Thank you, Audrey, for taking the time and effort to finish it properly. I suggest we all go inside while we can still feel our fingers.'

'Hang on, what's this?' Lila had finally got hold of Spirit and was on her knees, unwrapping something from around his throat.

'Has he got tangled up?' Sam asked, crouching beside her.

'No, I don't think so. It was tied in a bow. It's a—'

'Scarf,' Hannah finished. 'My scarf.' Her rainbow scarf that had gone missing. Had Spirit taken it, like he had Audrey's pen and Daniel's stapler? It was brightly coloured, after all.

'How on earth did it get round the dog's neck?' Reenie said. 'I know you all think he's got hidden talents, but bow-tying is taking things to extremes.'

'I don't know,' Hannah murmured, reaching her hand out. When Lila handed her the scarf she turned and ran up the steps, not prepared to stop and explain in case her sudden inkling was wrong, or she was going mad, or only imagining that one place she definitely remembered seeing it before she'd lost it was on the hook in Noah's parents' house. She broke into a slow jog, winding her way through the gardens to the door at the back of reception. She burst through it, her eyes scanning the empty space, and her heart sank.

Not, then, as she'd thought. He wasn't coming. She closed the door, trying to get her breath back.

'Hannah.'

He was standing in the entrance to the snug, jeans and a grey-blue jumper setting his eyes alight, his hair untamed. His gaze found hers.

'Noah, hi.'

'How did Audrey's cleansing spell go?'

'OK, I think. I mean, who knows if it worked? But Audrey seemed pleased, so maybe the ghosts are gone. You don't seem that upset to have missed it.' She stepped towards him. 'But you still came for dinner? I wasn't sure you would.'

He moved closer too, until they were next to the tall, twinkling Christmas tree. He lifted the scarf out of her hands and wrapped it around his own. 'I wanted Spirit to lead me to you,' he said. 'I wasn't sure where Audrey had taken you all. I tied the scarf round his neck, then Chloe started talking to me and by the time I turned around, he'd gone. I didn't see which direction he'd headed in, so I couldn't follow. I hadn't meant this to be quite so cloak-and-dagger.' His lips flickered into a smile.

Hannah's pulse refused to settle, even though her breathing had returned to normal. 'It's a night for cloak-and-dagger, though, so I'll allow it. Except – what do you mean, you hadn't meant *this* to be cloak-and-dagger? My Christmas meal?'

'Why did you think I wasn't coming tonight?'

'Because . . .' She didn't know where to start. With her assumptions, with Noah's mum, or with the fact she'd seen Noah and Beth on the doorstep together?

'Mum told me about your conversation in the car,' he said. 'That you thought I was with Beth. That night in the spa, when you said we couldn't—'

'I saw the photo of you together on your phone; you called her babe. I just assumed. It never occurred to me to ask you outright.'

He shook his head. 'And it never occurred to me to explain. These last couple of months haven't been easy in so many ways, but then – I didn't expect this.' He gestured between them. 'To feel the way I did about you, so soon afterwards. You thought I was with Beth when I kissed you?'

Hannah shrugged hopelessly. It felt like a dream, because he *was* with her, wasn't he? 'I don't know, Noah. None of this seems straightforward.'

'Why not? Because you're going home soon? I assumed that was why you backed off in the spa, why you said, outside The Ship, that we couldn't do this.'

Hannah shook her head. 'I thought you weren't free. You're still not—'

'What, Hannah?' He ran a hand down the side of her face, tucking an errant strand of hair behind her ear. 'You feel this too, don't you? How could you not?' His gaze searched hers, his touch like flames against her skin.

She heard voices behind her, the others coming in from the garden.

Noah took her hand and led her into the snug, weaving between the tables and chairs to the farthest corner, the bench that was partly hidden behind the curve of the bar.

Hannah sat down and Noah slid in next to her, then turned to face her.

'What's that?' she asked, pointing at a foil-covered parcel he'd put on the table.

Noah dipped his head, and even in the dim light she saw his cheeks redden. 'Chocolate and mallow log with bitter cherry sauce. All my own work, so I have no idea if it's edible.'

Hannah sat back. 'You made this for tonight?'

'You said someone else always brought the dessert, and I . . .' His voice dropped as he leaned in closer. 'When you talked about it that night, it made me . . . I wanted – want – to provoke that kind of reaction in you. I can't stop thinking about you. When I found out why you'd backed off before, I had hope. Hope that you want this, too.'

She swallowed. His face was so close to hers. She could see the different shades of blue in his eyes and smell coffee on his breath. She wanted to taste it on his lips.

'I saw you,' she said. 'Yesterday. We were doing the Secret Santa Tour, and when we got to Mousehole a van-load of Christmas puddings had spilled in the road and caused a hold-up. I went to see what was going on, and I saw you. With Beth. You put your arms around each other, so I thought . . .' She took a steadying breath. 'I thought that you'd got back together.'

Noah exhaled. 'She was saying goodbye, before she left for London. We've been in touch over the last few weeks, while she's been clearing her things out of the house, but that was a final goodbye. It's over between us. It has been since November.'

Hannah sighed; a giddy, untethered feeling worked its way through her.

'Who spilled the Christmas puddings?' Noah asked, a smile lifting his lips. 'Not Charlie.'

'No, it wasn't Charlie.' Hannah's own smile broke through. Noah's was irresistible; she couldn't help but mirror it. 'Why did we never talk about it, Noah? Why didn't you say, *I want to kiss you?* Then I would have said you couldn't, you were a bastard for even trying, and you could have told me you were single, and everything would have been cleared up.'

'You didn't say *I want to kiss you* either. I thought I'd taken it too far that night, that I was misreading the signs.' He laughed, rubbed a hand down his face. 'And I wasn't sure if it was real, or if it was a rebound thing. It's not, Hannah, you have to know that. The amount of time I've spent thinking about you.'

'But even in Mousehole, when we spent the day together, you never said it outright. I bumbled my way through a ridiculous speech about how nothing could ever happen between us, and you didn't ask me why.'

'I'd convinced myself by then that you didn't want anything more than friendship, but I still wanted to spend time with you. I couldn't help it.'

Hannah laughed, some of her giddiness escaping. 'I couldn't help it either. I wanted to be with you all the time.'

He inched closer. 'Do you think we should try that kiss again?'

The words sent a thrill down Hannah's spine. 'I think we owe it to ourselves to see what it would have been like, if we hadn't been holding back for entirely unnecessary reasons.'

'Let's never tell Gerald about our lack of communication skills.' He was centimetres away, getting closer, but then his smile faltered. 'Hannah, even now, I don't know if this makes sense. You live in Edinburgh, we're so far apart—'

'Not right now, we aren't.' She cupped the back of his head and brought his face to hers, brushing her lips gently against his before taking full possession. This kiss, this real, proper kiss, had been a long time coming, but she knew without question, as his hands found her waist and he brought her body closer to his, until they were pressed against each other in the darkest corner of the Crystal Waters snug, that it had been entirely worth waiting for.

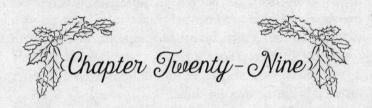

# Chapter Twenty-Nine

Hannah's friends' Christmas – with an entirely new set of friends – was even more celebratory than she had been expecting. When Noah and Hannah made it out of their hiding place in the snug, Daniel led them all through to the private dining room on the other side of the hotel.

'Noah.' Daniel slapped him on the back, then looked between him and Hannah, his eyes narrowing. 'You're too late to help us vanquish the ghosts, but you don't look too disappointed.'

'I'm glad your hotel is back to normal,' Noah said, shaking Daniel's proffered hand.

Daniel exhaled. 'Time to put the past behind us and look forward to Christmas. Speaking of which, Hannah, do you want to take the lead?'

She shrugged off her coat and hung it on a hook in the corridor with the others. She had forgotten she was wearing Lila's dress – at least she had done once she'd come in from the cold and her legs had defrosted – but when she stepped back into the room, Noah's eyes widened in stunned appreciation. She smiled and told everyone to sit at the large round table that she and Charlie had decorated earlier that day.

There were silver and blue crackers, and a central table display of mistletoe and herbs from the hotel gardens – rosemary and sage, and a red-berried plant whose name Hannah didn't know but wasn't holly, the foliage interspersed with twigs that had been spray-painted silver. It smelled heady and aromatic, and she hoped it would awaken everyone's taste buds for the meal to come.

She and Daniel opened bottles of champagne as everyone found seats. There were nine of them altogether – she had asked Hugh to join them – and it felt like a perfectly sized gathering. Noah gestured to the seat next to his, and she nodded before pointing at the corridor. 'Back in a sec.'

In the kitchen the mouthwatering smells were overpowering, and Levi assured her everything was on course. She checked the progress of the sauce, the cod about to go in the oven, the clean scallops waiting to be seared.

'Everyone's ready,' she said, taking her apron off the hook on the wall.

Levi put a hand on her arm. 'We're doing this. Your menu, your prep, our cooking. Go out and enjoy it.'

'I can't,' Hannah replied. 'I know what you said earlier, but I was the one who wanted to do this.'

'And now you need to go and host it. You can't be stuck out here with us, and definitely not in that dress. It's my kitchen and these are my orders,' he said firmly, then grinned at her.

'But—'

'No buts. Go.' He flapped his hands until she'd put the apron back on the hook.

'Thank you, Levi. You have no idea—'

'*Go*, Hannah,' he said, laughing.

Hannah smoothed her hair away from her face, walked back into the dining room and took her seat next to Noah. Daniel nodded at her, and she picked up her glass of champagne.

'I wanted to thank you all for staying on after Audrey's gathering this evening, to have this meal with me. The menu's mine but I've had – am having – a lot of help with the cooking. Levi and his wonderful team of chefs and, also . . .' She glanced at Noah. 'It's tradition for someone else to bring dessert to my friends' Christmases, but I'll get to that later. I have had the best time in Cornwall, and it's been a lot more dramatic than I was expecting.'

Everyone laughed, and it gave her the confidence to carry on. 'So this is to say thank you for having me, for inviting me to stay and have Christmas with you, and for helping me discover that Porthgolow is as special, as meaningful – and magical – as I thought it was.' She raised her glass. 'To friends, and Christmas.'

'To friends and Christmas,' everyone echoed.

'Cheers, Hannah.'

'To the chef!'

'I can't imagine why you're thanking us,' Reenie said. 'We're the ones who get to eat the delicious food you've spent hours preparing. It should be the other way round.'

'This is truly delightful,' Audrey said, raising her glass so her champagne twinkled in the light.

Waiters brought out the first course: scallops with crispy pancetta and pea purée, and a wild mushroom and asparagus tart for Lila. Everyone dug in, appreciative noises soon taking the place of conversation.

Hannah felt Noah's hand brush her knee, but so lightly it could have been one of the ghosts – if they hadn't been sent on their way only an hour before.

'This is amazing, Hannah,' he said, his low voice vibrating through her.

'I'm so glad everyone could come,' she replied. 'I do feel like a bit of a cheat, though, sitting here while Levi finishes and serves my dishes.'

'You can't be stuck in the kitchen tonight.' He laughed gently. 'You need to be out here. Mainly because I would miss you if you weren't.'

Hannah leaned closer to him, her scallops forgotten. She was still reeling. Noah wasn't with Beth. He wanted her. She hadn't mentioned the future beyond the next few days: it was too soon for that, and too complicated, and she planned on enjoying every moment of this evening.

She picked up her glass, and realized that Noah didn't have one. 'You've missed out on the champagne. Why didn't you say?' She reached over for a spare glass, but he put his hand on her arm.

'I have to drive back to Mousehole after this.'

'What? You're driving all the way to Mousehole tonight, then coming back *again* in the morning?'

He frowned at her.

'It's Charlie's last Christmas food market,' she explained. 'The last chance to pick up all the fudge, pigs in blankets and Christmas pudding you need for the big day, not to mention try one of Benji and Jonah's festive Porthgolow Burgers.'

'You want me to come to the food market with you?'

'I'll be going back to Edinburgh next week. I can't live in Daniel's hotel permanently, as glorious as that would be.'

'That's a real shame.' Noah was matching her flippancy, but she could tell he meant it.

'Which is why we have to make the most of the time we have.'

'And I need to drive back to Porthgolow in the morning for the food market.'

'Or,' she said, lifting the champagne bottle out of its bucket and pouring some into the empty glass, 'you could stay here. There's plenty of room in my bed.' She held out the glass to him.

It was a second before he took it. Hannah's whole body fizzed at the intensity of his gaze, then he gave her a heart-stopping smile, and she wondered if she would make it to his dessert. She was almost tempted to say goodnight to everyone that instant and drag Noah to her room.

'What?' she asked, when she'd composed herself. 'Why are you looking at me like that?'

'Because firstly,' he explained, 'it's quite difficult not to look at you when you're so beautiful, and secondly, I am endlessly amazed at how straightforward you are. There's no game playing, no teasing.'

'I can do teasing,' Hannah said coyly. 'But what's the point in not being straightforward? There *is* lots of room in my bed – I think it's a king-size – and there are all sorts of reasons why it makes sense for you to stay in it tonight, but by far the most important one is that I really, really want you to.'

'That's good to know.' He moved his face closer to hers, his voice dropping. 'The feeling, by the way, is entirely mutual.'

'That's a relief,' she whispered, her lips inches from his. 'I'd hate to be talking at cross-purposes *again*.'

'Sometimes talking at all is overrated,' he said, and then he kissed her.

Hannah surrendered to it, though a small part of her was aware that it was highly inappropriate at the table, and that the chatter around them had stopped. She usually hated being the centre of attention, and wasn't entirely comfortable with PDAs, but with Noah it was different. She couldn't get enough of him, and the fact that he wasn't normally an extroverted person, that she knew he was also being ruled by his senses, made it even more electric. They felt the same. There was nothing holding them back, apart from a few hundred miles that she was determined not to think about tonight.

They broke apart to silence and Hannah risked a glance at Charlie: she gave Hannah a knowing look, her lips flickering into a smile.

'I'm not sure the mistletoe on the table warrants *that* kind of kiss,' Reenie said, her eyes twinkling with mischief, 'and you are supposed to be under it, but congratulations.'

'This is a new thing?' Lila asked. 'A Christmas romance?'

Noah cleared his throat. 'It's been a while coming. Ever since we met, actually, but we finally got our act together.'

'You're *perfect* together,' Lila said.

'Hear hear,' Hugh echoed, raising his glass.

Hannah blushed deeply, and was glad of Daniel's interruption.

'This calls for a top-up. I'll get more champagne.'

When she caught Audrey's eye, the other woman gave her a warm smile.

The glasses were refilled and empty plates were replaced

by full ones smelling of herbs and the sea, and Hannah was relieved that her food was more tantalizing than her love life, at least to most people.

Once the main course had been cleared away, Noah's hand found hers. 'You don't have to serve my chocolate log, you know. It's probably awful.' He laughed, but she could tell he was nervous.

'It's going to be delicious,' she said. 'I can't believe you went to all the trouble of making it. Did you find a recipe online?'

'I couldn't find one for exactly what you'd described, so I cobbled a couple together, which was probably a colossal mistake.' He rubbed his forehead. 'I think it's actually—'

'Shh.' She put a finger to his lips. 'Stop stressing. It doesn't matter what it tastes like.'

'There are seven other people round the table who might beg to differ.'

'Then they can have something else, but I don't think they'll want to.'

Noah's pudding was brought to the table with a couple of sparklers stuck in the top, and everyone cheered its arrival. Hannah sliced it into equal parts and then took her time pouring the dark, glossy sauce over the top of each bowlful.

She would remember this moment for ever, she thought. Being in Cornwall, its features in darkness just beyond the glass, her friends inside, her head and heart full of new experiences, pieces of her life that, in only a few weeks, had made her feel so much more complete.

She handed out the bowls, catching Noah's eye.

Daniel was the first to have a mouthful, his eyes widening as it hit his taste buds. 'Bloody hell,' he murmured, and

Hannah, unable to wait a moment longer, lifted her own spoonful to her lips.

The sharp, sour cherry hit her first, quickly followed by the sweet ooze of chocolate and marshmallow, the crunchy biscuit pieces adding the texture that brought everything together.

'Oh my God,' she mumbled, turning to Noah, her words echoing those of others round the table.

'Who made this, then?' Audrey asked. 'Because it is incredible.'

'Noah made it,' Hannah said. 'He made it and brought it with him, and I didn't even know about it until this evening.'

'Noah.' Sam nodded at him. 'Great work. Seriously.'

Hannah squeezed his hand under the table. 'This is perfect,' she whispered. 'Thank you.'

'It makes total sense,' Charlie said, matter-of-factly.

'Why's that?' Reenie asked, before putting a large spoonful in her mouth and closing her eyes in pleasure.

Charlie caught her cousin's eye and Lila laughed. 'It's one of Uncle Hal's sayings,' she explained. 'Hal who left Gertie to Charlie in his will. He said the best food was made with love and extra calories.'

'Love and extra calories,' Noah repeated. 'That sounds about right.' He turned to look at Hannah, and she wondered if he could see how fast her heart was beating. 'Though this particular cooking effort also included quite a lot of swearing.'

'Love, swearing and extra calories,' Charlie said, nodding. 'That seems to sum up quite a lot of life, to be honest.'

'Just as it should be,' Daniel added.

There were nods of agreement, and Hannah sat back in her chair, full in stomach and heart.

After dinner was finished, and after being plied with extra champagne and a lot of flattery from his girlfriend, Sam took the small, maroon-covered hardback she had given him and went to stand by the window. Hannah watched him transform, his posture straightening, his shoulders squaring, and then he opened the book. He paused the perfect length of time as he looked at his audience, his eyes almost golden in the twinkling lights, then his gaze fell to the page.

The room was still and silent, everyone already hooked, waiting for him to speak.

'"Stave One, Marley's Ghost",' he read out in a clear, deep voice that sent shivers down Hannah's spine. '"Marley was dead: to begin with."'

She sat back and, clutching Noah's hand in hers, let Charles Dickens's words, in Sam's beautiful, resonant voice, captivate her. She decided that, as Christmases went, this might turn out to be her best one yet.

Porthgolow was sparkling like a Christmas bauble when Hannah and Noah left the hotel the following morning. Hannah loved the feel of his hand in hers, the way his fingers were both warm and strong, just like the rest of him. She had enjoyed sharing her bed with him – to put it mildly. Their desire for each other had quickly overcome any lingering nerves and, afterwards, she had lain there long after the moon had disappeared from view, the earth rotating away from it, and watched Noah sleep, his dark curls against the pillow, his breaths steady and even.

'Wow,' he said now, when the beach came fully into view, the vans and marquees of the food market bright in the winter sunshine, sounds of laughter and engines, voices and

Christmas music reaching them halfway up the hill. 'This is all Charlie's doing?'

'She started it, and the whole village has embraced it. Doesn't it smell wonderful?' Hannah swung their arms between them. 'I can smell frying onions and curry spice – turmeric I think – and garlic, definitely. There's something sweet, like candyfloss, and maybe cinnamon too – on hot doughnuts? Oh God, I want to eat it all!'

'Even after last night?'

'Of course! We're going to eat our way round – it's not like we haven't worked up an appetite in the meantime.' She gave him a sideways smile and he grinned at her.

He was completely relaxed, the Noah she had spent time with in Mousehole, rather than the reserved, sometimes snappy version she'd encountered during their first week together. She thought now of what he'd been going through, his separation from Beth raw and heartbreaking, and how he'd stayed professional – if not always cheerful – and made sure Hannah and the hotel were the focus of his attention.

'Where first?' he asked. 'Did you say that Hugh has a stall?'

'Charlie told me that he sells his own beer from a tent close to the pub. We should go and say hello.'

'I can't believe that, for all these years, you've been using Hugh's fisherman's pie recipe – and that work brought you here.'

'Some people,' Hannah said, as they stepped onto the sand, 'might say it's fate that I ended up here; that I recognized Reenie's house in my photo and met Hugh again. *Some* people,' she continued, 'might even say that it was fate that you were assigned to this case, and that nobody else from head office was free to come. That everything's worked out the way it has.'

Noah turned to her, halting their progress. 'Some other people would say it was all down to you. You saw the job was in Cornwall, and a subconscious part of your brain knew you had history here; that there was a reason to come back. And as for me . . .' He shook his head.

'What?' She laughed at his pained expression. 'What is it?'

'That was all you, too. As soon as you arrived, you turned my world on its head. Fate had nothing to do with it. It was all Hannah Swan.'

'Oh, really? Well, so is this.' She stretched up on tiptoes to kiss him, and he wrapped his arms around her, the fabric of his coat collar scratching her jaw. 'Now,' she said, once they'd broken apart, 'let's go and find some food.'

The Porthgolow food market was a mini Winter Wonderland without the rides. Competing festive soundtracks were enlivening rather than jarring, all the vendors and customers were smiling, laughing, offering and tasting, and once Noah and Hannah had picked up a takeaway coffee from Gertie – Lila helping Charlie serve on what was clearly a busy day – they wandered between the trucks, trying to narrow down their choices.

'There's something wrong about having a burger for breakfast,' Noah said, as they passed Benji's Burgers and Jonah waved at them.

'It's not that different from steak and eggs,' Hannah said. 'Besides, anything goes at Christmas. The number of times I've had chocolate for breakfast on Christmas Day.' She shook her head.

'Yes, but it's only the twenty-third.'

'You need to let go of the rules. It's my opinion that post-mind-blowing-sex breakfast can be anything you want it to be, so that *combined* with it being two days from Christmas gives you free rein.'

'Mind-blowing,' Noah repeated.

'You think I'd still be here if it wasn't?' she asked innocently, then ran towards the water when he started chasing her, not that disappointed when he caught her easily and lifted her off the ground, all his running paying off, and silenced her laughter with a kiss.

In the end they chose Mexican breakfast boxes: spicy scrambled eggs with chilli wedges, sausage, and chunky, lime-infused guacamole. They found a space on one of the temporary picnic tables that had been set up on the edge of the market, and sat looking out at a sea which was, on this crisp, sunny day, sparkling like sequins. The sky was the palest blue, streaks of white cloud stretching up to the abyss. It was cold, but not achingly so, and Hannah's cheeks were warm.

'God,' she said, unable to keep the emotion from her voice, 'it's so beautiful here.'

Noah didn't reply. She glanced at him, but he was focused on his breakfast. 'When are you going back?' he asked eventually.

'I've got a train booked on the twenty-eighth. It's not going to take much longer than usual either, so – y'know. Happy days.' She had booked it yesterday afternoon, before she'd got changed into Lila's dress. Speaking to Hugh and then her mum had made her resolute, and she had finally stopped dithering. The whole thing had taken less than five minutes. And then, of course, Noah had shown up. But what could she do? Her life was in Edinburgh.

'Your mum will be glad to have you back. And Gerald,' Noah said.

344

'His newest employee, who only got *slightly* sidetracked on her first job.' She laughed, but there was no real humour behind it. 'We can finish the Crystal Waters costings in the New Year, can't we? Daniel's OK with where we're up to.'

'He's happy to get the final report in January, so we'll pick it up as soon as the festivities are over. I do wonder, though, if it's really what you want to do.' Behind them, the jaunty notes of 'Fairytale of New York' filled the silence.

Hannah didn't know how to respond, and Noah continued.

'I think you know what I'm saying, because I've said it before. You were thorough and interested, you listened and you had ideas. You're a great eco-consultant, Hannah. But are you passionate about it?'

'I haven't been doing it for long,' she protested.

'But last night with your meal, and this market,' he continued. 'You love being here. I can tell, because your whole face is alive with it. You recognize all the smells, you're interested in the flavours and the processes – telling that guy he had the best guacamole you'd ever tasted, asking how he made it. That's passion. And last night . . .' he added, dropping his voice. 'There was passion there, too.'

Hannah laughed, her cheeks colouring. 'That's completely different and you know it!' She resisted the urge to throw a spicy wedge at him – they were too delicious to waste.

'Of course it is.' His smile dimpled his cheek, making him look impossibly gorgeous. 'But there's a difference between being passionate about something, and being conscientious and efficient – wanting to do a good job. You trained to be an eco-consultant because of your dad, because saving the planet is *his* passion.'

'It was part of the reason. But I spent a long time getting that qualification.'

'And while you were doing it, what did you enjoy more? Studying, or working at the Whisky Cellar?'

She narrowed her eyes. 'You know when you said that you liked how straightforward I was?'

'You're not enjoying being on the receiving end?' he asked, then shrugged. 'I'm not going to apologize for saying it, but I also know I *can* say it, because you'll do what you want – listen to me or ignore me completely. You know all I want is for you to be happy.'

Hannah's throat thickened. 'At this moment I am very, very happy. Sitting here with you, my toes numb but my face warm, this view and this breakfast. I couldn't be any happier, I don't think. My future is . . .' She sighed. 'My future is a different thing altogether.'

'Because I'm not wrong?' Noah asked softly.

'Because there are things that I want now that I didn't want a few weeks ago, and I have to work out what to do about that.' She smiled, but she had some tough decisions ahead of her. Now, however, two days before Christmas, she felt justified in putting them out of her mind. *One step at a time, Hannah.* 'The most important thing,' she said, 'is how long do you think it'll be before you're ready to eat something else?'

He stared at her and held up his fork, on which was speared a potato wedge and a piece of sausage. 'I haven't even finished *this* breakfast. How many are you expecting us to fit in?'

'I don't know yet,' Hannah said. 'When we're done, let's walk the length of the beach and then decide what comes next. And there's no hurry. We've got all day – just you and me.' Those four words, in that order, were currently her favourite.

*

By the time they made it on board Gertie, their shoes and jeans were crusted with sea water, they were laden with bags from the fudge stall and the luxury Cornish chocolate stand, and Hannah had been sold a large tub of sweet and salty popcorn by the most persuasive salesman she had ever encountered.

'Hannah, Noah,' Lila said as they came on board. 'This table has just become free, do you fancy a cream tea?'

Noah groaned, and Hannah gave her what she hoped was a placatory smile. 'I'm not sure either of us could eat another thing right now. We just came to say hello.'

'Hello!' Charlie echoed, putting her chin on her cousin's shoulder. 'Fun day?'

'The most.' Hannah nodded.

'I think I'm going to pop,' Noah said. 'Your food market is dangerous, Charlie.'

'I'd guess that's more the company you're keeping,' Charlie replied, laughing. 'What are you going to do with all that popcorn?'

'Film night?' Hannah suggested. 'Perhaps we can persuade Daniel to put on some Christmas films in the snug, if there isn't any cricket.'

'*Die Hard*,' Lila said. 'And *Elf*. And *The Muppet Christmas Carol*. I'd be up for that.'

'Rhys is very persuasive, isn't he?' Charlie gave Hannah a pitying look.

'It's organic popcorn,' she said defensively. 'The sample was delicious.' Noah wrapped an arm round her waist and she felt instantly mollified.

'I told you, it's dangerous. And not just because I'm here with Cornwall's biggest foodie.'

'*Edinburgh's* biggest foodie,' Hannah corrected, feeling suddenly forlorn. 'I have no claims on Cornwall.'

'You have a claim on Noah now,' Charlie said, 'and he's as Cornish as they come. He's got the accent, the fisherman dad, the belief in piskies and suchlike.'

'And he's a classic sexy surfer-boy behind those glasses and smart jumpers,' Lila added. 'He's fooling nobody.'

'Steady on,' Noah said, but Hannah could see he was pleased with their assessment. 'But you're right about one thing.' He hugged her closer and planted a swift, slightly self-conscious kiss on her head. 'She's claimed me completely.'

'Oh, you guys,' Lila cooed. 'You're adorable. You do realize you're going to have to buy a plane, though.'

'What?' Hannah and Noah said in unison, Noah sounding especially horrified by the idea.

Lila shrugged. 'Travelling between Edinburgh and Cornwall is going to take up a *lot* of time. Flying's the only way it's going to work.'

'They can't do that,' Charlie said. 'I mean, aside from your ridiculous notion of them buying their own plane – all this acting stuff has clearly gone to your head – they can't even hop on the commercial flights between Edinburgh and Newquay, because it's against everything they believe in.'

Lila stared blankly at Charlie and she rolled her eyes.

'Because they're *eco*-consultants, Delilah. The whole reason they're in Porthgolow is because they're trying to make Crystal Waters more environmentally friendly. They want to save the planet, not add to the pollution.'

'But if the flights are going anyway,' Lila said. 'I mean – they can't be apart for long periods of time. Look at them. They're besotted with each other.'

'We are actually here, guys.' Hannah waved. 'Hello.'

'So what will you do?' Lila turned towards them, her arms folded. 'I can promise you it's not much fun having hundreds of miles between you and the person you love, even for a few weeks.'

Hannah glanced up at Noah just as he looked down, a frown on his face. It was the one thing Hannah hadn't wanted to think about, but even while she was hiding in her blissful bubble with Noah, she knew she couldn't be in denial for ever.

And then Noah said, 'I'd break the rules and clock up the air miles for you, Hannah. I don't want us to be apart.'

The sincerity of his sentiment, the magnitude of what he was prepared to sacrifice for her, made her feel giddy, and when she tore her eyes away from his, she saw she wasn't the only one who had been moved by his words. Both Charlie and Lila were blinking back tears.

# Chapter Thirty

Hannah woke on Christmas morning, the other side of the bed empty. She would be seeing Noah later, but he'd told her that if he didn't have Christmas lunch with his parents then they might refuse to speak to him ever again. Hannah knew how close he was to his family, and wasn't about to get in the way of something so precious. He had asked her if she wanted to come, and while Hannah was tempted, she felt that it was too much of an imposition – too much too soon. They had been together all of two and a half days. Besides, Hannah had accepted Charlie and Lila's kind invitation, and she wasn't going to change her mind again.

Noah had gone back to Mousehole the evening before, and would be driving to Porthgolow later that afternoon.

'You'll be able to do the route between Porthgolow and Mousehole with your eyes closed soon,' Hannah had said, as they stood next to his car.

'Not something I'd ever attempt, even if I felt confident enough. But I don't mind the drive.' He'd patted his expensive Land Rover, and Hannah had been reminded of the luxury-tinged awkwardness of that first night, when she'd climbed into the passenger seat and attempted to spark up a conversation. 'What are you grinning about?' he'd asked and, as she reached up to kiss him, she had wondered whether to be honest.

'I was thinking how much more I like you now than I did the night we met.'

Noah had rolled his eyes. 'You don't need to remind me how much of an idiot I was. I remember.'

'I know,' she'd replied, brushing away his frown with her thumb, 'but it made it all the more surprising, and welcome, when it turned out you were actually a good guy. An *amazing* guy, in fact.' She'd shown him just how much her opinion of him had changed, kissing him until Lila had whooped at them from the doorway and they'd broken apart, embarrassed.

Hannah snapped back to the present – she couldn't stay in bed daydreaming about Noah. It was Christmas Day, after all. She showered and dressed, phoned her mum and Mike to wish them Happy Christmas, then took Spirit and walked down the hill.

She strolled the full length of the beach with him, while the waves crunched against the sand and scribbles of white danced across a blue winter sky. She lost herself to the sights, sounds and smells of Cornwall, and let her thoughts drift through her mind like the clouds.

She had been worried about what to do with her morning, while everyone else was with their loved ones, opening presents and stockings. Hannah had made the choice to be here, and she had known she would be alone for some of the day. Audrey had checked out of the hotel the morning after their meal, in the same flurry of colourful chaos with which she'd arrived. She'd said warm goodbyes, swapped contact details with Hannah, and assured Daniel she would run her chapter by him before the book went anywhere near publication. He'd nodded and smiled and not completely hidden his relief at her departure.

Hannah had asked Levi if she could help in the kitchen on Christmas morning, to pay him back for his generosity, but Daniel had vetoed it, saying she'd done enough work. So instead she spent the morning with the Cornish landscape, and with the little dog that seemed perfectly content, despite not knowing quite where he fitted in the world. Hannah wished it was so easy not to care, but as she let her toes sink into the sand – the sensation pleasant after the initial shock of cold against her bare skin – she realized that her wants and desires were making their way to the front of her mind, refusing to be ignored. She just didn't know if she had the confidence to act on them.


The Christmas dinner Hannah attended was served, late afternoon, in the restaurant. Daniel had overseen the earlier meal held for the guests, checking they had everything they needed, and now, while they slept or relaxed or walked off their turkey and roast potatoes in the village, it was the turn of the Porthgolow residents.

Hannah sat at a table with Charlie and Daniel, Lila and Sam, Reenie and Hugh. The Kerr family, of which the prank-playing Jonah was a member, were at another table, and Myrtle was there with her friends, Rose and Frank. Charlie explained that her best friend Juliette and her new husband

Lawrence, who Hannah hadn't met, were in France with Juliette's family, but that she hoped she'd be able to introduce them to Hannah next time she visited.

The restaurant was the most decorated area of the hotel, as if Daniel had allowed a full Christmas explosion in this room alone: The large Christmas tree in one corner had no discernible colour scheme, the decorations a riot of different shades; silver and blue garlands hung from the ceiling, and there was even some tinsel – superior tinsel, she was sure Daniel would say – draped over the frames of the pictures adorning the walls. Each table had a candle in a shimmering silver candlestick in the centre, along with a holly sprig, the berries a pop of red. Crackers sat at each place setting, waiting to be pulled.

'This is beautiful,' Lila said as she took her seat. Hannah noticed she was wearing a delicate necklace with a tiny opal teardrop that she hadn't seen before.

'It's a bit special,' Hannah agreed.

The whole thing was offset, of course, by the view beyond the glass. The sun had already begun to slip away, but it was doing so spectacularly: a peach melba ball hovering above a choppy sea.

'Happy Christmas Lila, Sam.' They clinked glasses. 'Have you had a good day so far?'

'Blissful,' Lila said, stretching her arms up to the ceiling.

'Lazy,' Sam added. 'What about you, Hannah?'

'It's been quiet, but good. I've spoken to my family, and Noah's with his folks, but he's going to be here for your big moment.' She grinned.

Sam groaned and Lila patted him on the shoulder. 'He's got a few launch-day jitters. But he needs to remember that he's *amazing* as Robert Bramerton, and that it's a sparkling production, entirely fit for the prime slot on Christmas Day.'

'I can't believe I'm going to be watching the first episode of *Estelle* with two of its stars,' Hannah said.

'One star and one add-on,' Lila corrected. 'I'm barely in this series, and my role in the second one is small. Sam's the main attraction.'

'It's an ensemble drama—' he started, but Lila cut him off.

'He's great, Hannah, don't believe the modesty. I'm so glad we're watching it together. Do you still have that bucket of popcorn you bought at the food market?'

Hannah grinned. 'I've saved it specially.'

Levi's menu was delicious; a traditional Christmas dinner with every aspect elevated. Starters of pork terrine or wild mushroom pâté with crispy fried bread, or smoked salmon and dill mayonnaise, everything delicately assembled, every flavour zinging on Hannah's tongue. The turkey was succulent, the roast potatoes were a masterpiece, and the pigs in blankets were the right amount of crispy and salty. Lila's vegetarian wellington looked wonderful; the pastry perfectly flaky, the inside bursting with winter vegetables. Levi had even, on Hannah's suggestion, added some deep-fried Brussels sprouts, and she thought they might be her favourite part of the whole meal. She had asked him to keep a few back so that Noah could try them when he got there.

Reenie held court over their table, keeping them entertained with her acerbic wit and teasing them all equally; even Hannah, who had thought she would escape her attention.

'How's your holiday romance going, Hannah? I hope you're making the most of it.'

Hannah felt herself blush. 'It's going very well, thank you,' she said, and cringed at how prim she sounded. 'I mean, I'm loving spending time with Noah. I love – that is . . . uhm.'

'He's coming over later, isn't he?' Charlie asked, rescuing her.

Hannah nodded vigorously. 'He should be here soon. His family eats earlier in the day, and he wanted to watch *Estelle* with us.'

'Not just that, I'm sure,' Reenie said. 'Of course, everyone wants to watch this handsome young fellow strutting about on the screen,' she gestured towards Sam. 'But I'm not convinced that will be at the top of Noah's Christmas to-do list.'

'He remembers it being filmed,' Hannah said hurriedly. 'I think he's really looking forward to it.'

'What are you going to do after this?' Reenie asked.

'After Christmas dinner?'

'You're going back to Edinburgh next week, aren't you? What will you and Noah do then?'

Hannah expected to see a smirk, but Reenie seemed genuinely interested and, she thought, sympathetic, which made her feel suddenly wretched. 'I don't know,' she confessed.

'You didn't cook any of this meal, did you?' Hugh asked, changing the subject. 'I would have thought you could do with a rest.'

'Daniel wouldn't let me,' she admitted, pushing her conundrum to the back of her mind. 'Besides, paying guests were fed today too, so it makes sense that I wasn't let loose in the kitchen.'

'Don't sell yourself short,' Sam said. 'You're a proper chef; we all know that after the other night.'

'I'm lookin' for a new chef for the pub,' Hugh said. 'Colin's headin' off to New Zealand, of all places – though why he'd want to leave somewhere as beautiful as Cornwall, I'll never know – so I'll be advertisin'. I only hope I'll get someone with your skill, Hannah. That fisherman's pie needs to be right, or it's my reputation down the drain.'

'Your head chef gets to know your family recipe?' Lila asked. 'You act like it's a state secret!'

'I can't be everywhere in that pub at once, Delilah love. I need to put my trust in someone.'

'I'm very trustworthy,' Lila said. 'If you just tell me . . .'

Hugh was shaking his head, Lila pleading with him and fluttering her eyelashes, when Noah walked in. He looked self-conscious – as well he might wearing a Christmas jumper with snowflakes and a flashing penguin – but he was also, Hannah knew without a doubt, the most attractive man in the room. She shot to her feet, rattling the crockery on the table, and he smiled.

'Happy Christmas, Hannah,' he said. 'Happy Christmas everyone. I hope now is a good time for me to be here.'

'Too bad if it's not, isn't it?' Reenie stood up to give him a hug. 'Come and sit next to me.'

'You're just in time for pudding,' Lila said.

'Oh God, really?' Noah clutched his stomach.

'Did you have a good meal with your mum and dad?' Hannah asked, as Noah pulled up a spare chair and squeezed into the gap between her and Reenie.

'It was great,' he said. 'Even though they spent most of the time berating me for not bringing you. They both really like you, Hannah.' He said it lightly, but there was something in his expression that squeezed at her heart.

'What did they get you?' Lila asked.

'A new running watch,' Noah said, 'some stripy socks, which is a family tradition, and this.' He pointed at the jumper. 'I am, of course, delighted to see I'm the only one wearing a ridiculous festive jumper, which is what I told them would be the case before they packed me into the car to come over here. They've achieved their goal of embarrassing me.'

'As is every parent's right,' Reenie said, nodding approvingly. 'How do I make him light up again?'

Noah sighed. 'Press his nose.'

Reenie did, and the penguin flashed blue. She chuckled.

Hannah leaned towards him and said, 'What happens if I press *your* nose?'

He narrowed his eyes. 'I don't know yet. Let me have a think, and you can try it later.'

She laughed, gave him a kiss, and turned back to the table in time to see Daniel whisper in Charlie's ear and get up.

'He can't leave it alone,' Charlie said. 'He just *has* to go and check something in the kitchen, even during his own Christmas dinner.'

'Are you really surprised?' Lila sat back in her chair. 'Honestly, I'm surrounded by people who actually *want* to work. It's crazy.'

'You've ensured you never have to work again, though,' Reenie said. 'Acting isn't exactly taxing, and Sam's rich and famous now, so if this *Estelle* business isn't all it's cracked up to be, next year you can jack it in and become a lady of leisure.'

Lila gasped. 'Reenie Teague, you are shockingly rude!'

'And you,' Reenie said, 'are hideously gullible. Actors work a lot harder than some, as I understand it, even if they do get to swan around in luxury between projects.

And you know I love you, Lila, but you're the easiest to wind up.'

Charlie put a hand on her cousin's arm while she bristled.

'Where do you run, Noah?' Sam asked, but before he could reply the lights were dimmed, enhancing the sparkle of the Christmas tree, the candles and, beyond the windows, the faintest line of rose gold edging the horizon.

'What's going on?' Lila whispered, just as Levi emerged from the kitchen carrying a huge Christmas pudding, alight with a brilliant blue flame. Hannah was instantly captivated, and almost jumped out of her seat when there was a loud, 'Ho-ho-ho!' from behind the chef. She glanced in Hugh's direction, but he was still sitting in his chair.

'Oh for goodness' sake,' Lila muttered, as Santa walked out of the kitchen. A Santa who, Hannah saw, had no padding, but strong shoulders. The dark, intelligent eyes beneath the fur-trimmed bobble hat latched firmly onto Charlie.

Realization dawned on Hannah as everyone started clapping. A knot of excitement tightened in her stomach and she squeezed Noah's hand. He gave her a quizzical look, but didn't say anything.

'I'm looking for Charlene Quilter,' Santa boomed. 'Has she been good this year?'

Charlie raised her hand. Her cheeks were red, and she was shaking her head, trying hard not to laugh. 'Over here,' she called.

Santa walked over to her, then dipped his head, rummaging in the sack he was carrying. Hannah looked round at the incredulous faces of the people who knew him best of all, and wondered if any of them had worked it out. From the looks on their faces, she didn't think so. Daniel Harper, all cool confidence and easy charm; the suave, professional hotelier, dressed as Santa Claus.

He rummaged for a few more seconds then said a loud, 'Aha,' and dropped onto one knee in front of Charlie.

The room went pin-drop quiet.

Charlie stopped shaking her head and froze, her chest rising in a silent breath.

'Charlie,' Daniel started, pulling the beard down so his whole face was visible, and Lila whispered, 'Oh my God.'

'Charlie Quilter,' he said again, louder this time, as he looked up at her. 'I have no idea if you knew this was coming, but you probably did because I am incapable of hiding anything from you.' He put the sack on the floor and held out a navy blue velvet box, snapping it open to reveal the diamond ring inside. Charlie's eyes widened as the room filled with coos and 'aahs' and 'wows'.

'The last eighteen months of my life have been nothing short of brilliant,' he continued, 'and that is all down to you. I am so happy that you didn't put up with my bullshit, that you gave as good as you got and somehow found it in yourself to see the good in me.

'And I have seen nothing but good in you, from the way you run Gertie, to the kindness and generosity you show everyone you meet, and I am so lucky to be loved by you. Would you do me the honour – an honour I'm not sure I deserve, but will do everything in my power to earn – of marrying me? Will you be my wife, Charlie?'

Tears stung Hannah's eyes. Charlie had them running down her cheeks. The room was still and silent: a bubble of anticipation.

'Oh Daniel,' Charlie sobbed. She held out her hand, fingers splayed. 'Of course I will! Nothing would make me happier.'

Daniel's smile was a combination of elation and relief as he slid the ring onto her finger and then wrapped his arms around his new fiancée, tilting his head up for a kiss. The room erupted into applause.

'I bloody knew it,' Lila said, raising her hands above her head to clap. 'This has been on the cards for *months*. Doing it as Santa is genius – Charlie loves Christmas! Oh God, what an amazing couple they are. What an *amazing* proposal! And look at that ring.' Her face crumpled into tears, and Sam pulled her against him, grinning and kissing the top of her head.

'Not a dry eye,' Hugh said. Even he looked slightly overcome.

'The Porthgolow dynasty is cemented,' Reenie added, grinning. 'This, more than anything, has cheered me up today.'

'I can't believe you proposed to me as Father Christmas,' Charlie said, once she and Daniel had stopped kissing. 'You are a ridiculous, soppy, wonderful man.'

'Ridiculous, soppy, wonderful *fiancé*,' he corrected. 'I was bloody nervous, I have to admit.'

'Oh, as *if* Charlie would have said no,' Lila sniffed. 'You two are perfect together. I am so happy for you, and I can't wait to help you plan the wedding.'

Daniel and Charlie got up and accepted hugs and congratulations from everyone. The room seemed to shimmer with happiness, though that could have been the tears in Hannah's eyes making everything blurry.

'Did you know?' Noah asked, once they were all sitting again and the Christmas pudding had been remembered.

Hannah shrugged. 'I guessed a couple of days ago. Just some things Daniel said and did, the way he was behaving, that made everything slot into place.'

'It makes it a rather unforgettable Christmas.' Noah reached over and took a spoonful of her Christmas pudding.

'It does,' Hannah said, laughing. 'There are so many reasons that I'll never forget this Christmas, but Daniel's proposal isn't the main one.' She leaned towards Noah and planted a kiss on his nose. She hoped that small gesture was enough to show him what she meant.

The snug filled up while Daniel switched on the large flatscreen television built into the wall, and once everyone was settled with drinks, and Hannah's big bucket of popcorn had been distributed – Charlie miraculously finding some traditional red-and-white-striped paper bags from somewhere – he turned the lights down.

The Christmas tree sparkled in the corner, and Hannah snuggled against Noah, his arm around her shoulder, his fingers playing with the fabric of her dress. Spirit, Marmite and Jasper, who had been allowed to join them for this momentous occasion, were lying under the TV, acting as if they were the main event. 'Typical Marmite behaviour,' Charlie had said, shaking her head.

As the BBC announcer introduced the 'fabulous, eerie new drama', and *Estelle*'s atmospheric theme music was accompanied by cheers and whoops, Hannah found herself unable to focus. The day's events couldn't keep thoughts of the future at bay. She had found so much in Porthgolow that made her happy, and while she hadn't considered herself miserable in Edinburgh, the last few weeks had made her look at her life in a new light.

'You OK?' Noah asked, against the sound of hooves cantering across clifftops. 'Your shoulders are rigid.' He gently massaged her arm, his touch sending a wave of desire through her.

'I'm wondering what will happen . . .' She trailed off, unsure how to voice her worries.

'To the characters?'

Hannah shook her head. 'To Spirit,' she said, which, in all honesty, *was* one of the things concerning her. 'Daniel's had no luck tracking down his original owner, and with Jasper and Marmite already, and the hotel and Gertie to run, they can't take him. Lila and Sam will be travelling too much, and I know he doesn't want to, but I think Daniel's going to have to take him to a rescue centre in the New Year.' She looked up to see Reenie glaring at her, and dropped her head. 'We should watch the show,' she whispered.

She was silent after that, but her thoughts refused to settle, even though *Estelle* was captivating, and Sam shone as brightly as Lila had promised in his starring role. Afterwards, there was another round of congratulations, more drinks poured and toasts made. Hannah felt slightly removed, even though Charlie and Daniel had been at pains to include her in everything. While everyone was talking, she slipped out of the room and crouched down by the Christmas tree in reception, retrieving the gift she'd left there earlier that day.

'I've been thinking,' Noah said behind her, and Hannah spun round, surprised. 'What's that?' he asked, pointing at the present.

'I got you something. It's only small, but—'

'Hannah, you didn't have to.'

'It was before we got together. Before I met you in this very spot, in fact, and you'd sent Spirit to go and find me, wearing my scarf.'

Noah laughed, his eyes dancing. 'That was a stupid idea.'

'No it wasn't. What were you going to say? You came out here and said you'd been thinking.'

'Oh, yes.' He pushed his glasses up his nose, the gesture so unconsciously sexy that Hannah wanted to remove them and kiss him senseless. 'It's about Spirit,' he said. 'About him not having anywhere to go. I've decided that, as long as nobody claims him, I'll adopt him. I've grown up with dogs, my garden at home is tiny but there's the beach to walk him on – he can come on my runs if he's up for it. I'd hate for us to lose him.'

'So would I. And at least if I know he's with you, I can think of you in Mousehole together. You'll have to send me photos.'

'Hannah,' Noah said softly, 'I'm not letting you go that easily. Whatever happens, however long we have to spend apart, you're not going back to Edinburgh without a plan for us to see each other again. It's not happening.'

'It's not?'

'You and me. We're not just for Christmas. There's more to it – more to us. You feel it, don't you?'

'Of course I do. But—'

'No "buts". We're both good at planning: we can redesign hotels to exact, sustainably advantageous specifications, down to the last recycled bottle top. We can bloody well work out how to make the distance between Edinburgh and Cornwall *seem* smaller, even if it isn't. You're my missing piece, Hannah. We belong together.'

He bent his head and kissed her, the lights of the Christmas tree shimmering in the dim hotel reception, the celebrations continuing in the snug.

And as Hannah realized there was no point in worrying

about tomorrow when she could be kissing Noah today, the clock ticked round to eleven thirteen, and some faint but definite footsteps echoed in the quiet space, a breath moved Hannah's hair and, even in the middle of the deepest, most tender kiss of her life, she caught the unmistakable scent of lavender.

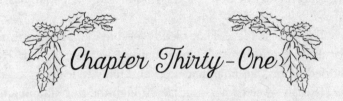

# Chapter Thirty-One

Hannah's train rolled into Newquay station on time; even though it was already dark and bitterly cold, she knew she was about to get a welcome that was infinitely warmer than the one she'd had the last time she'd been in this situation. She smiled to herself, remembering how Noah had been as cold as the weather, and how much had changed since then.

She wrapped her rainbow scarf around her neck, put on her coat and hefted her huge suitcase down from the luggage rack. A man with silver-grey hair took one end as she wobbled dangerously, and then lifted it down the steps for her. She thanked him and peered at his face, but there was no flash of recognition.

'Bit of a strange time of year to be 'avin' an 'oliday,' he said in a broad Cornish accent.

'Oh, it's not a holiday,' Hannah replied, keen to strike up

a conversation with this stranger. Keen, in fact, to tell anyone who would listen. 'I'm moving here.'

'To Newquay? In the depths of winter? You're a braver lass than me, and I'm not even a lass!' He chuckled, and Hannah grinned.

'It's Porthgolow, actually. I'm going to be the new chef in the pub there. The Seven Stars. I don't know if you've heard of it?'

'The village, I 'ave. That bleddy food market. Best burgers for miles around, mind. Got it marked in me calendar.' He smiled, doffed an imaginary cap and left her to it.

Hannah wheeled her suitcase through the tiny station and out into the car park. This time she didn't have to scout around for her lift, because he was there, leaning against his shiny Land Rover, Spirit on a lead at his feet, already barking. She dropped to a crouch and accepted the dog's fevered greeting, letting him lick her hands and burrow his nose into her neck. Eventually she stood up, and Noah gave her a wry smile.

'Missed him, did you?'

'A lot,' Hannah said gravely. 'Almost as much as I missed you.'

'Almost?'

'Well, OK. I missed him more, but it would have been nice to see you, too. My bed was cold.' She gave him her saddest expression, and he laughed.

'Come here.' He bridged the gap between them, tilted her chin up and gave her a kiss so passionate and purposeful, so full of promise for the months and years stretching ahead, that Hannah felt weak at the knees. This was her man, her future. Her happiness.

When the kiss was over, Noah put her case in the boot and opened the back door. Spirit jumped up willingly.

'Have you got him trained?' Hannah asked, her eyes wide.

'Barely. He's spent too much time with Marmite to be well-behaved. But we rub along OK. Your flat in Porthgolow's all set up?'

'Yup. I called Hugh yesterday and everything's ready, except – perhaps – for me.' She squeezed her hands together.

'What do you mean?'

'Can I really be in charge of my own kitchen?' she asked him, seriously.

'Hannah, of course you can.' He turned to her, the car keys in his hand. 'You were meant to do this. And you're lucky that Hugh got in there first, that you've got the flat above the pub and an entire kitchen to make your own. My mum would have had you at the deli, making coffees and lunch rolls, if she'd had her way. You will be brilliant as the Seven Stars head chef, and I know Hugh's over the moon about it.'

'Have you been spending a lot of time in Porthgolow without me?' she asked, feeling a twinge of envy.

'Don't look so forlorn,' he said, laughing. 'You've only been gone a month, though it's felt a lot longer. Charlie and Daniel are already thinking about their wedding, and Sam and Lila have rented a cottage in the village, so they'll be there too, at least until the second series of *Estelle* has finished filming.'

'Sounds as if there's loads I need to catch up on.'

'We'd better get going, then.'

As they drove, Noah told her about everything she'd missed while she'd been in Edinburgh, although in truth they'd spoken and FaceTimed so often that hardly any of it was new. She'd loved seeing him in his house, with the snow globe she'd bought him for Christmas – a Cornish port town blanketed by sparkling flakes, which she'd found in the depths of Myrtle's Pop-In and dusted off – on his desk, where he worked on saving the planet one project at a time.

She had told him, in turn, about her various goodbyes. Her mum was tearful but, she thought, happy that Hannah was finding her own way, even if it meant a drastic change of career path so soon after qualifying. Gerald had been shocked and disappointed to lose her, and threatened to take Noah off the books for the part he'd played in her jumping ship, and Saskia had been devastated she was moving so far away, until Hannah showed her photos of Porthgolow and they put a date in the calendar for her to visit in the spring. Hannah was also looking forward to her mum and Mike coming to see her sooner rather than later, and her mum's long-overdue reunion with a certain kind-hearted publican.

It had felt difficult, at first, to dismantle her life there, losing her walks through the Edinburgh streets, always interesting and full of life; her get-togethers with her friends; her family being so close by. But, as she put everything in motion for the move – changing her address with Royal Mail, cancelling her lease with her landlord, going through her flat and deciding what to keep and what to give away – her excitement mounted. And there were the messages, calls and photos from Noah and Spirit, from Charlie and Lila, to remind her why she was doing it and what was waiting for her at the other end.

Throughout the car journey she kept her hand over Noah's on the gear stick, squeezing it or tracing the shape of his knuckles with a finger, Spirit snoring loudly on the back seat.

It was the end of January, and even colder than it had been in December, but Hannah didn't care. Porthgolow Bay appeared below them as they reached the top of the hill, the houses lit up like a constellation, Crystal Waters gleaming on the opposite side of the cove. Hannah felt a flash of nostalgia for all that had happened there, all the emotions she'd felt during those few weeks.

Noah parked in the car park of the Seven Stars, its pub sign illuminated in the dark. He got out and came round to open Hannah's door before she'd had a chance to undo her seatbelt.

'Your castle awaits,' he said with a flourish, helping her down from her seat.

Hannah looked up at her new home. Hugh had warned her that, being above a pub, the flat on the first floor would be noisy, even once she'd finished her shift. But Hannah had been used to late nights at the Whisky Cellar and, living in Edinburgh, had rarely had quiet outside her flat. Besides, this was a sleepy village pub, not a nightclub. She had assured him she felt nothing but excitement for her new job and accommodation: she would wake up to the sound of the sea, its ever-shifting moods right on her doorstep.

'OK?' Noah asked quietly.

'I am every inch OK,' she said, turning to him. 'You're coming for dinner, aren't you? Are you staying, you and Spirit?'

'If you'll have us. Unless you want to get settled in tonight?'

'That is exactly what I want to do.' She tugged the lapels of his coat, bringing him closer. 'And I want to do it with you. I don't mind how we split our time between here and Mousehole. I won't be working every evening, and you'll *always* be welcome here, Noah. I came back for you: I want you to be part of my life. And I know it's an hour's drive between here and Mousehole, but—'

'Don't worry about that,' he said. 'I was all set to plan for the gap between Cornwall and Edinburgh, so Porthgolow to Mousehole is nothing. I think you were the one who said I could drive the route with my eyes closed.' He looked down at her, a dark curl falling onto his forehead and a smile whispering on his lips.

'I've changed my mind,' she said. 'Please don't try it, Noah.' She tugged harder at his coat, bringing him closer.

They kissed and kissed, making up for the missed days and weeks, while the waves beat out a rhythm on Porthgolow beach and Crystal Waters sat, like a modern-day lighthouse, on top of the cliff. Hannah was aware only of Noah, of his taste and his touch, his hands pressed against the small of her back, his lips on hers, warm and content in their bubble of two. Eventually they broke apart, and Noah brushed a strand of hair out of her eyes before taking her case from the boot and opening the door to let Spirit down.

'Inside?' she asked.

'Lead the way,' he said.

She held out her hand and he took it, and with Spirit close at their heels, they walked into the warmth and welcome of the Seven Stars.

This, Hannah thought, as Hugh came around the bar to greet them, was her new life. She had left everything behind and started afresh, throwing a fair amount of caution to the wind. And while it was very early days, she knew from the excitement that thrummed through her when she thought of running her own kitchen, from the happiness she felt being back in Porthgolow, and the way her pulse quickened when she looked at Noah, that this was exactly where she was supposed to be.

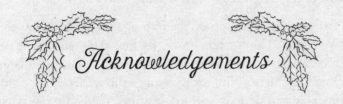

# Acknowledgements

I started *The Cornish Cream Tea Christmas* just before lockdown arrived, so most of it was written – not to mention all the edits, proofreading, and other stages that come after that initial first draft – in our altered world. This has made it more of a challenge but has also proved to be another reminder of all the incredible people who have helped make this book a reality.

Kate Bradley, my brilliant editor, has been a voice of reason, warmth and good humour throughout the whole thing. She took my first draft and showed me how to make it shine and sparkle, as all good Christmas books should.

My agent, Hannah Ferguson, has also been amazing and has supported and inspired me at a time when it was easy to feel isolated. The whole Hardman and Swainson team have adapted quickly, and I've found their guidance invaluable.

The HarperFiction team has been as dedicated as ever, ensuring my book is as polished as it can be, making it look beautiful and getting it into the hands of readers. Thank you to Penny Isaac for her copy-editing wisdom and attention to detail, and to designer Holly Macdonald and illustrator May Van Millingen for the stunning Christmassy covers. Thank you also to Katy Blott and Lara Stevenson, Kim Young and Fliss Denham.

I arrived at Book Camp on the 16th of March, which was the day the UK Government made its first daily statement on Coronavirus. It was a scary time, but being isolated in a large house in Somerset with my favourite writing friends felt right, somehow, and we managed to get words written despite what was happening. So a massive thank you to Cesca Major, Rachael Lucas, Holly Martin, Katy Colins, Emily Kerr, Pernille Hughes, Ali Harris, Tasmina Perry and Basia Martin – and also to Kirsty Greenwood, Isabelle Broom, Jo Quinn, Cathy Bramley and Liz Fenwick who were with us virtually. That week will always be woven into the fabric of *The Cornish Cream Tea Christmas*.

To David, who has kept me sane – and not just while I was writing this book. My Zoom Diet Coke Break man, and the only lockdown, and life partner I ever want.

To Mum, Dad and Lee, for just being the best. Always.

Now more than ever, books are providing a much-needed escape, and I say that as a writer and a reader. If I didn't have readers, then my stories – the places I create and escape to in my head – wouldn't ever be brought to life, and I am so happy, and so lucky, that they are. Thank you for picking up this book. I hope it is the sparkling, romantic and Christmassy read you were hoping for.

# Cressy's Christmas away from home...

I have only had one Christmas away from home, but it was in Australia so I did it properly. Kate, my best friend since secondary school, had the opportunity to do the second year of her degree out there, and when she asked if I wanted to come and see her for a month over Christmas I jumped at the chance. The two of us had spent six weeks between A-levels and university backpacking up the East Coast from Brisbane to Cairns, and it was one of the best things I'd ever done, so going back was an easy decision.

Australia celebrates Christmas during their summer, so it is as far from icy paths and bitter winds, mulled wine and hearty, warming food as you can get. Sometimes when we stepped out of Kate's air-conditioned Sydney apartment it felt like we'd opened the oven door rather than the front door. The week before Christmas the temperature reached 40 degrees.

One of Kate's Aussie friends, John, invited us to stay with his family for a few days, and so we made the six-hour drive from Sydney to the rural town of Wagga Wagga, and on Christmas Day itself had cold cuts of meat and potato salad, champagne and strawberries. We went for drives through beautiful forested landscape where kangaroos and emus roamed like sheep, and on walks where you had to tread carefully because venomous snakes lived in the long grass.

When we drove back from Wagga Wagga to Sydney, it was through land recently scorched by bush fires, blackened husks of trees and pockets of still-burning ground, the air thick with smoke. Back in Sydney, we took tram rides into the city, drank iced coffee, went to Irish bars and pizza restaurants, and had two days watching Australia vs South Africa at the Sydney Cricket Ground – where I got more sunburnt than I have ever been in my life. I shook out my duvet every night to check for funnel web spiders.

The best part of the whole trip was New Year's Eve. Kate, John and I, along with a couple of other friends, went to Sydney Harbour to watch the firework display; magnificent plumes of light and colour filling the sky over the water and the distinctive shape of the opera house. Then we bar-crawled our way around the city, talking, laughing and playing pool until four in the morning, when we got a taxi to the beach. We sat on the sand and watched the sunrise, the sea glowing pink as the New Year dawned.

It was unlike any other Christmas that I've had, and I will always remember it. Not least, the one Australian Christmas card that has stuck in my mind: Santa and his sleigh on top of the roof of a house, about to load presents down the chimney. Except in place of Rudolph, there was a sprightly kangaroo, and rather than the house – complete with decorated tree in the window – sitting in a dusting of snow, this particular destination was surrounded by sand. It was good to experience something totally different, but also to realise that, even on the other side of the world – and with a few necessary adaptations – some things about Christmas will always be the same.

Fern
Britton
*Picks*
Exclusively for
TESCO

**EXCLUSIVE ADDITIONAL CONTENT**
Includes an author Q&A and details
of how to get involved in *Fern's Picks*

### Dear lovely readers,

With Christmas fast approaching, I am thrilled that our next Fern's Picks read is *The Cornish Cream Tea Christmas* by the wonderful Cressida McLaughlin.

*The Cornish Cream Tea Christmas* is a delicious festive treat, the perfect book to read by the fire on a cold winter's night. Hannah Swan's new job is taking her – and her geeky colleague, Noah – to the Cornish village of Porthgolow for the first time. When bad weather cuts off Porthgolow, Hannah and Noah are looking at a Cornish Christmas.

However, as guests at the Crystal Waters Hotel begin to suspect that it is haunted, the pair must get to the bottom of what is going on. This is a heart-warming and romantic novel set on the beautiful Cornish coast, with a fantastic spooky twist that I know you will love. I can't wait to hear what you think!

With love
Fern x

# Christmas Q&A with
# Cressida McLaughlin

### What would your ideal Porthgolow Christmas look like?

It would involve a stay at Crystal Waters and a trip to Gertie and the Christmas food market. The closest I've got to Christmas in Cornwall was a holiday in October, where we had a mix of beautiful sunshine and stormy weather. I enjoyed the wind and rain as much as the sun, especially watching huge waves crash against the harbour walls of the picturesque coastal villages. So, cosying up in the Crystal Waters snug with a glass of wine, good company and Christmas music playing as the storm rages outside would be perfect. Also, there's no better way of getting into the Christmas spirit than going to a festive food market, so I'd love to spend a day browsing the stalls, eating all the samples and, of course, having a Christmas Cornish cream tea on board Gertie. I've never been to a food market on a beach, so I think there'd have to be some paddling too, even though it would be freezing. I don't think it's possible to go to a beach without paddling.

## Why did you want to include ghosts in your latest book?

I've always been fascinated by the idea that ghosts exist, and I love a good haunted house tale. It's not a standard theme for an uplifting romance, but the tradition of telling ghost stories, around an open fire with everyone's faces cast in an eerie, flickering light, is so Christmassy. I really liked the idea that Daniel's sleek, modern hotel wasn't entirely free of the history of the site it was built on, and as the heroine, Hannah, is also searching for something in her past, the two storylines mirrored each other. Also, I love how ghost hunts can be both terrifying and hilarious, and those scenes were so much fun to write. The atmosphere is automatically heightened as the characters sit in the dark together, waiting for things to go bump, so other feelings come to the surface, too . . .

## Tell us about your perfect, non-traditional Christmas meal.

I love fish, so I'd be very happy with a fish dish for my Christmas dinner. A couple of years ago my family went for a whole salmon instead of beef – it's been a while since we had turkey – and I could have gone on eating it until there was nothing left except the bones.

I would choose scallops, or a classic prawn cocktail, for starters, and for dessert pretty much anything that's not a Christmas pudding. Vanilla ice cream with toffee sauce and brandy snaps would be perfect. It was so much fun expanding my foody repertoire for this book; of course, Charlie cooks up some special festive treats onboard the Cornish Cream Tea Bus, but with Hannah staying at Crystal Waters, and having a passion for food herself, I could be really indulgent with the culinary details. Sometimes it's torture writing these books – I spend the whole time hungry and craving all sorts of delicious things and, very sadly, I don't have a Gertie nearby that I can pop to for a cream tea.

## Why do you think Cornwall is such an inspiring place for writers?

There's something so unique and magical about Cornwall; it's got its own language and so many myths and traditions, and it's right at the edge of the country, so it's a bit of a pilgrimage to get there – from Norfolk, anyway. The coastline is so beautiful, with perfect blue water and sandy beaches, hidden coves and cliff walks, the views of land meeting sea stretching on for miles. It can be romantic and intriguing and atmospheric, beautiful or sinister, sparkling or stormy. For me, it's endlessly inspirational, a canvas on which any kind of story can be mapped out and I don't think I'll ever tire of setting my books there; trying to do the landscape justice with my words and creating characters who find their inspiration and happiness within its borders.

## What's next for Porthgolow and the Cornish Cream Tea Bus?

The next book in the series is called *The Cornish Cream Tea Wedding*. I don't want to give away any spoilers about whose wedding it is, (You'll be able to guess if you've already read *The Cornish Cream Tea Christmas*), but it's a couple I have come to care about deeply, and who deserve a happy ending. Their wedding will be seen through the eyes of someone slightly outside the Porthgolow crew – the wedding planner. Elowen – Ellie – Moon, is determined to plan the most beautifully intimate, bespoke wedding for the happy couple, and get her business back on track at the same time. After a tough year, she's moved in with her sister, so she can rent her cosy cottage out to boost her income. Between planning the wedding, pining for the garden she's left behind, dealing with her new tenant and being roped in to her sister's plans to help a grieving old man, Ellie's summer turns out to be even busier than she'd planned.

# Questions for your reading group

- Who is your favourite character in *The Cornish Cream Tea Christmas*, and why?

- If you had one festive day in Porthgolow, what would your top three activities be?

- What was your favourite scene in *The Cornish Cream Tea Christmas*?

- There are so many delicious treats in the novel. If you could pick one Christmas treat from Gertie, what would it be and why?

- 'The soothing wafts of Michael Bublé's Christmas album filled the bus'. If you could only play one Christmas album for the entire festive season, which would you pick?

- Hannah and Noah spend their Christmas in Cornwall, but if you could spend Christmas anywhere, where would it be? You might escape to warmer climes, or cosy up by the fireplace in an Alpine ski resort?

- What did you think about the ending of the novel, was it what you expected?

# An Exclusive Extract from Fern's New Novel

# Daughters of Cornwall

**Callyzion, Cornwall. December 1918.**

I leant my head on the cold glass of the train window, drinking in the outside scenery. Bertie had described all this to me time and time again. He had insisted on reciting all the romantic names of the Cornish station stops.

'As soon as you are over the bridge, you come to Saltash. The Gateway to Cornwall.'

'Why is it called Saltash?' I had asked.

'No idea. Then after Saltash it's St Germans, Menheniot, Liskeard—'

I interrupted him. 'I'll never remember all those names. Just tell me where I need to get off?'

'I'm getting to that, Miss Impatience.' He inhaled comically and continued. 'Saltash, St Germans, Menheniot, Liskeard and then Bodmin. I shall be waiting for you at Bodmin.'

'Will you really?' We had been lying in the tiny bed of our Ealing home. 'I'm not sure I have had anyone wait for me anywhere before.'

'What sort of blighter would I be if I didn't pick up my beloved fiancée after she's travelled all that way to see me?'

'You'd be a very bad blighter indeed,' I smiled.

He held me closer, dropping a kiss on to my hair. 'I can't wait for you to meet my family. Father will adore you. Mother too, though she may not show it at first, she's always cautious of new people. But Amy and you will be great friends. She's always wanted a sister. My brother Ernest can be a pompous ass but he's not a bad egg.'

'It'll be wonderful to feel part of a family again.'

'You are the bravest person I have ever met.' He squeezed me tightly, his arms encircling me. 'My stoic little squirrel.'

I am sorry to say I had already told a few lies to Bertie about my upbringing. Needs must sometimes.

'My parents were wonderful,' I fibbed, 'and I miss them every day, but I feel they would be very happy for me now.' Shameless, I know.

'Do you think they'd approve of me?' he asked.

'Oh Bertie,' I smiled. 'They would adore you.'

In the peace of my carriage, I searched my little bag for my handkerchief, angrily wiping away hot tears as, with a jolt, the mighty train wheels, powered by coal and steam, started to slow down.

The train guard was walking the corridors as he did before arriving at each station.

'Bodmin Road. Next stop Bodmin Road.' I readied myself to disembark.

Standing on the platform, I watched as the train chuffed its way down the line and out of sight on its journey towards Penzance. The Cornish winter air blew gently on my skin, and I took in lungfuls of the scent of damp earth.

Bertie had told me that it was warm enough down here to grow palm trees.

'You are pulling my leg.' I had laughed.

'No, I'm telling the truth. We have one in our garden. I will show it to you.'

I picked up my bag and walked past the signal box painted smartly in black and white, towards the ticket office where a sign with the word TAXI pointed. Even now, the half-expected hope that Bertie would be waiting for me made me breathless with longing. I imagined him running towards me, his long legs carrying him effortlessly. His strong arms collecting me up easily, lifting me from the ground so that my face was above his. The look of love shining between us.

'Excuse me, Miss.' A man with a peaked hat was walking towards me. 'Would you be Miss Carter?'

'Yes.'

'I thought so. You looked a bit lost on your own.' He had a kind face, but not too many teeth. 'Welcome to Cornwall.'

# Available now!

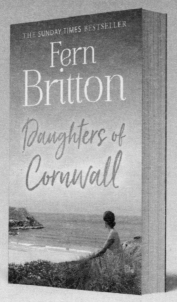

Look out for more books, coming soon!

For more information on the book club,
exclusive Q&As with the authors and
reading group questions, visit Fern's website
**www.fern-britton.com/fernspicks**

We'd love you to join in the conversation,
so don't forget to share your thoughts using
**#FernsPicks**

# Our next book club title

It's been a year since Lottie's fiancé walked out, leaving her heartbroken.

But things start to look up when Lottie is asked to organise a last-minute Christmas wedding at the beautiful Lake District estate, Firholme. That is until she meets the couple, and discovers that Connor, the man who broke her heart, is the groom-to-be.

As snow falls on the hills, can Lottie put aside her past to organise the perfect winter wedding? And will there be any festive magic left to bring Lottie the perfect Christmas she deserves?